Praise for Faith Hu

"Rich, imaginative, and de:
her Soulwood series shines.
coupled with the bone-chilling tension makes this story an
unforgettable read."   —RT Book Reviews

"I love Nell and her PsyLED team and would happily read
about their adventures for years."   —Vampire Book Club

"Faith Hunter does a masterful job . . . and has created a
wonderful new heroine in Nell, who continues to grow into
her powers."   —The Reading Cafe

"Once again, Hunter proves she's a master of the genre."
                                                —Romance Junkies

"*Blood of the Earth* by Faith Hunter is the best first install-
ment of an urban fantasy series I've read in about a decade.
Highly recommended."   —Rabid Reads

"There is wry humor, mild levels of snarkiness, cross-
pollination with Hunter's characters and events from her
Jane Yellowrock series, and passages setting a breakneck
pace that may cause you to forget to breathe."
                                        —Kings River Life Magazine

"A heck of a lot of fun, a neat mix of the supernatural and a
police procedural."   —*Locus*

Praise for Faith Hunter's Jane Yellowrock novels

"A lot of series seek to emulate Hunter's work, but few come
close to capturing the essence of urban fantasy: the perfect
blend of intriguing heroine, suspense, [and] fantasy with just
enough romance."   —SF Site

RIFT IN THE SOUL

A Soulwood Novel

Faith Hunter

ACE
New York

ACE
Published by Berkley
An imprint of Penguin Random House LLC
penguinrandomhouse.com

ISBN: 9780593335796

First Edition: March 2024

Printed in the United States of America
1   3   5   7   9   10   8   6   4   2

*As always, this book is dedicated
to my Renaissance man.
You mean the world and the sun
and the stars and the moon to me.
The joy of being with you on this life
journey cannot be calculated.*

ONE

I stepped on the dirt by the driveway and sniffed the winter air. A cold snap had come through at dusk, and the scent of the Tennessee River only yards away rode high and warm on the night, rising in a swirling mist that obscured much of the landscape. There wasn't time for a deep read of the land, but I needed a feel for it, so I bent and touched the soil with a finger-tip, sending my thoughts through the upper layers of dirt and lawn, skimming the surface.

The earth around me was unsettled, as property walked by the undead usually was, but there was no sense of danger. Nothing hurtled through the earth and grabbed me, no wild energies, no fear, no vines or roots, so that was good, but the soil felt different from the last time I had read it. The sense of death was stronger and there was a mixture of something disturbed, dis-quieted here, so I pushed a little deeper. I caught a hint of fire and excitement, of an unresolved exhilaration, as if the earth rode the brink of something wild. It felt the way it must feel to be at the top of a roller coaster, ready to plunge down. Though I had never been on a roller coaster and couldn't imagine why I ever would want to.

The important thing was that nothing dangerous leaped at me. That was a good start.

I opened my eyes and studied the property owned by Ming Zhane of Glass, the Master of the City of Knoxville. There were several dark circles near the rear of the otherwise pristine lawn, like burned spots, places that might correlate with the sensation of fire. There were burn warnings all over the eastern half of the state, but I could envision Ming demanding autumn's fallen leaves be burned. Her blood-servants would have complied.

While I was down low and out of sight of the house, I pulled the mini-psy-meter from a pocket. It was about the size of a cigarette case, and while not as sensitive as the larger model, it would do in a pinch. Before leaving HQ, I had checked the device against the ambient magics of the witch and the were-creatures of Unit Eighteen, and so a quick reading was possible.

Of the four psysitopes, the device settled firmly in the reading for vampires, so whatever this visit was for, it was likely not a situation with mixed paranormal-creature politics.

I stood, stepped back onto the drive, and glanced at the other cars. Their lights were off, drivers barely visible in the thickening mist. When I gave a thumbs-up, they climbed out of their vehicles, closed their doors, and walked to me across the concrete.

Regional Director Ayatas FireWind, the man I had taken to calling my boss-boss, gave me a small nod, telling me to go ahead. They had my back. Rick LaFleur, Special Agent in Charge of PsyLED Unit Eighteen, glanced at the house and back to me, his black eyes telling me to be careful. Even had there been no mention of a body, the two bosses would have come as my backup because, as Rick said when the call came in, "Weird shit is happening in the vamp world."

I looked back at the potted tree strapped into the passenger seat of my newish car and contemplated bringing the tree with me. Instead I closed the car door I had left open, shutting off the interior lights. Full dark fell on us. Ming's people hadn't turned on the security and landscape lights, which was a little odd. The mist from the river swirled higher and closer, more dense. I locked the car with the small fob.

I reseated my Glock 20, not that I expected to need it here. Ming had requested my presence, personally, to report a dead body, and when the new Master of the City of Knoxville wanted to report a crime, Unit Eighteen listened. Thanks to her, I was lead on this interview, and should Ming be bringing a case to the unit, and not vampire politics, it was possible that I would be lead on my very first case. Rick was betting it was vampire politics, but either way, anytime there were vampires, there was danger.

The two bosses had attended the coronation of the Emperor of Europe only a week past, and they had brought back tales of weird vampire actions and unusual personnel changes. They had even seen a vamp laughing with her fangs out, which they couldn't explain. Vampires could not laugh—laughter was a human emotion—while in predator state. It wasn't possible. Yet they had both seen her laughing.

Since LaFleur and FireWind had returned from New Orleans, vamp rumors of the wild and crazy kind had begun to circulate in Knoxville too. None of the reports were believable, and none had involved video evidence, but everyone wanted a look-see at the locals.

T. Laine, Unit Eighteen's resident witch, had called it "wackadoodle stuff."

"Comms check," FireWind said.

"Ingram here."

"LaFleur here."

"Copy, FireWind, Ingram, LaFleur," Jones said, back at HQ.

Rick and Aya positioned themselves in front of and behind me, and together we crossed the concrete drive to the front entrance. Ming didn't live in a castle like Dracula, but she owned a megamansion and several acres on the edge of the Tennessee River. Prime real estate. An attached six-car garage, greenhouse, big barn, and outbuildings. I smelled manure and hay and that familiar scent of horse I remembered from my upbringing at the God's Cloud of Glory Church. It brought a sense of peace that tried to replace the natural uneasiness of a law enforcement officer visiting a vampire lair after dark.

The men separated, leaving me in front. My bosses standing behind me, I knocked on the front door and rang the bell.

Nothing happened. Minutes went by.

I knocked again. Aya checked his watch. He still wore a watch, and not just one of those wrist computers / cell phones. Checking it was ingrained. Rick stared at the security camera, his long white hair catching in the misty breeze. He tilted his head and said, "Someone's coming."

Rick LaFleur was a black wereleopard. There were indications he had sharper senses even in human form and they got sharper closer to the full moon. Were-creatures also got skittish at that time of the month and, while we waited, I counted ahead to the three days when the were-members of PsyLED Eighteen would go furry. I'd rather not have to deal with Rick's big-cat on Ming's property, and I was safe on that point.

The door opened. Standing inside should have been the butler. Instead it was Cai, Ming's human primo, her number one blood-servant, but a vastly different Cai from the last time I saw him. Cai was slim, wiry, Asian, and skilled in several martial arts forms. He moved with that liquid grace of the well-trained fighter, and had all the charm of a steel blade. He did everything for Ming, from keeping her schedule to supposedly killing vampires who got out of line. That was hearsay, but had seemed likely. Until tonight.

Tonight he was grinning. A happy human grin, like a maybe-a-little-drunk kind of grin. And there was blood on his cheek and the neckline of his white T-shirt. "Ming's guests." He threw his arms to the sides in welcome. "Come in come in come in," he said, running the words together. "Ming is . . ." He gestured off into the darkness of the house, turned, and walked away, leaving the door open and three law enforcement agents standing there.

"Is that an invitation?" I asked.

"We assume so," Aya said, stepping past me, moving right, his weapon suddenly in his hand.

"Though we don't know what the invitation is for," Rick finished for him, stepping inside, to the left, his weapon also drawn.

Right. It might be an invitation for me to be supper to the vampires.

"This is the same kind of behavior we saw in New Orleans among many of the blood-servants, and Ming's people have no reason to still be celebrating so long after the coronation of the emperor," Aya said softly.

I drew my weapon but didn't chamber a round. I should have. But I didn't. Somehow this didn't feel like an ambush. Which, of course, would make it a really good ambush. I pressed a light switch on the wall and the foyer brightened.

"I don't see a DB," I said, looking around. "No blood spatter on walls or floor. No stink of decay on the air. But Cai did have blood on his shirt."

Patterns at my feet drew my eye. The foyer had been re-floored in white marble. In the center, tiny pieces of gray marble, brass, and glistening steel had been inlaid and formed a pair of blades, the sharp steel blades crossed. The single-edged blades themselves had been embedded in the floor; they appeared real but were strangely shaped. One blade looked as if an ax had been crossed with a machete and then a dragon had taken a bite out of the sharp edge. I knew nothing about fighting with blades, but even I could tell the dragon-bitten section was for snagging an opponent's blade out of their hand. The other blade was similar but without the snagging-dragon-bite, and a longer cutting edge. They were different but they were also clearly a pair of blades intended to be used together. The ends of the blades, where they should have attached to real handles—hilts?—were made of brass or gold and were shaped like dragon snouts, as if the steel was erupting from their mouths. Above and between the crossed blades was a green, faceted square.

"Ingram," FireWind snapped. There was an edge of "pay attention" in the tone.

"What's that?" I pointed at the floor.

"Ming's new crest," FireWind said, his tone still sharp. "Since she became MOC."

As if my up-line boss hadn't just snapped at me, I holstered my weapon and started taking pictures, sending them back to HQ. Aya grunted in approval. I was learning how to read him. I flipped on more lights and took shots of the parlor to the left and the hallways leading off into darkness. According to county records, the clan home of the Master of the City was nearly twelve thousand square feet, so I wasn't getting much of the house, but it was the first time I'd been in a position to film it.

As I worked, Rick explained to me, still a newbie, "It's customary for the Master of the City, the most powerful Mithran in the territory, to have their crest inlaid in the entry floor of the city's Council Chambers headquarters, to remind friends and visiting enemies alike who they would have to fight and conquer. Ming is both the MOC and head of the only vampire clan in Knoxville, so her home does double duty."

Ming had been given MOC status by Jane Yellowrock. I remembered that. When I had taken photos of everything I could without wandering around, I pulled the psy-meter from my pocket and quickly took a reading of Ming's foyer. The readings were all over the place.

At a warning signal from Rick, I slid the device away.

Cai wandered toward us from the main sitting room. "You're still here?"

"Ming demanded to see me," I said. "She said she had a body for me. Get her. Please."

"Oh. Sure. Sit sit sit sit." He waved to the sitting room. Then he said, "No. Wait. Tea. I should make tea. Come come come come. This way."

I looked at FireWind, who had a faint smile on his face and gestured I should take point. Cai led the way to the kitchen, which was decorated in black and white with emerald touches here and there. Two six-burner stoves, each with three ovens, and the commercial refrigerator and commercial freezer made my heart thump hard with envy. This was a bakers-canners-chefs' paradise. It would make the Nicholson mamas at God's Cloud of Glory Church turn green.

Cai put on a kettle and got out a fancy tea tin and six cups with saucers. He started humming, something that sounded like a dirge, then suddenly he was whistling what sounded like the music for the old *Gilligan's Island* TV series.

I looked at the bosses. Both were trying not to appear amused but not doing a good job of it. I wasn't amused. Things felt wrong here. As the water heated, Cai wandered along the counter and out the door at the far end.

"What in God's good heaven is happening?" I asked, my voice soft.

No one replied, but Rick and Aya began to open cabinet doors and drawers and I realized they were conducting a search. For which we didn't have a subpoena. Aya pulled a bottle from a small refrigerator and spun it slowly. "Nineteen forty-seven Cheval Blanc. A bottle sold at auction for over three hundred thousand dollars recently."

A bottle of wine? That bottle was worth more than I owned altogether in the whole world.

Rick opened the commercial refrigerator and said, "The blood-servants are eating well. Whole suckling pig, baby potatoes, and asparagus." He shut the door.

Feeling emboldened, I checked out the stoves and the ovens. They were not just functional, they were works of art, and I ran my hands across the decorative steel corners. The stoves had to cost a fortune, but vampires were often quite rich.

I turned off the kettle, which was steaming, but I didn't make tea. I wanted to read this place, which meant I needed something made of wood that had been here a long time. The floors were marble tile; the cabinets looked new and were painted black inside and out.

Aya closed a second wine fridge and opened a huge pantry. Now I had pantry envy. And it had wood floors.

I held up a hand to let him know I was about to go to work. Walking past him, I slipped off one shoe and placed my bare foot on the wood floor.

Cold and ice met my questing energies. I pushed through, to the underside of the wood planks, and then to the wood supports beneath. Wood, unless petrified, always had a form of power that I could read. Here there was nothing. The wood that constructed this house was truly dead. It no longer had energy, no longer had a . . . a soul, for lack of a better word. I slid my shoe on, stepped back into the main kitchen, and made hard eye contact with each man, trying to communicate, *Problem. Magical problem.*

It wasn't like we had ESP or anything, but they had hunted on my land. There was a bond between us. Rick, who had holstered his weapon, redrew it.

Ming of Glass entered.

I took a step back.

Ming's hair was down, a long straight sheen of hair, blacker than night, falling to midthigh. She was dressed in a purple fuzzy robe tied at the waist. She was barefoot, wore no makeup, her eyes closed. Her fingernails and toenails were painted, each a different color, with flower appliqués like a hippie or a townie teenager. She carried no weapons, not that vampires needed to. They *were* weapons.

And the Master of the City was dancing, moving to music only she could hear.

The Ming of Glass I knew would never have appeared looking like this. I had a feeling she slept perfectly coiffed, with a dozen blades on the bed beside her. She was dangerous and dignified and scary. Not fuzzy robed. Not barefooted. Never. As she spun in a slow circle, I spotted earbuds.

She whirled again, her robe flapping open to reveal naked legs, which shocked me. Thanks to my upbringing, even partial nudity sometimes made me uncomfortable.

Ming started singing, something that sounded as if it came from Bollywood, the notes not Western and the rhythm differ-

ent from the jazzy and bluesy stuff Rick LaFleur listened to and
different also from the music FireWind liked.

She opened her eyes. And saw me.

"Maggoty Girl! You came!"

Ming of Glass popped across the counter faster than I could
see and threw her arms around me, hugging me. I went stiff and
still and forgot to breathe until she unwrapped from me and
opened the wine fridge.

"You requested my presence," I said, my voice breathy, not
the firm tone I wanted. "About a dead body."

She flapped her hand at me, pulled out a different bottle from
the one Aya had touched, and opened it with vampiric speed using
a steel corkscrew I hadn't seen her pick up. She tilted up the bottle
and drank. When she lowered the bottle, she focused on the two
men. "Put them away." She pointed the bottle at their weapons.
"You two. Go to the front room. Maggoty Girl. You will come
with me." Ming tottered away and pushed through two doors that
swung closed behind her, like doors in an old-fashioned western.

"Ingram," FireWind said softly. "Video. Now."

"Oh. Right." Ming was acting strange. Everyone would want
to see and hear. I turned my cell to record and tucked the cell
into my upper jacket pocket, giving the camera a good view. We
had already checked comms, so we had an audio recording and
now video backup.

After a last glance at the bosses, I pushed open the doors,
following our hostess, revealing a different small parlor from
the one I had seen before. Ming was sitting in a puffy chair in
front of a gas fire, the flames turned down low but putting off
heat. She tilted the bottle up again and drank. I walked into the
room. The doors swung closed behind me.

Ming of Glass pointed at the chair to her side and I sat gingerly, on the edge. There was a thick rug beneath my chair and
the chair had no exterior wooden parts, nothing I could draw
power from.

"Maggoty Girl. What have you done to my scions? They are
walking into the sun. Three burned at dawn today. Two the day
before."

"I haven't done anything," I said carefully, remembering the
circles on the river side of the property. Walking into the sun
was a term vampires used when they killed themselves at dawn,

letting the sun burn them to death. "No one in PsyLED knows what's happening, only that there have been reports of Mithrans across the country acting—" I stopped. Not crazy. Not as if they were all in the midst of mental breakdowns. Either might get my head ripped off. "Acting unlike their usual selves. I did nothing at all, not to anyone."

"Our blood-servants are . . ." She waved the half-empty bottle in the air. "Volatile. At first they were happy. Now many are leaving us. We have had to negotiate new contracts with them. It is costing us much money."

"That sounds . . . difficult," I lied. "You said there was a dead body?"

Ming turned her black eyes to me. She was vamping out, her pupils already dilated, the white of her sclera bleeding scarlet. Her fangs snapped down on the little hinges. My breath hitched and stopped. Ming was in full hunting mode. I started to call for the guys. My fingers twitched for my weapon.

Ming smiled behind her fangs.

I froze as she leaned closer. She could hear my heart racing. She could smell my sweat-fear. I didn't know much about vampires, but I knew I was in danger. If I called for help, Ming could rip out my throat before my bosses could react. Before I got out more than a squeak. And I was taking too long to reply. I had to deal with this.

Possibilities flitted through my mind. I forced out my breath. Inhaled.

"Ming of Glass," I managed. "Master of the City of Knoxville. I see you are . . . disturbed." That should let Rick and Aya know there were problems. "PsyLED Eighteen has been called here about a dead body. How may we assist?"

I always carried some of the life of my land within me, but I hadn't had time to go to the roof of HQ and sit in my garden spot, a raised bed full of Soulwood soil. I hadn't replenished myself.

"Yoooou," Ming said. "Maggoty Girl. You brought *life* to the undead Mithrans. And because of you, my city is cursed."

"I didn't do anything. What could I have done to cause you, the . . . the illustrious Ming of Glass, discomfort?"

Ming leaned in a hair closer and breathed in the air I exhaled. I clamped down on the desire to run. Vampires were fast, and running would mark me as prey. I'd not make one step before I triggered her predator instincts.

I wasn't on Soulwood. I wasn't even standing on the ground or on wood that came from local trees. But Soulwood wasn't that far away. I began to gather the power of Soulwood to me. The land, as always, *hungered*. It wanted sacrifice. If I had to fight her—

Ming shifted. Raised the hand that wasn't holding the bottle and pointed her index finger at me. She touched my forehead with her fingertip. It was icy, cold as a dead body. I didn't pull away, but it was a close thing.

The vampire pressed her finger harder into my flesh, feeling my life force, my own magic. It rose fast against her. But I held it tightly. Her single touch was different from what vampires usually felt like. It wasn't nearly so maggoty, not the sensation of a rotting opossum corpse (from which I got the name Maggot) or the feel of icy death. It was *different*. Ming wasn't just *emotionally* different. Something about the vampire was *magically* and *physically* different. Just like the impressions of her land.

The swinging doors behind her opened slowly. Rick stood there, a gun aimed at the back of Ming's head in a two-hand grip. Aya stepped up beside him. I reined in my relief, holding it just as tight as I did my fear and my power.

"I feel the life of the earth in you," Ming said. "I wonder if there is a similar life in your sisters, in the children born on your land, land you call Soulwood." Ming drew back her finger and stared at its tip. Licked it. "*Dogs and leaves*. You taste of nothing but *dogs and leaves*. All of your kind should be exterminated."

Whether she meant those words as a threat against my family or not, I took it that way. Instantly my own *hunger* rose. I wanted to feed my land with her. To drain the undead life out of her. Far off, my land woke from its winter slumber, alerted by my fear-defense-attack mode. The power of my land stretched toward me, searching. I reached toward it, and the tendril of power wrapped into me. Calm flooded through me from that single coil.

Within my land, the Green Knight of the vampire tree came

to attention, but I had left its rooted sapling in the car. The tree would have a difficult time reaching me. Reaching Ming.

"You left a message for me at PsyLED Unit Eighteen," I said, "that there is a dead body here. You asked for me specifically to pick it up. Tell me about the body."

Her eyes narrowed as she stared at her finger.

"Please," I added. "Is it a human or an undead?"

"Undead?" Ming asked. "What is undead? How can the undead have a soul? What can the undead *doooo* with a soul?" She held her hand up in the air, studying her fingers with the colorful, childlike nail polish on them. "How did my soul return to me? Where was it kept for so many centuries? There are those who say otherwise, but I know it was you." She dropped her hand and scratched a single long cut across her chest between the robe's lapels. A line of blood appeared in the trail of the fingernail. She had ripped her own skin.

There was something seriously wrong with Ming of Glass.

I fought to keep my breathing slow and deep, my heart rate steady and calm. I was in the presence of a predator, one not herself. Like a rabid dog. Or a bull with mad cow disease.

I clenched my fists and pulled on Soulwood, preparing my earth magic, keeping that slow trickle of blood in my line of sight. I might have to fight her and I had left my best weapon in the passenger seat of the car. But if I needed to kill her, to drain her to death, all I had to do was touch that trickle of blood. The *hunger* of the land grew inside me.

"Did you force my soul into me?" Her eyes moved to my face. "Your life force is not human. Are *you* the danger to me? Should I drink you down?"

That was a threat. Even though she was nuttier than a candy bar, Ming could rip me apart with her bare hands.

That thought triggered my brain out of paralysis, into action.

"You owe me two boons," I said, clutching at that memory, not knowing what it really meant in terms of a balance of power against her threat, but willing to use what I had. "You will not violate your own blood word."

She shrugged slightly, her robe slipping to reveal one pale shoulder. "Yes." Before I could respond, she continued, "There are strange trees growing on your land." She touched her chest and scratched at the drying blood, freshening her wound in a line of bright scarlet. She licked her fingertip again. "They bleed. Charlainn tasted the tree and she . . . she felt joy. And now she is dead by the dawn."

I had no idea who Charlainn was or when or why the vampire woman had tasted the vampire tree. The tree was a poorly kept secret that grew on church land and my land and had a mind of its own, sentient and self-aware, and had taken to calling itself the Green Knight. I hoped to control the tree enough to keep it from killing people for its dinner. I even had a dream of monetizing it for lumber. Maybe. Someday. "Go on," I said.

"You are a people eater. I have heard you are purple, but I see you are not."

There was nothing amusing about this bizarre conversation, but laughter welled up in me, nervous, half-panicked. Soulwood filled me. Steadying me. I felt the Green Knight in the distance, alert.

"What happened to you?" I asked her softly.

"I found my soul. We all found our souls." Bitterly she said, "Every Mithran everywhere has our souls and we cannot . . ." Ming turned her head halfway around to see Rick's gun aimed at her. It was one of those not-human movements they can make, and the hair stood up on the back of my neck. As if the weapon didn't matter, she swiveled her head back to me. "We cannot make them go away. Souls are destroying us. When your sister's babies were born, did they bring back our souls? Did your tree bring back our souls?"

Vampires didn't have souls. Everyone knew that. Ming thought vampires now had souls? She had always been unstable, but this was a new take on vampire psychological instability.

"No baby did anything. Have you called J—" I stopped just in time. "Have you called the Dark Queen? She might know something. Have you contacted her?"

"Cai called. It went to voice mail. So he called again. And her lady-in-waiting took a *message*."

Jane Yellowrock had a lady-in-waiting? She was more likely to need an armorer than someone to paint her nails.

"When her secundo, the one called Eli Younger, called me back, he wove a tale of angels and demons, but I know . . ." Ming stopped and drank deeply again and tossed the empty bottle across the room. It hit the wall and clattered to the floor. I managed not to flinch.

When Rick and Ayatas returned from New Orleans and the coronation, they had referred to the vampires being a very different sort of strangeness from their usual eccentricity, as if very drunk. They had been right.

Cai opened the door to my side, looked at the gun aimed at the back of his mistress' head, and walked casually across the room to Ming. He held out his arm to Ming and she took it, embedded her fangs in his wrist, and drank. Cai laughed and stroked her hair. It was unexpectedly personal and suggestive, the way he touched her.

When she withdrew her fangs, she licked his wrist to clot the blood and close the wound. "Thank you. You will take the foolish nonhumans in the kitchen doorway into the front parlor. Keep them there."

My spine went straight. I did not want to be alone with a crazy Ming of Glass.

"Have the boy's body taken to the driveway so they may remove the filth."

"Yes, my mistress," Cai said.

"And call Yvonne. Have her bring the cards."

Ming pulled her lapels together and looked at me. Some of her old imperiousness seeped back into her eyes. "Forgive me. I have been remiss. Would you care for tea?"

"Thank you?" I said, not certain how to respond.

Cai walked to the swinging doors. In a single lunge, he swiped out with both hands and grabbed Rick and Aya by the throats. Fast. Faster than any para. Nearly vampire-fast.

"Put them away," Cai said of their weapons, his voice as nonchalant as if they were standing at a bar having friendly drinks. "You'd be dead by the time you fired."

Cai shoved and pushed both men back through the kitchen. I could hear their shoes sliding on the floor. We had known for a long time that Cai was far more than human. Cai's strength, against two other paranormals who also had greater than human strength, was proof of that.

"When you ate the witches and the enemy Naturaleza, did you find their souls and give them back?" Ming asked.

Very few people knew I had helped the earth itself destroy a group of vampires responsible for terrorizing the city of Knoxville with dark magic and a cursed deck of cards called the Blood Tarot. Just how much did Ming, with her vampiric, blood-sucking technique of "bleeding and reading" victims, know about that case?

"I don't have anything to do with souls," I said, still choosing my words carefully.

"I think you are more than you are aware."

The door behind me opened and Yummy walked in.

Yvonne?

Yummy had a real name. Occam had dated her before me. He had to have known her name. Her name had to be in the records. I had never looked.

Yummy was blond with a swimmer's shoulders. Or a boxer's. Broad and strong while still being lean and hard. We were friends of a sort. She was smiling a weird smile, and if the hair on the back of my neck could stand up any higher, it would have poked into the ceiling.

In Yummy's hands was an antique painted metal box sealed with two narrow leather straps.

TWO

"Sit," Ming commanded her. "Watch," she demanded of me.

Yummy pulled a small table between us and placed the tin box on top. It was about five inches by three by two, and was well-preserved beneath the thin straps, painted with a strange combination of coins, cups, daggers, a horse, pyramids, the Sphinx, and, in the background, a tower. Yummy pulled a small stool to the table and sat at its corner, removed the straps, opened the box, and lifted the lid to reveal a deck of cards.

The cards were old, the paper thick and heavy, the inks deep and dark on one side with a faint brown stain on one corner of each card. The pattern on the back was of a sword crossed with a stick, a cup to one side, and a coin to the other.

My eyes flew to Yummy's and her smile widened, making her look more human than I had ever seen her. *Tarot.*

Was this a *Blood Tarot*? One of three left in existence in the entire world?

Unit Eighteen of the Psychometric Law Enforcement Division of Homeland Security had been looking for the Blood Tarot deck that had been missing since the case Ming had mentioned. Well, *I* had been. It was my assignment, when I wasn't on an active case, to find the one deck we had lost in the midst of fighting off a black magic working.

Rick LaFleur had a tattoo spell inked into his body with a Blood Tarot. His life and magic were bound up in it and by it.

"Yes, we found the Blood Tarot that you and your unit lost," Yummy said through that strange smile. "No, I didn't tell you. Yes, Ming thinks it's at the center of what's about to happen to us. No, I don't know anything else."

About to happen? Prophecy? There is no such thing as

prophecy. Thought the woman who grows leaves . . . I shoved
that all away and asked Yummy, "You're a mind reader now?"

"Turns out I might be a lot of things," she said, sounding
both enigmatic and wry. Yummy's hair was different, long
blond streaks in it, and though she wasn't dressed as oddly as
Ming, she was wearing peculiar clothes—green and pink plaid
flannel pajama bottoms, red and white striped socks with Santa's
face on the outer ankles, and a fashionably torn, oversized sweatshirt in a hideous shade of sunshine gold. Visible through the
holes in the sweatshirt was a tight, stretchy, bloodstained T-shirt,
some of the blood fresh.

"Shuffle the cards," Ming ordered, pulling the edges of the
purple fluffy robe over her knees. She had regained her imperiousness since drinking from Cai, but the robe, the wildly
painted fingernails, and the long hair kept me on my toes.

Yummy shuffled the cards thoroughly and placed them in
the center of the table. "Cut the deck," she said to me.

"Ummm. No?"

Yummy's eyes flew to mine, going wide with warning.

"The chur—" I stopped. The polygamist church where I was
raised believed tarot cards were evil. And while I didn't sub-
scribe to a lot of the superstitions I'd been brought up believing,
I knew this deck was different.

It had been created with spells and blood and death. The
Blood Tarot decks were shrouded in mystery, with origins far
older than the commonly accepted history. They were blood
magic.

But I wasn't a churchwoman.

I looked into Ming's eyes and quickly away. Every cell in my
body screamed for me to get away from her and from the deck
of cards. I had no idea why the cards brought out such a strong
reaction in me, but fear reactions, while triggered by the body's
survival system, were seldom logical. I forced my breathing to
slow, but my hands were sweating, the churchwoman welling up
in me.

"It . . . It may be dangerous," I said.

"It *is* dangerous," Ming agreed. Her words lashed out: *"Cut
the deck."* It wasn't a request. The command was filled with
compulsion.

I squeezed my fists together in my lap, fighting her demand.

I had no backup. If I ran, I was likely to be killed, despite the reminder of the boons Ming owed me. If I refused, I would likely be dismissed and I'd never know what was going on.

Churchwoman.

I wasn't. Not anymore. I was more. So much more. I was a special agent with PsyLED. I was an investigator, which meant I had to look at things of the world in ways different from the church's fear and loathing. And I was a plant-woman with power of my own.

And Ming still had a wound on her chest.

The energies of Soulwood, the pure magic of the Earth herself, pushed into me.

"Maaaggoooty . . ." There was threat in Ming's voice.

Reaching out, I touched the deck with a fingertip, exactly the way I would read unfamiliar or dangerous land. Nothing happened. I traced my finger across the card, analyzing. It was room temperature, the paper slightly fuzzy, and each of the deep pigments of the inks ingrained in the paper had a slightly different feel. The gold felt metallic—real gold, then. As I stroked the top card, I felt the magic in it. A tingle of power, a sensation of energy. It was vaguely the way one of T. Laine's amulets felt, as if the power was restrained within, created for one use, one intent. But this felt like even more. Perhaps . . . purposeful? Biding its time?

I drew in a breath. *Sentient? Possessed?*

I wanted to pull the small portable psy-meter out of my pocket and read the cards, but I figured that would be considered rude and I didn't want to get eviscerated.

I lifted a third of the deck and placed it on the table. The back of the card I revealed was different from the first, the inks different, as if it was even more aged. I covered the top third with the bottom portion.

"And ask a question," Ming said.

"What's going on?"

Yummy removed the top card and placed it face down in the center of the table, her hand hovering over it a moment, as if in indecision. Quickly she placed twelve other cards around it in a circle, making a pattern, like a clock face.

She turned the center card over. It was a skeleton with a sickle standing in a pile of bones, some partially wrapped like mummies. Three white pyramids were in the background, a gold triangle on top of the largest. A sphinx was visible, though faded.

Yummy said, "No matter how we shuffle, no matter if we use only the Major Arcana or mix in the Minor Arcana, Death is revealed in the prime position."

"That's Death?"

"Yes." She gathered the cards and inserted them randomly into the deck, then shuffled seven times. She placed the deck on the tabletop. I asked the same question as I cut the deck, and she placed the cards into a cross shape, with three cards in the center in a fan, all face down. She touched the top card and said, "Celtic Cross spread. The third card is the one on top, and is the best course of action; the second card is the problem; and the card on the bottom is the person asking the question. You."

She flipped the top card. Death was revealed, upside down. "As always," she said, sounding grim, "but this time as potential rebirth."

Yummy flipped the middle card over. "The second card is eight of wands, suggesting that death and rebirth are moving fast."

She flipped the bottom card. "The Empress. In this case that's you."

The Empress card was of a woman sitting in a gold chair, wearing Egyptian clothing, a gold scepter in one hand, a spotted big-cat to one side. Behind her was flat land with grain crops and winding streams and the same pyramid in the distance. Like Death, it was an older card, older than the card in the middle.

Yummy flipped the other cards over, glancing at each one, but appeared uninterested. She gathered the cards and repeated the shuffling process, shuffling six times before saying, "Ask a different question."

"But first we will have tea," Ming said.

Even as she spoke, Cai pushed through the swinging doors from the kitchen, this time carrying a tray over his head. The fragrance was familiar, delicate and aromatic—a very expensive loose-leaf oolong called Tieguanyin tea. The best varieties sold on the market for three thousand dollars per kilo and it was named in honor of Guan Yin. Guan Yin was the Buddhist goddess known as the goddess of mercy. I knew this because Ming had sent me a small tin and I had tried it a time or two. I'd never tell her, but I liked my own decoctions better than the fancy tea.

But because vampires did nothing by chance, this tea was probably a reminder that the vampire Master of the City had somehow figured out that I was responsible for killing her vampire enemies.

But the two boons? That put me firmly in the lead. The *hunger* of the land sat within me. Waiting. Eager. Not something I would ever admit to, but a power I held, ready and waiting for an attack I hoped would never come.

Cai poured tea into tiny cups with even tinier handles. Ming lifted hers and I waited to sip the pale green tea until she pulled the cup away from her mouth. Then I tasted. Hoping I was doing it all in the right order. "I'm honored that Ming of Glass would share her Tieguanyin tea. It is delicious."

"It is my favorite tea, gifted to those who please me most. The tea is even better with a drop of my Cai's blood in it. Would you like to try it?"

My cup clattered into its saucer. "Ummm." I stopped, aware my heart rate had sped up again, my mind racing.

Cai leaned around the corner through the swinging doors. There was fresh blood on his lips. Rick's blood? Aya's? No. Cai would have drank from a vampire. Another vampire waiting around the corner. If I ever, ever, ever cursed, now would be the time.

"I am honored," I lied, knowing she could smell the lie.

Cai entered the room again.

"But I should refuse your kind offer," I said quickly. "I don't know that my kind do well with blood." And if I had a drop of his blood, that might tie him to my land, it might make him mine, and Ming would probably be really angry that I stole him. If I was right. "Especially strong blood like the blood your primo must surely have, after drinking from a Mithran as strong as Ming of Glass."

Yummy raised her eyebrows in amusement and I wondered if the flattery was too much.

"I do see the difficulty in drinking Cai's blood," Ming said. "It may unsettle your . . . *tree*."

It was so much in so few words.

I lifted the tea again and sipped, knowing that I needed to

punch back, politely, or be considered prey. I smiled slowly. "Trees have wonderful self-defense mechanisms. Some of them have thorns. Some strangling vines."

Cai walked back into the kitchen, and I could hear him whistling through the door.

Wackadoodle.

We drank slowly until the teacups were empty. Even Yummy, who clearly didn't care for the tea overmuch, finished her cup. Ming placed her empty cup into the saucer and I followed suit. Yummy placed hers down last, though I had a feeling she had been finished with her tea for a while. Her eyes still looked amused.

"Yvonne," Ming said. "The cards."

Yummy shuffled the deck.

To me, Ming ordered, "Ask your different question."

I cut the deck, sat back from the table a fraction of an inch. Placed my hands in my lap, one curled on top of the other. I pulled on my energies, and Soulwood answered with strength and comfort. "Why are the Mithrans different now?"

Yummy's pale eyes met mine in shock. I had a feeling no one had asked why. They had just blamed the life in their bodies and the return of their souls on me. I was an easy target, an easy out.

Ming breathed in slowly. She had been vamped out all this time, but now her fangs clicked back into her mouth and her bloody eyes bled back to white.

Yummy laid out the cards in three rows of seven. "The Romany spread," she said. Quickly, she pointed to the various rows, telling me about the horizontal rows A, B, and C, and the columns A through G, followed by the number of each card in the spread.

I didn't take in much of it, but with this many cards, I could tell that the Blood Tarot, if it really was a Blood Tarot deck, was composed of two decks of cards, or one deck that was augmented with other, newer cards. The fancy cards, what Yummy called the Major Arcana, were older, much older, than the rest of the deck.

"The cards in the center column are the querent. That would be you." Yummy pointed to the one closest. "Your past." She indicated the center card. "The middle card is your present. And the bottom is your future." She flipped over the card for my past. It wasn't Death.

Yummy's eyes met Ming's.

"What?" I asked.

"Not Death. For the first time it isn't Death," Yummy said.

She sounded breathless, which, had I not been in danger, would have been funny, since vampires didn't need to breathe. Right now, it just made my spine tighten even more.

"Instead," Yummy said, "we have the Tower upright. Complete and utter disruption. Abandoning former ties."

"Like I did when I left the church."

"And as we Mithrans are going through now," Ming said.

"Nell is the one who broke the chain of Death with that question, with this reading," Yummy said as she flipped over the middle card. It showed two angels flying above the Earth, blowing trumpets. "Judgment. You are becoming free of what held you back."

"But my question was 'Why are the Mithrans different now?' So if this stuff is really magic, then you vampires are the ones becoming free."

Yummy flipped over the top card. It was a globe being held in the hands of two children. The children were naked, winged, and flying in the air.

"The most auspicious card in the entire tarot," she whispered to me. "The card of the World always shows the globe of Earth held in the hands of twin children."

I flinched before I could hold it in. My sister Esther had just given birth to twins. But it was unlikely that vampires would be interested in plant-children. And the twins on the card looked like stylized cherubs, not plant-people.

"This card of the Major Arcana means great success in all areas of life." She smiled at Ming. "If this is the answer to her question, the good fortune is to be in all areas of our lives."

"*If* we survive this change," Ming said. She turned her black eyes to me and said, "I will answer your question. The change within us began recently with an upheaval and the return of our souls. It is still happening now. We are still in danger *now*. One hour before dawn, all of my Mithrans younger than a half century are chained in their lairs and watched over by their most trusted blood-servants. This is the only way they can be prevented from walking into the sun and burning. Shackled by who we are becoming, we wait out this change together, hoping we will all survive.

"Also," she continued, "there are enemies in my city. The body we found is proof of this."

Without turning over any of the other cards, Yummy gathered them into the single deck, placed them in the tin box, and strapped it closed. I assumed that meant our card session was over. I had survived.

Ming settled her vampire eyes on me, but I didn't feel any attempt at mesmerism. She wasn't trying to roll me. "Many people and creatures want the Blood Tarot," she said. "Black-witches, blood witches, power-hungry humans, weres of any stripe, Anzu for reasons of their own. The dragons of light—the arcenciels, who do not want a powerful tool in the hands of anyone—wish to find it. The skinwalker and the Dark Queen. My enemies, both Mithran and Naturaleza."

Were-creatures and skinwalkers. Unit Eighteen had three special agents who were werecats. FireWind was a skinwalker. And FireWind had been breathing down my neck asking questions about my search for the Blood Tarot. Soul was an arcenciel, and she had been on vacation for far too long, long enough that Unit Eighteen was growing concerned. And Mithrans and Naturaleza were both vampires. One group kept humans like pets, the other liked hunting and killing. Until tonight, they all had felt like maggots to me.

"With the Blood Tarot," she said, "I have great power. All others want the cursed deck. I have it. Therefore, you will work with me, for me, and I will protect you."

Instead of answering her demand to work for her, I said, "You said your enemy was after the cards, but you didn't offer a name. Who?"

"The most dangerous *searcher* of all: the Grand Inquisitor, Tomás de Torquemada," Ming said. "He is near us. He *searches* for the final death of the undead and for the Blood Tarot. He *searches* to bathe in the blood of his enemies. He *searches* for the end of this world and the rebirth of the next. And he intends to ride the dragon."

Wackadoodle, I thought, just like T. Laine said. Except that the forms of the word *search* had been oddly accented.

"I owe you two boons," Ming said, "yet I offer a third if you will do one thing for me. A small thing for one such as you."

"I won't promise you anything," I said.

She was still holding me with her eyes, but she didn't try to roll me, which might be the most strange part of this entire evening, because all vamps wanted to roll people and drink them down. It was what they did. I didn't break the contact either.

She took on a pleading expression. "I ask for little of you. Yet I offer a third boon," she said. "Find Tomás. Kill him. And kill the four and the four who guard him still, for even with souls to guide them, they are now no better than they ever were."

"I'm a special agent with a law enforcement agency. I'm not a hired killer," I said.

"Protecting the public is part of your job, yes? He seeks my land, he seeks my head, and if he is successful, he and his scions will take the Blood Tarot and ride the dragon. If you do not kill them, your city humans will die. And your own kind will suffer as well."

"I'm not a hired killer," I said again.

"So you say." She tilted her head, that birdlike thing they do. "But the time may come when you hold his head and his restored soul in your hands and you will be forced into a choice: to allow him to die true-dead, or to save him. Make the choice that brings safety to yours and to mine."

I answered in the way law enforcement had to in the presence of a powerful, not quite sane vampire. "Ming of Glass has offered information. PsyLED Eighteen has listened and understands. You said there was a dead body on your property. Where is it?"

"It is yours," she said.

I hoped she didn't mean that the dead body was my own.

"You may go," she commanded.

Not taking my eyes from hers, I got up and walked away from the table. No one followed. I had been in Ming's clan home before, and though the foyer floor was changed, the walls were pretty much where they had been. I said softly, hoping comms was still listening, "I'm heading to the front door."

FireWind and LaFleur met me at the foyer, a smear of blood on Aya's sleeve, the knuckles of both hands bruised and torn. The three of us left the house, a heavy river mist coiling around us. As the door closed, I pulled my cell, turned it off, and then slapped my hand against my chest as if to start my heart beating again. "That was horrible. Did you get all that?"

"Yes," FireWind said, ushering me toward the vehicles through the heavy fog.

I pointed to his bloody hand. "Fight?"

"Cai was insistent that we leave you," he said wryly. "We tried to dissuade him, but he was stronger than usual."

"And faster," Rick murmured.

"Dead body?" I asked.

"Haven't seen one," Rick said. "And Cai didn't mention one when we were beating on each other."

"Let's get out of here and back to HQ," FireWind said.

"If you can wait just a few minutes," I said, "I should read the land deeper this time. And I want to touch one of the burned circles at the edge of the property."

Both men pulled their weapons as I got the vampire tree and my new blanket from the passenger seat of my car. No vamps or humans followed from the house, but the mist had grown heavier, the air wetter. I could see maybe a foot in front of my face with any certainty, but the land was a good enough guide. I bent and touched the ground, scanning the lawn before zeroing in on the closest burned circle. "There's no one on the estate but us and vampires and Ming's humans, and we're alone on the lawn," I said. Leading the way, I walked into the swirling fog.

A foot out from the burned land I unfolded my backup blanket (an old army blanket Occam had found in a surplus store) and laid it on the wet grass. I sat and crossed my knees, the potted vampire tree in my lap. "You bite me and I'll make you regret it," I told the plant.

It was a testament to my life that neither of my bosses thought the threat to the tree was odd enough to comment over.

I touched the ground with one fingertip, and when nothing felt wrong, I placed my palm flat on the wet grass and dug into the dirt with my fingertips. It was vampy ground, a little dead-ish, a little bloody, needing some supplements and vegetable matter, maybe some mushroom compost. But when I placed my fingertips in the blackened circle, things were very different. In the dirt were traces of fire and the horror the grass felt at being burned, but the roots were still alive. Whatever had burned here had burned high and fast, not deeply, not slowly. And mixed in among the grass' pain was a strong sense of ecstasy, and beneath it, a fainter sense of awe and joy, the kind I might have felt had I watched a particularly beautiful sunrise. The vamps had died . . . happy.

I pulled my hands and consciousness from the dirt and handed the potted tree to Rick, accepting Aya's hand to pull me to my feet. I tossed the blanket over my shoulder. "One more. Just to be sure." I walked through the fog toward the next burned spot and tested the ground with a fingertip before I squatted, my weight on the backs of my calves, my arms forward around my knees, and pushed all ten fingers into the dirt.

"Dead leaves, living roots," I said. "And she was . . . The vamp who died here was singing as she burned."

"These circles are from dead suckheads?" Rick asked. "From burning in the sun?"

"Yes. And they weren't tied down to burn at dawn for punishment. They died happy." I stood and brushed off my hands. "Okay. Let's go back to HQ. Things are very wrong here."

Wackadoodle, I thought as we approached the drive and the parked cars. And we still didn't have the promised dead body.

But we didn't make it back to the cars.

Yummy appeared out of the mist, standing near my vehicle on the driveway, a bright green floral satchel in her left hand, a sword in her right. Parked behind our cars was hers, a Ferrari LaFerrari gold flake 2015 convertible she had "confiscated" from an enemy. She had been standing on the driveway, and not in the grass, so I had missed her appearance.

I took the last step to the concrete drive. I felt them step onto Ming's land. A dead sensation whipped through me.

"Vampires," I whispered. "There." I looked to the fence downriver from Ming's. I grabbed my best weapon away from Rick, the vampire tree. Stuck my finger into the soil, calling on Soulwood, pulling the wakened energies to me.

Rick cursed and tossed off his suit jacket.

Aya pulled multiple weapons.

Yummy pitched her satchel to my feet. Pulled her sword. Dropped the scabbard.

Everything *fast*.

To me she said, "Smallsword. Get it." She pointed at the satchel that had landed at my feet.

She screamed into the night, "I am Yvonne Colstrip, blood

child of the Warlord of the Dark Queen, the scion of Ming of Glass! I offer blood challenge to you all!"

A vamp in ninja black plunged out of the night. Landed to my side, but stumbled on the uneven ground and somersaulted away. He carried two swords, to Yummy's one. I ducked to the ground and opened her floral satchel. A smaller sword rested on top. I pulled it out.

She ripped it from my hands. Somersaulted, leaping into the air.

The intruder vampire stood. Vamped out. Small fangs. Black clothes with some kind of belted tunic dress over them, also black. Bearded. Mean looking.

Another vamp plummeted out of the darkness. Landed to the first vamp's side. They could have been brothers, dressed similarly, bearded. "I stand as second for Carlos Contreras." He pointed one of his swords at me. "You are her second?"

Second? Oh. In a duel. I shook my head fast.

"I stand as second," Cai said. He was positioned on the fog-wet grass, holding two swords, like the others. But Cai was wearing boxers and a white tee. And more blood, as if he had taken a quick sip before rushing out to the lawn.

Carlos attacked Yummy. Three quick strikes before he danced back.

Yummy had blocked them all. I had never seen Yummy fight. Not like this.

Rick was naked and going furry, but it would take several minutes. His tattoos shimmered in the night, the ones that had been applied with blood magic against his will, using the Blood Tarot, and had later been chewed on by werewolves, leaving behind a scarred magical mess and gold-inked cat eyes that sometimes glowed. Like now. All that could not be a coincidence, but was a worry for another time.

Aya aimed a weapon but didn't fire. "PsyLED cannot legally interfere with this because Yvonne Colstrip challenged him. That makes it vampire business, not law enforcement, unless Yummy asks for help or one of us is injured. Do not interfere, Ingram." He glanced at my tree and back to the fight. "With commonly accepted law enforcement methods."

So that meant methods not usually accepted were okay? And that my service weapon—for self-defense—was okay too? We were walking a fine line.

Yummy whirled her weapons, moving in and away again. The clashes of steel sounded harsh and low, muted in the fog.

One-handed, I checked my Glock 20. It was loaded with silver-lead rounds. FireWind had said I couldn't use it, but I had other weapons, less obvious ones, that I could exploit. The *hunger* deep within me, deep within the land, spiked.

I rested the Glock in my lap, not a secure position, but a good one for fast use. I sent my earth energies across the upper layer of the ground, and counted vampires, slightly maggoty bits of undeath. Yummy, Carlos, his second, and at least three more vamps were on Ming's property.

"Aya, there's three more standing close to the driveway, hidden by the fog."

"Copy that."

Yummy raced forward and engaged her enemy. When she danced back, she was bleeding. Her blood splattered on the ground. If I wanted to kill Yummy, I could. But it was the other one I wanted.

Yummy and Carlos dashed forward and back, lunging and cutting and blocking. Not near enough blocking. More of her blood flew. Cai stared at Carlos' second, looking like the dangerous Cai I remembered, not the blood-drunk one who had wandered around during my visit. Even in his undies.

Yummy stabbed forward and up with her short blade. Whipped down with the longsword. She nicked the vamp's chin. And half severed his hand. All in one move. Carlos dropped his shortsword and sprinted back. I found the blood trail he left and gathered it to me through the earth.

Rick stepped around the front of my car. A black leopard, full of killing grace and rippling muscle. He stood at my side and screamed into the night, coarse, half roar, half screech, all leopard. Carlos' second practically levitated into the air and landed several feet away from the wereleopard.

No grindylow showed up. I figured that meant no humans would be in danger from Rick's were-taint. Grindys appear to kill any were-creature who passes the taint to a human.

The fight moved away a bit, into the fog, closer to the river. The hidden others moved closer.

"Aya. Two of the other vampires are approaching."

THREE

I pulled on the earth force and wrapped my gift around the blood droplets from Yummy's opponent. I whispered to the vampire tree, "Don't eat them. They are not dinner. I'm only taking a little."

Hunger rose in me. The *hunger* of the land. I held it in place, forced it down. Breathed through the need in me.

Gently, I sank beneath the ground and found tree roots, pliable and strong. I pushed them up from the ground. Following the man's life force on the earth, I found the pattern of his movements, his sword technique. I shoved at the roots. Caught his toe. Tripped him. Not enough to harm him. Just enough to offset his rhythm.

It wasn't a fair fight. Yummy wasn't as good as he was. And she wasn't in fighting armor. My friend was losing.

And I'd stopped fighting fair a long time ago.

Aya and Rick changed position, the leopard edging toward the battle, Aya back to provide cover, ready for anyone approaching from behind or to the sides.

I felt a vamp leap. "Aya. Above!" I shouted. He raised his weapon overhead and fired three shots. Ducked to the side. Fired three more straight down. The vamp said something in some language I didn't know.

Aya said what sounded like, *"No me importa."* He fired three more rounds.

I slammed into the ground. A heavy weight on top of me.

And then I was flying. Rushing. Away from the fight.

Pain. Claws digging into my arms.

I had a single moment of clarity. A vamp had dropped onto me from the far side of the car. Picked me up. Leaped away. I was being kidnapped.

"I smell it upon you," the vampire said in heavily accented English. "Give it to me."

In midair, I wrapped my energies around him from the potted tree I still held. His power felt different from other vamps I had fed to the earth. Less maggoty and more like deep cold water. Icy water. The vampire tree grew a vine two feet long. It wrapped around his neck, stuck thorns into him. And sucked his energies down. The vamp staggered. Slowed.

He crashed to the earth in a heap.

I rolled off his undead body. Breathing too fast in fear, in shock, my heart thumping hard. *Hunger.* Putting my hand to the ground, I drained his undeath. *Hunger* as if the land starved, rose, and rushed through me.

"Stop," I whispered to the tree and to the land. I wrapped my fingers around the vine and tore it free of the vamp's neck. A trickle of vamp blood fell from each thorn. Thorns that hadn't been there only moments ago. Thorns on a vine that hadn't been there either.

My own *hunger*, the land's *hunger*, fought to take all of him. To feed him to the earth. Fighting my own need, I took him to the very edge of true-death. Stopped before the vampire was true-dead. Still undead by a hair.

Breathing hard, I placed my hand to the earth. I didn't want to claim Ming's land. Didn't want to make it mine. But the land wanted what I could offer, what I could give it. The land wanted the body and blood and soul of the vampire beneath my hand. The earth always *wanted*.

I pulled my palm away. Realized I was crying and wiped my tears and snot away. Breathed slower, or tried to. Found myself. Found my own desires and needs. We had been attacked. We could legally respond.

I shoved my conscious thoughts through the ground and up into the sleeping trees. I found an owl who was watching the battle and, trying something new, gently entered its consciousness. The fight scene was crisp and clear as if lit by bright lights.

Carlos stabbed Yummy. She fell. I yanked Carlos' undeath, pulled the icy cold energy to me through the ground, a gray green energy that looked like no soul I had ever seen before. I yanked it into the tree. Which was now far too large for the small pot. Vines were growing as it tried to reach the ground.

Tried to take root and claim the land for itself. For the Green Knight. I grabbed them and held them to me.

Feeling everything through the land, seeing it all through the owl's eyes, sharp and harsh and detailed. Rick was snarling, fighting the duel's second. Aya staked the vampire he had shot. He hadn't used silver rounds. Why?

Aya aimed at the vampire fighting with Rick.

Ming appeared at the fight scene. Popped there. Vamp-fast. She beheaded the vamp at Aya's feet. Grabbed Rick by the scruff of the neck and threw him across the lawn. With a single flash of steel, she took the head of the second. "Finish him," she demanded of Yummy, the sound so loud my own ears ached.

With a single flashing swipe, Yummy took her opponent's head.

Ming bent and cut off the vampire's fingers, then placed them in Yummy's hands.

My stomach turned.

The owl fluttered its wings at the blood and focused in closely.

Ming rifled the vampire's pockets and handed Yummy more stuff. And then yet more from the vampire at FireWind's feet.

"Cai," Ming said, the single word arrogant; she was accustomed to being obeyed.

The man in his underwear lifted and carried something from the front door. It was a naked human body, blood smeared all over the clear plastic it was wrapped in. Duct tape held the wrapping closed, and there was no trail of blood. Either vampires had drained it totally dry or it had been dead long enough not to drip.

The body we were called here for in the first place. Hours of wackadoodle and a violent attack ago.

The owl lost interest and launched from the branch. It flew along the road and I got a view of two white vans, the kind used in package delivery in neighborhoods, vans tall enough to stand up inside, big enough to hold many people. The vampires' transportation. The owl flew farther, seeking a place to hunt. I dropped away and I was back inside my body, in the dark, with a near-true-dead vampire.

Four pawed, Rick trotted through the undergrowth. Stuck his muzzle out at me and sniffed.

"I'm okay, boss," I said softly, the words painful in my bruised throat.

Rick whined an interrogative.

"I didn't kill him. If Ming wants a prisoner to question, this one is still undead. But he cut me with his nails, and the land isn't happy with him."

Rick huffed. Raised his head. He screamed into the night.

I nearly peed in my pants.

I was sitting in my car, Aya in the driver's seat, a baggie of ice from Ming's kitchen against my throat. The window was down so the rest of the unit could talk to us, but the car was running and the seat was warming the misery out of me.

The tree was on the hood of my car, a bloated, misshapen, wrinkled, and weathered-looking trunk three feet tall, twisted branches with leaves so thick they rustled in the cold air. Vines coiled out of the pot to pool on the hood, wicked thorns on every branch and vine.

Lightning flashed overhead, odd lightning, pearly and prismed through the heavy fog. The water droplets glowed before the light vanished. It flickered again. Fog and lightning, especially lightning that flashed the colors of the rainbow, were a strange combination.

Even FireWind studied the sky. Then the flashing light was gone and the mist closed in again. His face high, his expressions went through a series of changes.

It occurred to me that the flashing lights could be an arcenciel. No one in Knoxville had seen a rainbow dragon in weeks. Maybe months. Including the assistant director of PsyLED, Soul. And people had been looking for her.

Frowning, my boss-boss pulled a cell phone from a pocket and thumbed through apps. He was waiting on several things, among them: the ETA of the forensic CSI team, and any information about white vans passing traffic cameras. So far there had been nothing about either. CSI was on the way but saw no point at speed, and the vans had seemingly vanished. He pocketed the phone. He raised his eyes to the tree on the car. "That thing is . . . ungodly ugly."

I took a sip of water. Swallowing was painful, but it was getting better as my plant-body healed itself. FireWind had been afraid the tissues would swell and close off my air, but they were relaxing. "Yeah. I need a place to plant it," I said. "And I need a new tree at HQ. How about in the roof garden."

"You jest." His tone was so dry my hair might have crackled.

I didn't answer, but I did give him a side-eye smile. We had tried that once, and though the tree had been very happy to claim the space, the rest of the building hadn't been so joyful when it outgrew its soil and its welcome. "I'll plant this one on the edge of my property," I said placidly.

Rick, fully clothed, rounded the vehicles and took a place in the backseat. "Ming's people seized the nearly dead fanghead in the woods. I assume they took him to her clan home."

I presumed Rick meant Ming's punishment room, and that the vampire who tried to carry me off would be killed. I wondered if it was like the punishment house on the church grounds where I grew up. Or even worse. I wished I felt some small shard of sadness for his torture. But he had been trying to take me away.

"You didn't attempt to ask for assertions regarding his health and safety?" Aya asked, again with that dry, wry tone.

It was a sticky situation. Legally Ming was Master of the City and her land might (or might not) be considered much like an embassy. Politics were still on miry ground in the United States regarding vampires and other paranormals, though the Dark Queen's newly created ambassadors and her assigned legal teams were working to codify the vampires'—and by extension other paranormals'—right to exist.

"No," Rick said. "They gave him some blood at the scene. He took a breath. And I left. I can't testify to anything. And though I did get his scent, I never saw his face."

I thought about that one. I had seen the vampire's face up close and personal as I ripped the vine off his neck. I kept that to myself. Vamp relations were minefields. I looked over at the killing site, the battlefield where Yummy had beheaded the vampire she had challenged.

"Ingram. Why did the vampire try to take you away?" FireWind asked. "We don't have anything you said after you were taken off scene."

I touched my ear. "My comms set is gone. I hope I don't have

to pay for that, since I lost it while being abducted and attacked."
FireWind didn't reply. "The vampire said something about
'smelling it' on me. No explanation of what *it* was."

"The Blood Tarot?" FireWind asked, not expecting an answer. "Did you smell it on her when you were in cat form?" he
asked LaFleur.

Rick, his white hair moving slightly in the night air, bright
in the fog and the faint lights, turned to us, his eyes unfocused
and haunted. "Yes. Yummy smells like it too. Strange smell.
Like old death and herbs and black magic." Rick had been tattooed with a Blood Tarot.

That sounded horrible. I smelled nothing when I sniffed my
hands but dug in my glove box until I found hand sanitizer. I
cleaned my hands with the goop as best I was able, the residue
smelling like synthesized mango. While I cleaned myself, I
asked, "The dead body? What do we know?"

FireWind said, "White male, nude. Around five-ten, one
fifty, muscular build with little body fat. Patchy facial hair,
blondish, blue eyes. Signs of torture, but odd, not like the usual
electric burns or cigarette burns, no broken fingers or pulled-out
fingernails."

I didn't react. I had never seen the kinds of torture FireWind
was describing, but I had seen lots of awful things, and the after-
effects of those things on the abused, at the church.

"Ming said he isn't human," Rick said, "and beneath the
bleach, I smelled . . ." His words trailed off. "I smelled something familiar, but I can't place it. Something odd."

"For now, we'll take her word," FireWind said. He didn't say,
"That allows us to keep the body rather than turn it over to local
law enforcement," but I heard the words in his tone. "CSI has
already taken the body to UTMC for a forensic PM."

The University of Tennessee Medical Center was the only
local hospital that had staff and forensic pathologists who
worked on paranormal creatures.

The exterior landscape lights came on and Ming exited her
home. "Ming," I said, indicating the front door. The Master of
the City was wearing a bloodred dress, a tight sheath that fell to
her ankles. Her hair was up in a chignon, like women wore back
in the sixties. She carried the two blades she had used in battle.
Behind her walked Cai, dressed in his typical all black. They

looked like vamps again. Dangerous. Killers. Not blood-drunk teenagers on spring break.

She walked from the concrete toward the battlefield, where Yummy still knelt on the ground beside the dead vampire. Ming's delicate shoes were silent on the grass, her body shifting the fog into swirls, the currents of the air amplified by Cai's passage behind her.

She walked straight to Yummy. Ming extended the swords to Cai, who took them. The MOC bent over and pulled a bloody necklace from the stump of the vampire's neck and hung it around Yummy's neck. Yummy made a sound suspiciously like a sob.

Bare-handed, Ming rested her hands on Yummy's head and spoke, so softly I couldn't hear her words. When she was done, she held out her hand to Cai, who placed the smallsword in her hand. I reached for the door handle to halt whatever was about to happen.

Aya stopped me with a lifted hand. "Wait."

Ming used the blade to cut her wrist and held it to Yummy. The young vampire drank from Ming. "Oh," I said. "She's healing her."

"Yes. And more," Aya said. "I think much more."

Yummy pulled a small blade and slit her own wrist, holding it up for Ming to sip from. The Master of the City took a small sip and licked the wound closed.

Cai held out something to Yummy. It was a floral duffel bag that matched the satchel she had dropped on the driveway before the fight. Yummy stood, rising slowly, as if she hurt, and bowed from her waist to Ming. Her clothing was crusted with blood, most of it her own. Ming turned and, with Cai behind her, walked back to her clan home and inside. The door closed.

"What's happening?" I asked.

Aya sighed. "Nothing good, I fear."

Yummy cleaned her blades on the clothing of the dead vamp nearest, picked up the duffel bag, and limped toward us. On the way, she sheathed the long weapon from the scabbard she had tossed to the ground. She stored the short one in the satchel and approached my car.

Yummy opened the back door on the driver's side and stuffed her belongings on the floor behind Aya before she climbed in and shut the door. None of us said anything. Yummy looked worn, tired, and sad in the faint light coming from the landscape lights outside. Her blond hair was bloody and she was missing a hank at one shoulder where a sword had cut it off at some point during the battle. Her eyes were unfocused, staring into the distance at the back of the driver's seat.

Finally she took a breath and breathed it out, leaned in toward me, focused on my eyes, and said, "Hi, roomie."

"What?"

She laughed, but didn't sound amused. Maybe a little manic. "I personally challenged Ming's attackers instead of allowing them to challenge Ming properly. And I reeked of the Blood Tarot. The ones who got away will believe that I possess the cursed deck. Therefore, I've been . . ." She shrugged slightly, and when she spoke she sounded all formal and vampirish. "Removed from service."

Her expression was empty and strange and I glanced from her to FireWind, who was watching her. He looked pensive, and a little sad, as if he knew what she meant.

"At the same time, I've also been charged with keeping you alive," she said, on a sigh, as if she hated what she was saying next. "So, with your permission, I'm moving in to keep you safe from Torquemada's assassins and guards while they try to kill me, giving Ming time to locate them and kill them."

I nearly dropped the ice bag at my throat. "No."

"Yes." Her shoulders slumped. "Ming wants you alive. She finds you 'important and of value,' and she 'owes two boons' to you." She sounded as if she quoted Ming.

Before I could formulate a reply stronger than my original "No," she continued, this time sounding more formal.

"A dead body that had been rinsed in pure chlorine bleach was sitting upright at the front entrance when we woke tonight, like some kind of message. There was nothing on the security cam footage. It just appeared. None of us could find a scent on it anywhere. And, as good citizens of the city, we have given that body to PsyLED. Before Nell turns me down again, I have information you need."

"What sort of information?" FireWind asked.

"Tomás de Torquemada wants the Blood Tarot. There were sixteen confirmed guards traveling with him. Three died tonight, and all three deaths have now been laid at my feet. Photographic confirmation of the kills has already been released, with photographs of Ming, standing with her hand on my head, as if she was giving me her blessing to begin my own blood clan. This ruse raises my standing among the Mithrans who can be challenged for land and territory and for access to Ming. My implied release and elevation in status indicates—incorrectly—that I am being given blood clan status in Knoxville, directly under her command. It divides her enemies, so that some will come after me and some will come after her. I, however, have no primo or secundo. I am a blood clan of one. I'll have to take all challengers on one after the other."

"I wasn't born yesterday," I said.

"You're a baby," she said dryly.

"You're bait. She's sending you to me to keep her enemies off her backside. She wants you to fight vampire duels on my land. No," I said.

"*We* are bait," she corrected. "You were in those photographs as well, positioned in the shots to appear to be part of the deal."

A vampire had made me part of her machinations. "No. Not on my land."

"They'll find your land eventually, regardless of where I am," Yummy said. "Your magic is powerful and Torquemada wants anything and anyone powerful. He has always collected powerful creatures and forced them to work for his cause or to provide blood for him. Without me there, when they come for you, you will be alone. You and your sisters and the babies. And your Occam."

My cat-man had once dated—dating being a euphemism for sex and blood exchange—Yummy. I wasn't worried that Occam would cheat on me, but I also didn't want to have to see them together on my land, because not so terribly long ago, before we became friends of a sort, Yummy had made it clear she was available if Occam ever wanted to go back to her.

"Ingram," FireWind said. "If vampires can sense your land—"

"We can," Yummy interrupted.

FireWind gave his faint frown. "I can't force you to take her in, Ingram, but if you are in danger, according to PsyLED protocols, I have to put you and your family into protective custody."

"Dagnabbit," I said, cussing hard in church-speak. A vampire had put me between a rock and a hard place.

More thoughtfully, FireWind added, "Ming asked a PsyLED agent to kill her enemies. That agent refused. Therefore . . ." He stared hard at Yummy. "Ming guessed they would attack tonight."

"Not in such numbers or so early in the evening. Midnight was her guess. PsyLED was still here, and Ming wasn't anywhere near ready."

"So Ming had to revise plans," he said. "And since Nell was here, your impromptu strategy included her." His voice dropped lower. "One of *my* agents."

"Everything went sideways. No one expected anyone to make off with Nell."

"But they did," FireWind said. "And Ming used that abduction to plant one of her scions—"

"Sort of a former scion," Yummy interrupted again.

"—with Nell, taking the heat off the Master of the City and directing the violence to PsyLED. Why?"

"Layers and layers in her plans," Yummy said. "As I said. PsyLED was here, so you three got incorporated in them."

I said, "If you take me into protective custody, off my land, I'll be weak." My boss-boss looked at me, knowing what I meant. On the land, if there were duels, I could take the attackers, blood drop by blood drop. What he didn't necessarily know was that I might not be able to stop feeding the land. I might not be able to save Yummy from its *hunger*. The more I fed Soulwood, the more it *hungered*. Soulwood—which was part of me—had a mind and belly of its own.

"I said no." I was having to force the words out, and my voice was scratchy. I sipped my water.

"The others *will* attack," Yummy said. "It might be in groups of four, likely before dawn, looking for you, and for me, and for the Blood Tarot. I won't be here, and Ming and Cai will destroy any who come here. But they'll know I'm gone and that you were present when I was elevated in status. The photographs Ming released make it look like you were part of the deal. They *will* come to your land. It's unlikely you can kill four alone. Better if we work together."

Four vampire ninjas, I thought.

"Nell," she said, dropping all the vampire formality and talking like her regular self. "I'll follow and hide on your land, no matter if you agree. I'll keep the life in you safe. I've been given this responsibility by Ming of Glass, Master of the City of Knoxville."

Aya was watching me, his face austere and barren as a desert.

"I can stay on your land when I'm off duty," Rick said, sounding exhausted from the two shape-changes, his voice flowing to us through the darkness, on the other side of the open window. "I can roam in cat form." A hint of amusement in his tone, he added, "It isn't as if I have a social life."

"You will not be alone at night," FireWind said. "You have Occam. Margot can roam in cat form, if she's willing, since she can't give were-taint to vampires or your sister's family, and her lack of shifting control won't be a burden. That would give you enough paranormal protection to deal with an attack." FireWind looked at his cell and thumbed across the face. "I won't overrule you on your own home territory, Ingram, but I agree you need more security than you think."

"Fine." Not *Fine, sir*. Just *fine*. And not a happy *fine*.

I scowled at Yummy and said, "I'll know where you are on my land. I'll know if vampires come onto my land. *I don't need you*. And the land might *eat* you." The vampire tree might eat her. It had grown a lot stronger and a lot more possessive than the last time she came onto my land.

"Ming left me no choice. I understand that you'll eat the undead life within me if I overreach and cause you to face more danger." Yummy slumped slightly, and her face changed from something stiff and frightened but resolved to something more human and full of emotions I couldn't read. "I can live with the threat of death, bestie. I can die happy."

Bestie. Yummy was calling me her best friend.

We were more acquaintances than friends. We had shared tea. Talked about life. If that was a best friend in Yummy's life, her life was a barren shell.

On the hood of the car, the vampire tree fell over, scattering soil. I popped the trunk and got out, gathered up the tree and its too-small pot, and scraped the soil into it. I stashed the tree in the trunk, my hands brushing across it. Instantly some of the pain in my throat eased. I thought about saying thank you, but I had learned a lot about power struggles tonight and I wasn't about to thank the Green Knight just now. "Be good or I'll burn you," I ordered the tree. I closed the trunk and retook my place.

Yummy had stepped from my car when I did, her bags in her arms, and she had heard me threaten the tree. "What are you again?" she asked me.

"We've had this conversation. Not having it again."

"Debrief at HQ," Aya said, unfolding his long legs from my driver's seat. "We'll talk more there."

Rick walked away through the fog-laden darkness too. Yummy's Ferrari LaFerrari pulled into the road. I took my seat and backed into the road in front of Ming's clan home.

"I'm too tired to debrief," I said to my empty car. I put it into drive. "And I have a kid I was supposed to pick up and take home. Not that anyone asked me."

I called my sister Mud and told her I wouldn't be picking her up before bedtime. She was at Esther's Tulip Tree House—what the family had taken to calling the freakishly growing, deeply rooted living trees that had grown up around her log home when the babies were born.

Saving my voice, I listened through my earbud as Mud chattered about her day. She had been dropped off by the school bus and was having a great time helping her sister take care of the twins. Mud and Esther, once bitter enemies, were getting along famously since the babies were born. Mud loved them with utter devotion. She kept a bag at Esther's for overnighters, since my ability to be home at night during dangerous or hot cases was uncertain, and the judge at the guardianship hearing had agreed that Esther was an acceptable babysitter when I ran late.

Mud and I had spent a lot of time together over the last month, preparing for the court case that had given me full custody and assigned me as her legal guardian. That guardianship was not intended to keep her from her family or from the church, should she wish to return to it and to that lifestyle, and the judge had approved visitation to her parents, her sister-mothers, her sibs and half sibs, so long as she was not forced to stay there, and was not "programmed to marry as a child bride."

I knew she needed the noisy, joy-filled part of polygamous life. I remembered exactly how it had felt to be ripped away from everything normal and to suddenly be in an empty house, without dozens of people everywhere.

A week past, I had been given full—but conditional—guardianship and custody of my little sister by the court system of Tennessee. This legal approval had created inside me a confusing mixture of joy and terror each time I thought about it, and I had discovered that I mostly didn't want to think about it in a conceptual way, but only in the way of immediate problem-solving—like getting the church's support payments set up in Mud's name for college, and my own finances in better shape to care for her. I was good at that, the figuring-out part. Not so good at recognizing that I had succeeded in several of my goals for my sisters, and what it all might mean for everyone's lives.

I had succeeded. I had gotten custody.

And now vampires were after me. My sisters and the twins would be in danger. My steering wheel squeaked and I had to stop twisting it in fear and frustration. With my thoughts on what I had done and what I should do next, I followed the vehicles in front of me by muscle memory.

I could take my sisters to the church and leave them. I could take FireWind up on the idea of removing us all into protective custody. I didn't know what to do, except that I had spoken truly. We were stronger on Soulwood.

As I drove, Mud filled me in on the details about the babies. Noah and Ruth Nicholson—my sister had taken back her maiden name and given her kids her maiden name because her ex-husband had deserted them all—were thriving, both far ahead of testing standards. They were trying to roll over already when they shouldn't even be able to lift their heads, and, so far, neither was growing leaves. She prattled about Esther's Christmas decorations and the plans the Nicholson family had for the holiday late next week. I had put up a small tree at our house, but I hadn't decorated it yet, mainly because I couldn't force myself to drag out and use the old Ingram decorations, the ones left behind when John died, the decorations that his first wife, Leah, and I had hung when I'd "married" into the family at age twelve. They were things of my victim-past, and I wanted better for my first Christmas with Occam and Mud in what would be, by then, our home.

By the time my one-sided conversation with Mud was over, I had arrived at HQ and pulled in behind the golden Ferrari. Sighing, I got out of my car and walked toward Yummy and FireWind, who were standing beneath the security lights and camera at the unmarked entrance to PsyLED Unit Eighteen HQ. The two were having a heated discussion.

The door opened behind them and Occam stuck his head out. An unknown emotion flashed across his face and was gone, replaced by a tense smile as he looked me over from top to bottom, his eyes lingering on my throat. "Hey there, Nell, sugar. While these two argue about protocol, I have pizza for you upstairs. Come on up."

On cue, I felt faint with hunger.

"Wait, where's your tree?" he asked. "Do you want me to go get it?"

"The tree stays in her trunk until she can safely dispose of it," Aya said, interrupting his own conversation.

I took the opportunity to slip past the two arguers and inside. I squeezed Occam's hand, pulling him with me. We were careful about PDA—which I had learned meant public displays of affection—at work. There had been a long-standing rule about agents in one unit not dating, but since Eighteen was the only mostly para unit, that rule had been relaxed, though not ignored. FireWind's threat of transfer was always on the table, but we could have friendships as long as they didn't bring trouble to the job.

"What kind of pizza?" I asked.

"One veggie supreme, one meat lovers', and one spicy sausage and pepperoni with jalapeños, that one ordered for LaFleur."

"I'll make up something for his stomach."

Occam laughed and, as we reached the top of the stairs, buzzed us in, placing a kiss at my temple and plucking leaves from my hairline before the door opened. "I missed you, plant-woman."

"And I missed you, cat-man."

"This working split shifts sucks."

"At least he aligned our days off."

"The FireWind giveth and the FireWind taketh away."

"Let me clean up." I pushed into the locker room and saw myself in the mirror. No wonder Occam had reacted. I was covered with dried vampire blood and more leaves were hiding in my hair. Stress always brought on leaf budding, even in winter when a proper deciduous tree was leafless. I supposed that even as a tree, I wasn't proper.

Leaning toward the mirror over the sinks, I yanked leaves free and tucked them in a pocket. After drawing on my power, my eyes were greener, the leafy spring green that said I had been in contact with the earth too long again. My hair was brighter. A rich reddish tint in the tresses, brighter than the drying blood.

I stripped and showered, washing all the blood off. Looking under the door into the main room several times. Nervous as a feral cat.

I hated the unisex locker room, even though it had separate, lockable showers and changing rooms. It tripped what Occam referred to as my *PTSD triggers* from my childhood. I just thought it gave me the shakes. The men in the unit respected my need for privacy and had never, not one time, come in while I showered and changed. That was a kindness I could never repay.

When I was dressed, now wearing a pair of sweats, I retrieved the leaves I had groomed out of my hair during the day and just now, and flushed them.

Leaving my white shirt and black pants soaking in the sink to get the blood out, I returned to the hallway. Occam stood there, his gobag on one shoulder, a wriggling puppy in that elbow. In his other hand he held a plate of hot veggie pizza. I took a slice, biting experimentally into the greasy cheesy deliciousness and petting Cherry, who licked my hand enthusiastically. My throat seemed much better. I swallowed the pizza bite and said, "You're leaving?"

Currently, Occam was supposed to be off shift at eight p.m., working a ten-hour split shift. I was supposed to be off no later than six, but with Ming's summons, my shift had run way long.

"Naw. I caught a case. Should be a short one. Take a report and head home. FireWind updated me on everything, including you being abducted and Yummy staying on the land. I'm not happy that I wasn't at Ming's when you needed me, you know that, right?"

"I'm a fine agent and I didn't need help. And *you* know *that*, right?"

"I do. Just had to say it. My case is out in your part of the county, so I'll take Cherry. When I'm done, I'll send a prelim from the field, then check on your family, drop off the dog, feed the cats, and stoke the stove so you'll have some heat." Mud's tricolor English springer spaniel had become the HQ office pup, the only PsyLED unit to have a mascot. "And before you ask, she did great today. Tandy took her on walks and a run, and T. Laine fed her."

"T. Laine feeds her too much," I said, stuffing my face and sneaking Cherry a tiny pinch of cheese.

"True." He ignored me doing what I accused T. Laine of doing, glanced down the hallway both ways, and leaned in for a fast kiss. His lips almost moved the way they used to, before he was injured so badly that even shifting into his werecat on the full moon on Soulwood land hadn't healed him fully. "When I'm done with your critters," he said, his lips moving on mine, "I'll go furry, patrolling. Tell your sister not to shoot me."

Esther didn't like paras, despite the fact she herself was one, but she was getting used to the possibility that they may not all be devil spawn as the church taught. "I'll text her. I'll be back as soon as I can. No humans were killed tonight, so the action paperwork will only be four feet high, not ten."

He kissed me again and opened the door, coming face-to-face with Yummy. My stomach cramped in what I figured was jealousy. Then I smothered it, because Occam stepped back, gave Yummy room to enter, said, "FireWind," to the boss-boss, and padded down the stairs without looking at the vampire. It wasn't rude, but it was catty, and said all I needed him to say about Yummy.

"Are you finished in the locker room, Ingram?" FireWind asked.

"Yes."

"Yvonne Colstrip, scion of Ming of Glass, the showers are lockable," he said. "You may enter and shower while I'm in there, or remain bloody. Before you make a suggestive comment, I do not share showers, blood, or sex with Mithrans.

"While you are here, you will not be allowed anywhere in PsyLED premises alone except the null room."

Yummy laughed quietly. "Once upon a time I would have taken all that as a challenge. Now I just want to get this stinking blood off me." She followed him into the locker room and the door shut behind them.

FireWind opened the door again quickly. "Ingram, do you want me to take your clothes upstairs when I take mine up to be washed?"

The building was being expanded into the Southeastern Regional Headquarters of PsyLED, run by Rick LaFleur, and that required more IT and office space on the third floor. FireWind was overseeing the project and had installed a small laundry closet in the upstairs bathroom directly above, tying into the plumbing there so we didn't have to lose a shower stall in the locker room—*or* have workmen in a secure building. We had to trek upstairs to wash blood and gore out of our clothes, but at least now it was possible when necessary. Fortunately, today wasn't that day.

"No, thank you. I'll wash at home."

He closed the door again.

Rick buzzed in from the entry and went into the locker room also.

Two men in a locker room with me, with potential accidental nudity, would have given me the heebie-jeebies. Vampires were known to like . . . *things* . . . in numbers. Rick got naked before a shift. And FireWind was a skinwalker who also got naked to shift shape. Casual nudity would be unremarkable for any of the three in the locker room. I was a prude by upbringing and choice.

I took the stairs to the roof to check my rooftop garden and touch Soulwood soil. I paused in the entrance to the third floor. Electrical, electronics, and plumbing were in place, and the new office walls, aluminum struts, and supports were now filled with spray foam insulation and covered by a protective backing wall designed in some military complex to shield electronics from EM pulses and outside interference. The massive IT station would be well protected from outside electronic intrusion.

I opened the rooftop door and the night wind blew through, clear, cold, no river fog reaching this far from the river. The door closed behind me and I removed my shoes and socks, stepping over the low wood barrier into the dirt of my land. I breathed in the night air, let it out, and released all the power I had been holding. It shot out of me, through the soil, down the building into the dirt beneath, where I had mixed in a little Soulwood soil along the foundation. The power of the earth drained out of me and back to the land, my land, where it belonged. I worked my feet down into the dirt and rested into it. My throat relaxed even more, the pain diminishing to nearly nothing. Muscles that had been held tight relaxed. The latent *hunger* eased. As I unwound, two thoughts hit me.

A vampire had tried to kidnap me tonight. Because of the way I *smelled*.

And a vampire would be roaming my land at night for God knew how long to come.

I hadn't yet talked about either with Occam, but he had to know already. He'd turn on that protective mode, the one he had developed because, when he was a child, no one had protected him. I'd have to soothe that out of him, which could be all kinds of fun.

I rubbed my belly, feeling the rooty hardness there, remnants of the time I became a tree and nearly didn't make it back to human. Digging my toes deeper into the dirt, I raised my arms slightly to the sides and just breathed. I had no idea how much time passed before the door opened, and I couldn't have said how I knew it was Aya, but I did, and I knew he was standing in the dark, watching me with his peculiar yellow eyes.

"Do you know," he said softly, his words heavy with an accent from another time, another place, "when you commune with your land, you sometimes stretch out your arms, like a tree, reaching for the sun."

I dropped my arms to my sides and opened my eyes. "I know. But I also sometimes just curl in a ball on the ground."

"A root ball." There was laughter in his tone, but it was the sort of laughter that meant kindness and affection. I wasn't sure when Ayatas FireWind became my friend as well as my boss-boss, and oftentimes I didn't much like him being my friend, him being so prickly and all.

"Nell."

He used my first name.

"This can't be your first major case. It's too close to you and to your family. I know you were hoping."

"No." *I might have to kill someone on my land.* "I don't need to be lead on this case. I need to take care of me and mine."

I stepped from the dirt. I wiped my feet on the towel he handed me and put on my socks and shoes. He held the door for me and followed me down the stairs. It was nearly nine p.m. when we began the end-of-shift debrief in the conference room, and Yummy wasn't present.

JoJo was at comms. Tandy, being trained as an IT peep, was with her, and they were going through the shift-change sign-over protocols. They were a thing. JoJo glanced up at me for a moment, checking out my throat before returning her attention to the screens, pulling on the big gold hoops in her ears. She wore a single pair today that complemented the small braids with gold-ribbon weavings pulled tight in a bun on the top of her head. She was dressed in yoga pants and a tunic in the comfort of the conference room, the only room in HQ big enough to house the growing tech in our expanding regional headquarters.

A tiny *ting* sounded and Jo returned her attention to a small screen and frowned. She flipped a switch and said into a mic, "If you try to get into the security system again, I'll send FireWind to crush your tablet."

Yummy laughed, an unaccustomed sound over the speakers. "Ming's orders. Attempted and finished."

"Your skills suck."

I found the screen showing video of her. Yummy was sitting in an empty office, playing on her tablet, caught on the camera. She looked perfectly innocent until she looked at the camera and said, "Do they?" It sounded like a challenge.

Jo's eyes narrowed and she started tapping keyboards, probably starting diagnostics.

Margot, the team's truth-reader and a black wereleopard, entered and sat beside me. The probationary special agent was pulling a late-night shift, and for her this would be a start-of-shift briefing. She seemed quiet, though not peaceful, her dark skin catching highlights. She had supershort hair, nearly shaved, and the most perfectly shaped head I'd ever seen. She had also been an experienced field agent with another law enforcement agency before she was accidentally tainted with Rick's blood in a shootout. She had willingly transferred to PsyLED, an agency that allowed were-creatures to serve, and she—being a probie only by transfer, not by training and expertise—had way more experience than I did. She intimidated me.

She interlaced her fingers on the table and her perfect skin and manicured nails made me curl my own fingers under, hiding my brown rootlike nails in my lap. Beneath the table, I pulled an errant leaf off my thumbnail and pocketed it. My leaves tended to grow when I was on soil from my land, and I hadn't groomed myself after the time on the roof.

FireWind took his chair at the head of the table, Rick to his side, both facing the big screens over the windows, which were blacked out by mesh shades. Both men seemed amused at the tech contest between the vampire and the human IT person. I wasn't. Yummy was devious. Part of me liked that about her; part of me distrusted it.

"Dyson," FireWind said. "You are off shift."

"Yeah. I am." The unit's empath patted Jo's shoulder. "Don't let the blood-sucker get into your head."

Jo snorted. "As if she could."

When Tandy left, it was just the five of us: Rick, Ayatas, Jo, Margot, and me.

JoJo ordered Clementine to record and transcribe the meeting. Clementine was the software that saved us from having to type meeting reports, but it was confined to HQ; reports entered in the field still had to be typed in, though JoJo was experimenting with transcribing encrypted cell phone recordings and voice mails, and I was hopeful she could use it to transcribe the audio from my meeting with wackadoodle Ming.

Our tech guru gave the time and date and the names of all present, plus Ming's address, and turned the meeting over to FireWind. The boss summarized the events in Ming's clan home and the fight afterward. I turned over the info from my cell, and each of us told our part of the tarot reading and the skirmish.

FireWind said, "We have a preliminary on the DB from Ming's. Prelim cause of death is exsanguination, but there are no overt signs of vampire fangs at any of the usual locations."

He meant neck, groin, wrist, and elbow. But a careful vampire could hide signs of willing and even forced feeding.

And . . . there were other places a vampire could drink from, if the torture had been sexual in nature.

"Signs of torture have sent the ME back to textbooks for comparison data. External examination reveals a white male, age fifteen to twenty-two. Well-fed, no signs of recent weight loss, no signs of being on the streets—however, no signs of dental work ever. Worked with his hands. New tattoo of a bird in flight, possibly a crow. Not professionally done. Drug screen was negative for common classifications of street drugs. Detailed drug screen has been sent to a reference lab. Five-ten, one fifty-seven, muscular build. Patchy facial hair, blondish, blue eyes. Hair worn long in a ponytail. Postmortem will begin at eight a.m."

"Do we have any indication that Ming or her people killed the man?" Jo asked.

"No," FireWind said. "There was very little trace on the body. It had been washed liberally with bleach."

When we were done, JoJo checked her screen. "It's early and Alex Younger is a night owl. Suggest someone place a call for information."

"Would the Dark Queen's researcher and tech guy tell *us* anything?" Aya asked.

The boss-boss was her true brother, but the relationship was riddled with strife. And this was business, not personal, so I understood the question.

"Alex and I made nice-nice when we were at the coronation," Rick said. He shrugged slightly, his white hair resting on his black-clad shoulders, the T-shirt stretched over his too-lean body. "We didn't arrest anyone. Didn't call anyone fanghead or suckhead. I have Alex Younger's personal number." He pulled his cell and placed a call.

Rick looked confident. But Rick had bled on my land. Through that bond, I knew his latent uncertainty. He and Jane Yellowrock, the Dark Queen, had been a thing. Then he had betrayed her.

FireWind said, "Clementine. Halt transcription."

I had read my bosses' report from the coronation. The vamps had been acting different at the big soiree following the crowning of the vampire emperor of Europe, but with so much blood and alcohol flowing, and considering the importance of the event to the future survival of the vampires, no one had been surprised at out-of-character behavior. Not at first. Then scuttlebutt said the vampires had gotten back their souls, and the upheaval from that had only just begun.

Alex answered the call, which was a wonder. Getting people to pick up our calls was increasingly difficult. "Hey, Rick. What's up, my brother?"

Rick's face froze with shock. *My brother.* Alex Younger, Jane's adopted brother, had just used a New Orleans phrase of welcoming to Jane's old boyfriend. Rick blinked and breathed slowly. "You know. Same ol'. Vamps and blood and shit. You?"

"Same but weirder. What can I do you for?"

Rick smiled at the phrasing. "Appreciate you taking the call," he said. "PsyLED Eighteen is in conference with this call. We've some strange vamp activities here. The local Mithrans say they have their souls back. Several have walked into the sun while happy. The Master of the City is blaming Nell Ingram, the queen's friend, for making them feel different. There's also an underlying threat from a master vamp called Tomás de Torquemada, who wants a magical item from Ming of Glass."

"I thought he'd been beheaded or was still in prison," Alex said.

"We don't have independent verification of his presence in Knoxville, but our team was present during a confrontation between his scions and the scions of Ming of Glass at her clan home. One of our agents was injured, but is recovering. Ming appeared quite unstable."

"Looking." We could hear keys clacking in the background. "But while I'm running him, related to that instability, just before Thanksgiving, Janie—sorry, the Dark Queen—freed a partially bound angel and sent a demon back to wherever he came from. In thanks, the angel gave vamps back their souls and lifted most of the curses on all the paras. Don't go biting anyone, dude, but it might mean were-creatures are altered too."

Rick's head came up fast, his nostrils quivering.

Margot's reaction was more subtle, a faint tremor in her fingers. She was new at being a were-creature and she hated everything about it. Rick and Margot had been an item. Now they weren't. Margot had been very quiet and very solitary since.

Aya pulled his tablet to his side and began typing.

My land seemed to sense the change in their emotions, like a sleeping cat who opens one eye. After having my feet in the dirt, I could feel all the varied emotions in the room: loneliness, hope, fear. Lots of fear. It was chaotic and a little sad.

"No one said anything about this at the coronation," Rick said.

"FireWind here. We were at the coronation in an official capacity. The possibility of a change in all paranormals was information we should have been made aware of at that time. As a basic *courtesy*, we should have been told that."

"I disagree, dude, and here's why. One, Jane informed her sworn vampires, which was her job. Two, you guys share diddly. Now, if you want to go into a more formal information-sharing agreement, then we can schedule a summit between PsyLED and the Dark Queen's legal team. Till then you can stuff it."

The lines around FireWind's mouth tightened. "We are aware that the Dark Queen owes us nothing about internal Mithran politics."

It wasn't as if any law enforcement agency had a CI in any vampire headquarters. Confidential informants don't remain confidential long when they are some vamp's dinner to bleed and read and bind.

"There was no grindylow at Ming's," I said. "Cai is human, or human-ish, and Rick shifted." A grindy usually appeared when a human could possibly be turned. One should have appeared in the fight.

"You said an angel?" Yummy was standing at the door. No one had seen her move, but she was there, and had clearly been listening to everything. "An *angel* did this to us?"

At the word *us*, all the happy-happy drained from Alex's voice, replaced by an austere formality. "Identify yourself."

"I'm Yvonne Colstrip, known as Yummy, turned by Grégoire, Blood Master of Clan Arceneau and the Dark Queen's Warlord, former scion of Ming of Glass, free agent in Knoxville, currently in temporary agreement with Ming of Glass to do her will, but not bound by her."

"I am Alex Younger, the Dark Queen's adopted brother and her IT specialist. The Masters of the City Ming of Glass and Lincoln Shaddock, and by extension all the Mithrans in their combined territory, were notified about the regained souls,"

Alex said. "I made Ming's notification, speaking with the Master of the City herself. If she didn't tell you, you might direct your attention to the previously mentioned instability and potential sedition against the Dark Queen."

Yummy's face was a wide-eyed study in confused humanity. She pulled her cell and dialed a number as she wandered back to her assigned location. I figured she was calling Ming to ask for clarification. Or maybe someone else at Ming's to report in. Ming had known about the angel. Ming hadn't told her people. That sounded bad.

Margot leaned forward. "Margot Racer here, Alex Younger. As I'm sure you *know*," she said, a wry tone in her voice, "I'm a truth-sayer of sorts. One of Ming's Mithrans was in the room when you said all that. I felt nothing at all from her. Either my truth sense is inactive on her, or she was speaking the truth, or she doesn't know what the truth is."

Alex said, "Acknowledged, Racer. FireWind, I wish I could say I had more info on your fanghead Torquemada. Last I have for certain, he was in a prison under the Vatican. No confirmation on that since 2023. I have a text from Janie that says Leo talked about him being demon possessed, but no confirmation on that either. I'll do a little digging."

"Is there anything else you can tell us about Ming of Glass?" I asked.

"Is the suckhead still there?"

"No," FireWind said.

"Good. Ming sent Janie a blood-servant who might have been a troublemaker in Ming's clan, or one in need of training, or might have been sent to try to assassinate the Dark Queen, since he was killed trying. Both Ming twins are under suspicion by the Dark Queen for possible sedition. That and having a soul might make a difference in her mental stability."

"Thank you, Alex Younger," FireWind said.

"Later, FireWind. Hey, Ricky-Bo. Next time you're in town, Café du Monde. Your treat."

The call ended.

Rick smiled, looking bemused, and said, "That would have been helpful information to have before the visit to Ming."

Jo said, "I'll look into the sedition part."

Margot said, "I'll type up the phone call's focal points."

"Thank you, Jo, Racer," FireWind said. "Meeting adjourned. Ingram and LaFleur, you've both been on the clock since eight a.m. LaFleur, come in late tomorrow. Ingram, you're off shift. Go home. Have you decided that you're comfortable with Colstrip sleeping in your home? If not, we need to find a place for her to lair in the daylight."

"Can she fit in the trunk of her Ferrari?" I asked, not able to hide the snide note.

"It's less than two cubic feet of space," Aya said with the faintest twitch of his lips. "So no."

"I'll figure something out," I said, thinking of the closets upstairs. "What about food?"

"Ming promised she would send some of my humans at dusk to feed me." Yummy was standing at the door again. Whatever she saw on my face made her add, "I'll meet them at the bottom of the hill. I won't feed on your property." Her voice was expressionless, empty. Maybe a little lost.

Her expression made me a bad host, which I had been brought up to believe was one of the ultimate sins. Guilt bloomed in me. But guilt didn't mean I would let a vampire drink from her blood dinners in the house.

Yummy laughed, her change of expression mercurial. "Don't look so upset. I'm not insulted enough to drink you down. Not without an invitation."

FOUR

When we arrived at home, Occam's fancy car was parked in front and my cat-man was stretched out on the top step in cat form, my three cats and Cherry snuggled up against his warmth. Cherry thumped her tail hello but didn't get up to meet me. My critters liked my cat-man better than they did me. I wasn't resentful, exactly, but I did, from time to time, remind them who fed them and cared for them. I looked around my land, bright in the moonlight. The fog from the river valley, if it had ever reached this elevation, had blown away.

Yummy's Ferrari LaFerrari pulled in and parked to the side. I was sorta surprised to see that it made it up the hill. The gravel street got semiregular maintenance, but it was awfully bumpy and her car was made for street speed, not climbing unpaved hills. Yummy got out, carried her bags to the stairs, and dropped them on the bottom one. "Occam," she said, her tone neutral.

"Wait here," I said.

I dropped my things by hers and walked to the raised beds where herbs and flowers grew in summer, beds I had constructed by the sweat of my brow, with low narrow pathways between them. Though I had laid them out to be a pretty entrance to the house, they had another purpose. The lower pathways provided me cover, where I could duck down behind the beds and fire over them at churchmen who had once wanted me and my land. That was back before my bonding with the land grew so strong and the Green Knight showed up to help protect me.

I sat on a raised bed and put my hands to the earth. Soulwood, already awake, welcomed me with warmth and what felt like joy—if trees and roots and grass and dirt could feel joy. I was just about to tell Soulwood and the vampire tree about

Yummy visiting, but I wasn't fast enough. A surge of energy swept through the earth like lightning.

All around the vampire, vines with thorns sprouted, growing at hyperspeed. Before she realized she was trapped, each foot had been penetrated by a thorn, as the vampire tree tasted her blood.

She screamed, inarticulate, sharp. "What is this magic?" she demanded.

"It's my land."

"Make it stop, damn it. It's painful."

"Working on it." I hadn't read my land deeply in a week, and the tree was always rooting in closer, trying to keep me, and now my sister and her babies, safe. I sent my awareness through the earth and touched a nice-sized root I hadn't noticed. I thought at the tree, *You back off. We'ns got rules.*

The Green Knight appeared in my mind, in the vision world of green light he had created for us, standing at the fence that separated us. Usually he was sitting astride a pale green horse and carried a white halberd propped over a shoulder, trailing vines and bursting with green leaves. In the other hand he often carried a long lance the dark green of fir needles, the entire length trailing more vines, green leaves fluttering in an unseen wind. Green. All green. His skin was the palest green of spring leaves, his hair lighter today, and while he almost always wore pale green armor, this time he was helmetless, his gauntlets and his horse not in the image. Behind him a pasture stretched into the green sky, so many shades of green. A dark forest grew far behind his pasture. His green eyes were on mine. A long strand of grass with seeds on the end rested in the corner of his mouth, like he was a farmer tasting his land. On the end of the grass, thorns sprouted. *Stop it,* I thought. *She's a guest.*

He cocked his head at my words.

The tree, the physical embodiment of the Green Knight, had to be fed occasionally, and it wasn't a vegetarian. It wanted living creatures—mice, squirrels, birds—and now maybe vampires. It was a fast-growing, pretty pinkish hardwood, once an oak, now a meat-eating monster I had created in a burst of accidental magic while I was dying. I had no way to control it except by negotiation, and though it was learning English, it didn't communicate well except through images.

I sent a memory of Yummy in my house, my hand on hers, trying to say, to imagine a scene, that said to him, *She's mine. Not yours.*

In the background, I heard Yummy scream, that high-pitched ululation of death.

I felt Occam, standing beside me, changing form, transforming to human. His magic sparkled through the land where his paws touched it, and then where his hands and knees touched it. I felt him stand. Naked, he said, "Tell the tree if Yummy tries anything on you, Esther, Mud, or the babies, I'll rip her arms off."

I passed the information to the tree in a bloody visual. The Green Knight seemed to consider. Seconds later Yummy stopped screaming and began crying. I felt her move off direct contact with the land as she dragged herself up the stairs to the porch.

The Green Knight held out his hand, which had been empty only moments before, and poured out the green stuff he now carried. It was an image he had sent before, and which I didn't fully understand except maybe it was the green of life.

I sent other images of Yummy on the land, running, sitting, standing.

The Green Knight shook his head no.

I re-sent the image. *Yes,* I thought at him. *She is mine.*

He sent an image of a thorn with her blood on it. And then that thorn in my mouth. He wanted me to taste her blood, which was a form of cannibalism and I'd surely go to hell. He re-sent the image to me again, insistent.

"Occam, pick me one of them thorns with Yummy's blood on it, purdy please," I said, sliding into church-speak.

I felt him almost ask why, but instead, totally naked, he strode to the bloody patch of ground where Yummy had been trapped, and returned with a broken-off thorn. I took it in one hand and licked it, bitter, salty, cold.

The Green Knight cocked his head the other way, considering. Then he held out his hand, fingers spread, palm facing me, waiting until my mental palm lifted and touched his. There was no sensation beyond what might have been the night air flowing across the hillside.

The cold taste of Yummy's blood flashed through my brain and I realized that we had both tasted her blood.

An image of Yummy appeared near him, his fence between them. In the vision, Yummy was a stick figure with fangs. At her feet were two trees, one me, the other Mud. Yummy tied us up with vines and threw us onto her shoulders. She raced out of sight of the green world.

Ahhh. I thought. He wanted me to be alert. I envisioned the three of us as he saw us. In the vision, I called on the land. Vines erupted from the earth and trapped Yummy, who dropped our tree-bodies to the ground.

Palm to palm, he nodded once, then vanished.

I opened my eyes to see Occam, now wearing a pair of sweatpants and nothing else, kneeling beside Yummy. His wrist was at her mouth, and she was drinking his blood, still weeping, a note of fear in the sounds. I realized that I had never heard any vampire weep with fear.

I wasn't jealous that my cat-man was feeding his old girl-friend. There was nothing sexual about it. He was doing her a kindness. As I watched, the punctures and lacerations on her ankles sealed over. They didn't go away completely—I figured that would take the blood of another vampire—but they stopped bleeding.

She pushed his wrist away. "Thank you. They still hurt like a bitch, but they feel better."

"You're welcome," Occam said, sounding cautious and formal in his Texan accent.

"The tree shouldn't hurt you now," I said.

Yummy pointed to her ankles. "How did you do this?"

"Wasn't me." *It was a carnivorous tree. Not a wise thing to say.* "My land thought you were a threat."

"You *are* a witch."

"No. We've had this conversation before. Jane Yellowrock said I was maybe a fairy or a wood nymph. Whatever I am, my kind were mixed with humans long ago." Jane was Cherokee, and in American tribal lore, only the Cherokee had fairies and little people, possibly from the British who intermarried among them for so many centuries. Or the Knights Templar. Or the Scots, who were said to have settled here centuries before the Spanish arrived.

Occam, who had been silent for too long, said, "If you go

near the children, Mud, Esther, or Nell to do them harm, I'll kill you and feed you to the land myself. Do you understand?"

"Yes."

"Soulwood sent you a message," I said, gesturing to the bloody thorns, visible in the moonlight. "You've bled on the land. It knows your blood and your thoughts. It sent me an image of you tying up Mud and me to carry us away. It'll attack if you try, if you harm us. And I'll know it was you, even if I'm not here. You need to remember that. It will also try to protect you if you're in danger."

"Ming still holds my allegiance. For now. I suppose you know that too?"

Occam said, "You don't smell very happy about that. What's she holding over you?"

"My two chained scions and six blood-servants." Yummy pulled her hair to one side, the shorter hank of hair falling back toward her face. "They're my friends. She has all of them chained in her lair. She planned to take you when you came to the clan home tonight, but you brought backup. Every time she talks about you and your land and what drinking your tree did to Charlainn, she has another use for you. One is she has some crazy notion that you can fix her scions. Another is that you'll kill Torquemada. And she never told us about the angel bringing our souls back. An *angel*." She laughed without humor, a sad sound, and shook her head in wonder.

I said, "So we need to get your people free. She owes me two boons. Let's see what I can do with that." I patted my pockets and found my cell. Dialed Ming's number. When Cai answered, I said, "Ming owes me two boons. I'm calling in one now, and it's a two-parter. I want Yumm—Yvonne's—two scions and six blood-servants kept safe until they can be delivered to a place of Yvonne's choosing. Safe, healthy, and not missing any blood. No cuts, no drinking, no weakening. And Yummy is mine now. Not Ming's."

Cai cursed in his native language, whatever that was, and hung up.

"Why?" Yummy asked. "Why would you waste a boon on something like that?"

Discomfort wriggled into my soul. "You'un—" I stopped.

"Your friendship to me is deeper than your loyalty to Ming." My discomfort grew. After tasting her blood, I knew that Yummy had really meant it when she had called me her bestie. She liked me way more than I did her, but she had been growing on me. I shrugged away my awkward feelings. "You're free now. This way, you're safe and Ming can't retaliate against you."

Yummy's eyes were wide and glowing in the night.

"You might find you don't *want* to be a free vamp," I said. "'Specially now that you done challenged Torquemada's followers. It ain't easy being on your own. You'll have to figure out a place to live and a way to make money, just like a regular human, but—"

Yummy threw herself at me and her arms around me. After a good two seconds, I realized she wasn't letting go. I patted her back with one hand. The hug increased in pressure. I breathed out my uncertain embarrassment and hugged her. I could feel a hard lump at her chest, and remembered the necklace Ming had hung around her neck, taken from the neck stump of one of the attackers at the clan home. There was magic in the lump, but I didn't say that aloud.

"I have money saved," Yummy said into my ear, "and the gold from the men killed at Ming's. Everything they carried on them is mine now. Together it's enough to buy a small place in Oliver Springs and get it set for day-sleepers and humans. Thank you."

"Ummm. Yeah. Uh. You're welcome." I tried to find a way to push her back, but vampires were strong. I finally reached up, grasped her arms, and pushed. She released me and I stepped back.

"I'll patrol now," she said. "I'll be back at dawn. If I could spend one day in your home, I'd be grateful."

"My house isn't set up for day-sleepers. No windowless rooms. But I have a closet and quilts and stuff. You shouldn't burn. Too much," I added.

Yummy laughed under her breath. "You're too kind," she said, sarcasm in the tone. She gathered up her satchel and her duffel and looked at me.

"Door's unlocked," Occam said.

Yummy set her things inside and leaped off the porch to the ground. In an instant, she was gone. I walked to my car and opened the trunk, pulling the oversized vampire tree out by the roots and scooping the dirt into the empty pot. I'd need to vacuum the dirt out of the trunk later, but for now, I carried the tree and its too-small pot to the tree line and upended the pot into the woods.

"You'un listen to me, you green thing," I said to the tree. "You'un want to share Soulwood with me. I get that, in some strange twisted kinda way. And I'm willing to have a protective tree to carry around. But I want something small, something that starts small and stays small and don't try to grow to all sizes overnight. You can't do that, then you ain't goin' with me to work. Period. So here's a pot and you got a day or so to think about it. But the next time I'm using the land, and your dang tree Hulks out on me, it'll be the last time I carry one, even to protect myself."

Feeling righteous, I all but stomped back to my house and up the stairs to the porch. "Dang tree."

Occam came into the house behind me, chuckling under his breath, a chuffing huffing sound, all cat.

I stopped in the middle of the main room and turned to him, feeling all kinds of uncertain. About the case. About the dead body. About Yummy. About vampires maybe hunting me because I had touched the Blood Tarot. When I spoke, it was not about the major, dangerous things, but maybe the least important thing.

"I can't be lead on this case," I said.

Occam, visible in the dim light, his body lean and long, shirtless. Beautiful. He said, "FireWind didn't assign anyone lead, which is odd. Until we have a COD and a species, technically it doesn't matter."

"Good. 'Cause we'uns is alone."

"I noticed," he said, almost a purr.

It was rare we were alone at night in the house. Usually we had Mud in the house, and though consensual sex between unmarried people while children were in the home was the norm at the church where I grew up (my mother wasn't legally married to my father and was one of three so-called sister-wives), I wasn't comfortable with Occam at a sleepover while Mud was here. Tonight she was at Esther's, and since I had locked the door on any possibility of Yummy's unexpected return, we had time to ourselves. Private time.

Occam glided past me, all cat-man grace, and stoked up the wood-burning stove. He took my hand and led me to my bedroom, where he proceeded to strip me down. I pulled him to my bed, where we made love, an act I was liking more and more. After that, we reopened the bedroom door to let the heat in, and ate toast and jam, all homemade, in bed together, the three cats and the dog skittering in with us, sitting on the foot of the bed, alert for treats. And we talked about our upcoming wedding.

"You sure about not marrying in the church, Nellie? Don't make that decision on account a me."

"It's not on account a you'un. I broke with the church a long time ago. It's *our* wedding. I want what *we* want, and getting married on *Soulwood* at *our* home is what *we* want."

"Your mama is sure gonna blame me," he said.

"She'll be mad as a wet hen," I agreed. When we were alone, no one else to hear, our city accents went out the window. We talked slower, canoodled more, like cats in a basket full of blankets. "I jist wish that rose you gave me would have blooms, but it's barely rooted. I'd like to have lavender roses in my bouquet."

The rose Occam had given me was in a pot on the porch, a single stick, ready for winter, alive and happy. It would sprout come spring, not sooner. I wasn't delaying my wedding for a flower.

"We can order them, you know, get them flown in. It's what I did."

"I ain't buyin' no flowers, dagnabbit. Not when I can grow my own."

Occam's damaged lips pulled on one side, a teasing smile. The skin looked fine, but the nerves and muscles were still healing beneath.

I said, "You'un's pickin' on me, ain'tcha."

"Yup. I love you, Nell, sugar."

"I love you, cat-man."

I rolled over and he pulled me close, nuzzling against my bare back. It was the way we slept together, and it was comforting in a way I had never experienced before, certainly not with John, my first husband. With him, after relations, I'd roll out of bed and climb the stairs to my private cot to sleep, relieved it was over. With Occam, it was all different. Funny, romantic, silly, intense, full of feelings I'd never had before, and a sense of wonderment. I snuggled against him, into the quilts, and closed my eyes.

In my dreams came a memory-dream of the bones of the pregnant woman who had been buried on witch land, with a tree planted over her. The roots had curled down and found her skeleton, growing into her bones and taking on the shape of her body. We'd found her at a crime scene. I had known she was like me. A plant-woman. I didn't know her history, and I wanted to know it. In my spare time I was researching her and any connection to the church.

Since I'd found her, I'd had dreams of her, and of people like us, climbing into the earth, beneath the roots of a tree, to die, to be buried and be claimed by a tree. People of the Trees, maybe. People who could hear the trees talking, the old, old, *old* trees, which were no more, except here on my land, and in a very few places in the mountains, the trees calling, calling, calling us to save them. To protect them from the farmers, the lumbermen, to save the soul of the land.

I woke in the midst of the dream, an ancient tree screaming out its pain as it was harvested to build a rich man's home. Occam stroked my side, calming me. Sleepily he murmured, "It's okay, Nell, suga'. I gotcha."

It took a long time to find sleep again after that, my thoughts restless.

Occam rose before dawn, let Cherry out to do her business, ate himself some leftovers, moving quietly about the house, before he let himself outside. Outside, he shifted and went loping across Soulwood, sniffing for Yummy, following her. Checking up on her.

I drowsed, feeling all this, knowing when he shifted to human and put on his sweatpants from the gobag he wore when he thought he might need to shift again. He'd found Yummy, standing beyond Esther's house, uphill from the new chicken coop.

They talked, but I couldn't hear words, just the vibrations of their bodies and their emotional intent. Yummy guarded and reserved, maybe a little afraid. Occam forceful, as if he was in a battle, but a mental one. An argument. It drew me out of what was left of sleep and I got up, added some slow-burning wood to the stove, started water for tea, turned on the Bunn coffee maker, and got dressed. It was still dark.

I carried Yummy's things up the stairs and stood at the top, considering, finally putting Yummy in Esther's old bedroom, the one my sister stayed in before she had her own home, the one with the L-shaped closet. If a quilt hung over the doorway, and she piled lots of quilts to cover her while she slept, Yummy should be safe.

I was back downstairs and dressed in jeans and layers, whisking eggs and crisping bacon, when the phone rang. It was Esther.

"Morning, sister mine," I said.

"I done saw that cat-man outside. He took off his clothes and was naked and he turned into a cat. He was *naked*!"

People who thought that religious polygamists were sexually promiscuous or okay with casual nudity didn't know much about them. With the exception of her husband, Esther had probably never seen a naked man. "Naked, huh? Did you watch with your binoculars while he took off his clothes?"

"I did no such thing!"

But she had. I could hear the false indignation in her tone, and I knew the moment Occam had shifted to human, well beyond the easily observable vision of Esther's windows. He had been standing in a patch of moonlight partway up the hill to my house.

"Uh-huh. Listen to me, Esther. There's a rumor that some new vampires are in the area and they might . . ." I stopped. Considered. And chose a partial truth. "They might want plant-people and our land. So one of the local vampires will be patrolling the property by night, along with Occam and some of the people from work, trying to keep us all safe."

"They want plant-people? This is all you'uns fault, ain't it? You bein' with the po-lice."

Esther was fast at pointing fingers, usually at me.

"No. They can feel the power of the land and the power in us. And you should know that the vampires got their souls back."

"Well, that's good they got souls. Now when they die they can go to hell like proper evil beings."

I sighed softly, so my sister couldn't hear it. "An angel gave them back their souls. Seems like God has given them a second chance. If so, that means we have to give them a second chance too. And the angel broke the curse on were-creatures, whatever that curse is."

The silence over the phone was electric and fraught with more indignation. "That *stinks*."

I'd boxed her in with words and religion, but I didn't gloat. "Ummm." I sliced into a fresh loaf of homemade bread and put three slices on the oven top to toast and removed the jar of Mama Grace's homemade jam from the fridge.

"Fine. I'll play nice with the blood-sucker and your cat. Mama's coming over for coffee and devotionals sometime this morning, and she wants you here. I'll text you when she drives up." The call ended.

I sighed again. Mama bringing devotionals to my sister's, and me having to be there, meant the conversation would turn to my wedding and finding Esther a husband. We'd end up at odds. And I'd leave feeling mad and stubborn.

I checked my work messages. The PM on the dead body from Ming's was still scheduled for eight a.m., hours away. There was still no assigned lead on the case. Nothing new.

The door opened. Yummy stood there, the faintest light of dawn behind her as she stepped in. Closed the door. She was looking around my house, likely for her things.

"I put them upstairs. All my rooms have windows, even the shed, but the closet in the first bedroom to the left has a little L shape to the side and plenty of quilts."

Her expression turned sly. "By some standards, you making me sleep in a closet makes you a poor hostess."

"Church insults don't work on me. Besides, a host is a willing giver. I'm not willing and you're *taking* my hospitality. I'm more a hostage in my own home."

"You're smarter than you act sometimes. Will you eat my soul while I sleep?"

"I don't eat souls. The land does. So don't sleep outside where it can get you. Meanwhile, I put a pile of quilts and a hammer, nails, and hooks on the bed and you can hang a quilt to cover the closet doors. I suggest you cover the windows with quilts too and sleep wrapped in more of them."

At my feet the cats were everywhere, twining, making those indignant sounds they made when they wanted out. I walked around her and opened the front door, figuring they were feeling Occam coming. Cherry bopped my leg and trotted out after them.

Yummy frowned, staring at the stairway to the second floor. "You're enjoying this, aren't you?"

"I admit to a certain amount of satisfaction at the thought of you sleeping in a closet. Shower is at the top of the stairs."

Yummy walked up the stairs. I heard the shower come on, and I went back to the stove, where I sniffed Occam's coffee and poured hot water from the kettle over my strainer and leaves into the teapot. I scrambled a dozen eggs.

Occam knocked before he opened the door. He had a key. He had his space for his clothes in our bedroom closet, but I had a feeling that even after we married, he'd still always knock, so I would never be shocked and turn around to see a man in my house and have a sudden start of fear. He was thoughtful that way. "Morning, Nell, sugar. You look pretty as a picture."

I may have flushed a little with pleasure. "Morning, cat-man. I made us breakfast."

He pulled a long-sleeved sweatshirt off the hook near the door, covering up his scars and providing warmth. He stood on one foot at a time and tugged on socks, sliding his feet into slippers, all with that cat grace that sometimes made me feel clumsy. Even with the stove heating the place up and the new backup electric heater running on stored solar power, it was usually chilly in winter and layers were smart, even for cat-people.

Occam gently hugged me and kissed my temple. Such a strange sensation, that gentleness from a man. I leaned into him a moment, and then stood straight and dished up our meal. As I set the table, he poured coffee and my tea. I still wasn't used to a man helping around the house. It felt unnatural.

We ate in silence long enough for his hunger to fade. Were-creatures used the moon power to change shape, but there was still some energy spent in a shift. They were always needing protein.

The shower went off and hammering echoed down the stairs

as Yummy secured her day lair. Occam chuckled softly at the sound. From upstairs Yummy yelled down, "Don't you laugh, you, you, you *cat*!" Which only made Occam laugh louder.

I was nearly done eating and he was scraping his plate clean with a crust of toast when he looked up the stairs and then outside to check the position of the sun. With the sun up, we knew Yummy was in her closet lair and sleeping.

Quietly, Occam said, "I talked to Yummy."

"Why didn't you ever call her by her name?" T. Laine would have said it was a random question, but it mattered. "You dated her and yet you called her Yummy, same way I do."

"She told me her name was Abella. And then ChristyLu. And then something else, I don't remember. But when vamps challenge someone they use their true names."

"What happened after, when Ming put her hand on Yummy's head and gave her the stuff out of the loser's pockets and his jewelry?" And someone took pictures, and used them to tie me to Yummy. *Dagnabbit.*

Occam popped the toast corner into his mouth and considered my questions. I hadn't been with PsyLED long. I didn't know much about vampires. Yet. And it seemed they may have changed from what they used to be into something new, so this was different. Everything was different.

"Because of the challenge, his belongings were hers when he died." He tilted his head back and forth, considering. "From what Rick said, all the vamps killed last night were wearing jewelry. Rings. Necklaces. Probably had cash and other valuables on them."

I remembered the tingle of magic from the necklace Yummy had been wearing when she hugged me.

"Ming gave her own winnings to Yummy. That was a sign of respect and status," he said.

"It's part of the reason she can buy a house in Oliver Springs, according to Yummy."

"Ming's hand on her head was either a demand or a kind of blessing. Rick probably heard what she said. If he didn't put it in the record last night, it's probably there by now. But I'm sure her original intent was to abduct you and use you against her enemies and against Unit Eighteen. Which is why Rick and Aya were with you. They thought she would have ulterior motives, and if I went instead of them, I'd just kill her and be done with her. Which could have set off a paranormal war." He shrugged.

"I should have used one of my boons to keep us safe from the get-go. Okay. I'll check the records. Go on. You talked to Yummy."

"She's fascinated with your land. Said to keep Ming off it if possible. And if Ming tries to claim the land, or challenges you for it in some way, you better make sure she's dead first."

I laughed. "I'll take the advice of a vampire into consideration. But I do see her point."

Occam leaned in again and kissed me, this time on the lips, so sweet and tender it mighta made my toes curl up just a bit, his hand stroking along my jaw. "I love you to the full moon and back," he murmured.

"I love you too," I whispered, "deep as the roots, high as the tallest tree, with the full moon held in its branches." I snuggled into his arms, closing my eyes.

"I like that."

"Mmmm," I said.

"You didn't sleep much," he said. "I'm taking you back to bed."

"Is that an invitation?" A small smile curved my mouth.

Occam breathed out a laugh as he lifted me in a baby-carry and walked to the bedroom. "You got terrible timing. I gotta go into HQ early for a few hours, since Rick and Aya will be late getting in. I'll be off early unless we catch a case." He placed me on the bed and said, "Sleep a bit."

"Okay. You want venison stew for supper?" I said as my eyes closed. "I got the fixin's."

"Sounds tasty."

I knew, even in my dreams, when Occam drove off the mountain.

I was up and dressed by eight thirty, my weapon and harness in my gobag, me sitting on my sofa reading progress reports on the case. The PM had started at eight a.m., with the PsyCSI team on hand to remove trace evidence like hair and fibers that might have been missed when they took the body in. They also were present to take swabs from each wound, and watch the proceedings—because the scientific types were always curious and always learning. Saliva, blood, and urine had been collected and sent for testing. So far, the pathologist had three types of hair, which had been given to the lead tech of the PsyCSI lab: three hairs that were short, coarse, and brown with a black tip; five that were short, coarse, and totally black; and two that were fine and silky white.

The first two had been preliminarily identified as animal, likely canid. The white one had been determined to be animal, not human, but class, order, and family had not yet been determined.

The cutting and measuring and weighing of organs would be done by eleven. Maybe. So far, beyond the things FireWind and LaFleur had determined, we knew the unknown DB had been in good health until recently, and appeared to be of a lower socioeconomic background because he'd had multiple untreated dental caries—cavities. He was uncircumcised. The ME had ruled out torture of a sexual nature.

By nine a.m., that was all we had. And because I had no reason to go into work early, sadly I had no excuse when Esther sent a text inviting me to Bible reading and coffee with Mama. Feeling grumpy, I walked down the road to her house, letting my awareness pass along the ground beneath my boots, into the roadway, lightly out to both sides, skimming with my mind to the neighbor's property on one side and to my house on the other. Both plots of land were mine in the sense that my power had claimed them. My land. The Green Knight's land. No matter what the deeds and plots filed in the county offices said.

I didn't actively reach out to the tree for contact with the Green Knight. I kept my steps light. The sound of traffic was gone, rush hour slowing, and the only sound was the breeze in the limbs, a rushing like water, a clack of branches hitting. The breeze was cold and I tucked my hands into my pockets.

The vampire tree had been cut along the road to build Esther's house. Weeks later, trees lined both sides of the road again, fast-growing saplings, trees with thorns, the bark rough with vine-like things falling from the limbs to the ground, vines that had the capability of fast movement, vines with thorns to catch and kill prey. Meat it needed as much as it needed sunlight and water and nutrients to sustain it. Meat: like birds, deer, even humans and paranormal creatures, though so far it hadn't tried to attack anyone but Yummy.

I hadn't allowed the tree to root anywhere else. Currently it was all one massive tree with a single origin point and a single sprawling root system. I hadn't allowed myself to think about the tree if it tried to take over the world. It could. It was faster growing than kudzu, filling in open spaces between trees, with the means to defend itself.

The tree was a menace. That it was also a protector wasn't lost on me. Along the long drive, the new vampire saplings rustled with the cold wind. The warmth of the land rose into me. The tree had woken as well, aware of me and welcoming.

The division between Esther's land and mine was both hard as stone and tangled like roots, a place she had claimed, once with her blood and later when her water broke and poured through the porch floorboards to the ground below.

The Green Knight appeared different to her, but because she was afraid of her power, she didn't look at her land often, didn't interact with it the way I did mine. That made her protection more passive and therefore potentially less useful and more dangerous.

I rounded the curve in the road and spotted the trucks at Esther's. I stopped in the middle of the rutted street. I hadn't reached out to her land and hadn't sensed them, but I knew all of the trucks and all of the drivers. Knew they had driven over to "visit with the babies," knew why I had been invited to devotionals and coffee. The mamas were here. All three at once. And with them was my mawmaw, the family matriarch, Maude Hamilton Vaughn, Mama's mother. The mamas had brought out the big guns.

This was a wedding ambush.

Though it was dark as pitch, the bus had already picked Mud up for school. I was on my own.

I'd rather face down a dozen armed bank robbers wearing clown masks and armed with bazookas than the mamas working together.

Reluctance weighing me down, I walked toward the house, Esther's magical Tulip Tree House. The night the twins were born, the pinkish horizontal logs that had been sawn from willing vampire trees had put out roots, long, sinuous roots, trailing and draping to the ground, thickening into trunks. They had also grown upward and out, tall, strong, like living siding, with branches sprouting leaves. Not the dark green leaves with red petioles of my vampire tree, but burgundy five-pointed leaves like serrated maple leaves. When the trees first grew, the leaves were shades of green, growing in pairs, one pair one way, the next pair the other, so they shaped a round fan or funnel that captured rainwater and let it glide down to the roots. The leaves at the bottom were larger than my two hands spread side by side; near the tops of the new trees, they were smaller, and the treetops curled, rising above the roof to touch before they spread out, forming what looked like an unopened-tulip-blossom-shaped framework. A second roof of living wood.

Vines with the same leaf positioning had grown all around the trim on the windows and around the doorway like decorations. Saplings had sprouted around the acre of land Esther had claimed, while leaving lawn and garden space that would eventually become a playground for the kids. Earlier in the season, between two icy spells, every branch and twig had flowered in bunches of tiny white flowers, like a fairy house. Now, in early winter, the flowers were gone, but the trees still bore leaves the colorful reds and golds of different varieties of maples.

The trees made it appear a joyful place, suggesting that a happy person lived there, totally unlike its owner. Esther was a dour woman, demanding and complaining.

I walked from my land onto Esther's and felt the welcome. Climbed the stairs, my hand on the handrail, the pinkish wood smooth. A faint tingle of power acknowledged my presence. The sensation was like and yet unlike the power of the Green Knight as it presented itself to me.

I lifted my hand and knocked on the door.

FIVE

Mama Grace opened the door, gave me a version of the church blessing, "Hospitality and safety, sweet girl," and in the same breath called out, "Our Nellie is here." She enfolded me in her arms. Mama Grace was the youngest of Daddy's three wives, soft and rounded, and her hugs were pillowy, offering a sense of safety and peace. Though she was the youngest, and was usually surrounded by toddlers, most of them hers, Mama Grace, when she wasn't in the midst of child care, was the peacemaker in the family, a kind and sweet-tempered soul.

I entered the house and let myself be led to the small sofa, where I was shoved against Mawmaw and a baby was plunked into my lap. Not having children of my own didn't preclude a thorough understanding of babies. I'd been raised in a polygamist household where the more babies the better. This one was tightly wrapped in blue, so I knew which twin I had been handed. The church strictly adhered to blue for boys and pink for girls as babies.

"Hey there, little Noah. It's good to see you." I tested his ability to hold his head up and bounced him slightly. He met my eyes, his curious. He started wriggling, trying to get out of the blankets, far too young to be so coordinated and strong. I glanced at Mama, who was holding Ruth, and she carefully turned her eyes away. It was church-speak for "We'll talk about these babies later. It's private."

Mama Carmel brought tea from the tiny kitchen and set a mug beside each of us before she wedged herself in on my other side. I was truly trapped, and happy that Esther's place was too small for my other adult sisters, Priss and Judith.

I sipped Mama Carmel's tea, tasting chamomile and rose

hips and a trace of something else I couldn't place. The women all had their hair bunned up and were wearing proper winter church dresses: tiered or full skirts, square or high necklines, and full long sleeves. All wore aprons. The only difference between their clothing styles when I was a child and now were the colorful sneakers they all wore. There were two pairs of yellow, one pair of blue, and two shades of pink between them. Sneakers were new footwear for churchwomen, breaking centuries of tradition.

As if I had interrupted their conversation, Mama Grace started talking about the babies and how they needed to hold a sewing bee to make some new onesies and nightgowns. I listened, adding nothing. Talk drifted to Christmas. I spotted a small fake evergreen tree in the corner on a table, decorated for the season with glass ornaments and handmade crosses and miniature manger scenes.

I hadn't celebrated since John died, but now I had Mud. I couldn't put off decorating the tree. *Dagnabbit.* I stared into the tea and didn't even bother to hide my sigh. The room fell silent.

Mawmaw touched my arm. "I understand you don't want to get married at the chapel?" She was using her townie accent, the one she grew up with, not her church-speak. That meant this was really important.

I froze, my eyes on the tea. "Ummm. I . . ." I stopped.

Mama Carmel harrumphed.

I raised my eyes from my mug to my grandmother's face and her kind, gentle eyes. Mawmaw had married into the church, a townie girl who had fallen in love with a churchman and given up everything, literally everything and every person from her previous life, to marry him. She had been disowned by the fancy townie Hamiltons and not one of them had ever spoken to her again. Mawmaw was tough as nails and twice as strong. And there was a glimmer of something unexpected in her eyes.

Mawmaw might not be here as the family's big gun, but as my big gun.

"No," I said. "I don't want to be married at the church. My husband will never be part of the church. I will never be part of the church. We will be married on our land, at our house."

No one spoke, so I went on.

"On the front lawn if it's pretty, on the porch if it's raining or cold. While my family and my work friends and my other friends are gathered around."

"Fine. You'll need a dress," Mawmaw said.

The mamas and Esther gasped. Mama Carmel actually put a fist to her heart as if she had been stabbed. The family matriarch had just given formal permission for me to marry Occam outside of the church. A sense of wonder filled me. Tears I hadn't realized were gathering spilled down my face.

Noah gurgled and reached for me with a hand he had gotten free from his swaddling blankets. I put a finger to his and he gripped it with surprising strength.

Mawmaw handed me a cotton handkerchief. Church folk didn't believe in the wasteful use of tissue but in reusable, washable, sterilizable if necessary, hankies. I shifted Noah so I didn't break his grip, took the hankie, and patted my face.

"White won't do," Mawmaw said, "you being married before. And pink might clash with your red hair, assuming it's still red in a week," she added wryly.

When I used my power, it had an effect on my hair, making it redder and more curly for a while. Today it was a halo of scarlet curls that had been hard to comb out.

"But," Mawmaw continued, "I saw some pretty blue gray silk at the cloth shop in town. I had a bit of money put by in my cookie jar and picked up enough yardage for a wedding gown." She pulled a scrap of cloth from her pocket. "You like it?"

I pocketed the handkerchief with a mental note to wash and return it, took the scrap of blue gray silk in one hand, and ran it through my fingers. It was soft and thin and shimmery, without being glossy. It had a good hand, meaning it would fall and drape beautifully. "I do. It's lovely."

"You three"—Mawmaw lifted her mug at the others—"will make a dress that Nell likes."

It was said as a pronouncement, an order. And it meant I'd have a big say in the style of the dress. It wasn't going to have to be a tiered skirt with square neckline and puffy-styled sleeves.

"You've been looking at dresses in town? In magazines?" Mawmaw asked into the horrified silence.

"Yes," I whispered, my voice rough. "Mostly online. I took some photos. Something simple. Full skirted to my ankles, but not a circle. Petticoat to hold it out a bit. Tight sleeves and bodice, with a sweetheart neckline."

"Can you send a picture of your dream dress to your mama's cell phone?"

I nodded, not looking up in case more tears wanted to fall outta me.

"You'll have to stand for fittings, but these three ladies are talented seamstresses, and while I doubt any other three women in the church could pull a wedding dress together in time, these three can."

The mamas looked at each other and sat a little straighter. Mawmaw didn't give out compliments often.

"I'll handle the food." Mawmaw looked at me. "I assume you're using your own flowers?"

"Yes," I said again, fighting to sound normal and not as if my throat was closing up in teary gratitude. I held the baby closer and breathed in the smell of baby: milk, formula, a fainter scent of baby pee, and the indistinct scent of fast-growing plants. "Winter greenery in my bouquet."

Noah released my finger and reached up with his free arm. He managed to close his fist on a coil of my hair. He waved it around and pulled it to his mouth, making little sounds like he might be hungry. I eased my hair away and handed my nephew to Esther. She unhooked her dress top, positioned a clean cloth diaper so it would cover her breast and the baby's head, and snuggled him close, letting him nurse.

"So," I said. "I'm getting married two days before Christmas. Thank you, Mawmaw."

My grandmother hugged me and reverted to church-speak, pointing at the mamas. "You'uns got work to do on that dress." She sent that finger to me. "Nellie, you scoot on home and send your mama a picture."

I hadn't expected an attack in daylight. I hadn't expected an attack at all.

It was five to eleven and I was eating an early lunch. I had a sandwich a half inch from my mouth when I felt the first footfall on my land. Dropping the sandwich, I grabbed my shotgun, my PsyLED service weapon, and my cell phone and raced outside beneath cloudy skies. I moved so fast Cherry didn't even have time to try to get outside with me.

I laid the weapons and my upper body across a raised bed facing south, dialed Esther and told her to stay inside. Before she could demand more information I ended that call and dialed PsyLED. I shoved one hand into the soil. Tandy answered.

"PsyLED Eighteen. Dyson."

"Tandy. This is Nell. Not asking for help yet, but reporting a stranger on my land, entering from the highway on foot."

"Can you tell if they're armed?"

"No. Not yet."

"Liaising with local law enforcement. Sending a car by, no lights, no sirens."

Yummy was asleep in the closet. Mud was at school. Occam was on a case forty miles to the west. I was on my own.

I closed my eyes and concentrated. Felt the footsteps move up the hill, purposeful but not in a direct line, through the old woods of Soulwood in my general direction. Not toward Esther. The footfalls followed an animal path, a deer path. The footsteps felt the way a hunter walks, careful but not stalking, not predatory like a cat. And it was daylight, not dark. So, not a vampire.

I relaxed, letting my awareness gather around the intruder.

The birds in the trees around it called out alarms. From the land I got the sensation of boots. The feeling of human male. No rifle. A steel blade in one hand. Slashing. The awareness of trees shouting, screaming. He was hacking his way through the undergrowth. Harming oaks, black walnuts, and a few tight stands of poplar saplings. Striking in long diagonal cuts, high on one side, to his knees on the other. Some of the saplings would never recover, cut too low, damaging the trunks.

"Machete," I said. "He's too far from the road for a LEO to see him. Have the unit go directly to my sister's house."

"Roger that," Tandy said.

"Do you feel anything?" I asked him. Tandy was the member of the unit most closely tied to Soulwood. His gift of empathy had allowed him a deeper connection.

"No. Nothing. Yet."

In the background I heard him giving my address and a description of Esther's house: "It looks like a hobbit built it." The description was way off, but I let it slide, my own thoughts concentrating on the man slashing his way through the property. I was fairly certain he was a hunter ignoring private property, looking for a good place to build or raise a deer stand.

But just in case . . .

I envisioned the Green Knight, showing him the invader's position, but the tree already knew about him. I felt vines erupting from the ground in front of the trespasser.

In our shared reality, the knight was fully helmeted, his visor down, gauntlets in place, a sword in one hand and a shield on his left arm. He was sitting astride his green horse. The massive beast stamped its front hoof and snorted, breath a white cloud, its breastplate a golden green with an iridescent shimmer.

All through the ground I felt the earth awaken. Soulwood, *hungry*.

"Tandy," I whispered. "Tell the deputy to stay in his car. Do not, I repeat, do *not* step out of the car. Tell him I have security cameras tracking the trespasser."

"Copy." I heard a faint click as he took me off the recording. "Nell. Is your land . . . moving?"

He was feeling the land awaken. Tandy loved the land like it was family.

"Yes."

I heard another click and Tandy said, "Affirmative, Ingram. Deputy to remain in her vehicle unless shots fired."

"Good," I said, and sent my consciousness into the earth again.

The huge warhorse was shoving through tall grasses. Dark trees appeared ahead. Oak, maple, poplar, spruce, fir, all in various shades of green, summer trees, not winter trees, but known to me. I oriented myself to his location. He was approaching the bottom of the hill, closest to the main thoroughfare that headed into Oliver Springs. The horse changed leads and shoved his way into the trees. The vision shifted and altered. These were real trees. Trees on Soulwood, along a narrow trail with cut and splintered saplings. As if his ghostly image moved through them in reality.

My own connection to the land sharpened. I recognized the birds and squirrels and sensed a fox hiding in a den.

The greens of our shared nonreality changed and grew in

clarity. I saw and felt everything through the eyes of the Green Knight, who must be combining the visuals of every animal and the sensation of every plant in the area to share this view. This was new. A change in the way we sensed the land. Together. This was . . . fearsome.

I concentrated on the interloper. The human was closer now. He was angry, frustrated. He was also armed with a handgun and multiple mags, which I hadn't sensed before. Not breaking my concentration, I informed Tandy of the weapon.

The man sweated, droplets flinging from his face as he swung his arm back and down, to cut and cut his way through. He bled from abrasions against tree bark and the punctures of thorns. He grunted for breath in air that was cold and damp, and with each step, wrenched his boots from earth that had become sucking mud, though it hadn't rained enough in the last weeks to be muddy.

The trees and undergrowth around him grew more tangled as vines erupted from the ground. He stopped and held out his cell phone. Then a mechanical compass. He tried to adjust his position, but the trees were too tangled. He was lost. Soulwood was creating barriers, all without my assistance.

A vine snagged his pants from behind, thorns piercing through to skin.

I had blood. I had sweat. The land was claiming him. Its *hunger* grew.

But what if he was simply trespassing to find a place to hunt? Deer season had opened only weeks ago.

I studied the man's clothing through the eyes of birds, a disorienting experience as they cocked their heads and looked at the man from one eye.

Jeans. Jacket. Hoodie. Boots. Not the strange black clothing of the men who had accepted Yummy's challenge. He looked like a hunter. No rifle, but still, a hunter.

On his cell phone, he punched buttons and sent a text. Nothing I could see or hear. But overhead and all around him, the tree canopy began to whisper and shift, a soft susurration of threat. The birds fell silent. The fox curled tight in its den.

I felt a car pull onto the road and roll up near Esther's home. A stranger, a vehicle the land didn't recognize. The Green Knight looked back and I saw an officer pulling her vehicle to a stop.

She lowered her windows. Female cop. Following orders. Esther stepped out on her porch and exchanged words with her. Esther carried a glass of tea out to the officer and then stood at the unit, the two women chatting. The mamas' vehicles were already gone.

I reached out to the Green Knight. I thought at the vampire tree—sending mental pictures of a man wounded, lost, forced out of the forest, to take back word of an impregnable plot of land, asking him to let the human go. The Green Knight sent back images of humans throwing burning torches into the woods. Of fire and destruction and death everywhere.

If this man was with the vampires looking for Yummy, following the orders of the vampires who attacked at Ming's, the tree might be right.

The knight sent me images of the intruder disappearing into the earth as Soulwood ate his energies, body and soul. Then another of the man eaten by the tree.

I was a cop now. I couldn't. Not even if it was in my best interests. I sent back images of the trespasser being trapped, then handed over to local law enforcement for questioning.

The knight stopped moving through the trees. Information was important. This was a negotiation he could consider.

To seal the deal, I added details. I sent the knight a vision of caging the man with the machete. Taking his phone. Using vines to carry him from the property to the road, where he would remain trapped until the officer could arrive. Holding him still. If he was a hunter, the officer could confiscate his weapons, arrest him, or send him on his way.

The Green Knight turned his head to me, nodded once, and began to move through the trees, slower this time, until he saw the man on Soulwood land. The man was hacking at the undergrowth. Behind him, vines and small trees shoved through the ground, weaving together. From the sides they grew around until they had made a curved wall, a woven, impenetrable prison. And then the vampire tree began to grow thorns.

Power arced through the ground in slow waves. Vines elongated.

Two thorned vines snatched out and wrapped around his arms, yanking them to the sides. Stretching him out.

He shouted, grunted, fought. He dropped the machete. His cell phone was pulled from his fingers.

A third vine slid around his waist, found and removed a handgun.

The man screamed in pain and terror, the sound echoing.

The officer started to open her door.

"Tandy," I said into my phone. "Tell the officer to stay in her car. A bear woke up and is chasing the man back out to the road."

"Copy."

A fourth vine wrapped around the prisoner's mouth. His scream cut off. He went silent, gasping. The vines pulled his hoodie over his face, cutting off his vision.

The Green Knight looked back at me.

I nodded. "Take him to the road."

The vines began to pull him back to the main street.

The knight gave me that single nod, stiff in his helmet. The warhorse turned in a tight circle and disappeared.

I pulled my hand from the earth and opened my eyes to a dark, cloudy sky. I was shaking. My stomach churned, as if I'd eaten Scotch bonnet peppers on a dare. I pressed my dirty hand to my middle and said, "Tandy, the guy's going back to the main road. The officer and I need to meet him there in about twenty minutes."

I heard the click again. "Willingly?" Tandy asked me on the private connection.

"More or less." That was all I could offer to explain the unexplainable.

I felt the deputy's unit turn around and move back down the street toward the main road.

"Ingram out," I said to Tandy. The connection ended.

I tried to catch my breath, tremors all through me. My sister called, and it took two tries to answer. "You'un wanna explain what jist happened?"

"A hunter came onto the land. He was . . . scared off." Another lie at my feet.

She ended the call without reply because my sister was fearful of the land and what it could do and what it meant about her power. Power that the church would label as witchcraft, making her a creature who should be burned at the stake.

Shaking, I went back inside. As I shut the door, a wind blew through my land carrying leaves and twigs and the first rain-drops. I had fifteen minutes before I needed to head down the hill to interrogate the man who had come onto my land. I washed the dirt from my hands and went to the fridge, opening a jar of peaches Mama had put up this past summer. I ate three slices with my fingers for the sugar rush. Outside, the skies opened up, and rain, in a driving sheet, traveled across the cleared acres, the heavy drops hitting my metal roof as if dozens of drummers sat up there, banging.

I turned to the table. My lunch plate was empty. I remembered dropping my sandwich. I looked under the table. Not even a crumb.

Cherry was draped across the couch, her eyes guilty.

I shook my head. Why fuss at a dog for eating my meal when I had just lied to everyone and had a man—possibly an innocent man—wrapped in vines, a prisoner, just down the hill? I ate peaches standing at the sink until I stopped shaking. Got my work gear and headed to the door.

My cell rang. FireWind's picture was on the front for a Face-Time call. I locked the house and tapped the screen. "Hey, FireWind."

"Ingram. Are you all right?"

It hit me that everyone who claimed a place on my land might have felt traces of my feelings, of the land's reactions—tension, fear, guilt, *hunger*—and that Tandy had to have informed them all what was happening. It was his job. Occam was probably having kittens in worry.

"I'm good. I'd rather be making tea than going down the hill to interrogate a trespasser."

"Margot is near your place on an unrelated case. I'm sending her to take this, instead of you." FireWind's tone made that an order, but a kind one. His face, from the angle I could see on the small phone screen, was intent on driving.

"And if he's a foreign blood-servant for attacking vampires?"

"If he doesn't speak English, Margot will have to call in a translator. And then Margot, with her truth sense, will ferret out the truth beneath whatever story he comes up with. If he tells a cockamamie story about being attacked by trees, he may end up in lockdown."

My boss-boss meant in a psych ward. Seventy-two hours of evaluation and meds strong enough to bring a patient out of a psychotic episode.

I dropped my gear and turned back to my kitchen. Added water to my kettle.

On his side, the ambient noises suggested heavy traffic. "Nell?"

First names. Yeah. He was being kind. "Okay," I said. "Thank you."

"I was going over your report about Ming having the Blood Tarot. Were there any indications about how she got it? Or where?"

Frowning, I rinsed my mug and got out creamer and honey. "She didn't say. Didn't hint. Just that she had it."

"What did it feel like?"

"It had power. Like a faint vibration of magic. T. Laine might have gotten a lot more off of it, but it wasn't my kind of energies, so I didn't get much beyond that. Except the deck was comprised of two different sets of cards. The face cards, the ones she called the Major Arcana, were older, the inks deeper, and the energies on them were heavier."

"The Major Arcana were from an older deck?"

"That's what I got from the limited amount of time I touched them."

"PsyLED needs access to the deck."

I knew what my boss wanted from me in reply, some kind of deferential agreement. FireWind had been alive for a lot of years, working in the military, as a cop, had been a hunter and a guide, a warrior in the Old West, probably other things he had never told anyone. He still carried expectations of acquiescence to authority. Which I wasn't good at providing. And since I wasn't on the clock, I decided not to be good at acquiescing today.

I said, "Yeah? I think that's a good idea. Whyn't you'un walk up to Ming of Glass' clan home at dusk, knock on the door, and politely ask the MOC for it."

Aya burst out laughing, which re-formed his face into a study of delight. Aya laughing was always a surprise, because he didn't laugh or even smile often. He changed the subject. "There is a tree growing on your land, at the church where you grew up, *and* in the pot you carry. The one you carry in a pot grew incredibly quickly when you were attacked. And you talked to it when you threw it into your trunk. Have you learned any more about it?"

"It eats meat. I call it a vampire tree because of that. And I talk to all plants."

He made a soft "Mmmm" sound and changed the subject. "According to what we have so far from the PM, there was no vampire saliva in the wounds of the man we collected at Ming of Glass'."

"Okay. That all we got right now?"

FireWind didn't reply, letting a silence build between us, his eyes not on the screen but on the traffic. Eventually he said, "No. CSI retrieved three kinds of hair from wounds deep in the body. Two of them were *gwyllgi*."

Everything inside me went still. There were two results to the inbreeding in the church, two different mutations that plagued the families. One branch—the Nicholsons among them—mutated into plant-people. Some families mutated into Welsh *gwyllgi*, also known as devil dogs, or Dogs of War. We had fought and killed and captured a lot of *gwyllgi*, sending the young ones to the Montana werewolf pack to learn how to control their shape-shifting and their desire to hunt and kill humans.

FireWind said, "I am concerned about you taking part in this case. You are too close to it. You've been injured already. I want you to take the rest of the day off, and when you come in for your next shift, limit your time spent on it to checking facts and Clementine's voice-to-text notes." More gently, he said, "Understood?"

"Yes," I said, my voice wooden. Unexpected nervous laughter started to rise in my chest at the thought *wooden*, but I smothered it down.

"What happened on your land twenty-seven minutes past?" he asked.

Before I thought it through, I said, "What happened in the horse pasture at Stella Mae's ranch when you danced with the stallion?"

Our last major case had involved investigating the death by paranormal means of country music superstar Stella Mae Ragel, and I had seen the big boss display some unexpected gifts, standing in a corral in the middle of the night and . . . charming might be the best word for it . . . charming a very feisty stallion into loving him.

"You were there? That night?"

"Yes. Passive magic. Dances with horse. Like in that old movie with Kevin Costner but with a horse instead of wolves. So far as I've been able to find out, it isn't magic that comes with being a skinwalker."

"Perhaps it's an Indian thing," he said. "Isn't that what you white people say about my kind? That we can commune with animals?"

"I'm a farmer. I commune with the land. Tit for tat. So let me remind you I'm *off the clock*," I said, letting him hear my anger in the words. "If you'un wanna chitchat, you can wait until we're at the office. Or you'un can call for a visit, moon in the night sky or not. But unless it's an emergency, how 'bout you'un not bother me again on my *time off*."

"You do have a waspish tongue, Ingram." It could have been in insult or condemnation but he sounded amused.

I quoted from Shakespeare, "'If I be waspish, best beware my sting.'"

Aya chuckled softly, the small camera catching his black brows rising. "That passage ends on a randy note. Shakespeare was at times indelicate.

"I won't block you from reading the case files, including the COD when the forensic pathologist files it. Enjoy your day off, Ingram. And perhaps reread that scene before you quote it to the wrong person."

The call ended in a snarl of hope and dissatisfaction on my end. Hope, because FireWind wasn't blocking me from knowing about the case; dissatisfaction, because FireWind had been teasing me about my Shakespeare quote. What had I said?

To keep from thinking about *gwyllgi* hair on a DB picked up from the clan home of Ming of Glass, I carried my mug to the coffee table in front of the sofa and rummaged around for my copy of *The Taming of the Shrew*. I flipped around until I found the pertinent lines and read:

PETRUCHIO: Come, come, you wasp; i' faith, you are too
    angry.
KATHERINE: If I be waspish, best beware my sting.

PETRUCHIO: My remedy is then, to pluck it out.
KATHERINE: Ay, if the fool could find it where it lies.
PETRUCHIO: Who knows not where a wasp does wear his sting? In his tail.
KATHERINE: In his tongue.
PETRUCHIO: Whose tongue?
KATHERINE: Yours, if you talk of tails: and so farewell.
PETRUCHIO: What, with my tongue in your tail? Nay, come again, Good Kate; I am a gentleman.

"Oh dear." There was a time when I had been so unworldly that I hadn't understood what the passage might mean. Now I saw it was possibly an improper sexual innuendo. I sat on the sofa and sipped my tea, not sure if I was amused or embarrassed or both to have quoted it to my boss.

I skimmed *The Taming of the Shrew*, comparing it to the way women were treated in my youth in the church, and even in my marriage. And I wondered if I could turn it around and apply Petruchio's methods on the men in my life. Or perhaps I had already been doing that.

I remembered Jane Yellowrock being the bigger shrew, never tamed, and wondered if she would have beaten Petruchio to a pulp for the things the fictional man had done to win the hand of his shrew.

I checked the clock and sent texts to Occam and to Mud, at school, telling them I was home for the rest of the day. I had energy to burn and winter gardening to do. There was a break in the rain, so I pulled on my yard clothes and my old gardening boots. When I was done with farmwork—not that it was ever really done—I'd fall on the couch with a good book and the afghan, turn off my cell, snuggle down next to Cherry, and fall asleep.

I put in hours of backbreaking work. By the time I was ready to stop, the rain had started again. I showered and napped to the sound of pounding rain.

I slept. And I dreamed. Of the earth and the deeps of the spirits of the mountains and hills that slumber. And the bones of the earth that spread and cracked and sprouted. I dreamed of the People of the Bones. The first people. I dreamed of skeletons and graves and the death of sacrifice.

I dreamed of the People of the Straight Ways. Ancient seafarers and farmers and engineers, the killers of my own people.

Dreams of famine and war and pestilence. Of great floods that destroyed an entire worldwide oceangoing civilization.

Twisted, confusing dreams, warped images, potent smells, and swift, strange sounds.

Dreams of the man in the woods, the man who had been shackled with thorns and vines and filled with fear and horror, shivering, as Soulwood and the Green Knight together tasted his blood. Through them, I tasted his blood. Traces of vampire. A blood-servant. His heart pounding with the terror in his blood. Trapped. Trapped. *Trapped.*

I woke, my heart slamming in my chest. It was five p.m. Early night had fallen.

Someone was coming down my steps.

There was something on my land. Vampire. Evil. *Danger.*

SIX

"Yummy?" My voice was gravelly with sleep and my hands uncoordinated as I untangled my legs from the afghan and tried to stand.

"You're awake?" Yummy called from halfway down the stairs.

"Yes." I found my boots in the dark and yanked them on while I talked. "We're in danger. While you slept, I trapped a blood-servant in vines not too far from Esther's and he was picked up by the police. Now there's some vampires on the property, prob'ly lookin' for him, unless he knew to ask the local LEOs for a phone call and a lawyer."

I tied my boots securely. I needed to pee, but there wasn't time. With the lights off—because I knew my way in the dark—I found my gear.

As I worked, Yummy dashed back up the stairs, calling behind herself, "How many?"

The dreams had been all mashed up together. "Two? For sure two. Maybe a third one keeping watch near the main road."

I checked my cell. I had two missed calls and four texts from Mud. My heart clenched painfully until I remembered that it was Friday. She would be spending much of the weekend with the Nicholson clan, going to church with her family and friends, according to the guardianship and custody agreement. While she had a taste of family, I was supposed to be working my every-other-weekend schedule. Instead I'd been told to stay home.

Sure enough, the first text informed me that Mud was going to Mama's for supper, and expected Sam to bring her home around seven p.m.

Occam wasn't back from work; he must have caught a case.

They were safe.

But if vampires could indeed feel the magic of Soulwood, Esther and the twins were in danger. If I hadn't been home for the day . . .

Yummy, with her vampire night-vision and strength, leaped off the top landing and was out the front door while I was still finding my ammo bag and gear bag. *Vampires. On my land.*

I checked my weapons and called Occam at the same time, telling him what was happening. He was stuck in Friday rush hour traffic and couldn't get here for at least half an hour, even with lights and sirens. I called it in to HQ, but no one in the field was anywhere near me. And human law enforcement had no weapons for fighting vampires. They would simply die.

Yummy, Soulwood, the Green Knight, and I would have to face this alone.

I went outside and closed the door softly. I hadn't seen Cherry or the cats and figured they were out back. There was a pet door at the back of the house, opening to the enclosed space of the shed-roofed porch and the fenced area set up for them.

Yummy was standing on the top of the front raised bed. It was no longer raining and the temperature had dropped and felt as if it was still dropping. Clouds raced overhead, throwing moon shadows, catching the vampire's pale face in its glow. Before I could go back for a coat, Yummy said, "Tell your land I heard your call. I fight beside you." She sounded vamp-formal, serious and . . . maybe deadly. Even in the fluctuating light her face was different, manic, and more . . . human? "I fight with you and with this land. This land is mine to protect now. I am your Warlord."

It sounded like a vow. That was different too. "Okay. Why?" My breath blew out, a cloud of winter cold.

"Because, you *idiot woman*. I woke smiling tonight, for the first time in *decades*. Your land pierced me and took my blood and now I'm . . . I'm fucking *happy*."

Which didn't sound happy at all. The words should have been angry. But Yummy didn't look enraged or dangerous. She looked blissful, ecstatic. Gleeful. Almost mad with life and joy, like a religious convert caught in the spirit.

"Point me," she said. "You drive down. Lights off."

I pointed. Yummy took off on foot.

My new car had autolights, which would give my position away, so I got into John's old truck, set the weapons on the floorboard, and backed out of the drive. Once the hill's gravity had me, I put the truck into neutral, turned off the motor, and rolled down to Esther's on the old winter tires, steering by pure muscle, breaking by willpower and liberal use of the handbrake. As I rolled, the Green Knight pushed into my mind. It was harder for the knight to reach me without my hands in Soulwood dirt, with my body on rubber and steel and composite materials, but he made it work. Somehow.

He was dressed as he had been before my nap, his horse armored, but this time there was no sword. He carried a war ax. Across his back a mace had been secured, the head sticking out at his elbow, wicked and barbed and, oddly, black as real iron. He showed me six vampires near Esther's house. *Six. Not two.* Four were watching from the center of the road that led to my drive. Two were trying to cross the tiny lawn to the Tulip Tree House, close to where Yummy had stood the previous night while patrolling. While carrying the fresh scent of the Blood Tarot.

In the dark around the two vampires, vines and thorns were whipping the air. Slapping at the vamps, slicing them with thorns. Trying to trap them. The vampires cut them with swords, one long blade, one short. There was plant blood all over the vampires—white, green, and ruby red. Not just the vampire tree's blood, but also the blood of the tree that had mutated just for Esther.

Esther's tree and the vampire tree were fighting together.

I rolled around the curve and the four vampire watchers turned to me, barely visible in Esther's security lights.

Yummy stepped into the yard. She raised her blades into the air and screamed a challenge. "I am Yvonne Colstrip, the former scion of Ming of Glass, now Warlord of Nell Nicholson Ingram, protector of Mindy Nicholson, Esther Nicholson, Noah and Ruth Nicholson, and guardian of Soulwood! I offer blood challenge to you both!"

Oh Lordy Moses. That was bad.

Using all my strength, I stopped the forward momentum of the truck and jammed it into park.

Yummy raced across the land and engaged the vampire closest. Steel clashed on the night air. Sitting in the uncertain safety of the truck, I pulled one of my toys and my cell phone out of the ammo bag and turned the one-hundred-thousand-lumen flash on. It lit up the watching vampires like a torch, blinding three of them. The fourth watcher had looked away in time.

In the first instance of the flash, I got a good look and a dozen pictures in burst mode. They had been standing there, the three watching Yummy and two unfamiliar vampires fighting in the yard. The sixth one was watching me. None of the watchers moved except to turn their heads from the light. I kept half an eye on the fight and sent the photos to HQ.

I turned off the lamp. The vampires returned to standing in what looked similar to military "at ease," hands clasped in front. They each wore a tunic dress, leggings, a hoodie, and gloves. Swords hung by their sides. Medieval-type clothing, like something the Crusaders might have worn.

From Esther's land echoed the clanging of steel and the rare grunt of breath. Yummy was fighting one vampire as the other fought the vines.

I shoved my Glock into my waistband and stepped out of the truck, my feet on soil claimed by the vampire tree and Soulwood. Instantly I knew that neither of the attackers had bloody wounds. Again I aimed the lamp at the vamps who were watching the fight. Flicked it back on. In the brilliance of the flash, the ground between us looked as if it was crawling, the dirt and rock quivering and shaking. The vampire tree was about to destroy my road, *dang it*.

The back door opened and Esther emerged, raised a shotgun to the sky, and fired.

Everything stopped except Yummy.

Faster than my eyes could focus, she stabbed the vampire she was fighting in the heart with a shortsword. Whirled and took his head. Her body still spinning, before the other combatant moved, she took his head.

I slid my eyes back.

In the light of my flash, there were only three vampires.

An arm wrapped around my neck. Again. Lifted me off the ground.

My breath stopped.

Well, *damn*, I thought, figuring this needed an actual cussword.

"You have touched the Holy Deck," he said into my ear, "you and the woman vampire. You stink of the magic of the Holy Deck. You stink of this land and great power, evil power. *Witch* power. He will have you all. And then he will burn you at the stake."

The pressure on my throat increased and my breathing passages closed. Darkness stole my field of vision. I had the sensation of movement. I was being pulled away.

Fear should have claimed me. Anger tore through me instead. I dropped the light. Didn't fight the arm. I reached over my head and scratched the man's face with my fingernails. I drew blood.

He is mine, the tree and I thought together. *Hunger* roared up through my fury.

The vines beneath the roadway burst through the gravel and twined up his legs. He tripped.

We went down. I landed on top of him. I twisted my arm and touched the earth.

His undeath was mine. His soul was mine.

Life force and the undeath force, opposing magics, fought within him. His vampire magic, his undeath, battled his newly returned soul, a soul that was tattered and filthy, and had been even when he was human. The vampire part of him was a perverted, distorted thunderhead of energy, boiling with lightning and rage, trying to drink down his human soul's life force. Traces of clear blue spirit peeked through wild clouds of blood-tinted undeath, as if the last glimpse of the sun warred with darkness, with lightning, and with a pelting blood rain.

The storm within him was formless, chaotic, and bloody. His vampiric undeath and his human soul were at war.

I shaped my power, my gift, into a glowing glove of sunshine and light, a glove netted with fingers of brilliance. I gathered up the tarnished, enraged soul, tangling it with the darkness of the raining blood and the wild winds of the undeath. I began to shove them together into the earth. Claiming this spot of ground, this ancient roadbed, the roots and vines that twisted and burst through.

The strangling arm released and I sucked in a breath. Another.

I heard pops of vampire travel and sent the vines up to grab anything that moved.

A shotgun boomed again.

Beneath the vampire's still-struggling body, the vines gathered. The earth roiled and juddered. I breathed again, gagging out a ragged laugh, which hurt.

I had been carried up the street. Couldn't see Esther's yard, but caught a glimpse of my sister through the bare trees, standing on the porch, shotgun aimed at the yard. There was no sound of swords, no sound at all. Good thing. I was pretty sure I wasn't able to stand right now.

I nudged the vines and roots and the body they had claimed until the tangled mass rolled off the side of the road into the drainage ditch. I didn't need a forest blocking access to my house, and a tree would surely grow up where the land absorbed the vampire. The plants complied and, without my help, pulled him farther to the side. The vampire began to disappear, bits and pieces, blood and gore, his shoes. The earth vomited back up pieces of gold and silver into a little heap.

That's new. For a moment I rested in the power of Soulwood, letting it trickle into my throat to heal me. My breath came easier. I made it to my knees and then to my feet, and gathered up the rings, a bracelet, and a gold necklace made of a natural crystal, maybe smoky quartz.

Breathing hurt, and I touched my sore neck, figuring I was bruised. I was also freezing, both from the cold and the shock of . . . of being attacked. *Again.* Of killing someone. Where his body had lain was a small sourwood tree, easily identified by the sour stench. The stinky sapling was growing fast, inching up half a foot as I watched. But I hadn't added any of my blood, so the tree wouldn't mutate. I hoped.

I stood with my feet wide apart until the world stopped spinning. I touched my belly. The woody knot of roots was bigger. *Dagnabbit.* I tottered down the street like a drunk.

The vampires were gone. Yummy was sitting in the dirt, vines and roots all around her, tendrils waving in an unseen breeze. She was crying. There was a little pile of gold between her knees. Oddly there was an old rusted ax-head there too. Her longsword and her shorter sword were on the lawn beside her and were being cleaned by vines. Small coils of mutated maple vines and leaves were wiping the blades meticulously, almost tenderly. Esther's tree might be adopting Yummy, which was a scary thought.

Esther was still standing on the porch in her housecoat, her shotgun cradled. She wore a mulish expression and her eyes narrowed as I stumbled out of the darkness into the round spot of the security light.

"You'uns all right?" she asked.

"I think so." I approached John's old truck and fished the still-glowing flashlight out from where it had rolled against a tire. With it I found my Glock and my cell phone. I dialed Occam first. "I'm okay," I said, before he answered. "We're at Esther's. Three dead vampires. Three missing vampires." I figured I couldn't keep it a secret anymore. "I killed one of them when it attacked me. Will you call it in?"

"You sure you're okay?" he growled, his cat strong in his voice.

"I'm . . . I'm good enough."

"You used your service weapon?"

"No. I used the land."

He was silent for a moment. "We'll figure something out. I'll call it in. My ETA is ten. And FireWind's on his way too."

"Oh."

Occam might have heard the misery in my voice, because he chuckled. "Later, plant-woman." He disconnected. Plant-woman. Not Nell, sugar. Not when I'd killed someone. My shoulders went back. My cat-man knew what I needed. Even when death was involved.

I trudged to Esther's.

"Is that vampire your'uns?" She gestured to Yummy.

"Yummy. Meet Esther. Esther, meet Yummy."

"She kilt them two vampires and then the vines and roots started pulling 'em down. Is my tree eatin' 'em?"

"Yes." It was the simplest explanation.

"That gold theirs? Hers now?" Esther demanded.

Trust my sister to always think about money. "Yes." In the dark, I wrapped the necklace the vampire had worn around my wrist. Reaching the porch, I held out to my sister the gold bracelet and the rings the land had given to me for the vampire I had killed. "These are yours."

She took the bracelet in a finger and thumb as if it was covered in poison. "Real gold?" Her voice was a hint nicer now.

"Yes. Get Sam to sell them for you."

"I reckon that would be nice." She tucked the jewelry into her robe pocket. "What's wrong with *her*?" She gestured again at Yummy.

"I don't know. I'll find out." I staggered to Yummy and plopped on the ground beside her, still talking to Esther: "You go on inside and take care of the babies."

"You'un don't have to tell me twicet."

I sat close to the vampire on the wet ground, vines all around her, waving as if in a summer breeze. Tears were sliding down her cheeks. Not some kind of emotional breakdown with a flood of big bulbous tears, but more like a trickling spillover, the way water ran over a low-head dam in drought season. As if she had forgotten how to cry but was having a good go at it anyway.

The necklace worn by the vampire I had fed to the earth resting in my lap, I said, "Yummy. Talk to me."

She picked up the ax-head that had erupted out of the ground and tossed it against the foundation of Esther's house. It landed with a soft *thunk*. "He was here," she said. "I saw him. He was watching as they attacked me. He didn't stop them."

"Okay. One of the watching vamps is someone you know and . . . care for?" I was guessing and way out of my league to be asking a vampire about her love life.

She nodded, dejected.

Lights pulled up the road and I recognized Ayatas FireWind's headlights. I was going to have to tell lies to my boss-boss. Or maybe I'd just finally break down and tell him everything I hadn't told him the last time my powers and my land did stuff I wasn't supposed to be able to do. I'd told him most everything once before. I wasn't sure what I'd kept back that time and the lies would eventually trip me up.

Behind FireWind's vehicle, Occam's fancy car wheeled in, and had to slow down to keep from hitting FireWind's car, which was moving more slowly. Behind them was a bread-truck-type vehicle with PSYLED CSI on the sides.

Yeah. This was all going to be one batch of snarled, jumbled-up lies.

"Yummy." I touched her arm. "Here's what you tell the cops. My sister's home was attacked by enemy vampires. You killed two. You think I killed one. You have no idea why their bodies are disintegrating into the earth."

She made a pained sound that might have been laughter. "So just tell the truth. Got it."

"Hide the gold or it might get confiscated."

She gathered up the jewelry and put it in her pocket. I hung the crystal necklace around my neck and put my hands flat onto the ground. I told the vampire tree in pictures that we were okay. Told the tree we didn't need his help. Told the tree to eat nothing and no one or I'd . . . I'd do something mean to it. I got a flash of the Green Knight. His helmet and gauntlets were gone and so was the horse. He was at the fence where he usually stood when we talked, but this time he held up his bare hand. Centered on it was a handprint in blood.

When Esther had met the Green Knight and the land of Soulwood, the one and only time she'd sought them out, the knight had appeared to her like this, one hand up, her own bloody print inside his. "Got it," I said. "You protected her. And you protected me. And I'm good with that. Just no more eating people tonight."

He shook his head and sent me a vision of the bodies being dismantled and pulled into the earth. Soulwood's work. Not his. The land *hungered*; I couldn't stop it.

I blew out a frustrated breath.

"You talk to the land. And it talks back," Yummy whispered.

"More or less," I said, withdrawing from Soulwood and the Green Knight. I opened my eyes and saw her face, curious, grieving, conflicted. Shivers gripped me and I realized I was probably hypothermic from the cold; the wet ground, which I hadn't noticed until now; and shock. My throat was sore, but not as bad as the last time. Not as bad as it had been just a few minutes past. "You'll tell me about whatever has you so upset later?" I asked her.

"Yes. I'll tell you everything."

Together Yummy and I stood and walked to the road, side by

side. I stopped at John's truck and pulled out his old work coat. It was filthy and way too large for me, but it would warm me up. Eventually.

Every on-duty member of PsyLED Unit Eighteen was showing up, along with a few who were off duty. Their vehicles parked in an untidy line, up and down both sides of the narrow lane, and when they got out, they all uniformly adjusted their weapons and holsters from the discomfort of driving in a harness. And getting ready to draw their weapons if needed.

Occam strode down the center of the road and up to me. He put an arm around me and pulled me close. Gently. "You're bleeding, Nell, sugar," he said.

"Not my blood. The other's guy's blood."

He exhaled a quick breath of relief, gave me a squeeze, and reluctantly removed his arm. This was work. He knew our boundaries. "Is he gone?"

"Very gone. Heart and soul."

FireWind and T. Laine stopped in the center of the street, blocking traffic, their vehicle headlights and flashlights illuminating the yard where the bodies were decomposing.

Tandy walked right up to the edge of the greenery, a look of confusion on his face. Tandy could feel the land and he knew it was feeding, satisfied, and maybe a little smug. "It's happy," he said softly, the Lichtenberg lines on his skin bright in the headlights all around. "Proud."

"Yes." Proud it helped to save us. Proud it was eating three sacrifices, body, blood, and soul.

More people spilled out of vehicles. Official chatter. Introductions. Acknowledgments. I overheard a tech say that the PsyCSI team was on-site so fast only because a unit had been driving through town after working a scene in Chattanooga. The team of three were already pulling on sky blue P3Es—paranormal personal protective equipment—gathering evidence bags and tweezers and kits of various kinds.

Though para crime scene had funds approved to build in town, doing anything at all in government took forever, and all we had in town was a local office with minimal testing and evidentiary space. All the real testing on trace evidence went back to Richmond to the main PsyLED offices.

From the way they moved I could tell they were confident

and experienced, but they weren't ready for this site. I'd done my own evidence collecting before. This site was going to present some problems.

I nodded to FireWind and then to the CSI team.

He understood instantly and walked over to them. "There's some kind of active energies on this place. If the vines try to trip you or hurt you, get back to the road fast. Whatever you do, don't sit or lie on the ground."

"It's got a curse?" a woman asked, stepping into the light of the units all around. She looked vaguely familiar, a black woman with broad shoulders and a shaved head. I moved closer. The tech wore a name tag that said DORA WINCOME, HEAD TECH. I remembered her from the "death and decay" crime scene, but she hadn't been in charge.

"Yes," FireWind said. "Some kind of plant curse. Congratulations on the promotion, Wincome."

"Thanks. I worked hard for it." She gestured at the small yard with the moving plants and vines. "We got null sticks. Will that help?"

FireWind said, "Interesting thought. We haven't tried it. Kent?"

T. Laine walked over, put her hands on her hips, and said, "Just for the record, you're authorizing me to risk losing a null stick on an experiment?"

"Good point. Let's try this first." He pulled a Swiss Army knife from a pocket and tossed it into the yard. In seconds, vines pulled it underground and it was gone.

"Ingram. If we lose a null pen here, can you get it back?"

"I don't know." I had never gotten gold or old farm equipment back until now, and I was pretty sure some of the victims who had disappeared on Soulwood had been wearing gold wedding bands, and had pocket change on them. I wondered what I'd find on the surface if I went to the places where the men had been absorbed by Soulwood. And then I wondered how Soulwood had learned that gold was important. Had it had something to do with the fact that Esther had been wearing her wedding band when I introduced her to the Green Knight? Had he gleaned something from her?

I thought about the pocketknife FireWind had tossed onto the ground. Nothing happened. The knife did not reappear. But . . .

"I can try," I said. I accepted a null stick—one of the costly and difficult-to-recharge null sticks used by law enforcement to keep us safe at paranormal crime scenes—and sat on the edge of the yard. I placed the stick on the ground, and instantly thorned vines attacked. I yanked the stick out of the vines and rolled off the property. "Nope. It sees them as dangerous magic." I looked at FireWind. "And maybe it liked the taste of your knife."

His lips crinkled on one side in amusement.

"Fine," Wincome said. "Sandra, Jack, get cameras set up and we'll photograph and film what we can."

I gave the null stick back to T. Laine. Another bout of shivers hit me. I went and sat in John's old truck, turned on the engine and the heater. FireWind joined me, which I thought was nice. Until he started taking my official statement and I had to decide how to tell him about the third vampire. With the fresh bruising around my neck, my being attacked wasn't something I could hide. I settled on, "I got away from the guy who attacked me. I scratched him pretty good. Might have caught his eye. When I looked back, he was lying on the ground in a patch of vines and saplings." I pointed to the spot. "I'm pretty sure the land took him."

"Your weapon?"

I handed him the Glock and he sniffed it. "You haven't fired this recently."

"Not since I cleaned it after Occam and I went to the range the week of Thanksgiving."

"DNA under your nails?"

I held out my hand. There was dirt under them all, garden dirt, Soulwood dirt. And under one there was some blood mixed into the dark earth. FireWind manually rolled down the window and called for CSI to come take a sample. I sat silent while the tech did so, wondering if vampires were in a national database somewhere.

When the tech left, my boss said, very quietly, "Will they ever find a match, Ingram?"

"I have no idea," I said honestly. "He may have committed crimes at some point in history."

"But he never will again."

I scowled at him.

"'O, it is excellent to have a giant's strength, but it is tyrannous to use it like a giant,'" FireWind said. It sounded like a quote, maybe from *Measure for Measure*, one of Shakespeare's least known plays. If so, the boss was again using Shakespeare—the one thing I had studied so hard all my years of aloneness—against me.

I said, "'The trust I have is in mine innocence, and therefore am I bold and resolute.'" Still using a bit of a Shakespearean tone in my words I added, "I did him no harm by my own hand but that scratch, boss-boss."

"'Truth is truth, to th' end of reck'ning.' We shall never know," the boss said.

With that bit of word jousting, he left the old truck and walked back to the CSI team.

Yummy, standing alone among us all, watched from the trees. She used her cell several times, texting and placing calls, and twice I thought she was weeping.

It took half an hour before there was nothing left of the attackers, but meantime, CSI, and therefore every unit in PsyLED, knew that a patch of "cursed" land had eaten three dead vampires, leaving no leftovers, and that there was nothing anyone could do to get the evidence back. The techs mostly got pics of the land feasting and the plants in Esther's yard blooming like it was spring instead of the start of a cold snap. As they filmed, the temps dropped into the twenties and the newly bloomed flowers wilted, browned, and drooped to the ground. The winter chill finally convinced the earth to stop trying to put out new growth. Vines stopped punching through the topsoil. Everything quieted.

But all the attention meant that my kind and I were becoming fully documented by PsyLED.

When the last of the excitement was over, the team's vehicles and the CSI truck left, except for FireWind and Occam. My catman sat in his fancy car and waited for me, patient, furious that I had been attacked again, happy that I was a fierce woman. That's what he'd called me the one time he came to check on me. "You're a fierce woman, Nell, sugar. Fierce as any person I've ever known."

It had made me proud and teary-eyed as I'd watched him return to his car.

Alone, I walked the property around Esther's one last time, seeing all the new growth. Stopping near the far edge of the property, I saw a new tree, and got an itchy feeling under my skin. It wasn't an itch I could scratch until I had sunlight, so when FireWind called me over to Occam's vehicle, I went.

"Ingram," FireWind said. "I know I told you to take the night off, but I need you and Occam to go with me to UTMC and look at the dead body that Ming gave us."

I frowned. "Okay. But why?"

"I'd like to get your thoughts."

"Mud is gonna kill me. She's stuck at Mama's."

"I'll call Mud."

My face musta shown all kinds a shock, because FireWind laughed softly.

"I'm not a monster, Nell. I'll call your sister."

SEVEN

UTMC was the only hospital within miles that had a psycho-metric ward with a staff trained to deal with paranormal patients. It was also one of only a few in the nation to have a paranormal forensic pathologist on staff. The hospital got most of the weird forensic PMs—*weird* meaning anything that the coroner couldn't explain—that came through the county, and when UTMC was done, the bodies were shipped to the county morgue for storage.

I had seen plenty of dead animals when I lived at the church. Butchering them for the table was a weekly part of life. And I'd killed people. Didn't mean I liked seeing dead bodies.

And it also didn't mean the weekend pathologist liked seeing me.

It was Friday night. Dr. Gomez was on duty. She wasn't the pathologist who had trained with witches and a vampire doctor, but she worked with the pathologist who had been. And she had worked with Unit Eighteen enough to learn a lot more about paranormal creatures.

Gomez had very dark copper skin, a curly do that was currently pulled back in a clip, and a frown worthy of a churchman as she watched FireWind, Occam, and me walk down the dimly lit hallway toward forensics. To me she said, "I haven't been clocked in for four hours and *you* show up."

FireWind gave that rare, beautiful smile, the one that could charm, the one he never directed to his team. FireWind gave *us* orders, saving the charm for people he couldn't order around. "Dr. Gomez. Good to see you again," he said.

Gomez let him waste the smile and didn't take her eyes off me. I wasn't sure why she had it in for me, but we always seemed to hit things on the wrong foot. She gave a harrumphing sound. "You want to see which body?" she asked me.

"John Doe fifty-three," FireWind said.

Each year the unidentified bodies were numbered by the coroner according to gender—John or Jane Doe, based on visible genitalia if there was anything to see—and the order found. So far the county had fifty-three unknowns, most of them biologically male. Some had been identified. Most never were. The adults who died of natural causes were eventually cremated, their boxes of ash buried in one of two vaults, the location not made public. Adults who died by violence and under suspicious circumstances were embalmed and buried in graves marked by their number, so that if their killers ever went to trial, the bodies could be exhumed. Though we hadn't had an unidentified child since I came to work for PsyLED, their bodies were embalmed and buried in marked graves for the same reason. And also so that if they were ever ID'd they could be returned to their family for emotional closure and proper burials.

Gomez said, "We've had a record number of unidentified human remains this year. Never thought we'd get to fifty-three. The county morgue is full, so we've held on to some overflow." She turned her back on us but let us follow her into the morgue and then into the cold room, a large refrigerator with shelves, each with a body on it, each in a clear plastic zippered body bag. The bags were new—cheaper disposable bags than the HRPs—human remains pouches—used in the field. Cheaper because we needed more of them. Cheaper because the city and county tax dollars had to stretch to cover items that the burgeoning drug and homelessness problems and inflation created.

We three stayed at the open cold-room door, the chilled air almost as bad as the cold outside, where the temps were dropping faster and lower than forecast. The stench of sickly sweet old blood, old death, and misery blew out on the refrigerated air.

Gomez wheeled a stainless steel gurney to the left side of the cold room and dropped it down, about two feet from the floor, setting a brake with a foot pedal. She grabbed the corners of a clear bag and muscled it from a low shelf onto the gurney. Pressed a different pedal on the gurney and it rose to about three and a half feet high. She released the brake, which thumped loudly in the room, and wheeled the gurney out into the bigger room where the autopsies were performed.

I stepped back, shivering in my winter jacket, feeling the necklace I was still wearing, icy against my skin, reminding me to look at it soon. There hadn't been time when I stopped by my house to pull on dry work clothes. FireWind, Occam, and a silent Yummy had been standing in the main room, waiting, not willing to leave me alone. I'd been hurrying, too fast to think about the necklace.

"Since you're not family, you don't get the full compassionate viewing," Gomez said, "with a sheet covering. This is the cop viewing." Gomez unzipped the cheap HRP halfway around, the sound loud, echoing through the room. The scent of bleach poured out, sharp and cloying, but better than the stench of death that surely rode beneath it. She pulled back the upper half of the body bag, revealing, from my angle, a blondish head with large, looped, black thread stitches sealing the middle of the scalp together, roughly ear to ear. She turned on a bright light, glaring directly over him.

I walked to the side of the gurney. Not looking at his face, not yet, but taking in the torso and arms Gomez had exposed. The naked flesh of his chest was white where the harsh light hit it, blue on the bottom where the blood settled with gravity. Livor mortis, they called it. His chest was sealed in a Y-shaped incision, also closed with thick black thread in looping stitches.

The signs of torture were evident. Cuts. Long tearing cuts that seemed to circle from high on his back and sliced around low, to his hips or ribs, on the sides. Whipped. He'd been scourged. I reached to take his hand and Gomez stopped me, handing me a pair of blue nitrile gloves.

I pulled them on, wordless, and took his bruised hand, stiff and cold, and forced it to rotate to get a better look. His fingers had been broken. There was a blackbird tattooed on his inner arm. Amateurish work, not that I was a specialist in tattoos.

I replaced the hand next to his side and moved around the stretcher to his feet. Without asking, I unzipped the body bag all the way around and peeled back the plastic at the bottom corner, revealing his feet. There were no puncture wounds, but one foot was horribly bruised and swollen. I maneuvered it, the movement proving the bones of his foot were all badly broken.

My breath sped up. Tremors started in my bones. It took everything I had to not step away and clutch myself with both arms.

I pulled the lessons about postmortems I had learned in Spook School to the surface of my mind, dredging them close. But what I was seeing on the victim made me think of . . . other things. Other places. Old memories. Memories that now trailed that schooled information to the surface of my thoughts, sliding up from some dark place inside me.

I rolled the plastic up. Revealed his lower legs. The left one showed bruising in three linear spots on the shinbone. Taking the heel and toes, I rotated the foot and leg. I heard the shinbone crunch. The man's calf displayed far more livor mortis than the other leg. More bruising, from when he was alive. I set the leg down. Smoothed the clear plastic back over his legs and feet, as if to soothe him. But it was too late for anyone to soothe this poor man.

I walked to the head of the gurney, feeling all the eyes on me. Their assessment and patience was a heavy weight.

The man's blue eyes stared up, milky.

I closed my own eyes. Blinked against tears. Forced a breath in and out.

I tried to speak. Had no voice. No breath to say what had to be said. I tried another breath. A tear slid down my face.

I pulled off the gloves and dropped them on the dead man's chest. Cleared my throat. Wrapped my arms around me. I felt Occam move toward me. Felt FireWind hold him back.

"Ingram?" the boss-boss said gently.

"His name was Arial Holler," I said through my tight throat. "He's a church boy. A few years older than Mud. Seventeen. Maybe eighteen. Churchmen don't get tattoos. It's a desecration of God's sanctuary, in the eyes of the church." I tried to swallow. Couldn't. Arial Holler had likely been a Lost Boy, cast out from the church. I managed to speak again. "They used the Boot on him."

"What's the Boot?" Gomez asked.

Tonelessly, FireWind said, "The Boot refers to a family of instruments used by the Spanish Inquisition and all through the Middle Ages for torture and interrogation. They are of various designs to cause crushing injuries to the bones of the foot and/

or leg. Some are vises, often with iron spikes, that squeezed feet. Other forms are made fully of iron. With those, the torturer used iced and then scalding water."

"Scalding . . ." Gomez spun and yanked open the cold-room door. The sound of a zipper was sharp and rough on the shining walls. She said, "Would that cause wounds like this?"

FireWind followed her. From the confines of the cold room he said, "Yes. Exactly like this."

"I've got more." Gomez's voice was harsh and grinding, dry as stone.

"Open the others, please."

The sound of zippers echoed off the sterile walls.

Occam walked up to me and pulled me to him, his cat warmth like a furnace against my cold body. I laid my head on his chest and shoulder.

Time passed, FireWind and Gomez speaking softly. The sound of zippers came again.

"Nell?" FireWind asked more loudly from the cold room. "Would you be so kind . . ."

Occam released me. I walked into the cold room and looked at the man on the first shelf. Only his face was exposed. "Not a church member I recognize. Not a . . . Not a church member I know." I looked at the others. "That one. Maybe? The last two? I . . . I'm not sure. I don't think so, but I don't know." *But the first one was a Lost Boy.*

Those words wouldn't come.

"Then I'd say you have a serial killer who likes medieval torture devices running around the city. Because I have five male bodies of various races and ages whose feet, roughly speaking, have similar signs of a medieval torture device. All within the last week. All were homeless so far as we know, most unidentified, and with kin who haven't bothered to file missing person reports or come claim the bodies."

I was supposed to go to the church to pick up Mud. But I couldn't. Not with a Lost Boy at the morgue.

Back at HQ, I sat in my cubby, typing up reports, lots of reports, of the events over the last two days. I also read the post-mortem reports of the other men tormented by medieval torture devices before being killed. No one spoke to me. No one bothered me. Occam walked by several times, and once placed a bottle of water on my desk, but he didn't speak. I didn't look at him. My brain was too busy on too many levels, processing too many things. The attack at Ming's. The attack at Esther's. The bodies in the morgue. The ties to the church and to the *gwyllgi* mutation.

About nine p.m., I became aware that FireWind stood at the door to my low-walled cubby. I let him stand for a whole two minutes as I typed up the last paragraph and ticked the last boxes on the form. I saved my work and closed the file. Spun in my desk chair to face him.

He was a beautiful man. Golden brown skin, amber eyes, long silky black hair that he usually wore in a single braid down his back. Tonight he wore it in two braids and they hung over his shoulders in front, nearly to his waist. It was a very tribal look on him, and nothing else about him took that impression away, not his crisp white shirt and black pants, not his shiny black office shoes. Not even his glowing yellow eyes.

Aya stood in my office opening, but was turned to the side, so as to leave the appearance of an opening, a way for me to get out. Standing with his body turned, so that I didn't—wouldn't—feel trapped. It was another of the odd little kindnesses I never expected from him.

"Sir," I said without inflection.

"Ingram. May we speak?"

It wasn't an order. I cocked my head.

"In my office if you will?"

Again not an order. A request. "Yes, sir." I stood, followed him down the hallway between cubicles, leaving my weapon locked in the drawer, my cell in my pocket.

In his office, the blinds that covered the glass walls were open, but he closed the door, took a seat in front of the desk he still currently shared with Rick, in the corner, his back to the wall. A visitor's chair. A supplicant's chair. I had a moment of mad mirth at the thought that I could take his chair, behind the desk, a position of authority. Instead I sat in the chair beside his. He had placed them at an angle, mostly facing each other, several feet apart. Well staged for an informal chat.

"Sir."

"Talk to me, Ingram. What does the church have to do with this?"

I don't know. I don't want to know. Didn't say that. "The church has a secret." I shrugged. "They have lotsa secrets, or used to. But this one's a secret mostly inside the church. They don't talk much about it."

I laced my fingers across my lap to keep their trembling from being seen. I kept my eyes on them as I spoke, and knew I had slipped into church-speak. I didn't care.

"We'uns in the church tried mighty hard to keep from breeding too close. But the church land was less than a thousand acres, and not many townie women wanted to marry in with us. We sent our young boys off to war, off to the service. Off to homestead. But there were too few wars to fight to keep the numbers of men in check.

"The teenaged males who hit their majority, who don't fit well into church life, are traditionally . . . kicked out of the church as soon as they reach eighteen. Sometimes sixteen, if they are gay, or too studious, or violent troublemakers. They're expected to join the military or go to work as tradesmen in nearby towns when they're ejected. They're called the Lost Boys.

"Lost Boys are picked up from their homes in the dead of night and dropped off in town to live or die on their own. Some make it. Some disappear. Some die.

"Some churches in town help them. Most people ignore them.

"When the director in charge of the Knoxville FBI office, Thomas Benton the Fourth, who had Lost Boy heritage, discovered he could shape-shift into a devil dog, he knew where to go to find more like him. An entire generation was removed to his purposes—young church boys and Lost Boys.

"A man called Ephraim was in charge of the Lost Boys program when I lived there."

And I killed Brother Ephraim, fed his body to the land, and then fought his filthy, diseased soul, spirit, and stone-hard will until Soulwood and I finally figured out a way to kill that evil energy.

It was brutal. I nearly died.

Aloud I went on. "After the loss of so many to the devil dog taint, none of the church families needed to remove young men for a while, or at least not in such large numbers as once upon a time.

"Arial Holler woulda been in the last batch, the batch used by the local FBI director Benton to create his own devil dog army. But Arial wasn't from a family that had devil dog genes. He was in the church branch that had . . . plant genes? But he didn't change into anything. He was on the street or had a low-paying job somewhere. He kept his head down. Stayed out of trouble so far as I know."

I met the boss' eyes. "Unit Eighteen knew it was possible that some with the devil dog taint escaped. When Benton was killed and his breeding program halted, I'm guessing that someone was paying attention. I'm also guessing that someone was or is trying to find the devil dogs. And since pain is one way to force a shape-change, that might be one reason Arial was tortured. Or he was tortured for information about the family lines, or about the church. Something."

"And the presence of *gwyllgi* hair on the body? And the method of torture used by the Inquisition being used on him?"

I sat up straighter in my chair. Gripped my hands tight. "I'm guessing a *gwyllgi* dog was, or several were, present for the torture. Because of the Boot, I'm guessing that Tomás de Torquemada was there too."

"Elucidate."

I liked that Ayatas FireWind didn't use small words, thinking my lack of education meant I was stupid. "Whatever Torquemada is here for is tied into the church in some way. And into this." I reached around to the back of my neck and lifted the chain away from my skin, pulling the necklace over my head. I held it out to him. "It's a quartz crystal, naturally terminated. It looks like a space for an arcenciel has somehow been carved inside the crystal. It's impossible. I know that. It has to have been cut open, carved, and then resealed. But I looked at it under really bright lights in the locker room. It looks solid to me."

He held it to the light, studying the shape of a miniature frilled and feathered dragon on the inside. "Where did you get this?"

I lied through my teeth, using just enough truth to satisfy

most truth-sayers and the skinwalker nose in the chair opposite me. "When the vampires attacked Esther's place, one of the dead vampires lost it. I put it on and forgot about it until I got cleaned up and then mostly forgot about it until now."

"The assistant director of PsyLED is missing," FireWind said, tilting the quartz. "Has been missing for some time. Soul is an arcenciel."

"Yeah. And maybe some vampire either worships them or wants them and devil dogs for some plan, some crime, something. And since I'm guessing wildly here, that vampire is Tomás de Torquemada. I don't know, really know, anything, Aya," I said, speaking his name as a way to show I was talking to my friend, more so than to my boss. "But it scares me."

"I am dismayed as well." He twirled the crystal in the light. It cast shadowy rainbow patterns on the walls, a prism of color, and the movement somehow made the shape inside seem to move. "This is from a crime scene. It should have been logged in. Please do so, and bring the necklace and the COC to me. I'll sign in for it, study it, make some calls. When you are done, take off. It's been a difficult night."

I shrugged, got up, accepted the necklace from FireWind, and went back to my cubby. A COC was a chain of custody, a form filled out for every piece of evidence and trace evidence from a crime scene. One more form to fill out. Just one more.

But there was *always* more paperwork to fill out.

Feeling the guilt in my heart, I called Mud to tell her I loved her. But she was too busy with a birthday celebration for Bethany, one of our half sisters, to care that I'd not see her today. I reminded myself that she was safer at the church right now at night than with Esther. But guilt at not being with her was a persistent beast.

Occam and I were both expected to work our odd hours this weekend, so when I rolled out of bed to let the dog out the front door at five a.m., he grumbled but didn't follow me. We kept the doggie door locked at night, the better to keep the critters from getting skunked, which wasn't likely in winter but it was a good habit to keep. In the dark, I dressed in overalls, an old padded flannel jacket, and a sturdy pair of boots. I set out stuff for tea making, put on a pot of coffee, left Occam a note, and slipped out the front with Cherry.

It was freezing, hoarfrost raising the top layer of soil. My breath made a white cloud in the darkness. I scratched Cherry's head and, as the puppy did her business, I knelt and touched the ground. The land beneath me was somnolent, resting, satisfied, and unconcerned.

Yummy was walking the church boundary. FireWind was in one of his cat forms, following her, stalking her, crouched and intent, which made me smile. I wondered if he was going to try to leap on her. Margot, alone, in cat form, walked slowly along a branch in the densest part of the forest, approaching the cage of thorns that had held the human until the land turned him over to the police. I wondered what she would smell there, reminded myself to check the arrest report, if there was one, or find out if the trespasser had been committed to a psych ward.

Satisfied that all was well, and no strangers were on the land, I walked down the hill to Esther's, Cherry at my side, gamboling up the road and back, sniffing, marking territory on everything.

Esther was awake, finishing her five a.m. feeding, the babies needing to be burped, which I helped with. I liked the plant-babies, but I was really glad they didn't grow leaves. After the burping, Esther put them back in their cribs and I made tea. When she returned, she said, "You'un brought that dog in."

"Ummm. Cherry's waiting at the door, just like she does when Mud is here. She's very agreeable."

Esther scowled at me, a mighty scowl because of my placid tone. "You'un know I usually get an hour's nap after they go back down, right?"

"Yes. Tea's made. I'm not staying. Is Mud sleeping here, at Mama's, or with me tonight?"

"With you'un. She'll be here at six p.m."

"I'll be home at nine p.m. I'll pick her up."

Esther looked pointedly at the door and back to me.

I laughed softly. "Right. I'll be walking around, okay?"

"Doin' cop stuff or plant-people stuff?"

"Plant-people stuff. I'll be quiet."

"Better be." Esther opened the door and waited until Cherry

and I were outside before shutting it firmly. She had never been real chatty even in the best of times. Tired and sleepless, taking care of twins mostly alone, she was crankier than usual.

I approached the saplings that had given me pause last night. I turned my flashlight on them. They were growing from an old root ball from an American chestnut tree. The root had never really died, and it put out tiny saplings every year, but the saplings never survived. The trees weren't extinct, but no American chestnut tree had exactly survived either, dying off from a fungal blight called *Cryphonectria parasitica*, which had been brought to America from Japan in 1904. Between then and 1940, something like 3.5 billion of the trees, the giants of the Appalachian hardwood forest, considered the finest chestnut tree in the world, had died. Many of the root systems, underground and protected from the blight, were still alive, and tried to grow every year. This root system was over a hundred twenty years old.

And now, after last night, its saplings were twenty feet tall, and though its leaves were turning in the icy weather, the saplings looked unexpectedly healthy. They were growing up from every root for twenty feet around the old stump. Had the sacrifice of three vampires so close to its root system cured it? Or had the Green Knight? I wouldn't know until spring, when they lived or died, but just seeing the trees sent electric delight all through me.

I clicked off the light, whistled Cherry to me, and walked up the road to the ditch where I had rolled the vampire I'd killed. There had been an acre of young scrub trees at the side of the road before. Now, after feeding the land with the life of the vampire that had tried to drag me away, there was a whole acre of healthy hardwoods looking to be a hundred years old, none growing in the roadway but crowding in close, and many of them carrying the reek of sourwood, and others I could identify by the bark and the shape of the trunks: white oak, a patch of red oak, poplar, some dogwood, and smaller trees here and there. The branches were bare, leaves heavy and fresh on the ground.

None of the trees should have been able to grow at this season. My land might be developing a taste for vampire blood. Which could be a good thing unless it started attacking the local vampires, and I had to claim them all to keep them safe. I didn't want to have many more vampire friends.

I reached out to the land and found Aya and Margot. They had driven up together and were changing shape near Aya's car, which was parked near the end of the road near my drive. Yummy was sitting in a tree nearby, watching me. I said softly, "I have coffee. Come sit on the porch."

Overhead, cloud-to-cloud lightning flickered. I wondered if we'd have snow, and maybe a snow thunderstorm.

Dawn was a long time coming, the sky obscured by heavy clouds, only the barest hint of paleness graying the horizon when Yummy joined me on the front porch swing, sipping coffee while I sipped tea. "Is coffee enough?" I asked.

Yummy breathed out a laugh. "No. But I've gone longer without blood."

"When will Ming send your blood-servants and scions? You know I don't have room for 'em. They ain't stayin' in my house."

Yummy, who had cleaned up and changed clothes at some point, pushed off with a toe, sending the swing into movement. "She released my servants immediately after you claimed your boon. There's a house in Oliver Springs I've wanted for twenty years, and my people sent an offer to the owner, who happens to be a night owl." She laughed, a sound of wonder in the tone. "She already answered. Can you believe it? The paperwork will take a bit, but because the building was empty and it was a cash offer, she already agreed."

"That was quick."

"Money talks. Lots of money talks fast. My people will begin repairs and painting and we'll move in immediately."

She pushed us again, and I waited, hearing something different in her voice, in her tone.

"They started work on my lair already. My very own lair," she said, sounding wistful, as if she had dreamed of that for a long time. "It's a large room with its own bath in the basement. They'll seal off the basement's exterior windows with steel shutters tomorrow and I should be able to move in at dusk and sleep there tomorrow—not today, if I can get you to invite me to stay another day."

Mud was at the Nicholsons' so I shrugged and said, "Sure."

"But I do have a question. What duties will you require of me?"

"Huh?" Overly succinct, but it got the point across.

"When you used one of your boons from Ming of Glass, you asked for my scions, blood-servants to feed all three of us, including my personal blood-servants, demanded they all be kept safe until they could be delivered to a place of my choosing, alive, healthy, and not missing any blood." She glanced at me from the corner of her eye. "Not an exact quote but close enough. And then you said, 'Yummy is mine now. Not Ming's.' So what do you require of me?"

"Nothin'," I said, a sense of horror flashing through me. "I was just giving you my protection so you would be free to do whatever you want. Barring abusing and killing humans, you're free. I don't own people."

"I have a counterproposal. I don't want to be free. I want what I already claimed, to be your Warlord. To have access to this land to run on at night. To dance on." She smiled at me, that wonderment still on her face. "Your land makes me happy. I want the protection you offer, and to offer all my protection in return."

Her lips drew down in what looked like wistfulness. "And I want our friendship."

I didn't have a lot of friends, almost none outside of work, and her simple statement lit a small flame of warmth in me. "Okay. With the stipulation that you owe me nothing and can stop coming anytime you want to."

"So you would permit me to build a blood clan family in Oliver Springs? To make allies with other Mithrans?"

I frowned at that, but managed not to sound suspicious when I asked, "What other Mithrans?"

"Oliver Springs is in Ming's hunting territory, and so I'll always owe her allegiance, but I was hoping to reach out to Lincoln Shaddock and build some bridges there. It's said he has a new bloodline that brings scions out of the devoveo sooner than normal, sometimes much sooner. My two scions have been in the devoveo for five years."

The devoveo was a long period of madness experienced by vampires when they became undead. The average time in the devoveo was ten years, but some of them never got their minds back at all.

"Who are your scions?" I asked.

"Charlie and Felicity. They were my first blood-servants, and when they were injured in a fight, I turned them. I'd like to see if I can negotiate with Shaddock to let them drink from his best bloodline."

I looked at the sky. We didn't have long for this. "So you want to be under my protection, keep a lair in Oliver Springs, have your own blood clan, run on my land, make overtures to the Master of the City of Asheville, and still owe Ming of Glass allegiance. That's a pretty fine line to walk, politically speaking."

"Yes."

That wasn't much, but it was all she was going to give me. "I have a teenaged sister I was just given guardianship over. You being on Soulwood will bring dangers to her I can't even begin to describe."

"My not being on the land will bring dangers to her, without me present to defend her, that you can't begin to understand."

Without moving my body I lowered my eyes. Thinking. Remembering the way Yummy fought. The way the vampires fought. *I may need a vampire ally. Jane Yellowrock had vampire allies.*

I asked, "Why were you crying after the blood challenges last night? Who did you see that upset you so?"

Yummy looked to the east, and moved from the swing into the corner of the porch that gave the most protection from the morning sun. "I've told you the story of how I let myself be turned out of love, but after I came out of the devoveo, I realized my maker wasn't interested in me, not the way I wanted him to be. After a few years of being his least important scion, I went on vacation to Europe. In Italy, I flirted with danger. Hunted in the streets. Attended some Mithran balls and danced and drank with some gorgeous but very dangerous people. At one of them, I met a priest who was also a Mithran." She tilted her head. "Maybe I was trying to get myself killed true-dead, but for whatever reason, I followed him that morning and watched as he entered the Vatican."

"Where the pope lives? *That* Vatican?"

Yummy offered a ghost of a smile. "Yes. That Vatican. I got

a room nearby, one with a rooftop that showed me the secret entrance he had used to get inside, and I watched. I discovered that there were Mithrans, including the priest I had met, coming and going, through the secret entrance. It became a game to me, to see how many there were, what their schedules were, where they lived."

I kept my tone deadpan. "You were spying on vampires in the Vatican."

"Yes. But I got caught. To save myself I claimed I had seen one of the priests and was *enamored of him*."

She threw the back of her hand across her forehead like a damsel in distress and I almost laughed. "Go on," I said.

"I was, sort of, enamored of him. He was really pretty. We had a—I guess you could call it a fling. And I discovered that his duties as a priest were to guard Tomás de Torquemada."

"Oh. That changes . . . everything."

"Yes. It does. My priest was one of Torquemada's original guards. His name was Don Inigo Manrique."

I didn't know much about movies, but I had been introduced to the movie where one of the main characters said, "My name is Inigo Montoya. You killed my father. Prepare to die." I kept my face neutral, but something must have shown, because Yummy smiled slightly. "I laughed like a fiend when I saw the movie, called him long-distance, and teased him unmercifully. It's when we started talking again. But I'm getting ahead of myself. History first.

"Some priests were turned, back in the days of the Grand Inquisition. Tomás—among others—had powerful blood. But Tomás had been changed late in life and became dangerous. His death was faked and he was placed in a cage for several hundred years. That cage was kept at various locations all over Spain until the early 1900s, when he ended up at the Vatican for a hundred-plus years.

"My little fling with Inigo was very intense, but it didn't last, and when I got tired of Europe I went back to New Orleans. I kept in touch with him—letters, the rare overseas phone call, then emails—but I didn't dwell on Inigo until last night. He was one of the ones in Esther's yard, watching me fight."

"All the caged vamps got their souls back too, right? Including Torquemada."

"If they ever had souls, yes. I made a few calls after I saw Inigo. It seems all the Vatican's prisoners were either killed or released after the coronation of the Emperor of Europe. It's been said, in Rome, that Don Inigo Manrique himself opened the cage doors and let Tomás go. Despite that fact he knew, *knew*, with every fiber of his being, that Tomás was a violent dangerous creature."

Yummy knew all the people who had been tied in with our enemy Tomás, those close to him and those on the periphery. She knew more than she had said. "Who did I kill?" I asked.

"Domingo Ponçe attacked you at Ming's and is now dead. Miguel de la Peña you killed at Esther's."

"Did they come to my land because I smelled like the Blood Tarot? Or because someone at Ming's sent them here?"

"I'm sure Tomás has access to someone at Ming's. It's likely a double agent. Ming uses double agents all the time. When she released me, she informed the vampire world that you have the Blood Tarot."

I dropped my head into my hand. "Dear heavens."

"Yes. Prayer is a good idea. I can tell you this, from the letters with Inigo, letters I read back over on my cell while I walked your land tonight. Even in a jail cell, Tomás had access to all the secret libraries of the Vatican. Anything he wished to read or research was brought to him. For centuries."

She looked out into the darkness, seeing much more than I could, her vampire eyes watchful and thoughtful. "In the last fifty years, there was the discovery of certain encoded words hidden within the Hebrew text of the Torah."

"The Torah?" I asked. "The Five Books of Moses?"

"Yes. The Pentateuch. The first five books shared by Christians and Jews. Some say all the secrets of the future are encoded in them. You don't know about this?"

I shook my head and shrugged at the same time. "I'm guessing my family know about it, and the church, but I haven't been part of them for a long time, and as a child, I wouldn't have been told about esoteric things." Evil things, according to the church. *Magic.*

"With new computer sequencing patterns called ELS— equidistant letter sequence—and a special program called Sof-SofTorah, the Vatican began searching for things. Inigo told me the researchers discovered things in the diagonal strips across the text, or in columns, amazing things: prophecies, warnings, some about wars, some naming individuals. End-of-the-world things that far exceeded anything prophesized by Nostradamus.

"Tomás became fixated on what he called the Prophecies of the Torah's Coda. The fact that the scriptures of the Jews held secrets for centuries that they had uncoded, and now could be read by anyone, was both infuriating and energizing to him. I think because he found mention of the Blood Tarot in the Torah, Tomás traveled here."

"How did he know the Blood Tarot was in Knoxville?"

"Someone has been searching for the cursed deck. It was a blunt-force search, no finesse. It left a trail."

I had been assigned by PsyLED to hunt for any mention of the Blood Tarot after we lost it. I was the searcher with no finesse. Sooo. *I* had led Tomás to this city. To my land. My eyes met Yummy's. If I hadn't been sitting down, I might have fallen to the porch floor.

"Nell?" Yummy asked, alarmed. "What's happened? Your scent just changed."

I shook my head. "Just putting things together," I said. "Go on, please."

Her mouth turned down and her eyes blackened as her pupils widened, but she didn't vamp out. She said, "Inigo knew I was still with Ming."

"So he attacked Ming, unexpectedly ran into us, and lost the fight. When Ming sent out word that you were free and hinted that I had the Blood Tarot, she redirected his activities away from her. And since they had already located me through my *blunt searches*, they attacked on Soulwood." I didn't react. Not at all. But my heart froze and then caught fire. Fury lanced through me. I knew Yummy could smell it. "Why didn't you tell me all this last night." It wasn't phrased as a question. It was phrased as a demand.

"I was busy healing last night. I didn't put it together until tonight."

I didn't reply. Just looked at the lightening sky, the sun hidden behind the horizon, its faint light behind the clouds.

She said, "Inigo was one of the original four who protected and guarded Tomás. And tonight, he watched Tomás' lesser

Mithrans try to kill me to obtain the cursed deck. He may have wanted to help me, but he didn't. Or couldn't.

"I don't know what happened with the vampires since the oldest, Roman Catholic ones got their souls back. Do they live in horror for what they did under the Inquisition? I don't know, but Inigo looked different."

"The undead life of the two vampires I drained felt odd. Spiky? Maybe warped?" I tried to bring it to mind, but it had been a subtle thing.

"Once a psycho always a psycho," Yummy said. "Tomás was a sadist for his version of the church when he had a soul, was a sadist for the church when he lost his soul, and will be a sadist for the church even with his soul returned. Again assuming he was born with one."

"And Inigo?"

"Don Inigo Manrique was a priest, a priest who had to drink blood to survive, which was a sin, maybe a bigger sin than being with me. He lived with terrible guilt, a dark and brooding man, which had seemed exciting when we first got together, back in Rome. I was an idiot. I thought I could help him, change him.

"When I realized he would never put me first—and that though he was not allowed to participate in the holy mass or his priestly duties, his loyalties would always be to the church and the vamp he guarded—I left him. At the time he was still in love with me. I don't know what he feels now, but I do know he hasn't been with anyone since I left Rome. He could still be carrying a torch, but that seems unlikely since he was willing for me to die. The thing we had, even if it was a rebound fling on my part, was powerful."

She took a breath and let it out. She edged to the door and put her hand on the knob, ready to dash inside. But she wasn't done. Not quite. "With Tomás here in the States, with the Torah Coda prophecy about the Blood Tarot, to Ming we're both useful as bait and as redirection to buy her time. And then you used one of your boons to help me, and that messed up a lot of her plans." Yummy smiled. "I bet she was apoplectic when you used a boon."

"And now Tomás de Torquemada, the scourge of humanity, the grand inquisitor, the face of the devil on earth, is at my door," I murmured. Unknowingly, I had done it to myself with my blunt search.

"Inigo once said that if Tomás gets his way, all that do not worship the one true God and the Holy Mother who gave him birth will die and only the pure will survive."

"Religious genocide," I breathed out.

"One last thing. An important thing." She raised her arms and lifted something off her neck. It was the necklace she had worn since Ming placed it around her neck; it matched the one I had left at HQ. "I don't know what this is or means, but Tomás wears one around his neck too. I once had a photo on my cell of a painting of Tomás. If I can find it, I'll send it to you. In it, Tomás is wearing an amulet just like this. It's bound to be part of Tomás' plans and needs.

"Nell. Ming knows all this. Ming has a Blood Tarot deck. Tomás and his entire coterie have invaded her city. I don't know what Ming will do."

"Ming isn't sane right now," I said. "She could ignore him, go to war, or try to force us, force me, to fight for her. That's what she meant when she asked me to kill him, isn't it? She wanted me to solve her problems."

"Yes. Ming is crazy. Batshit bonkers."

"If I had gone to Ming's alone when she summoned me, I'd never have been allowed to leave, would I? I'd have disappeared."

Yummy didn't reply, which I figured was an answer of its own.

I watched Yummy, squeezing herself into the tiniest corner as the light brightened around us, and remembered the burned spots in Ming's grass. "Are you? Sane? Bonkers?"

"I may be batshit crazy. I still get a really nasty sunburn if sunlight so much as brightens a room I'm in, but I can laugh and be vamped out at the same time."

"Go inside and get in your vamp hole before you burn to death."

In an instant, she was gone and the door hung open. The faintest whiff of scorched vampire hung on the air.

I pulled my cell phone, sent an abbreviated report to HQ, grabbed an empty plastic coffee-grounds jug, and walked to the tree line. I dug up a baby vampire tree sapling and stuffed it into the pot with a good helping of Soulwood dirt. "You'uns grow big like the last twig, and it'll be the last time I take you anywhere," I warned the Green Knight.

Nothing happened, so I went inside, where I crawled into bed next to my cat-man for a morning nap before I had to face PsyLED and a job that might kill me and mine.

Work was not at my desk, as FireWind had suggested, but in the field.

A city contractor crew discovered a body while excavating a foundation to support a new electric supply line. The county had a massive, doubly redundant electrical grid managed by the Tennessee Valley Authority, one that connected the various city power supplies to various top secret government and military contractors, all of which needed a steady power supply to run their top secret tests. The benefit of the electric grid redundancy to the rest of us was that power outages were usually localized and quickly restored.

One of those electric grids was being rebuilt, and digging with a backhoe had resulted in the discovery of a body with a brick in its mouth, an iron stake in its chest cavity, and its decapitated head between its legs. It was weird enough that both the lead Knoxville PD investigator and the head of Knoxville CSI had shown up on scene and determined they needed to toss this case somewhere else. They called PsyLED to take a look in case the body was vampire, witch, were-creature, or some other paranormal.

Occam and Margot were off on some other case that might be a witch spell gone wrong. Margot was from a witch family and could sometimes sense witch magics. So FireWind, who needed a witch at the scene with the "brick-in-its-mouth body," called T. Laine in on her day off and sent me to help. I was assigned as second on the case because I wasn't a witch. And I wasn't senior enough yet. I wasn't insulted. I was relieved.

Lainie, however, was not happy to be called in on her weekend day off, and by the time I arrived on scene, she had already arrived, dressed out, stomped over to the crime scene, and crawled into the trough. Over my winter coat, I pulled on a white crime scene uni like hers and slid into the hole with her.

"Well, this sucks," she muttered to me. Her fists were on her hips as she stared at the bones revealed by the backhoe. "I hate it when the city crime scene techs get something right on my day off."

She looked up to the surface and spoke to the investigator on scene. "Detective, for now this is ours."

The city investigator nodded, said, "Good by me. I'd rather deal with drive-bys than weird shit. I'll leave you a uniform to keep the lookie-loos and the media in line. I'm a cell call away if needed."

"Come on, Ingram," T. Laine said. "PsyCSI gets to finish digging this out."

Back on the surface, she called our own paranormal crime scene crew, telling whoever answered the call that we had a cold case, skeletal remains, a partially opened gravesite, and needed their expertise. While we waited, we crossed the street to a row of stores with a little mom-and-pop coffee shop and bought a box of coffee and cups for everyone who would show up. Then we sat in my car to watch.

This team was once again led by Dora Wincome. The lead tech looked as grumpy as Lainie, so maybe it was her day off too. Being in charge meant longer working hours than the usual eight- to twelve-hour stints of most law enforcement. And more paperwork. Dora must never sleep. From her expression, I gathered that being in charge was a pain in the behind.

Also by her expression, and the glares she sent our way, it was clear she recognized us from the last crime scene at my house. She was still glowering her displeasure when the skies opened up again. Following a singular cussword I could read on her lips, Dora and her crew put canopies up over the exhumation site and, with only a few more nasty glances at us, and all of them wearing sky blue P3Es, they crawled down into the ditch.

Over lunch I called Mud to chat, and to make sure she was helping her sister and taking care of the critters at our house. It was Saturday, but her chores still had to be done, and Mama Grace had driven her over and stayed to visit. The two women were currently ensconced at Esther's, cleaning, washing baby

clothes and cloth diapers, folding clothes, and making lunch so
the exhausted mother could get a break and take a nap. Cherry,
who was usually a high-energy dog, had preferred to stay home,
and since there was access to the backyard to do her business, I
was good with that. That necessary call over with, and since the
rain hadn't let up, T. Laine and I did a lot of research and caught
up on reports while Dora and company worked in the mud. Lots
of mud.

T. Laine and I kept warm, stayed dry, did research, and
brought in lunch for everyone, paying on the PsyLED Eighteen
credit card.

Two hours in a steady downpour later, a thoroughly unhappy
PsyCSI team had the body exhumed, all evidentiary materials
bagged, and the skeleton in a body bag on a gurney in the back
of their transport vehicle.

T. Laine and I climbed from our nice warm car into the back
of the PsyCSI unit, and Unit Eighteen's resident witch began
species and paranormal identification of the skeletal remains.
Immediately after placing her hands on the bones, Lainie said,
"Female. No residual magic in the bones, so not a high-power
practicing witch. Not a were-creature." She flipped the skull
over and looked inside at the upper teeth and what remained of
the palate. "No hinged fangs, so not a vamp."

Dora Wincome cursed with interesting imagination, words
that once would have shocked and embarrassed me but in which
I had recently taken what Mama would call an unhealthy interest. Not that I wanted to cuss, but the use of words to relieve
stress or attack others was fascinating.

"You telling me that our crime scene people worked in those
miserable conditions for nothing?"

"Not nothing," T. Laine said. "Somebody thought she was a
para and murdered her. All I can tell is that the body wasn't any
known, or at least currently detectable, powerful paranormal
creature. Maybe she had been bitten by a vampire and her family killed her to keep her from rising. Or she had been born a
low-power witch. A woman punished for magic of some kind,
since she was staked and her head was between her legs. That's
not nothing."

"Yeah, yeah," the lead tech said. "Point made. And from what I see, she'd been in the ground for decades."

"Ingram. Any chance the church did this?" T. Laine asked.

"I'll have to ask Mama to nose around. See if burials of 'evil women' were done this way in the past, off church grounds, unmarked."

Wincome sighed. "So we'll turn this over to the locals and my report will read, 'The skeletal remains are that of a female, likely human, no signs of magic used in her death, no magic was in the stake or the brick, and that makes it a mundane murder investigation.' Agreed?"

"Agreed," T. Laine said. "I'll make mine the same and send it in from home. I might be able to steal a little me time from what's left of my day off."

"I hear ya," Dora said.

I jumped out of the CSI unit and walked through the pattering rain toward my car. Our part in this was over, but the body worried me. As my hair and shoulders absorbed the rain, I looked back at the long line of foundations to be dug for the new power lines. Would any more bodies be found? And had the church been involved?

As T. Laine and Dora Wincome turned the body back over to the city, I drove out of the parking area and headed back to HQ, only then remembering that I had dug up a new twig of the vampire tree and potted it. And left it in the trunk all day.

Change-of-shift report at seven p.m. was held in the conference room, which had become, by default of size, the main IT room too. When day shift turned over to night shift, everyone who was working gathered, including Occam and me, our split shifts overlapping. The crew consisted of FireWind, LaFleur, Occam, JoJo, Margot, and me. Tomorrow there would be a different mix. Weekends at PsyLED were either boring as all get-out or lively and bloody.

JoJo had dug up info about Tomás de Torquemada, but only bits and pieces might be valuable to the case involving the Lost Boy and other homeless men who had been tortured to death. The grand inquisitor was born to the wife of Pedro Fernández de Torquemada in 1420, in a place called Valladolid, Castile, which was an old-fashioned name for Spain, and Tomás' death date was listed as September 16, 1498, at Ávila, Castile. He was the Roman Catholic Church's first grand inquisitor, who had a penchant for torture, rape, maiming, and burning witches at the stake. JoJo said, "His name is synonymous with the Christian Inquisition's horror, religious bigotry, and fanaticism."

His methods had been adopted by the church a few times over the centuries. I had been threatened with burning at the stake. And if some of the elders had their way, I'd have been tortured first. All at age twelve.

I thought about the beheaded skeleton of the woman with the stake in her rib cage and a brick in her mouth. I needed to talk to Mama, but I'd have to be doubly careful because Occam was lead on Arial Holler's case, which put him into direct confrontation with the church leaders. I had no doubt that I'd be drawn into that one, too close to the participants or not.

As JoJo read the report on Torquemada, I looked down at her words on my laptop screen and skimmed his early years as priest and theologian.

JoJo said, "In August 1483 he was appointed grand inquisitor. And that's when the horrors began, most of it supported by public opinion, at least early on."

Public opinion was worth nothing, to my way of thinking. Public opinion was usually governed by self-interest and mob rule. I didn't offer that, as I was sure that FireWind would suggest that my personal opinion was worth just as much as public opinion. Nothing.

"At some point before 1494," Jo said, "we believe Torquemada was turned by a vampire, perhaps willingly. But he was already an old man and in poor health, and we believe that his turning was not as successful as he might have hoped. In June 1494, due to Torquemada's health—again probably the result of being turned late in life—combined with widespread public criticism, Pope Alexander VI appointed him four assistant inquisitors, but their real job was to restrain him. The assistants/guards were Don Martin Ponçe de Leon, Don Inigo Manrique, Don Francisco Sanchez de la Fuente, and Don Alonso Suarez de Fuentelsaz, all of them bishops."

Without looking up, I said, "Those four were turned at some point, and they faked his death and their own and moved him elsewhere, but they're still with him, and according to my source, Tomás was eventually imprisoned in the Vatican."

"Your source?" LaFleur asked.

"Yummy. Yvonne Colstrip."

JoJo continued, "I don't have many contacts in the Vatican, so I called Alex Younger, who does have a contact there, and we've learned that, in addition to the original four guards, the church added four more in 1649, for a total of eight. Those are: Alvaro Cardoso, Miguel de la Peña (now dead), Domingo Ponçe (now dead), Escobar Sarmiento. There were an additional eight added in the 1700s, for a total of sixteen, all still undead when they came here from Spain a week ago. There were four killed true-dead at Ming's, including Domingo Ponçe; three killed at Ingram's sister's place, including Miguel de la Peña; and that leaves nine, and Tomás himself as tenth."

Rick said, "Normally PsyLED would not take an interest in vamp-on-vamp attacks, but since homeless men in the city have been tortured to death by methods similar to those used by the Spanish Inquisition, and since one of our own has been attacked twice, things are different. We need research into all these known 'guards.'"

A *ding* sounded and JoJo said, "Shit." Her eyes were on the central screen overhead. It was showing the outer door of HQ. "We have visitors."

Standing at the door were Cai, two unknown vampires, and their mistress, Ming of Glass.

EIGHT

FireWind's face took on an expression of mild amusement as he stood. His long black braid swung forward and back. "Jones," he said to JoJo, "can you harden our electronic defenses, keep track of every one of them while they are here, and then sweep the entire place when they leave?"

"Affirmative." The screens overhead went black, and Jo clacked so fast it was like a dozen castanets clattering at once. As she typed, she rolled her chair into a corner and arranged a single laptop, the screen not visible from the room.

"Excellent. Everyone arm up. Make certain there are sufficient chairs in here. Someone make fresh coffee and tea. Those off the clock may go home."

"I'll stick around," Margot said.

"Me too," Rick said.

"LaFleur. With me," FireWind said.

So much for bosses' days off. Ain't no way I'd ever be a boss. The hours were terrible, nearly as bad as being a mama with twins.

Rick, his long white hair swinging, followed FireWind down the hallway.

I darted into my cubicle, slung on my shoulder harness and the suit jacket to cover it, made sure my Glock was loaded with a magazine of silver-lead rounds, grabbed the brand-new vampire tree twig, and raced to the conference room. Occam and Margot were moving chairs, so I set my vampire tree on the table and dashed to the break room, where I started setting up for a proper tea and coffee service, or as proper as we could get with our own travel mugs and disposable cups, various sweeteners, and powdered creamer.

On the overhead speakers, I heard the discussion between Rick and Aya as they went down the stairs. The outer door opened.

"Ming of Glass, Master of the City of Knoxville," FireWind said. "How may PsyLED Eighteen assist you?" He made the question somehow both polite and unwelcoming at the same time. I envied him that skill.

Ming said, "Ayatas FireWind, leader of the paranormal law enforcement departments over many states. We have information to share."

There was a lengthy silence before FireWind said, "Be welcome in our offices."

Over the speakers, I heard Ming say, "You two, cover the exits. Cai, you will come in with me."

JoJo muttered, "Whatcha think? Shall I put the external camera views up to let Ming know we're watching her people?"

"Yes," I said, sticking my head around the corner. "And let her know the conversation is being recorded." I had nuked water. Started a pot of coffee. Found some stale cookies. Occam entered behind me, pulled out an ugly floral plastic tray, and set some plastic spoons on it with some napkins from a fast-food joint. I truly hoped Ming didn't want anything, because everything we had was woefully beneath her standards.

I texted Yummy to tell her Ming was at HQ. I didn't know why I texted her, but it seemed like something she might want to know.

I caught a glimpse of Ming following Aya down the hallway and waited out of view. The overhead speakers went silent. I heard a chair being adjusted in the office.

"We are pleased to offer Ming of Glass a chair and refreshments," Aya said, his tone wry, indicating she had already taken a seat. "Do you wish your blood-servant to sit as well?"

"Yes. He will sit beside me with his electronic device and explain. Where is Maggoty Girl?"

I huffed a breath and walked into the conference room. Ming was sitting in my chair. Which meant it would feel like maggots crawling all over it for weeks. "Nell Nicholson Ingram greets Ming of Glass," I said.

"I do not need names," she said, imperious. Ming pointed

around the table. "That one is the human who finds secrets in the ether. That one is a truth-sayer and is the new wereleopard. That one is Nell's lover."

I didn't blush, but it was a near thing.

"You are Rick LaFleur and Ayatas FireWind, werecat and skinwalker. Just after dusk tonight, someone attacked the clan home of the Master of the City of Asheville, Lincoln Shaddock. He was not in residence, but was en route to visit his wife."

I sidled farther into the conference room at that one. I hadn't known Shaddock was married. In fact, I knew that Shaddock and Ming had shared blood in the past, and I assumed that meant sex, so if he was married he'd have been doing some hanky-panky, not that vampires thought about relationships as being monogamous. And if he was married, why weren't they living at his clan home? So many intriguing questions I wanted to ask, but I was Maggoty Girl and therefore unimportant.

"I dispatched fighters to assist Linc," Ming continued, "and the Dark Queen's staff was informed. It is my understanding that she had already sent him both Mithran and human replacements for those lost in a recent battle, and assistance from New Orleans, and provided new housing for them in the city. His own people held off the attack as the Master of the City returned with haste, and as his new scions and humans arrived from Asheville. Cai."

Cai again looked much like the Cai I had first met, austere, distant, dangerous. He stood and held out a thumb drive to Aya. "Video feed of the attack."

Aya's hesitation was brief, but Ming saw it. "There is no subterfuge, skinwalker, no hidden electronic attack on the thumb. If I chose to attack this place, it would be far more direct."

Though her calling him a skinwalker, twice, was surely a deliberate demonstration of just how thorough her dossier on him was, Aya accepted the small drive with a slight bow. "My apologies." He handed it to JoJo, who unplugged some hardwired devices and plugged in some others before putting the video up on the screen overhead, next to the screens of the vamps standing watch outside. As she worked, Cai opened a small laptop and went online via his cell phone connection, ignoring us all.

On the screen, with the early night of a cloudy sky as backdrop, the footage began. We watched as vampires rappelled down a cliff wall and attacked steel-shuttered windows. Ming said, "It was clear that the attackers had not reconnoitered the clan home by day, as they were unprepared for the presence of the new steel shutters introduced just prior to the reign of the Dark Queen."

Other camera angles of the same attack appeared. There were three vampires and a dozen humans, all with weapons. Security lights around the house blinked on and off, at times blinding the attackers. There was no sound, but two attackers fell, shot, I assumed.

"The attack went on for some time," Ming said, "long enough for Linc to return, for his fighters to arrive. Long enough for me to send him reinforcements, though they have not yet arrived. Long enough for his wife to arrive and join him in the fight."

The way she said the word *wife* suggested some long-standing jealousy, the kind one would find in a polygamous household, but no one commented. Maybe no one but me even heard the note of complaint, indistinct as it was.

We all watched on the screen as Shaddock's scions from elsewhere in the city arrived, and as vamps and humans were killed left and right. Standing on the cliff edge, watching, was a lone man in church robes. "Tomás de Torquemada," Ming said, extending an index finger, the nail painted a bloody red. "He directed the attack until Shaddock's female appeared."

There was a moment in the video where Tomás was there and then was simply gone. In his place stood Shaddock and a shorter, middle-aged, nicely rounded, platinum-haired woman, her silver hair flying in a wind that glimmered with power I could see, even on the camera video, as bright sparks of light.

FireWind said, "PsyLED was led to understand that Torquemada came for the Blood Tarot. What do these vampires"—he gestured to the screen—"want with Lincoln Shaddock? And why does Ming bring this to the attention of PsyLED and not the Dark Queen, who handles such cases of attack between Mithrans and Naturaleza?" I noticed he didn't mention the five tortured homeless men.

"I speculate three things," Ming said. "First, Tomás always wants things and beings of power. Second, Linc has the scion

Amy Lynn Brown, the Mithran who has blood that brings
Mithrans back from devoveo. It is my assumption that Tomás
has found reference to her in the Coda." She said the word *coda*
like a title of some great portent. "Third, I speculate he wants
Maggoty Girl."

"Because you told the world that I had the Blood Tarot," I
blurted.

Ming smiled in satisfaction but didn't look my way. "I believe he hopes the blood of Amy Lynn Brown will heal him.
Tomás did not come through the devoveo . . . intact. His body is
old and his mind is broken. When our souls came back to us, some
of us had been undead for too long. Others were damaged, frag-
mented by the lives they had lived, the lives they had taken, and
the loved ones they had lost. Others were poisoned. Some of
us have not learned to survive the return of our fractured humanity. All of us have remembered joy and happiness, the kind
that only one with a soul can experience. The angel's *gift* was
more than many of us can bear." Her eyes flicked to Margot, our
truth-reader. "Even I require much more blood than before my
soul returned, to maintain my self-possession."

Was a lack of blood the reason she had acted so bizarre the
night she called me to attend her? That made a vampire kind of
sense.

I glanced at Margot, our probie and former FBI agent, who
had truth-sensing abilities and who had been sitting silent, in
the corner, watching and listening. She met my eyes and gave
me the faintest nod. Crazy as it sounded, Ming was speaking
the truth or at least the truth as she knew it.

Ming turned her head in the way that made my skin crawl
and looked at me, standing in the doorway. "I will accept tea."

Occam and I brought in the tray and poured hot water over a
tea bag in a small foam cup. Ming stared at it, and though her
mouth didn't turn down, she somehow emanated a sense of disgust. With one carefully manicured hand, she lifted the bag by
the string and dunked it several times. She sipped once and set
the cup aside.

"Maggoty Girl. Though you refused to kill him for me, I
made certain you were a lure to divide Tomás' forces. I do not
regret this. You diminished his numbers appropriately. You will
continue to do so."

Cai said, "My mistress. The local witch coven, the Everhart-Trueblood coven, have joined in Shaddock's fight. The Mithrans are departing with haste."

"All of them? *All* of the Everharts are fighting with my Linc?" she demanded.

Cai turned his laptop to her. Ming studied the screen, sat back in my chair, and stared into the distance. She made a little twirling motion and said, "Show them."

Cai repositioned the laptop and FireWind and LaFleur leaned in, watching with fierce concentration on whatever was happening on the screen. Unable to see, and feeling superfluous, I followed Occam into the break room and together we poured and then returned with cups of coffee. Their attention was still on the small screen; no one touched the coffee.

FireWind said, "The witches helped drive off the Mithrans and now are cleansing the land around Shaddock's clan home. Why?"

"Marriage," Ming said, the word imbued with disgust, before changing the subject. "Tomás will return here, to my city. They will not stay away. There is too much here that he wants, and with the minds of his closest scions shattered, he can coerce them to do anything he desires."

I thought about Yummy's former boyfriend and her tears. Yeah. She had felt the difference in him.

"This fight," Ming said, "is part of the information I offer, freely. As your people say, with no strings to attach. Lincoln Shaddock's wife is the matriarch of the witch clan, Bedelia Everhart Shaddock, and all of her witch daughters except for the first, who died at the hand of Jane Yellowrock for calling a demon, were fathered by him."

JoJo gasped a little and started typing like a madwoman. FireWind narrowed his eyes as possibilities flashed through his mind. I thought about witches who were also half vampire and wondered how that had happened and how that would affect their power levels.

"FireWind. The Dark Queen is temporarily unavailable to assist me. As her brother, you will assist me in her stead. For this information and much like it, I require you to kill Tomás de Torquemada."

"Ming of Glass, Master of the City. Your information was

not delivered without strings. You have attached the string of murder to it. PsyLED is a law enforcement agency. My sister and I, while sharing blood, do not share responsibilities. You know this. We will not execute anyone, even the old psychopath masquerading as a priest. He belongs to the Vatican."

"It is the Vatican that released him," she said. "If he remains undead, he will kill many." Her eyes rose from the screen to FireWind's face. "He has killed many, even in this city you claim."

"If we find proof that he has killed humans," Aya said, sounding as if he was in a negotiation, "we may take him down and transport him to the Dark Queen. That is all we can do, though should he die resisting us, that would be an . . . an unfortunate accident."

"Boss," JoJo said, "the fanghead out back is gone."

I stiffened. My land sent a shock of something electric through me, alerting me. A vampire had just stepped on the dirt tied to me. "He's on the roof. He's coming down from upstairs."

"She's right. He ripped off the door," JoJo said. "And the fanghead from down front just ripped off that door."

Ming vamped out, her eyes going scarlet and black, her fangs clicking down.

Aya pulled two handguns I hadn't even noticed him wearing and stepped into the hallway where he could aim in both directions.

Rick aimed at Ming. Occam aimed at Cai.

Margot leaped to a crouch on top of the office table, her stance catlike, also aiming a gun at Ming.

JoJo was standing behind her electronics, a stake in one hand and her service weapon in the other.

Cai laughed.

Ming stared at me. "Mmmmaaaaggot."

I had pulled my weapon and aimed at Ming until I realized Aya was alone. I was closest to the door, so I grabbed my potted tree and ducked around the standoff, into the hallway, taking the L to the right. Aya aimed toward the exit doors. I grabbed a handful of Soulwood dirt, dropped it into a pocket, and placed the pot on the floor.

The vampire who entered through the roof entrance had stepped into my soil there. I knew where he was. I held up one finger to FireWind, whispered, "He's moving slowly." I raced to the end of the short hallway.

Gunfire erupted from the conference room, but I didn't turn to see.

FireWind fired.

I focused on the vampire coming toward me. When he appeared around the corner, I shot him, midcenter chest. He wasn't expecting it, so he didn't pop away. The single round was enough to take him down to one knee.

I got in two more shots as he rose and tried to make it back down the hallway. At least one more of the rounds hit him. He disappeared around the corner. His blood was on the floor, a trail I could sense. He was heading to the nearest window, which he opened and dropped from. Landed on the soil two stories below. My connection to him faded as he limped off.

The soil in my pocket felt warm. I ignored the sensation and turned to the fight in the hallway. Which was over. All the vampires were gone.

I was breathing too fast. My heart felt as if it would rip itself from my chest. I was deaf.

I walked toward the open L where FireWind had been standing.

There was a lot of blood. Occam came to me, and I saw his lips move. Asking me if I was okay. I nodded. "You?"

His lips moved again, and I lip-read, "Okay. Everyone is fine."

That was wonderful, but it didn't sound right. "No one got hurt? At all?"

Occam frowned. There was blood in his blond hair. "No. None of our people. And that's mighty strange."

Down the hallway, Aya and Rick were getting the interior door set in place and Margot and Occam—both extra-strong werecats—went to the roof to secure the door there. JoJo was on the phone talking to someone.

I was alone. I looked at my tree, still sitting on the hallway floor in its little pot. It looked fine. Except there was blood on the pot. I picked it up. I had no idea which vampire—or Cai—had contributed the blood. But they had attacked for no reason. And they hadn't used weapons of any kind. They had just attacked, fists, claws, fangs, with no way to win against overwhelming numbers, silver rounds, and trained shooters.

That was really stupid.

Unless it was all a diversion. Holding the pot, I went back down the hallway to the place I had shot the vampire. I followed his blood trail down the connecting hallway and into the office where he had jumped. It was the fancy office once used solely by Rick and now currently shared by Rick and Aya. I stood in the entrance, thinking.

If they left a listening device, JoJo would find it. But if the vampire I shot—or one of the others—took something . . .

I walked back to FireWind, who was hammering at the door-frame with his fist to force it back onto its hinge, and asked, maybe too loudly, "Did you leave your computer on the desk in the office?"

FireWind whipped around so fast, I jumped back. He and Rick both strode down the hallway, turned on the lights, and stood in their office door. The desk was bare. The window was open. There was a smear of blood on the desk and the window casing.

My hearing was coming back, because I heard when FireWind said, "They can't get into the laptop."

Rick said, "We hope. This is a clear violation against PsyLED by the Master of the City. This should fall under the auspices of the Dark Queen."

"Yellowrock is otherwise engaged."

Rick's voice was tight when he said, "Honeymoon. The ceremony was over a few hours after dusk."

The pot waggled in my hands at that. Jane Yellowrock was married? How had I not known that? "Tonight? Coincidence?"

FireWind tilted his head, his braid sliding. "Interesting timing. We will report this up-line to the Department of Homeland Security, and to the proper Dark Queen channels. However, as no one was injured, we will not disturb the Dark Queen on her wedding night." Aya looked back at his office. "In addition to working up this crime scene, we need to do a thorough sweep to see what else they may have taken, and what they left behind."

I thought about poor Dora, and her lack of time off, and was glad I wasn't the one who had to call her. Fortunately for everyone, she liked Rick, and since Rick had no social life to speak of and no romantic life anymore, he stuck around and charmed her.

The vampire visitors had taken a lot of rounds, silver rounds that meant they would have to have surgery to excise the silver-lead rounds and then receive copious amounts of blood to heal. And if Cai had been hit he would need the same. I wondered if Ming had been sane enough to plan for that in advance.

Our search proved that the visitors/thieves took nothing else and the three listening devices they left behind were child's play for JoJo to find and dismantle. She was also able to remotely scramble FireWind's laptop the moment someone opened it, a tech program I had never heard of and that she had probably developed. The crime scene and blood cleanup would take a lot longer.

Long after the end of our shift, Margot, Occam, and I typed up our reports. I finished early and, for reasons I didn't fully understand, beyond intuition, I wandered into Margot's cubby. I waited at the door until she typed in her report and spun in her chair to face me fully. She didn't speak. Her dark eyes simply waited, watching me.

"I'd like to be nosy," I said.

Margot snorted softly. "Girl, you are always nosy."

"Why are you so unhappy?"

Margot didn't jerk or flinch, but shock crossed her face. I thought she wouldn't answer, but she laced her fingers across her flat belly and tilted her head. The head tilt was a very catlike gesture.

"I was a nonwitch in a witch family. I was a black child in advanced classes, with a bunch of white children. They weren't all racists and bullies, but the ones who weren't were too frightened to stand up for me. I was in advanced classes in prelaw at Yale, and in the top twenty percent of my class, when a white boy, the top linebacker of Harvard Crimson, decided he wanted to try a piece of dark meat. I put him flat on his back, dislocated his elbow, and ended his football career."

"Good," I said.

"I was sent packing for that offense. I finished my degree at a state school. Went into the FBI. On my first rookie case I stated that the defendant was innocent. When I was proved right and the case had to be started over, my truth sense came to light. I was promoted quickly, as much for my truth sense as my other abilities."

"That sounds like a good thing?"

"No. I was feared by my coworkers, hated by my trainer, who had staked his career on the defendant I proved innocent."

"Margot, why are you telling me this?"

Distinctly, she said, "I have never fit in. Not anywhere."

"You fit in here better than I do. You're a werecat, like the others."

Margot stood, gathered her things, and walked away, down the hall and through the doors to the stairwell.

"That didn't go as planned?" Occam asked from his cubby nearby.

"No. She's lonely."

"I know. Let's go home."

Together we left the bloody scene, but the office wasn't closed. Though there were no open cases requiring overnight activity, and HQ could have been closed, Rick and JoJo volunteered to remain behind to oversee CSI and cleanup. We drove off, leaving the second floor fully lit and manned by tired and irritated techs wearing sky blue unis, with a construction crew waiting in the parking lot to replace the doors.

We were halfway home when I had an idea. I told my car to call Occam and said, "We'uns got an hour. Mind if we go to Ming's? Providing LaFleur or FireWind approves? I got a question I wanna ask Cai."

"Do you think that's wise?" my cat-man asked. "I mean, considering they just attacked us?"

"I can't think of a better time."

He was silent as the road passed under us. "Nell, suga'? Why not?"

I could almost see his expression, amusement in the sound.

"I'll call HQ," I said. I ended the call and told the car to call Unit Eighteen's headquarters. I asked Jo to speak with whomever was still there and in charge, and was connected to Rick LaFleur.

"Nell?" he asked. I liked that about Rick. He often used first names instead of the formal last names required by FireWind.

"Permission to ride by Ming's and speak to Cai?"

Rick asked, "Why now?"

"Ming will be doing MOC things, probably well fed since the attack and the fight. Cai will be in charge of security. I'd like to see if he'll talk to me. Maybe let me see the Blood Tarot again."

"Permission granted. Keep Occam with you. Record the interaction. Be safe, Nell." The call ended.

Together we went to the door and Occam rang the bell. When he tried to step in front of me, protectively, I said, "Maggot should be welcome. Ming wants me to kill her enemy."

Occam stiffened. Stepped back. And frowned heartily at me. I chuckled, seeing one of my own expressions on his face.

The door opened and Cai eyed Occam standing behind me, and then me. "Does the Maggot come to issue challenge to Ming of Glass? My mistress is not at home. She is traveling to assist Lincoln Shaddock in Asheville."

Putting as much asperity in my tone as a churchwoman accused of using store-bought canned vegetables, I said, "Maggoty Girl is not stupid enough to challenge Ming of Glass. I want to know what the Blood Tarot has to do with all this mess you vampire people are in."

Cai's eyes narrowed, as if trying to unify conflicting data. "Maggot should know that Ming of Glass was visited last night by a federal official from ICE. Brenda Jabroski is a Mithran hater and has decided to confront Ming because my mistress lacks *documentation*. This woman claimed that Soul approved this visit. But I have discovered that Soul is missing. For how long?"

I kept my face from reacting, but the roots buried in my hands twitched.

"Three weeks or more," Occam answered.

"Jabroski's paperwork was signed by Soul yesterday."

Occam dialed HQ and asked, "JoJo, is there a Brenda Jabroski from ICE in Knoxville?" A cold wind blew against us as we waited. Occam asked, "Will you look into the name, a possible affiliation with other agencies, and any people who might have a beef against Ming? Thanks." He ended the call and said, "There is no Brenda Jabroski with ICE. Someone gave you false documentation and impersonated an ICE officer."

Cai gave Occam a formal nod, as if at some ambassadorial function. "Thank you. You should know that my mistress has said She Who Guards the Rift is no longer rational. The rift has affected her mind. Soul is delusional, and therefore my mistress believed this treachery."

The roots in my fingers twitched, but I kept my reaction off my face.

Cai looked back along the entry hall, as if listening to something we couldn't hear. While his expression and tone had been formal, I realized he wasn't dressed in his formal attire, but in a pair of jeans and a T-shirt torn at the shoulder. And he was barefoot.

Imperious as that miffed churchwoman, I raised my voice and said, "Cai! I would like to see the Blood Tarot. And we would like to be offered a beverage. Tea for me and coffee for Occam."

Absently he said, "Sure." He waved to our left, turned in the direction he had been looking, and wandered away, moving with an irregular gait. Briefly, I met Occam's eyes and followed Cai into the house, through the wide entrance of the main parlor to the left. It was an ornate room, with upholstered furniture and gewgaws everywhere, probably all antique and expensive. We didn't sit, but instead stood, our backs to the corners of the room, facing the entrance.

Half a minute or so later, Cai returned and placed the metal box with its leather straps on the tabletop. He held up a finger as if remembering something. "Tea. Coffee." He wandered away again.

I sat and opened the straps and the box, revealing the deck. I lifted it out. I hadn't held the deck in my hands the last time. The power of the cards was almost a vibration, something I could feel through my skin. Knowing that, according to the church, I was sinning to so much as touch a magical object, I aped what I had seen Ming and Yummy do. Unfortunately, my hands didn't have that particular skill. "Can you shuffle the deck?" I asked Occam.

He glanced at the door, seemed to listen to the silence of the house, and sat beside me on the settee. He shuffled the deck, his hands moving better than after he'd been burned. He was almost fully healed. When the deck was well shuffled, he placed it in front of me.

Clumsy by comparison, I shuffled them once more and placed them between us. "Cut the deck and ask a question," I said.

His cat eyes were glowing in the semidarkness of the room. "You know I don't believe in this hokey stuff."

"Me neither. Ask a question. A serious one."

"What's going on with the vampires." He stated it, as if demanding of the deck as he cut it.

I laid out a cross pattern face down. Then I placed three cards in the middle and turned the center face up. It was Death.

"Death on top. That's what Ming and Yummy said happened every time, no matter the question, until I showed up." I turned over the next card. It was a man, hanging from a tree. If this deck really had some kind of arcane power, maybe that was supposed to be the Green Knight / vampire tree. With a dead man hanging from it.

The next card was three coins. "Any idea what this means?"

"Not a one, Nell, sugar, but I'm calling FireWind. That deck was removed from a crime scene. We might have legal recourse to walk out with it."

Shrugging, I flipped the other cards while he called FireWind. I had no idea what the cards might mean. I took a pic of the overturned cards, though, so maybe T. Laine could read it or maybe knew a witch who could. Occam finished up the call and said to me, "I'm going to your car. There's the necessary paperwork in my case. FireWind says that unless they come back and physically take it from us, we can confiscate it."

"Will that get Cai in trouble?" I asked. "Ming's crazy. Will she kill him for this?"

"I can write up the paperwork without mentioning his name, but I'm sure she won't be happy."

I began to put the deck away in its fancy metal case. The paint on the tin felt slickery, like the paint on the Major Arcana cards had, and the tin vibrated with the same magic as the deck. Occam returned and began to fill out paperwork. While he worked, I took pictures of the parlor, every nook and cranny. When I found a small book on tarot readings, I opened it and took pics of each page. The book was really old, and hard to read, with *f*'s and *s*'s looking alike, but it might be helpful.

Cai didn't return. We never got our coffee or tea.

An hour after we had entered the clan home of Ming of Glass, Master of the City of Knoxville, Occam placed the paper authorizing us to retrieve property improperly removed from a crime scene on the center of the coffee table. We walked out with the Blood Tarot.

Mud leaped up the porch stairs like a gazelle. His eyes glancing back at me, Occam followed her, graceful as a house cat at the end of a lazy day of watching birds at a window. I trudged along behind, stiff as a tree trunk, tired, and a mite grumpy.

From out of the dark, Yummy popped up beside me, and I cussed, "Dang it, Yummy!" My gear bobbled and I nearly dropped the tree. Occam didn't flinch except to reach back and steady my tree. Probably smelled her coming on the night air. He'd spent twenty years in his leopard form, locked in a cage, and he'd retained some heightened senses.

"Give me your keys," she demanded of him.

"Take your own car," Occam said.

Yummy slapped his hand, snatched the keys out of the air, and popped away. A fraction of a second later, she dove into Occam's fancy car.

He dropped his gear and raced toward it, but Occam had only the speed of a cat, not the preternatural speed of a vampire.

Engine roaring, Yummy skidded out of the driveway and spun the car to point down the mountain, shooting gravel into the air. She floored it, Occam's car going into a sidewise skid before it found traction. Occam stood in the dark, his arms to the sides. "What the ever-lovin' hell?" he yelled. "Her car is right there!" He pointed at Yummy's even fancier car.

I knew it wasn't funny. Not at all. But I still had to hold in a laugh.

Mud didn't hold it in. She gurgled with mirth.

Occam looked back at the road and the fast-moving vehicle lights bouncing down the hill, disappearing into the night. "She's not willing to tear out the undercarriage on her own car, but she's willing to rip out somebody else's? Why didn't she take yours?" he asked, irritation making his voice catty-rough.

"Mine isn't built for street speed?" I suggested. There were benefits to driving a regular car, one that couldn't hit one-twenty on Knoxville's pikes.

"She could have at least left me *her* keys." Hissing under his breath like the cat he was, he returned and climbed to the porch.

Mud was the only one of us with keys out. She unlocked the door and Cherry bounced out, sniffed everyone's crotch, and tore into the dark. Mud squeaked, grumbled what sounded like "Stupid dog," and went into the house, where she turned on a light. One light. Her abstemious upbringing made sure she didn't waste anything, especially power.

Occam paused to allow me to enter before him and our cells rang, at the same moment. We had a conference call from FireWind. Occam gave a cat hiss. "He isn't calling to invite us to coffee."

I glared in the general direction of the cell tower I had allowed to be erected on the highest point in my land. It provided good rent money monthly, but it meant I was never off the grid anymore. We stood on the porch in the dark as the rings echoed into the trees, the cold wind blowing over us, now with a promise of ice in its touch.

I pulled the door closed and we tapped our phones, said our names.

"FireWind in HQ with Jones," our boss-boss replied. "Jones?"

JoJo said, "It took some time, but I tracked down Soul's cells, including four burners, one of which pinged in Richmond, Virginia, at PsyLED national HQ; one in Seattle; and one in New Orleans. The fourth one is at her apartment here in town."

No one asked JoJo how she got the contact numbers of burners purchased by the assistant director of PsyLED. Not a peep. Not even from FireWind.

"I called all of them. They all went directly to voice mail," Jo said. "According to her log, Soul went on personal leave three weeks ago, and none of the cells have been used except the one here in town, five days ago."

FireWind said, "I requested uniformed officers do a safety

check. No one is at home. They looked in the windows, all of
which were left with the blinds turned open, not something Soul
would normally do. There is no sign of Soul or indications the
house was the location of a struggle, but there are two pieces of
luggage on the bed, open, with clothing inside. I'll send one of
our people there soon, but first we have two videos."

Occam and I still stood in the dark, on the porch, and the
chill had already crawled through my work clothing. This didn't
sound confidential or classified, and I didn't think a call from
our boss meant we had to stand in the dropping temperature, so
I pushed through the door.

The cats all twined around Occam's feet, *yowring* in welcome, halting us in the doorway. Cherry bounded back inside
with a high-pitched yelp of happiness, welcoming her people and
her cat-man. She nearly tripped us both and leaped from the
doorway toward the sofa, missing by enough to send her flop-
ping with a thud to the hooked rug on the floor.

Mud giggled from the kitchen and called the dog to her, the
sound of dog food rattling into a bowl.

"The first is security camera video from thirty minutes past,
just after you left her clan home. The video was provided by
Alex Younger," FireWind said as we dumped our things on the
couch and the dining room table. "We'll discuss the importance
of the Dark Queen's IT people having access to the security
cameras at Ming's later."

On the small screen was external security cam video of
Ming of Glass and Cai standing ten feet or so from the front
entrance. Both were wearing fighting armor and carried swords.

"Cai said Ming was in Asheville," Occam said.

"I am aware. There is no audio," FireWind said.

"Her stance suggests she's issuing a challenge," JoJo said.
"Or maybe answering one?"

On-screen, Ming and Cai rushed into the night. The screens
went black.

"And then there is this video," FireWind said. "Jo?"

Her reply was garbled and sounded far off. The cell screen
went black again.

My house was cold, so I checked the stove and decided there
were enough coals to light some kindling. I piled cedar curls
and heartwood pine shavings in the center, muted my micro-

phone on the phone, and opened the stove's airflow vents with a clang.

The cell screen brightened again. "We received this from one of the city's finest, on scene at Ming of Glass' former clan home, recorded ten minutes ago."

Occam and I exchanged a glance. *Former clan home?* I mouthed.

The video showed flames and flashing lights and people in heavy firefighting uniforms. Smoke obscured everything. There were dead bodies in the driveway and what looked like blood in pools and trailing away. The video moved from showing the drive and the dead vamps to the house, which was in flames, fire billowing from the windows. It looked like a total loss. I hoped Ming had a hidden underground lair or she'd be looking for new quarters before dawn.

The cell camera moved around more to show the barn and several outbuildings also on fire. The battle had been devastating.

"This is not PsyLED's case. Not yet. But keep your cells close," the boss-boss said.

I activated my cell's mic. "Joooones," I said, changing it from JoJo to her last name midword, "and FireWind. Yummy stole Occam's car about five minutes past and left here, moving fast."

"I got a feeling Yummy took my car to get to Ming's," Occam said.

"I see. Occam, do you wish to press charges for car theft?"

"Not unless she damages my baby," he grumped.

"Keep me apprised. We'll do the same."

The conference call ended.

The flames caught in the firebox of the old Stanley wood-burning stove. I added more wood. Mud was standing in front of the refrigerator, pulling out jars of veggies we had opened at our last meal together, lima beans, chicken stock, a covered pottery bowl full of the remains of a roasted boned chicken, a half jar of diced tomatoes, and a bowl of diced celery, onions, cabbage, and garlic from the garden. Competent as an adult cook in a diner, she began to assemble soup out of what we had on hand.

Tired as I was, I cleaned off a workspace and got out buckwheat flour and spelt flour and began making fresh noodles for the soup. Occam brought in more wood, made sure the pipes were not frozen, and set the table. As we worked—already a well-honed team—Mud told us all about the goings-on in the church: whose baby had colic, who had gotten poison oak from winter firewood, and who was having marital issues. Then, proud as a peacock and trying not to show it, she told us the latest goings-on in the new women's council, a group of women headed by my own mama as an elder for the women, created to resolve disputes in households between sparring wives, disobedient children, and abusive husbands.

The church had problems—huge problems—but they were trying to do better, be better.

Minutes before serving, Mud's chatter ran down and the house went silent. I dropped the soba noodles into the broth and filled the mugs on the table with hot tea. I took in Occam at a glance. He was watching us from the dark near the bedroom door, leaning against the jamb, his arms crossed, wearing jeans and a Henley, his feet in socks. He looked good enough to be on the menu too. His hair was lighter than it once was, streaked with blond, and in the shadows my cat-man looked completely healed from burning, though I knew he wasn't, not yet, not quite.

He gave a small nod. We had planned this part of the conversation on the way to pick up Mud from Esther's.

Casually, I asked, "Mud. Has anyone at the church said anything about the devil dogs lately?"

"Nope," she said lightly. "But if them critters show back up, Sam and the boys got plans to trap 'em."

"Not kill 'em?"

Mud looked up fast, her wide eyes the shade of gray mine had once been. "That there would be murder."

"I'm not accusing," I said gently, ladling up the soup. "But if they don't kill 'em, what will they do with them?"

Mud frowned. "Ain't nobody said."

I made a small sound, as if her information was insignificant. But it might be important.

NINE

It was after ten, and Occam was getting ready to leave, the keys to John's old truck in one hand. Mud was upstairs preparing for bed. We had a moment of alone time, our arms around each other, my head against him, listening to him breathe. It was not a human sound, a hint of purr in it, calming. He rubbed his jaw against my redder-than-usual curls, a cat gesture, as if scent-marking me.

"Soon you won't have to leave," I said. When he didn't reply except to tighten his grip on me, I added, "And the church ain't got rules about cohabiting without legal marriage. You could stay."

"We done talked about how we wanted to start and how we wanted to go forward, Nell, sugar."

I heaved a sigh. "Yeah."

My phone rang. I heaved another sigh. *This can't be good.*

Occam turned me around, cradling my spine against his chest so I could pull my cell from a back pocket. "FireWind," I said to Occam. I answered, "Ingram."

"Ingram. A firefighter saw indications of an arcenciel in the sky over Ming's. Would you be willing to read Ming's land again, specifically searching for signs of Soul?" he asked.

"Yes. Tomorrow."

FireWind took too long to respond before he said, "Why not now?"

I pushed away from Occam and paced along the room toward the kitchen. "Lemme get this right. You're wanting me to go to a vampire's property, right now, in the middle of the night. Just after a battle where people died on that land, their blood and bodies all over it, and after a fire that killed plants, all of which will be screaming with shock. While I'm off the clock."

"I—" he started.

"First off, once the fire trucks leave, any vampire on the property will be riled enough to kill first and think later. Second, I can't learn anything about Soul until the sun rises and the vampire blood that currently contaminates that ground boils away. Now. Ain't my job to remind you what you shoulda thought about a'fore you called me," I said to my boss-boss. "Your'un the boss, and your'un job is to look after your'un agents. What you'un just did wasn't looking after me. It was putting me in danger."

I was pacing a lot faster, and began to circle the kitchen table. I mighta been stomping a bit. I could feel Occam's attention the way a mouse might feel the stare of a predator, but I knew whatever expression was in his eyes, it was not directed at me but at the man I was fussing at.

"You wouldn'ta sent Rick or Margot or Occam on the full moon to do something that could get them injured because a their nature. You'da thought first. But where I'm concerned, you didn't even think about it. I done told you about me and what I am and how it works to be a plant-woman. You need to remember my nature too. And I am mighty *dadgum tired* of reminding you. On top of that, I'm tired of defending myself. So. Tomorrow." I stomped some more, scowling at nothing but seeing the cats race to the top of the stairs and sit, hunched, watching me.

"Yes. Tomorrow," FireWind said after a silence that stretched out too long. "My apologies."

"Tomorrow. After I deal with the church and my sister. I'm on the clock at eleven. I assume that will be acceptable?"

FireWind said, "Certainly." He sounded stiff and uncomfortable. "Good night, Ingram." He didn't wait for me to respond before he ended the call.

Occam had put down his gear and my keys and moved back into the kitchen, a different expression on his face from the one I was expecting. Maybe . . . *pride*? I wasn't used to seeing pride on anyone's face, and my own face burned with embarrassment.

I stopped stomping and went to my small refrigerator, where I removed an open bottle of Sister Erasmus' wine, pulled the cork, and splashed a little into two of the oversized pottery wineglasses that might actually have been intended as candleholders. I offered one to Occam and drank back what only a very kind person would have called a ladylike sip. I looked at my fiancé, whose face held a small smile, and demanded, "What."

"You do like yanking his chain," Occam mused.

He was leaning against a cabinet, ankles crossed, the wine and pottery in one hand. He looked relaxed and huggable, not that I told him so. Not with my cheeks still red and burning.

"So?" I said, the tone defensive. "Sometimes a man's chain needs a bit of yanking." And then I turned all kinds of red all over, because after not understanding Shakespeare, even I caught the accidental double entendre in my words.

Occam's lips pulled as he smiled, the scarred muscles twisting his face. "Sometimes," he agreed, teasing me just a little. "But what I was referring to is you standing up for yourself. That's the sexiest thing in the world, Nell, sugar."

I glanced at my—our—room and back to my cell. It was late. It was sooo late. My shoulders slumped. "And I'd act on them words right there," I said, "if I wasn't so tired and if Mud wasn't so big eared."

"I heard that," my sister shouted down the stairs.

Occam rumbled with cat laughter. "There's always tomorrow, Nell, sugar. And I think I need to shift and run around, get some exercise."

"You're'un jist guarding the property until Yummy gets back to patrol."

"Cats don't *have* to sleep all day and all night. We just want to. I ain't gonna rest while you're unprotected."

I crossed to him and laid my hand on his chest. He raised his arms and drew me in. Kissed the top of my head, and let me rest against him again. I yawned and he kissed my head once more. He stepped away, plucked off a few leaves that had sprouted while I fussed at my boss-boss, and tucked them into my shirt pocket. Without another word, he stripped down to pure-T-naked.

"That is so not fair," I said.

Laughing in a half purr, he walked to the front door and into the dark.

Sunday morning usually meant taking Mud to church (or making sure she got there), as per the custody agreement. Instead this Sunday I was awakened before dawn by the arrival of Yummy in Occam's car. I felt my cat-man on the property, racing in to confront her, and figured I better get to her first.

Wrapping a robe around me, I walked out to the front porch, Cherry darting out between my legs as the door closed. "Don't you get skunked," I ordered her.

"I beg your pardon," Yummy said, which was Southern for "I'm insulted. I suggest you rephrase."

"Not you. The dog. Though it's too cold for skunks to be out and about. Did you tear up Occam's car when you stole it and tore outta here like a bat outta heck?"

"Hell. It's 'bat out of hell,'" Yummy said distinctly, as she climbed the stairs to the front porch. "No. I didn't tear up his car. And on the way here, I filled it with gas and checked the tires. I also left a fifty-dollar bill on the passenger seat for the *loan* of his car." She reached the porch and dangled Occam's keys, one finger through the key ring.

I spotted Occam at the edge of the property, near the road, and knew he had heard her words. Cat ears were far superior to my own. I nodded at him to stay outside, accepted the key fob from the vampire, and went inside, hanging his fob and keys on the hook by the door.

Yummy followed me in and stopped at the door. Mud was standing in the kitchen, yawning, filling the teakettle—water thudding into the bottom—and adding another log to the stove with heavy wood-to-metal *thunks*. She was wearing pajamas, pink, with little white and black goats on them, clothing outlawed for women in the church, who had to wear nightgowns. On her feet were fuzzy bunny slippers, pink rabbit ears curling up to her ankles. She looked up at me, scratched her scalp, and mumbled something that might have been, "Morning." Or not.

"Yummy is here," I told my sister, "to get her things from the guest room. You okay with her coming in?"

Mud looked up at that and her eyes spotted the vampire at the door. "Long as she ain't gonna drink my blood or nothing."

Yummy laughed, an odd sound coming from her. So human. So . . . vulnerable. "I promise."

"Shut the door," Mud demanded. "Whatchu think we're doin'? Heating the entire farm?"

"Tea or coffee?" Mud finished.

Yummy stepped inside the door and closed it, not quite certain how to act with this grown-up, grumpy, challenging Mud in the room. "Tea. Please. With a splash of lemon if you have it."

"Nothing fresh," my sister said, "but we have candied lemon."

"That might be . . . interesting," Yummy said, the tone in the last word barely hiding disgust. She added, "Thank you."

As Mud prepared tea and started Occam's coffee, I said to Yummy, "There were nine guards left before you took off last night, ten bad guys left, counting Tomás. Update on what happened?"

Yummy moved into the room and took a place at the table. She stank of fire and burned hair. Her blond hair, one section cut by a swordsman, was now also singed in spots and black with smoke. Her clothes showed signs of smoke damage, and there was blood all along one sleeve and down one side of her shirt. Vampires were very flammable, so whatever she had been doing had put her in danger, probably a lot of danger, but she moved fine, not as if she had been stabbed or burned badly enough to cause pain.

"Ming killed four," she said. "That leaves five guards, and Tomás."

"Your boyfriend still among the undead?" I asked.

"Yes. Thank God," she added, sounding wry, very tired, and maybe a little mocking, since her boyfriend was a vampire, a priest, a torturer, and she was thanking God he was still alive.

"Did Ming kidnap Soul?" I asked, hoping for honesty or at least a shocked reaction I could interpret.

Yummy's brow creased, her expression visible in the dim light. "The assistant director of PsyLED is missing?"

"Might be. We think so."

"If she was taken, Tomás has her. Not Ming. Her clan home isn't—wasn't—big enough to hide a secret like that, and her scions have been overly chatty since we got our souls back. I'd know."

"Nothing's ever easy." I looked to the east, where the sun would rise around seven. "Where are you sleeping today?"

"In my new place." She smiled, looking happier than I ever remembered seeing her. "I haven't had my own place since I was first turned. My people worked all day yesterday and all night to prepare my underground lair. And nine blood-servants left Ming after the fire to sign on with me, so feeding my family should be no problem."

"Where is Ming staying?"

"She has a place in town. Small but adequate." Yummy's tone suggested Ming's lair was very small and barely adequate and that she was amused at Ming being discomforted.

Feeling Cherry running across the lawn, I opened the door as she bounded up the stairs and back inside.

"Mind if I get my things? Since you're up?" Yummy asked. "And then we should talk."

That sounded ominous. "Sure." Softer, I added, "Don't laugh at the bunny slippers."

"I'd never laugh at bunny slippers."

As she gathered her things upstairs, I put tea on a tray and carried it to the front porch, Yummy behind me. I took a seat on the swing, one of the teacups in my hand. My eyes were on the dark southern sky as Yummy took a seat beside me, silent as the predator she truly was.

She sipped the tea. I grinned, waiting.

"It's . . . different," she said after she swallowed the first sip. "I remember the taste of lemonade from when I was human."

She didn't say she liked it. It was a carefully worded truth, without presenting insult to the offering. She set the mug aside and angled to me on the swing. "I'll be here every night, patrolling, until Torquemada is stopped."

"Why?" I asked. "I didn't ask you for nothing. It isn't like I'm the Master of the City."

"I told you. You're my friend. And it's been a few decades since I had a real friend."

Yummy didn't wait for a reply. "I'll be patrolling for as long as it takes." Without making the swing move at all, which was unsettling, she was suddenly standing, her gear in her arms. She leaped over the handrail, dropped to ground level, climbed into her Ferrari, and, seconds later, disappeared slowly down the hill.

Troubled, chilled to the bone, I went inside to discuss decorating the tree with Mud. Like maybe throwing a small party. Or something. But Mud was sound asleep on the couch, so I covered her with a blanket and went to my room.

Trying to move as silently as Yummy had, I pulled gardening clothes out of the closet and dressed, knowing that my next visit would be no easier. But when I walked out of the bedroom, Mud was standing in the center of the room, wide-eyed, pale, her hair sticking out on one side. "We'uns need to go to Esther's. I done had a bad dream."

Esther's Tulip Tree House was dark, so Mud (wearing her church dress over jeans and zipped into a heavy padded jacket) and I (wearing hogwashers, John's old jacket from his truck, and boots) sat on my old ratty pink blanket—what was left of it—at the boundary of the land between Soulwood and Esther's acreage. She would be up with the babies soon, for the five a.m. nursing, burping, changing, and soothing. All alone. When we finished reading the land and her lights came on, we'd go lend a hand.

All but Esther's one acre of the one-hundred-fifty-acre farm John had left me in his will was technically Soulwood, but the night my sister's water broke and she fed the earth, her influence over the land had spread. Elsewhere, the vampire tree wore thorns and looked dangerous, but here it had mutated to match Esther's particular DNA, and though the tree still had thorns, they were hidden beneath leaves and, in warmer weather, fluffy blooms, a concealed weapon. The tree was pretty. I didn't know whether to be amused or envious that my prickly sister got the pretty tree while I got the ornery warrior one.

I pulled off my gloves and placed my hands on the frozen ground. My plant-woman sister did the same. Together we worked our fingertips into the ground, the frozen layer on the surface thin, but hard. Beneath that, the warmth of the land flooded up to touch my flesh, crawled up my arms, and into my torso, alive, slumbrous.

Beside me, Mud sighed. "That's nice."

"Mmmm," I agreed.

The land wasn't angry or protective, wasn't gathering power or building toward anything sudden or direct. Soulwood was lazy and stretching in its winter sleep. I let my thoughts flow through the land, not particularly deep, just enough to know that Soulwood was safe and was protecting Esther's home.

Just at the edge of her land, I brushed across something new, yet ancient and aware. I reached out to stroke across it and knew instantly what it was. The American chestnut's roots, the one I had sensed and seen when the vampires fed the land with their undead blood.

Letting my senses move upward from the root ball system to the new sprout/saplings, I experienced health and strength and a burgeoning life. I had been right when I first noticed them. This root system and the trees growing up from it were all completely healthy. The blight was gone. Gently, I pushed more life into the young trees, not enough to make them leaf out again, but enough to give them a boost to help them survive the cold of winter.

Beside me, Mud removed one hand from the ground and gripped my wrist. "Do you see the new tree?"

"Yes." I told her about it in a few sentences, and together, her hand around my wrist, we watched the tree's roots from underground, new roots spreading from the old root ball, all of them healthy and living.

I guess some would call it meditation, or communing with the land. To me it felt like coming home. I dropped my head and exhaled in peace.

At some point later, I was aware of movement. My other plant-sister was on her porch.

"You'uns gonna sit out there till sunrise," she called, "or you'uns comin' in to help me change diapers and wash a load of clothes? I got spit-up, pee, and stinky mama-milk on me and I need a hot shower and a break."

Without opening my eyes, I called back, "You'un got tea?"

"'Course I got tea. I'm a Nicholson, ain't I?"

Mud laughed. "You better have eggs and bacon, then, sister mine."

"I got 'em. You cook 'em."

"Then we're your girls."

I smiled and pulled my thoughts from the land, opened my eyes, plucked leaves out of my hairline and one out of Mud's. Gathering my blanket and my sparse gear, I stood.

Mud grabbed my hand and turned my nails up. She plucked leaves off my fingertips, her head bent over my hand, her voice soft. "That bad dream I had? It was about vampires and blood."

"Okay. I'll . . . I'll hold that worry close." It was a church saying, more mindful than "I'll keep it in mind."

Together, we walked into our sister's pretty tree house and closed the door on the winter.

An hour later, with Mud still at Esther's playing with the babies, I went back home. Occam was in my bed and I kissed him awake. He wrapped me in his arms and pulled me under the covers of my—our—bed, happily half purring; I rested against him for long enough to know he was very happy, and that made me very happy, and so I spent half an hour making us both even happier.

The phone call from the church came just as I was about to take my first bite of my second breakfast. Before I could even get hello out, my brother said, "Nellie, we're getting ready to start services, but there's a truck at the gate. Three men inside are saying they your'un friends."

"I ain't got no friends," I said. "At least none that would go to the church." *But what if this is Ming's blood-servants? Or worse, Torquemada's?* "Let's see what they want. Get the guards to send me pics of the vehicle, the men, and if they feel like it's okay, let 'em in. If they want to go inside and worship, let 'em. Otherwise, pull a couple young'uns outta church and set 'em to track and spy."

"Nellie, what's going on?"

"Heck if I know, brother mine. Jist giving intruders rope to hang themselves with if they're intending harm."

"It's Sunday. Don't cuss." The call ended.

"Heck ain't cussing," I grumbled. My phone started dinging with pics, which I flashed through as I forwarded them to HQ to run the pictures and the vehicle plates. Three people in one old truck, slender men, fitting with no difficulty onto a bench seat. No one looked familiar.

I checked what I was wearing and it was vaguely work acceptable. Jeans and a button shirt over a tee. Black boots. Better than the hogwashers I'd worn earlier. I slid my badge clip onto my belt and took a dark work jacket with the word *PsyLED* on the back in big white letters.

Occam put something in my hand when I finished texting the pics to whomever was on duty at comms this morning. "You want me to go with you, Nell, sugar?" he asked.

While I'd been busy, my cat-man had rolled my eggs and bacon up in a wheat tortilla, making a wrap I could eat while I drove. He had only recently introduced me to the bready wraps and they were so convenient for on-the-job meals.

I took a bite. Occam had smeared on a bit of jelly. "'Ish is goo'," I said, swallowing. "No. I got this. I'll see you at HQ." I scratched Cherry's head, kissed my man, grabbed my gear, and walked toward my past, stopping to pick up Mud from Esther's, so she could attend Sunday services, as my custody agreement required.

My nosy sister beside me in the cab, I flashed my ID at the guards, recognizing most of them. It was an odd mixture of younger and older churchmen from several different factions, including two from Jackson's faction, Balthazar Jenkins and Obed Jackson. That had to be my brother Sam's work, trying to heal the schisms that had been developing among the membership. Balthazar and Obed stared at me with hate in their eyes.

I scanned the others. One of the men was Jedidiah, Esther's ex-husband, the man who had abandoned her when she grew leaves.

Mud made a face at him and he looked pointedly away, pursing his lips as if trying to keep from saying words he might regret later. The man had learned a lesson or two about how he treated me, especially where others might hear. Rather than riling him, I spoke instead to my half cousin on Mama Grace's side.

"Hello, Joel. How's Dinah and Miriam?" Joel had recently married a new wife, and the transition from a single-wife to a double-wife household was often fraught with arguments, jealousy, and pain.

"They seem to be getting along well enough," he said, gruffly. "Thank you for askin'."

"Where are these men who say they're my friends?"

"At the devil tree," he chortled, "getting stuck and cussin'. Evil tree is good for something, but I ain't happy at the young'uns Sam set to keep watch, hearing them words."

"Mmmm." I didn't say anything about the other things the boys might see and hear in their own homes, like women crying in the night from neglect and abuse. I wanted to say it all, but I'd learned as a child to pick my battles and keep my allies. "I'll see about getting the men off the church grounds."

"Mighty thankful."

I rolled on in, through the gates and past the line of young vampire tree saplings that had created an inner barrier. I didn't know if it was intended to keep the people inside safe, or to eventually close off the gate and trap them. If I ever had time to read the church grounds and try to evaluate the tree's possible plans, I would.

My cell rang, and Tandy said, "Ingram. I have the license plate you sent. It belongs to a David Jones Meechum, a city law enforcement officer, who has just been informed his personal vehicle's tags have been stolen. He's taking care of running the tags that are currently on his own vehicle just in case they were stupid and swapped them."

"Did he recognize any of the men inside the truck?"

"Negative."

I knew it was a stupid question, but I went for it anyway. "Any luck with facial rec?"

"Working on the driver, but unless he's on a list, uses social media heavily, games online a lot, or recently came to the States, we aren't likely to get a hit."

"Yeah, I— Hey. Send them to Cai and to Alex Younger?"

"Brilliant," Tandy said. "Making those calls momentarily and will send. FireWind is interested in the church. He was in the area. His ETA is ten."

"Dagnabbit." Reflexively, I sped up, then slowed. My sister chortled and gave me the side-eye in amusement. I was surely going to hell for cussin' in front of her. "I'll see he's let in." I ended the call to Tandy, pulled over, put the vehicle in park, and dialed the only number I had for the men at the gate. Jedidiah. It went to voice mail. So I called back. And then again. On the fourth try, Jed answered.

"What."

"A very important person in law enforcement is interested in these men. He'll be at the gate shortly. Give him trouble and he'll remember you dumped Esther. He likes Esther." I was so going to hell, now for lying. "Let him through and give him directions to the tree."

Jed was no longer on the line. I could hope he made FireWind mad enough to arrest him. Maybe punch him. And hope some-one caught that on their cell phone and let me see it. It would never happen, but a mad Nicholson could hope. *Stupid man.*

As I put the car back into drive, HQ called. "Ingram," I an-swered, spinning the wheel.

"Cai didn't answer," Tandy said, "but Alex says the men are blood-servants to Tomás de Torquemada's Mithrans. I called Yummy's primo blood-servant and she is sending names, which I'll share with Alex Younger and his brother. They're handling official correspondence for the Dark Queen while she's on her honeymoon. Hopefully, we'll soon have dossiers. Your backup ETA is five minutes. FireWind suggests that until he arrives, you observe and not engage."

"Copy that. Thanks."

Mud disconnected the call for me and said, "Drop me off at Mattie's and I'll take the back way to church."

I put the car back into drive and eased around the unpaved roads until the tree near the chapel appeared. It had changed since I was here last, which was before the first hard freeze. The tree bark and leaves were a darker red, the once-green leaves with red petioles (which should have turned brown and fallen already, had it still been an oak) lingered on the limbs, though the outer leaves had turned a vibrant scarlet, as if cold weather had been delayed here, at this one spot, but was finally catching up with the tree. But the tree wasn't asleep. It was very awake. Vines were moving as if there was a wind, but the leaves were motionless, the air strangely still.

I rolled into Mattie's driveway, parked my vehicle facing out, and turned it off.

I took in Mud's chopped-off hair, her ugly square-necked church dress, school sneakers, and white socks, and decided she looked proper enough for services, once she pulled off the jeans. I scanned her hairline and fingertips and said, "No leaves. No vines. Take off the jeans. Hug Mama for me. Have fun."

She made a face, slid out of the jeans, and slipped out the door. Once she was safe, I watched the tree and the men claim-ing to be my friends.

One of the visiting men was armed with a small and very illegal submachine gun of some kind. He was probably supposed to be keeping guard, but he was having a hard time paying attention to his surroundings with the tree so close and vines waving in the calm air.

Two other men were trying to take cuttings. Like Joel said, they were having trouble, and kept stabbing themselves on the thorns. One man managed to cut off a single leaf and stuck the cut end in his mouth as if sucking sap. He made a terrible face and I wanted to laugh. Then I remembered that a vampire named Charlainn had tasted a tree and liked it. Had Torquemada's men heard about that and wanted a taste? Why?

Not that it mattered right now.

The machine gun guard said something and went to their vehicle. He came back with an ax.

I didn't laugh. *This should be interesting.*

The guard handed his gun to a bleeding man and approached the tree, standing back and a little to the side, out of the arcs of any moving vines. He assumed the correct stance, proving he knew how to torque his body with an ax stroke. He swung back and then forward, cutting into a low tree branch, as if he expected to cut off the branch and take it with him. On the surface, that plan might be smart.

He cut again, the ax landing with precision, a hair below the first cut. He knew what he was doing. Most modern men trying to chop a tree cut wildly all over, without hitting anywhere near where they wanted to. Cutting with an ax wasn't a video game. It required muscle training and muscle memory, real skill. He swung again.

I expected the tree to do something, but it didn't, vines waving but otherwise inactive. The vampire tree was bleeding red in the wedge the lumberjack was making, the scarlet sap running down the bark. By the sixth cut, the tree had had enough. When the man stopped cutting to adjust his grip, the tree struck out with a vine and whipped at the man's face, drawing blood. That opportunity was what it had been waiting for. It had the blood of all three.

And so did I. I could take all three men and feed them to the land if I wanted.

Hunger bore down in me, the *hunger* of the tree, the *hunger* of the land. It *wanted*. It needed a sacrifice. It had been so long since there had been war on this spot, the death of many to feed it.

The man with the ax swung in a different arc. He cut a vine free. It fell on the ground, writhing like a headless snake. One of the other men stepped to it and lifted it by the cut end. He opened a cloth backpack and dropped it inside. The man with the ax had made a large wedge in the limb, though he was still being scored by waving vines.

I dragged my gaze away from the man chopping the branch. I forced myself to breathe, though I wanted only to drop into the earth and drain them all. Four minutes had passed since I arrived. I gripped my cell in one hand and wrapped my other hand around my weapon. Knowing what was coming.

The vampire tree had been playing with the men. It attacked. Vines snapped out, snagged into clothes. Roots writhed to the surface. Wrapping their ankles. Trapping them. Piercing them. Tearing flesh. There was so much blood as it pierced them, I could nearly taste it. And I realized I had gotten out of my vehicle and crossed closer to the tree. I had to stop myself.

I dropped to the ground and put my palms flat. I shoved my consciousness into the earth.

The Green Knight was waiting for me, he and his warhorse fully decked out for battle. He carried a sword and a shield. Furious, his breath and the stallion's blew in an icy green mist. Around him, the meadow was a trampled battleground, the fence he always stood behind broken, split, as if it too had been chopped with an ax, the ground no longer lush with green grass but browned to a dead olive shade and crushed into brown sludge.

His hands were red from the blood of the binding, when I'd introduced Esther to him and we put our bloody hands to his. And the face of his steed was marked with the blood of Mud's handprint.

The horse pranced, ready to fight, ready to make war. A battle lance was in a deep sheath on the back of his saddle with the point high, and on it fluttered a white banner marked with a tree and three scarlet handprints.

"Stop," I whispered. "I need their knowledge. I need to know what they know. I need them to be alive."

The Green Knight shook his head, his eyes invisible beneath the closed visor.

"Ayatas FireWind can take them in. Into a jail. I can question them. We have their blood, so if they get away, we can find them wherever they walk the earth. They will still feed the land."

The horse snorted and tossed its long green mane. Shook its head violently. The knight raised his head and stared over my shoulder. The last time he'd done that, he pierced me with his lance and nearly scared me into a heart attack.

"Nell?"

It was Sam's voice. "Nellie. Open your eyes. We got problems."

I opened my eyes, my unfocused gaze landing on my hands, buried in roots that also twined up my arms. I was slumped over, my knees bent, my hair scarlet, curled, and tangled with leaves all around my face.

I raised my head to see Sam, standing a few feet away from me, staring at my hands buried in the roots, the roots growing into my flesh. He was dressed in his Sunday best, holding a shotgun. Around him were men of several factions, all armed, all surrounding the vampire tree and its prisoners, watching it, facing away from me, fearful of the tree.

A car slowly rolled into the clearing. I knew by the sound Ayatas FireWind had arrived. The silence of the morning fell upon us as he turned off his vehicle and got out. The men divided their attention between Aya and the tree, turning slightly as if to cover the tree and this new, potential threat. None of them looked my way.

I felt Aya's boots on the earth as he walked slowly to me, his steps wary of all the men with guns. He leaned over me and draped an open blanket around my shoulders, over my arms, covering my hands, and over my head where leaves sprouted. He whispered, "Occam is on the way. He will cut you free. Or . . . can you make it let go?"

My mouth was too dry to reply so I shrugged and shook my head. Aya opened a bottle of water and held it to my lips. His normal aloofness always made the kindness surprising. I drank, tilting back my head. I met his eyes and he lifted his brows as if asking if I'd had enough. I gave a tiny nod and he pulled the bottle away. I sat straighter, watching the churchmen through the strands of hair curling wildly over my eyes. I sent a pulse through the earth, pulling the power of Soulwood to me, Soulwood, which was mine, and which the tree knew had power. Through the Earth herself, I thought at the tree, *Let go. Let the men go. They are mine. I need them. And release* me, *you blasted tree.*

FireWind stood in front of me and faced the tree and the prisoners and the churchmen. "I am Regional Director Ayatas FireWind, PsyLED," Aya said. "These men are wanted by the law. I am deputizing you, you, and you"—he pointed to three men, not Sam, which was probably smart—"to help me bring them in. When the tree releases them, capture them, take their weapons, cuff them, and search them. I will escort them off the property in my custody."

The men of the church were looking at the tree and a new ring of saplings that were growing around the prisoners. They knew about the saplings that surrounded the property. They had known for a while that it would make two good things: a cash crop and a watchdog, if it was willing. They knew and accepted that the tree ate meat sometimes. They hadn't really, consciously, accepted that the tree could act of its own volition, in their interests, and trap enemies.

Let them go, I demanded of the tree. Soulwood boiled up in me, heated and fecund and teeming with life. *We can find them again if needed.*

In the back of my mind, I heard the horse snort. Or maybe it was the knight.

The tree withdrew its thorns and vines from the prisoners. At the same time, the tree released my outer arms to snake back into the earth, and began to pull out of my skin. I hissed with pain and the motion stopped.

At the tree, the churchmen moved in and began to search and secure the intruders. I felt Occam step onto the land. He knelt beside me and repositioned the blanket over my right hand. With a sharp steel knife he cut the roots away from my hand, leaving bleeding pieces protruding from the ground and from my bleeding flesh. Then he freed my left hand, slid his arms under my knees and behind my shoulders, and picked me up like a baby. "I gotcha, Nell, sugar. I always gotcha."

I wrapped one arm around him and held on tight.

TEN

Occam's body heat was a furnace at my side. I was hypothermic. I wondered if I'd go into tree hibernation if I stayed cold too long.

He bent and sat me in my car's passenger seat, climbed into the driver's seat, and, very strangely, drove to the chapel. He got out, and I watched him walk inside, his boots loud on the wood steps and the front porch floor. I was confused, hurting, not thinking straight, until he walked out with all three mamas, loaded up Mama Grace and my mama in the backseat, and sent Mama Carmel to have Sam bring her to the Nicholson home.

Tears gathered in my eyes at his forethought as he silently drove us all to the Nicholson house. Behind us, Sam followed with Mama Carmel and Daddy squished in his truck's bench seat. We rolled to a stop and Occam came around, lifting me from the seat and carrying me inside to the kitchen table, where he sat me in Daddy's chair and turned to the mamas and Daddy and Sam gathered at the doorway. "We'll need some alcohol, some sharp garden snippers, and maybe some needle-nosed pliers. And then we all need to have a chat."

"I'll get the pliers and the snippers," Sam said.

"I'll get the medical kit," Mama Carmel said. "Grace, we got any clean diapers? From the looks a things this'll be messy."

"I'll put on tea and coffee," my mama said.

"I'll set and rest," Daddy said, turning my mama's rocking chair to face the table. He lowered himself into it, using one carved arm and his cane. He looked better than he had before the surgery, but he was still a mite pale. Daddy was a preacher now, in the church, a man ordained by God to speak. He was also an elder, chosen in the men's council, as his wife, my mama, had been chosen in the women's council as an elder.

Daddy was a man with authority, and that advance in status had given him a purpose and the will to fight through the changes in his world and force his injured body to continue to heal.

Occam pulled a bench to the table and straddled it. He lifted my hands and studied them, angling them high and low, back and forth, before placing them on the tabletop. "You want me to try and pull them out or just cut them off?"

"I tried to pull them out. It hurt a lot. But maybe not so much now, with them cut away from the tree?" I tried to make fists. My hands didn't want to bend, the joints stiff, creaky, and woody. This time, the invading roots felt as if they had attached to and wrapped around my bones. My hands looked strange too, bigger than normal, with things that looked like bones in places no normal human hand had bones. "I am Groot," I said, releasing my fists.

"What?" Mama asked.

Occam smothered what might have been a snicker. Sam laughed aloud. Sam had been away to college and he had clearly watched secular movies there.

"Never mind," I said. I wasn't about to explain that Occam, Mud, and I had watched a film with a small tree character recently. Sentient talking trees were a little too close to reality for me to explain the humor without possibly sounding morbid.

Occam placed my hands on the clean, folded cloth diapers and inspected them again. He poured moonshine over the pliers, over my entire hands, and held me still when I hissed. He gripped a thin root high on my right hand. "Mama Carmel, you hold her wrist and her fingers steady," he instructed. Her hands took mine where he indicated and, gently, Occam exerted pressure. That one came out, an inch long of straight root, with shorter multi-legs.

"Nell? You okay?" he asked.

"Not bad," I lied, my breath fast and my heart pounding. "Go on."

"I'll watch the door," Sam said, "to keep anyone from walking in."

The surgery was swift, brutal, and, for me, impossible to watch. The pain was excruciating, my breath came in gasps, and tears ran down my face to splatter on my coat. But I couldn't go to a hospital. There was no research on plant-people. No medical professional could have done any different from Occam.

Maybe a gardener . . . When I laughed at that thought, it sounded wet and pained. Occam studied my face before he bent back over his work.

Mama Carmel acted as restraint and nurse, and Mama Grace cleaned up the bloody mess, my bloody flesh, and tossed each bloody rootlet into the woodstove. Occam couldn't pull out everything and had to snip some off. My mama watched, ran errands to the root cellar when they ran out of moonshine to clean my wounds, and offered general comfort, rubbing my shoulders and the back of my neck. When he had done what he could, Occam cleaned me with more moonshine and ordered me to make fists again.

I healed differently each time I read the earth too deeply and each time I communed with the Green Knight too long, especially in combat, which this had been. And this reading, so close to the heart of the vampire tree, may have left lasting damage. I worked my fists open and closed. "Still stiff," I said, "but lots better."

Occam frowned. "You need to see a surgeon."

"You know a good tree surgeon?" I asked.

Mama Grace and my mama laughed. So did Daddy.

Mama Carmel frowned hard, patting the blood off my hands.

Occam's own expression faded into a steady nothingness. He bandaged my hands and wrapped them with sticky wrap.

When he was done, he swiveled on his bench and faced the family. "Got something I need to say. Nell can speak for herself, but not for me, just like I don't speak for her. That ain't changing when we get married. We're being married at our home, because that's what we want. Nell will get the wedding she wants, no matter whether you folks agree with that or not. It ain't likely we'll be able to have children. That doesn't matter to me at all, and I don't think she cares either, because her family is our family, and Mud is her sister and my sister, and we'll have plenty of nephews and nieces and halfsies to love and help with. Far as I'm concerned, you'll always be welcome in our home and at our table, but Nell will have rules and everyone will be expected to follow them. And one of the rules will be to protect her, Mud, Esther, and the twins. The trees and the land are already doing that. But Soulwood is only part of the equation. The rest of that equation is family." He looked around at them. "We good?"

"We're good," Daddy said. In the Nicholson home that was law. "Your kind ever go feral?"

"Yes. Just like humans do. And we die for it. The grindylows police us and they have a second sense, and an ability to move through time and space I'll never understand, to attack any were-creature acting in a way that might spread were-taint."

"You got a were-creature who might be interested in Esther? She's a plant-person like Nell. And she's lonely too," Mama Carmel said.

"I weren't never lonely," I said, falling deeper into church-speak. "Or not much," I amended.

"No, ma'am," Occam said. "Sorry 'bout that."

"Jedidiah's courting a girl," Sam said. "And every man knows that Esther has a quick temper and a cuttin' tongue. She scares most churchmen, even ones looking for a third wife or concubine. She'd bring discord into any home."

Everyone at the table knew he was right. Esther had a lot working against her when it came to finding a husband, and she had been born and bred to believe all she'd ever be was a man's helpmate and baby-birther. That thought hit me hard. What did my sister dream of besides a husband and babies and chickens? Did she have desires and hopes that she had long ago buried? Had I pushed her hard enough to consider something different?

Occam checked his cell and met my eyes. "FireWind has the men from the tree back at HQ and in the null room for interrogation."

"For what reason? The church let them on the property. All they did was chop on a tree limb."

"We have video of them participating in the attack on Lincoln Shaddock's clan home. One of them injured another human. It won't hold up in court, but it's enough to hold them for questioning. FireWind wants us to go to Ming's and . . ." He let his words slide away.

I was supposed to read Ming's land at eleven this morning. I lifted a hand, my eyes on the damaged flesh.

". . . talk to Ming's people," he said. "You up for it? If not, we have reports to look at. PMs on the . . . the others at the morgue."

He was talking about the bodies tortured like Arial Holler had been.

"Hang on, cat-man." To my family I said, "Y'all might need to know that all the vampires, all over the world, got their souls back." My family didn't react except for mild puzzlement. "That means they're acting out of character even for vampires. Crazy as rabid barn owls. And some of them like the feel of my land. And they can feel the difference in us plant-people. Some of them blood-suckers already caused trouble on our land, and somma them already died there. I also ain't ruled out that they might want Mud, me, Esther, the twins, and could maybe settle on all a y'all or any a y'all if they can't get us. You'uns keep everyone close to home, safe, and guarded. And—" I stopped.

Carefully, I chose my words. "They have shown an interest in the family lines that bred into devil dogs. They killed Arial Holler. I ain't—haven't—had time to come by and tell y'all. We can notify the family while we're here, and see if they want to claim the body."

The mamas exchanged hard glances and then turned to look at Daddy.

"Ain't no need for police officers to tell the Hollers," Daddy said gruffly. "I'll handle it. And the family won't want the body. Arial was no longer a part of the church." Daddy hesitated, his chair rocking on the wood floor. "Was he . . . Was he . . . drank down?"

Daddy meant was he sexually assaulted. For a churchman, sexual assault on a woman was fine, but on a man, it was an abomination.

"No," Occam said. He offered nothing else. And neither of us mentioned the torture.

If the family didn't want the body, then they hadn't wanted the boy and the man he had become. This was a quagmire of church sin and church politics. Arial Holler had been a Lost Boy. Cast out. Unwanted.

"If you need my help, I'll come," I said. "PsyLED will come." Slowly, I added, "And if you need the tree to do something to help you, you can ask it."

Daddy rocked back in his chair and dropped his cane, which banged on the floor, echoing through the unusually empty house.

"I ain't saying it'll understand," I added, "but it might."

"Witchcraft?" Mama Carmel asked quietly.

"No, ma'am," I said, adding a hint of irritation to my tone as if that was foolish but I was too polite to actually say so. "You know. Like a trained dog." I hoped the tree wasn't listening to that one. "It evolved and it might be willing to work with you'uns." I'd sorta said all that before, but Daddy and the mamas weren't exactly open-minded about anything townie or paranormal, so repetition was useful.

"And, just so you'uns know, Esther and the twins brought an American chestnut tree on the edge of her acre back to life. It's healthy and everything."

"Long as they don't bring dinosaurs back I'm good with that. Feral chickens are bad enough," Mama said.

Daddy said, "Nellie, the world is changing too fast. Too dangerous. And I'm getting too old to protect my daughters, my family." Daddy looked away, as if the admission took a lot out of him. His eyes settled on Sam, still standing at the front door. Sam, who, though not the eldest son, had been selected as the leader of the Nicholson clan when Daddy passed the mantle.

"Mr. Nicholson," Occam said, "you're still healing. I know how weak and useless that leaves a man feeling, but you got a lot of good years left in you. I got the ones who live on Soulwood. I'll keep them safe."

Occam ignored my scowl that told him I could keep my own self safe. But with my hands full of roots, I *was* pretty useless.

"You and your family," Occam continued, "are enough to take on a few blood-suckers. And forgive me for saying, sir, but your boys ain't babies, and from what I see, your girls ain't either. You brought 'em up to be self-sufficient, self-reliant, and stubborn and hardworking as mules. The Nicholsons are a force to be reckoned with."

Daddy's shoulders went back, and his head, which had been bowed, rose. I had a feeling an outsider's encouragement might be viewed as real to Daddy, and not pity.

Mama Carmel added, "You'un listen to that man. You taught your young'uns well. They'll handle things around here till you'un get back on your feet, Micaiah."

Daddy nodded once, a firm gesture. I hadn't realized how much I'd missed that assurance, that self-confidence, during his illness and postsurgical recuperation. I sent Occam a look with all the love I had in my eyes as a thank-you.

My cat-man mighta blushed.

To Mama, I said, "I got travel mugs in the car. Any way we can get a tea and a coffee to go?"

Occam drove my car. We spent the trip to Ming's listening to an AI-quality voice reading from my tablet all the postmortem reports from Dr. Gomez. The men had died horrible deaths, each very different, but each involving several forms of torture with the Boot.

Each body had *gwyllgi* hairs, one as many as seven hairs, from several different devil dogs. Arial Holler had only the three hairs. The PsyLED lab had sent back more testing and confirmed that—though the preliminary testing had not shown up positive—the bodies all had trace amounts of vampire saliva on them in open unhealed wounds.

And worse, each of the men had ties to the church. Each of them a mother or grandmother who had once been part of the church. Most of the tortured men had likely been part of a devil dog bloodline.

We had proof that vampires and devil dogs had participated in killing humans.

We now had a serial killer case.

That also gave us full legal authority to work the case and apprehend the killers, but, unfortunately, we had no prisons that could hold vampires due to their speed and strength, no way to feed them, no way to keep them out of sunlight, and no way to keep them from mesmerizing humans and walking out under cover of darkness. Human prisons would have been deemed cruel and unusual punishment, and no punishment at all.

And we still had no idea where Tomás de Torquemada's lair was, what he wanted personally, or what his goal was politically, and therefore no way to predict his next move. As a six-hundred-year-old vampire, he would have layers upon layers of desires and plans. All we had was: five dead humans with church affiliations; vampires wearing crystals with a place inside to capture an arcenciel; vampires using the Torah's Coda to learn who knew what; vampires wanting the Blood Tarot; vampires following the scent of the Blood Tarot and discovering plant-people and strange trees; vampires working with Welsh *gwyllgi* shape-shifters, the result of genetic material passed through church bloodlines.

We also had a dead female body buried with her head between her legs. The last one seemed to have nothing to do with the first part, but I wasn't ruling anything out.

Ming of Glass' clan home was gone. There was nothing left but smoking ruins. Occam and I parked in the street, left a PsyLED sign in the window, and crossed under the fire department's crime scene tape. The wide acreage on the Tennessee River was burned: The fancy landscaping, the greenhouse, the big clan home with its multicar garage and horse barn with horse ring and jumps were all gone. The only things left were sooty white-painted fencing and tennis courts. The house had caved in on itself. The barn's back wall was still partially standing, but it didn't look as if it would remain upright in a stiff breeze. Far upwind, I spotted horses standing in a pasture. I hoped all the horses had gotten out of the barn.

Water from fire hoses dripped. Puddles of blackened water stood in low spots. Smoke was heavy and oppressive, rising and settling. Ash covered most everything. Being a tree-person meant I hated the stench of smoke, the feel of fire, the plant death on the air and in the land.

"What am I supposed to read?" I asked Occam.

I supposed he knew the question was rhetorical, because he didn't answer. We walked across the crunchy blackened grass to a single patch of unburned lawn, downwind and downstream from the house.

Occam refolded my newish army blanket and put it on the small patch of green. With my hands bandaged, I was fairly useless, and Occam was doing everything that required any manual dexterity.

Already ash had stained my work field boots and the hem of my work pants. And the blanket. I'd have to wash everything on me to get the ash and smoke stench out.

I stared down at the blanket, and then around at the grounds, and sighed. Reading damaged ground and burned and dying plants was always bad.

"You sure about this, Nell, sugar?"

"A'course not. Maybe it'll be helpful, but probably not. But I been thinking about the possibility that if I got some vampire tree inside me, then I may not need to carry around a potted tree."

That didn't seem to make him any kind of happy, but he unwrapped the bandages from my left hand. My entire hand looked pretty horrible and he shook his head. "You don't have to do this."

"I know I don't." We were on the job, but I kissed his cheek anyway, and that made him smile. "Don't tell FireWind I did that."

"Never, Nell, sugar." Carefully, he unwrapped my right hand.

I sat and got comfy. The sun was bright, but the air was still cold. Little clouds were scudding across the blue sky. The wind shifted and the familiar smell of horses came to me, and the sound of whickers on the breeze. I put all ten of my fingertips to the ground and reached into the earth with my spirit. Nothing tackled me, so I reached a few inches deeper and spread out, toward the road and toward the river, feeling the land beneath me.

There was a vastly different sensation from the last time I read Ming's land this thoroughly. It was burned. So much was burned. Plants were screaming. Roots were digging for moisture. All the plants in the greenhouse were dead except some sweet potatoes.

I reached beyond the scorched earth and found the places where the vampires had walked into the sun. There were no more of them since I was here last, and the sensation of joy and wonder had disappeared. I pushed farther out, widening my range. Down to the river. Then out to the sides. Beyond the fencing that marked Ming's territory.

I found bodies. They were buried on the far side of the fence, and they weren't buried deep, only about three feet underground. I was certain that they hadn't been here before. They were fresh, still in the early stages of rot. I pulled back out of the earth and looked up at Occam. "Do me a favor?" I asked. "Call Yummy's blood-servants and ask about the bodies buried over there." I pointed to a slice of undeveloped land just past Ming's white fencing, downstream. "Three. Maybe four. They could be the vampires that were killed here, but they don't feel like vampire bodies used to feel. No maggots."

Occam dialed his cell and walked away, speaking to someone human, someone who could and would be aboveground in the daylight and not catch fire. I tuned him out and went back into the earth.

When he returned, he said, "Yummy's primo says she doesn't know anything, but that people went missing after the vamps got back their souls. She thinks that property is Ming's. That's all we have. I texted JoJo about the deed, to find the owner, and about getting a warrant. I don't think your reading the ground would count as an acceptable reason to go digging up anything."

Occam's cell rang and he and Rick LaFleur had a short discussion about whether PsyLED Eighteen was concerned over the presence of bodies on vampire land, and whether it was worth the resources to get a warrant to dig them up at this time. If they were vampires, it would have to be nighttime work so they didn't burn in the sun. After a little back-and-forth, LaFleur finally said, "Jones says the property is indeed Ming's. Since Nell is reading the land at FireWind's request, without a search warrant, and without Ming's personal permission, for now we can't do anything. Come back to HQ."

We didn't make it to HQ before we were alerted to proceed to Soul's home. As requested by FireWind, the local police had done a more intensive safety check, and found the house empty. FireWind wanted us to check it out.

Occam parked on a busy street and we got out, an unexpectedly cold wind trying to blow right through me. I felt the chill most in my rebandaged hands and tucked them into my coat pockets.

Soul's place was a one-room efficiency on the ground floor of a converted older building in downtown Knoxville. Though the outside had been modernized, was freshly painted, and had been fancied up some, it was not the kind of place I would have expected the assistant director of PsyLED to have as a home.

"Are you sure this is it?" I asked Occam. "Why so tiny? I mean, I understand that it's a quick drive to HQ, but most people want big places."

"Her mailing address is in Richmond. She isn't here all the time, so PsyLED foots the bill. Cheaper than a hotel, and the security is top-notch."

"Oh. Okay. I guess that makes sense." Having two places, or maybe more, since she spent a lot of time in New York, Seattle, Arizona, and Texas, seemed wasteful to me, but that was the frugal churchwoman in me thinking, and I hadn't seen the financial statements so I knew nothing.

We took the three steps to the small porch and Occam opened the outer door by punching a code on a keypad. I noted the cameras on the outside, one of which pointed directly at us. I resisted the urge to wave. Inside, he knocked at the door of apartment 101 and we waited. When no one answered, Occam punched in another code and we let ourselves into Soul's home.

The place was empty and, if the dust was any indication, it had been for some time. The thermostat was set to fifty degrees, just warm enough to keep any pipes in the outer walls from freezing. The windows were sealed with top-of-the-line security.

There were no personal items on the counters, no papers, no carry bag. The furniture was minimal: a sofa, one lounge chair, a table and two wood chairs, and a big bed made up neatly with white linens. Two pieces of luggage lay on the bed, the clothes on top with a thin layer of dust. Somebody needed to change the HVAC's air filters. Not that I'd put that in a report.

Occam pulled on a pair of nitrile gloves and began to go through drawers and the one closet. I couldn't pull gloves over my bandages, so I caught the tip of a cloth handkerchief and pulled it from a pocket to cover my fingertips. With the folded square of cloth, I checked the minuscule kitchen and even tinier bathroom. There was no food in the cupboards except coffee and powdered milk creamer. Only tiny hotel items like soap and shampoo sat on the bathroom counter. There were no towels, no washcloths. It looked and felt unused.

I pulled open the shower door and got my first indication of something I didn't understand and couldn't assign to the average unused efficiency apartment. On the floor of the shower was a thin trail of what looked like clear, dried fish slime, flaky and half-disintegrated. Pulling on my earth magic, I bent over the clear stuff. With the exposed fingertip of my left middle finger, I carefully touched the crust and my brain was instantly flooded with images. Underwater: fish, sharks, caves. On land: jungle, rivers, the sound of a tiger's roar, the sensation of prey in my fangs.

I jumped back, finger tingling.

Something caught my attention near the ceiling. A trail of brown, the color of dried blood, started on the wall two feet below the ceiling and swiped up, across the shower ceiling. The spray was about thirty-six inches long, total, and appeared to be that distinctive pattern of arterial blood spatter.

Carefully, I reached up and touched it too. The same weird tingling shot up my arm again. "Occam?" I called. "I found something weird."

"I did too." He crowded into the small bathroom, a piece of old paper in his hand. "It looks like a page from a book. See the edge here, where it appears to have been sewn into one of those packets of pages that make up the sections of old books." He tilted the edge and it was clear that stitches had held the pages in place once upon a time.

"Signatures," I said. "They're called signatures." When he looked at me in surprise, I said, "All the old Bibles in the church are made this way."

"Sometimes, Nell, sugar, you surprise me with things you know. I sent a pic to HQ and they're trying to figure out the language so they can translate it. I'm guessing Spanish or maybe Portuguese because there's the words *del* and *de* in it."

I pointed at the two trails, of slime and blood. "I think I found Soul's blood. Both her human and her arceniel blood."

Occam's eyes tracked the spray, his face growing hard.

"I touched it with bare skin. It's not human. I saw visions of undersea stuff. Jungle stuff with plants that were glowing. Heard a tiger roar. Soul can shape-shift into a tiger, right?"

"Yes," he said, understanding. "We have a crime scene. And Soul is now officially missing."

We called our buddies at PsyCSI and, while we waited, we

were ordered by HQ to collect small samples of the slime and blood for our own use. "Just in case," Tandy said.

"Just in case" of what, we weren't told.

PsyCSI showed up at the apartment to process a possible crime scene. We left them working, one masked and wearing a blue uni as she collected samples of the clear flaky stuff and blood for the PsyCSI lab. They were also dusting for fingerprints when we headed to HQ.

The new doors at PsyLED Unit Eighteen headquarters were heavier and harder to open, the prehung doors were of a higher grade of steel than before, and the jambs had steel insets built into the walls, like internal bars at a bank that could be locked down. They sounded secure when they closed behind us. After they'd been torn away by vampires, lots of steel seemed like a good security upgrade.

The moment we got inside, Tandy assigned Occam a case over the sound system, so everyone could hear it. "Special Agent Occam. There's a large gathering of crows in a white oak out near Victor Ashe Park. You need to check it out." In a rare moment of levity, Tandy added, "Don't get distracted, shift into your cat, climb the tree, and eat the evidence."

"I don't eat evidence," Occam called out through the mostly empty HQ. "Not often anyway."

"Go bird-watch," Tandy yelled back.

We separated and dropped our things, including the vampire tree sprig that I had dug up and stuffed into a pot. Feeling clumsy, I secured my weapon and struggled out of my work jacket. When Occam reappeared, we covered the particulars of our day between us, shorthand or bullet-point style. Because Occam's car was still at the church, he'd have to take my vehicle and leave me stranded. Not that I could drive, because my hands were still a mess. His absence also meant I was now handling the Blood Tarot deck situation solo so he could—literally—go bird-watch.

Standing at my desk cubby, he pulled up the case's particulars on his tablet and read softly to me, "A local, walking the greenway, noticed some very un-crow-like activity and reported it. Parks and Rec and U.S. Fish and Wildlife all agreed it was un-crow-like and called the cops. The local cops verified the weirdness—whatever it really was—and ruled out radioactive contamination." He looked at me under lowered brows and said drolly, "I doubt I'll be there long."

The nation's atomic bombs had been designed and created in Knoxville, and R&D continued to this day on all kinds of secret projects. That meant there were secret leftover hotspots, and radioactivity was often reported locally. Not nationally. That information fell under national security protocols and the major news carriers were actively dissuaded from carrying the stories. But once Geiger counters ruled out radioactivity at odd scenes, PsyLED was always notified.

This was a common chain of notification, from one department to another until the *weird stuff*, as the Knoxville PD called it, landed in our laps, whatever it was, and someone had to go check it out. Usually it was nothing. Bird-watching, while amusing, wasn't particularly strange.

Occam took off, my car fob in his hand, and I went to work, hunting and pecking on my laptop with my unbound fingertips. Once typing out my report was over with, I went to the conference room to research, taking the Blood Tarot and its COC papers with me. I didn't admit aloud that I didn't want to be alone with the deck, or that it gave me the heebie-jeebies, but it did, so being in the big room was more comforting.

On the table in front of me I placed my laptop, my tablet, my cell, and lots of pictures that FireWind had printed out for me himself. Among the printouts was the tarot instruction book I had snapped at Ming's on our last visit there. A book that had been old and obviously valuable, and was now burned to ash. The instruction pages were in order on the table in front of me when FireWind appeared in the doorway and took a place at my side.

"Kent is on the way in. I'll help you take background readings on the deck, so her time at the office is limited." T. Laine was still on her weekend off, so she'd be unhappy to be called back. And . . .

The boss-boss would help me take readings. That felt weird, to have the *regional director* helping *me* on a case. It was all out of order. Things out of order made me nervous, but I shoved my

how to use magical equipment like the new portable null rooms that were currently being built.

"Kent?" FireWind asked.

"These were definitely not made at the same time or by the same person or coven. Physically, the major cards don't even feel like paper; they have the feel of a heavy cloth content, though that doesn't seem to affect the way they shuffle, which is odd.

"The major cards appear to have been reinked, with modern elements added in. For instance, these pyramids and the Sphinx are from the original inking, and there are flecks of blue still adhering, as if the Nile once flowed right up to them. The rest of the card has been heavily over-inked and enhanced with new energies, some of which I think were mixed with the blood of sacrifice. Same with all the other majors. The minor cards are not nearly as old, but still, several hundred years old.

"The energies originally used in the creation of each set are totally different, but someone, probably a really powerful coven, overlaid the older energies with new workings, ones that combined a *preservation* working with whatever the original makers considered important, into something new and darker. The blood sacrifice was probably not a goat." Her lips twitched down. "It was likely a witch."

None of us reacted. We had always known a sacrifice had been involved with the creation of the decks. That it was a witch wasn't a surprise.

Lainie shuffled each of the arcanas, then began shuffling all the cards into one deck. She glanced at my tablet, where I'd been recording the readings and anything of importance she said. Hunt and peck.

"The energies," she said, "combine differently when they're used together. Interesting." She placed the deck on the table and addressed FireWind. "Ask a personal question—an important question, because intent matters—and cut."

FireWind said, "What is Nell's tree's purpose?" He cut the deck and Lainie laid out a quick Celtic Cross pattern. She turned the top card over and said, "Death reversed. I'm not gifted in reading, but I'm pretty sure this is not death so much as rebirth, re-creation. Do you want me to read the other cards I've laid out?"

"Not necessary," FireWind said. "Nell and I were about to try a reading without the Death card."

Lainie removed the Death card and reshuffled the deck, and FireWind read the deck. The psy-meter readings had changed, with Psion 3 greatly decreased. Lainie reinserted the Death card, removed other cards, and the readings were still off, but now in Psion 4. She said, "Interesting."

"What would happen if we did a reading in the null room?" I asked.

"Experiment time," Lainie said, regathering the cards. "We don't all need to go."

"I'll assist," FireWind said.

T. Laine stood and led the way; I sat at the conference table a while longer and finally looked at Tandy. He had observed and filmed the entire reading, and I could see the little light that indicated Clementine was still recording. I pointed at Clementine's light, and Tandy touched a display. The light went dark.

"It's only recording in the null room now," he said. "You're upset. I can feel it."

The three lightning strikes that gave him the reddish Lichtenberg lines tracing across and through his skin, like forking veins in leaves, had also given Tandy the gift of empathy. It was deeper and more encompassing than Margot's truth sensing, and it often made him the unit's counselor whether he wanted that job or not.

"The Blood Tarot. It's black magic. Blood magic," I said.

"Yes."

"My power—" I stopped and thought about what I wanted to say, letting the memories of the land's *hunger* flow through me. The roots in my hands twitched with need and my bones began to ache. "My power, my oneness with the earth, caused an oak tree to mutate and grow into the vampire tree. It needs blood. Soulwood needs blood. So is my power blood magic? Am I a dark magic practitioner?" It was a question I had asked myself before and still had no answer for.

Tandy leaned back in his chair and laced his hands across his stomach. It was his "listening pose," and meant he was giving me his entire attention, his expression thoughtful. "Any power, any position, any authority," he said slowly, "any *energy* can be used for good or for evil. Atomic energy was created for war and for the deaths of millions of civilians. That power became *more*. Now it's nuclear bombs *and* clean nuclear power *and* nuclear medicine.

"People enter politics to do good, then get caught up in making money and holding on to control, forcing their world view and their people view and their religious view onto others, though they started out altruistic and wanting to make things better." He gave a small shrug. "For your magic? It depends on your goals and whether you let your focus narrow too much, whether you stop learning and growing and loving. And it depends on how and when you hold back and say no to the hunger you feel. Can you still say no to the desire for the blood of your enemies, Nell?"

I partially evaded his question. "The tree is having more and more problems not taking human blood meals."

"The tree isn't *you*, Nell. The tree is a new life-form. I'm only asking *you*. And possibly your land. Is Soulwood's desire for blood and for killing your enemies harder to fight?"

I shuffled the energies and desires in my mind the way FireWind had shuffled the cards. The tree's needs and the land's needs were not the same. I had been thinking of them as the same, but they were distinctly different and worked together only when necessary. The land wanted to grow and protect and, when possible, wanted the blood of battle and war. The tree and the Green Knight wanted to capture, feed, control, and force its will on the land and on me. But it had no real power to do that. I considered the warmth of Soulwood. As I did, it filled me, sleepy and languorous as a stretching cat.

It seemed to see the roots in my belly and in my hands. In my mind's eye, I held them up to the warmth of Soulwood, and the heat gathered there. The pain in my hands eased.

That was . . . different.

I answered Tandy's question. "No. It isn't. It's easier. Huh. Thank you."

Tandy tilted his body back to the screens and typed a fast line or two. "Just so you know, according to quantum mechanics, everything is created of the same particles as energy—light, matter, meditation and prayer, sound and vibration, space and time, electromagnetism. Magic is just energy used in ways some people can't see or understand."

I considered that as his eyes tracked things on his screens. I said, "When I commune with my land, I see underground. When I commune with the tree, I see a different reality."

Tandy's reddish eyes shot back to mine. He relaxed again and assumed his listening pose.

I looked at my woody nails and plucked off a leaf that was trying to unfurl. "I see a reality that's a lot like things in movies, like an overlay of imagery, a place that's matter, energy, and life *on* and *in* the land, in the earth itself. When I talk to the tree, it's a different reality. A green landscape and a knight and a stallion."

The empath said, "So . . . the tree . . . some . . . *thing*, some-*one*, is directing that energy, organizing it into patterns you can understand."

I looked up quickly to see if he was making fun. He wasn't. And now I let him hold my gaze. "Yes. It—he—calls himself the Green Knight."

Tandy nodded thoughtfully. "He's self-aware and acts with purpose?"

"Yes. He is the tree. And, like the tree, I think that there is no way to kill him."

"You've tried to kill the tree several times," Tandy stated.

"Fire. Axes. Chain saws. A bulldozer that the tree ate. It can't be killed. It's the cockroach of plant life. I have a feeling it would survive a direct hit by a nuclear bomb." I smiled to show I was joking, but part of me wasn't joking at all.

I swiveled in my chair and took in the screen where FireWind and Lainie could be seen working in the null room, the deck of cards on the table. Knowing Tandy had the comms in his ear, I asked, "What have they discovered?"

"Whatever working is making the Death card turn up first, no matter what, doesn't work in the null room. They've done five readings and it never showed up in the patterns that T. Laine laid out. The other energies of the deck are equally muted. In the null room, the cards are mostly just cards.

"T. Laine is calling in another witch. They'll experiment on readings inside and outside of the null room."

"Thank you," I said again.

Before I could react, his eyes went wide. Into the mic that sent feed to HQ's speakers, he said, "FireWind."

The door to the null room opened and FireWind walked

down the hallway with that ground-eating stride, his black braid swinging.

"We have a message from a Lieutenant Colonel Leann Rettell, DO, from the office of General David Schlumberger, U.S. military. Schlumberger heads the joint military version of PsyLED. She's on her way here."

Rettell was a medical doctor who worked for the military on paranormal events. She had helped us with the slime mold case.

"Why?" FireWind asked. "What cases do we have open that the military might be interested in?"

I said, "Maybe they discovered that the vampires are acting odd."

"But why send a doctor?" FireWind asked.

"Don't know, sir." Tandy turned the screen to allow Aya to see the email. "Maybe they think there's a biological component? Whatever their thoughts, Rettell is on her way to Knoxville. She'll be here at dusk."

Dusk was when vampires woke. I wondered if there was a correlation.

ELEVEN

As a probationary agent, I had learned that law enforcement was mostly paperwork and that there was always a backlog of it. Having retrieved the Blood Tarot, I had a lot of paperwork to attend to. I had been searching for the missing deck of cards for months, and there had never been a hint that Ming had gotten her hands on it. Now that we had it, I had to wrap up our re-acquisition in terms as legal as possible. It was harder than I thought, because I knew that while "finders keepers" wasn't a real thing, "possession is nine-tenths of the law" *was* a real thing. Ming had possessed the deck.

Upon the advice of the director of PsyLED, who had followed up our actions with a backdated order from Homeland Security, Occam and I had taken it. Legally, Unit Eighteen was as safe as we could be, under those circumstances.

Then, Ming's house had burned down, which would have destroyed the deck anyway.

All that could cause problems, so I had to "jot and tittle" every line of paperwork.

Once I completed the Blood Tarot casework, I read through Clementine's notes on several meetings and made some minor corrections. As I slowly typed with my index fingers, my hands felt better and better and I was ready for lunch, which Occam brought in from a local salad and soup place after his crow adventure.

So I could eat more easily, Occam removed the bandages and I got a good look at the damage wrought by the tree. After contact with Soulwood, which had taken place in my mind, my wounds were mostly closed over and no longer leaking a bloody fluid. The evidence of the roots that had traced under my flesh and along my bones was less pronounced. I didn't know if that was a good thing or a bad thing, but having the bandages off made eating easier. After lunch I joined Occam in his cubby and helped him write up the crow event, which he had first called a crow convention.

"It's called a crow gather," I said.

"That's a thing?" he asked.

"Country-girl stuff," I said. "Roosting gathers are common in winter to keep warm at night. Daytime gathers are usually smaller, and often involve a crow funeral. But *big* daytime ones? Like, really big ones like you saw? Those are rare. The church calls them a congregation of crows."

"There had to be hundreds of crows," Occam said. "When I got there, they were all shouting and screaming and chasing away humans. I watched from a distance, downwind so they wouldn't smell my cat." He grinned that wonderful lopsided grin and said, "And I didn't eat a single crow." His smile faded. "But here's where it gets weird, Nell, sugar."

"Crow gathers are often weird, cat-man."

"One crow took a perch on a dead limb, surrounded by all the others, and it started croaking and clicking and making all sorts of sounds I didn't know crows could make."

"Oratin' to them," I said.

"Not supernatural or paranormal. Just crow-weird."

I flexed my hands. Plant-woman-weird. "I was serious. Orating to them. I saw a small one once. It was clearly a passing of information. A sermon. Which is why the church calls them a congregation."

My cat-man went still, the way a cat does when it's watching prey, though his eyes were off in the distance. "I don't think we can just say that," he said at last.

"We need to find better words to explain the oration part," I said, "but I'm serious. Crows have congregations and orations. Usually deep in a forest, where no one can see or hear."

He shook his head. "I don't know why I should think that's strange. I turn into a cat on the full moon. But talking birds creep me out, Nell, sugar. Especially when I found trace evidence beneath the tree the preacher bird was on."

"What kind of trace?"

"Hairs. Dried blood. Maybe an animal death. No feathers, so not a crow. I collected it and sent it to PsyCSI. They're gonna hate us after the last few days."

We sighed at the same time, the way old married people do. Smiling, we went back to work.

We spent over an hour catching up on his backlog of reports, elbows touching often. By accident. And not by accident. The tedium of helping with reports didn't bother me at all. Being with Occam was something I desperately needed after the last few days.

Tandy had sent the pic of the torn book page Occam had found at Soul's to Alex Younger, and samples of the blood and dried slime went with PsyCSI, but no one had gotten back to us. Tandy was trying several translation programs, and midway through the crow report, his voice came over the speakers. "I finished translating the page," he said simply.

We left our cubicles and made our way to the conference room, beating FireWind by seconds.

Tandy had the translation up on a screen. "The book could be a very old Latin prayer book, nothing important in terms of archeology, but the fact that someone deliberately destroyed it is significant."

"How do we know someone deliberately destroyed it?" FireWind asked.

"Because on this side"—Tandy tapped a key and a mirror page appeared—"someone wrote a line in Latin. It translates as, 'Give unto us the Tarot de Sanguis.' The Blood Tarot. 'You get back the draco.' The dragon."

My hands twitched, bones burning. I looked from the translation to my boss-boss.

FireWind's amber-colored eyes went cold and deadly. "They know we have the Blood Tarot. We've had it for . . . less than twenty-four hours?"

"PsyLED had the deck—more or less—before we lost it in the battle," I said. "Then Ming had it. So they . . . what? Covered their bases? Torquemada's research people are good."

"There was a little dust on the prayer book page when I found it," Occam said. "Not as much dust as the table underneath it." He tilted his head, thinking, remembering. "I'd guess the page had been there for two or three days. I'll bet Ming got a similar demand that said, 'Give us the Blood Tarot or we'll burn your place to the ground.'"

"Which might explain why she called me to her clan home

that first night," I said. "Making *sure* Yummy and I smelled like the deck of cards. Yummy and I were bait, just like Yummy said."

"Torquemada," FireWind murmured, "perhaps hoped to get us to work against Ming of Glass."

Tandy said, "I finally heard back from Alex Younger and he verified that arcenciel blood is clear and sparkling, and they haven't heard from Soul in weeks."

I asked, "Isn't her leave over?"

"The assistant director requested an open-ended leave without pay," FireWind said, "and it was approved. She's entitled to time off."

"We don't *know* that Torquemada has Soul," Tandy said, "but the blood and the very old Latin prayer book seem to point that way."

"Or it's a way to point us in that direction when Torquemada wants the trackers to do something for him, without us knowing it's something he wants," Occam said.

FireWind, his face cold as ice, said, "All leave is canceled. Everyone is to be prepared to work through until we find the assistant director. Call in Jones PDQ. We need the Diamond Drill for this. Contact the local FBI for possible resource backup."

"I've already made a dent calling Airbnbs," Occam said, "and short-term listings that advertise inner rooms suitable for vampires. I'll put all my efforts into that today."

"I'll start calling hotels that have vampire suites," I said. Vampire suites were rooms that had steel shutters over the windows and were big enough to sleep several guests.

"Ask for Alex Younger's assistance," FireWind said.

"Done already," Tandy said. "And I got him to request the Dark Queen's authorization to behead Torquemada and his scions if necessary." Tandy shrank under FireWind's blazing eyes. "Sorry. I guess that was over my head."

"Yes. It was." The boss' eyes crinkled slightly. "I assume the request came from me?"

"Yes, sir. Shall I report myself for overstepping my authority, sir?"

FireWind chuckled, the tone resigned. "Not this time, Dyson. We'll need an original order with the Dark Queen's seal delivered to us, along with a personal call from her office to the mayor, the governor, Ming of Glass, and Lincoln Shaddock, plus anyone else you can think of. Good work, Dyson. Let's find where Torquemada and his merry band of priests—who may have abducted our assistant director—are laired. And get her back."

"There were two white vans at Ming's property when they showed up there that first night," I said.

"We ran a traffic cam search for them," Tandy said, "but caught nothing. There's a blue million white work vans in Knoxville, and nonpriests might have leased or rented them anywhere. The FBI might be willing to put resources onto it now that we have dead humans and a missing VIP."

"See what they say. Keep me informed."

The weekend workday turned on its head. JoJo and Tandy worked in concert, tracking the appearance of anyone who might have seen the vampires or rented a white van to them or had a van stolen, as well as gearing up the search for missing person reports, looking for people who might have disappeared into the underbelly of the vamp world. Others of the crew began to trickle in.

As a side project, I put together a list of things Torquemada had and needed, and things we needed to do to solve any case involving him. He had:

1. Soul
2. Empty crystals with arcenciel shapes in them. Speculation: he wants arcenciels and needs them in dragon form, not human form. Additional speculation: he captured Soul in human form, a theory that *could* be borne out by the clear slime and blood in the shower in her apartment. Except he offered to trade for her.
    *   Note: Two quartz crystals (that appeared to have space inside for arcenciels to be captured) are no longer in Tomás' hands. Yummy has one; Unit Eighteen has one.
3. Enough human and vampire power to attack and burn out a vampire master of a city
4. Speculation: Probably magical gewgaws they could use for magical stuff. Spells. (Fire spells?) Workings. Probably curses.

5. Five homeless men, all of them tortured and killed, most with church ties to the devil dog bloodline. The bodies had traces of vampire blood in open, unhealed wounds, as if the vampires had drank from the victims but not healed them. Vampire saliva healed human skin. Question: Did vampire saliva not heal devil dogs? Again, interesting thought. Additional and opposing question: Did a fallen Catholic priest not think his people should drink from humans with fangs in skin because of the sexual component to that sort of drinking? Did he torture to get blood another way? No data for an evaluation.

The next list was things Unit Eighteen (and I) needed to do:

1. Talk to Mama about how many young men were removed from the church
2. Find out what Torquemada might accomplish if he had an arcenciel trapped in a quartz crystal
3. Find out if the above answer shows us what his ultimate goal is
4. Save Soul

I figured the lists would get longer, and soon. Outside, the clouds grew heavier, the air colder. Lightning lit the dark sky here and there, an odd, pearly color as if reflecting off ice or snow crystals.

About two in the afternoon, I received a dozen pics via email from an unknown address. Normally I'd have dumped them all as spam, but the subject line said *From my mistress, Yvonne,* so I took a chance. In the zipped folder were six pictures of old paintings. I sent them to FireWind and went to his office, where he was sitting at his desk, typing on a new laptop. The door was open so I knocked and started talking. "FireWind, I just sent you a file. I think it's from one of Yummy's blood-servants and I don't know what it means."

Without lifting his head, he looked up at me, his yellow eyes bright. He returned his attention to the laptop and kept typing. "Sit," he said to me.

I considered barking like Cherry, but thought better of it, and it was a good thing because he touched the chair next to him at the big desk. I crossed around to sit beside him, facing the door. He opened the file and six photos spun out like a propeller and took up positions on the screen. He enlarged one and frowned. "Middle Ages, most likely. One of the old masters. Religious scene. Perhaps Jesus calling Lazarus from the tomb, small crowd."

He moved to another, then another. They were all religious, and FireWind pronounced them from the same period, possibly by the same artist. "Ah. This is curious. The artist used Torquemada as a model for a minor character in each. Why did your vampire send this to you?"

"She ain't my vampire," I said, my tone mulish.

My boss-boss cracked a faint smile. Trying to get my goat.

"It's in my report," I said. "Yummy dated one of the attacking vampires. She said they had secret stuff in the Vatican. I'm guessing she found these pics from her time in Italy and had her servant send them."

He went back through them again, and then again. And finally he said, "Tomás de Torquemada is in each of them." He pointed at an image on the screen. "There." He switched photographs. "There."

I said, "And in each one, he's wearing a necklace and it doesn't look like a cross."

FireWind enlarged each of the photos. The crystal around his neck seemed to hold a blue and purple winged creature inside, the color of paua abalone shells.

"Huh," FireWind grunted. Again we went through them. FireWind sat back. "It's a crystal, with what could be a dragon inside."

"Yes." I handed him my lists. "See my first list, numbers two and three. 'Empty crystals with arcenciel shapes in them.' If Torquemada already has an arcenciel in a crystal, why did he take Soul? How many does he need to do whatever he wants to do? And if he needs multiple arcenciels, why would he trade Soul for the Blood Tarot?"

"Excellent questions. Have you ever heard of 'riding the dragon'?"

"When Ming first called me to her clan home and tried to get me to kill Torquemada, she said something about . . ." I closed my eyes and ransacked my memory. "'He and his scions will take the Blood Tarot and ride the dragon.' No, I don't know what it means."

"Arcenciels are said to have the ability to go back and change the past. It's been said that if one can capture arcenciels in quartz crystal, or perhaps enough of them, they can 'ride the dragon' into the past and change it. What would Tomás de Torquemada want to change in the past?"

"Everything," I said instantly. Then I stopped and looked away from my boss-boss. "He would want to change . . . the fact that the Inquisition ended. That he lost power. That the church lost power. That the Protestant revolution took place and took power from the Roman church."

"That he allowed himself to be turned?" FireWind asked softly.

"Could be. He might feel he's a bigger sinner because he's a vampire than because he tortured and killed people in the name of God."

By three thirty p.m. we had Margot, Rick LaFleur, and T. Laine in-house, all on their days off. We were all talking on cells and landlines, sometimes simultaneously, while messaging agencies all over the world and searching databases. Outside, sleet began to fall. It was Sunday and I was ready for my day to end so I could leave work. I had to pick up Mud and we had a Christmas tree to decorate. And school tomorrow.

An hour later, we had found nothing. It was frustrating.

Overhead speakers announced the arrival of Lieutenant Colonel Rettell. The military liaison was on-site. Occam and I headed to the conference room. The rest of the unit were already in place and waiting, the sunset hidden by heavy cloud cover and the dark of night upon us.

It was nearly dusk. Vampire time.

While we all watched on camera, Rick trotted downstairs to let Rettell in the outer door.

In the glare of sunset it was hard to tell much, but the woman looked muscular, her spine straight as a board. She had long hair pulled back in a severe bun, and she was dressed in a uniform beneath a military coat, with a satchel over one shoulder.

On camera, Rick opened the door. Even in the wavering dull light, we saw him go totally still.

Margot stood up from her seat, her expression fierce.

"Racer?" FireWind said.

"He's trying not to shift. The woman—"

FireWind shoved away from his chair. Dove down the hallway. Slammed open the door, where the new stop-device held it. By the time he was halfway down the hall, Margot had leaped over the table, catlike, graceful, one foot landing in the center to propel her after him. Occam followed, his fingers shaped like claws. I reached for my weapon. Stopped when T. Laine held up a hand. Silent, we watched the screen.

Rick was holding the doorframe with both hands, his hands fully clawed and covered with black fur, like the black were-leopard of his cat form.

Aya ducked under his arm, too fast for a human, skinwalker-fast, and stood in front of Rick, facing him, his body poised to fight.

The woman had already backed away, hands up in a gesture of peace.

Growls echoed up the stairway to us. Rick's growls. Bass, rumbling vibrations shook the roots of my hands and deeper, juddering the hard rooty place in my belly. My hair moved as leaves grew in, tightly curled, so many my scalp ached.

"Lieutenant," FireWind said. His voice was soft but carried up the stairs, soothing, steady. "What are you?"

"Sorry," she said, nearly as calm as FireWind. "I thought you knew. Asiatic cheetah. Turned in Afghanistan in '06."

"Your sleeve shows you were active duty," Aya said, his tone still carrying that mesmerizing quality that was oddly, vaguely vampire-like in its power and intensity, "but makes no mention of your being a were-creature. We didn't bother to look deeper."

Rettell laughed. "Your bad. Tell Diamond Drill to pick up her game."

I shot my eyes to JoJo in the corner with Tandy. She cursed under her breath, fingers flying on the keyboard.

"How did she know what we call you?" I asked. Diamond Drill was a nickname, in-house only, so far as I knew.

"No idea," Jo said. "Unless the military can get into Clementine. I've shut her down, and will do a deep dive for anything that isn't supposed to be there."

That meant JoJo thought someone had drilled into her system and planted code that would send them anything Clementine recorded. But why would Rettell lead us to look? Because she had to know we'd pick up on that clue.

"You'll find something," I said. "But you need to look even deeper."

Jo raised her head and her fingers stopped tapping. "Decoy. Maybe more than one."

"She expected us to find it on the next deep diagnostic," Tandy said, "so she gave it to us, hoping we'd miss a buried one."

"Or two," I said. "Or three."

"Dayum, girl," Jo said. "You think sneaky."

I looked at the screens to see the small group moving up the stairs as if violence hadn't nearly happened. I spoke fast. "But why would the military want to hack into us?"

"Nosy bastards," JoJo muttered. "They think they need to know everything."

Occam glided down the hallway, his cat close to the surface, his eyes glowing in the lights. Behind him came Margot, equally ready to shift. FireWind and Rettell walked side by side, her gait steady and her demeanor unruffled, cat-smooth beside FireWind's skinwalker grace.

My official cell pinged and I glanced down to see JoJo had gotten to the good stuff hidden in Rettell's sleeve. I'd have nighttime reading.

The people in the hallway filed into the conference room and took chairs. All but Rick LaFleur. My up-line boss stood in the hallway, at the stairs, staring, looking as if he'd been hit by a sledgehammer. He was watching Rettell like a hawk. Or a hungry cat.

Or . . . or like a churchman looking at a woman he wanted.

I backed deeper into the conference room.

Occam was instantly at my side. "Nell, sugar?" he murmured. "You got leaves growing." He followed my stare to Rick. "Ohhh." He slid an arm around me, closed both our laptops, and began to guide me out of the room. "FireWind. Nell and I'll be leaving now. Have someone send us the minutes."

I didn't hear FireWind's response. Had the sensation of being pushed out of the room, to the right, away from whatever was happening in the conference room, and back to my cubicle. Minutes later, I was being pelted by sleet, then sitting in the passenger seat of my car, the heated seat on, and Occam driving us toward home.

I took a breath, breathed out hard, and took another breath. "I'm sorry."

"Why? I'm guessing you never saw a werecat who just . . . let's say, fell madly in love. Rick is smitten and he didn't control his reaction."

I frowned hard at the sleet beating on the windshield. I had seen barn cats and even bobcats mating. Sex and fury and loud desperation. Yeah. Rick had that look. Occam had never looked at me like that. I frowned harder and thought about whether I was going to say that to him. "That was normal werecat behavior?"

"Pretty much," he said calmly, slowing long before an intersection to avoid sliding on the icy road.

Except for brine and sand trucks moving here and there, the streets were deserted.

I thought about him and Yummy, and something green that wasn't leaves coiled through me. I yanked leaves off my head and from the tips of my fingers and added them to my pocket. It was getting full.

"She didn't seem interested," I said.

"Oh, she was interested. She's just been a werecat longer than Rick. She's better at hiding visual cues. But when a werecat is interested, all the cats around know it." Casually he added, "First time I saw you, it took a bit to get calmed down. Had a long talk with LaFleur about boundaries and your history. And then a talk with Soul about how to court a plant-woman." He took his eyes off the road for a second to glance at me. "Anyway, I was advised to take it slow and easy, to not pounce on you like a rabbit, and to remember that you deserve dignity and honor at every single moment. So I didn't pounce." A bit too proud for the situation, he added, "I stalked instead."

The clump of ice that had formed inside me at the sight of Rick's face, and again from the cold air, began to melt. My frown melted away too. Part of it was the heated seat. The rest was Occam, knowing just the right thing to say. "You stalked me?"

"Yep. You never knew it."

"Did you—" I stopped and gave a shrug as if to say it wasn't important.

"Did I feel like Rick when I first saw you? Damn straight. First time I ever got hit by a truck was the day I saw you."

"Truck. Sledgehammer," I said.

"Beg pardon, Nell, sugar?"

"When I saw Rick's face, I thought he'd been hit by a sledgehammer. Then I understood and it reminded me of a churchman on the prowl."

"Ummm," Occam said.

"I love you, Occam."

"I love you too, Nell, sugar."

I wanted to hold his hand, but he needed both on the wheel to drive. So I just turned in my seat and watched my cat-man, wondering if I was brave enough to see that look of need and desperation on his face when he looked at me. And that thought warmed me even more.

As we decorated the tree, Mud danced around it like a four-year-old. Cherry got what Occam called the zoomies, running up and down the stairs, confused but excited at Mud's exuberant happiness. We let the puppy run until she skidded into the tree, knocking it over and breaking the three glass balls Mud had put on. Now it had nothing on it but multicolored lights and three cats, who refused to leave it be. Because of the cat weight, Occam had been forced to tie the tree to the desk and one window latch to keep it upright.

The tree had no ornaments on it, but it was beautiful, the multicolored lights reflecting in the windows, the house lamps off except one near the stove. Outside, the sleet had turned to a snow-sleet mixture, whispering against the house and the metal roof and changing the landscape into a beautiful but treacherous frozen wonderland. I toed off a slipper and felt through the wood floors, into the land. It was lazy, drowsy, but still aware, and I'd know if anyone crept onto Soulwood. Even the Green Knight was peaceful, but my land was guarded from predators.

Yummy was wandering the periphery of the land, adding her strength to the land's protection. I could feel her serenity, an odd emotion for a vampire.

Mud, a plant-person and claimed by Soulwood, must have been feeling the peace of the land too, because she suddenly collapsed on the sofa. Cherry joined her, snuggling under her arm and bopping her knee. Occam sat at the big desk, his back to me, working on his computer.

The floors felt . . . happy. Tears gathered in my eyes and I blinked them away.

Sliding on my slipper, I took down three of my favorite pottery bowls—lovely leaf green bowls turned by hand at the church. I used to call them Leah's bowls, back when I thought of the house as still belonging to John and his first wife, and myself as an interloper. Now they, and everything else inside, were mine. And soon would be Occam's and mine. My cat-man, Mud, and I would be a family, a real family.

With an old steel ladle, I stirred soup Mama had sent over when Sam delivered Mud and Occam's car. The note on the soup jar had said, *In case your hands still hurt too much. Love, Mama.* She had also sent a loaf of bread, already sliced, for the same reason. Mama would have been horrified to know I hadn't baked bread in the last few days, so Mud had put the ingredients together and now we had four loaves rising. The soup was steaming in the old pot, heated up on the stove, which was putting out enough warmth to keep the house cozy most of the night. Overhead, the old fan was moving the heated air.

Home. I finally had a *real home.* I blinked away tears.

I dished the soup into the bowls, set the table, and poured hot lemon tea for us.

Occam looked over and met my eyes as he closed his laptop and joined me. He checked the wood in the stove, added a few logs he had split that fall, and washed his hands as I finished up. Quietly he said, "We got work for later. And I most likely can't get down the mountain tonight, with the ice so heavy. Mind if I sleep in one of the upstairs bedrooms?"

Cohabiting without marriage while having custody of a minor was frowned upon—though not outlawed—by the state. In contrast, the church was all for it. I didn't want my sister to draw any connection between my home and the three-wife Nicholson home. We were done with the polygamist life and she needed to know that.

"Upstairs might be best," I agreed. "Yummy had plenty of quilts in the bedroom across from Mud's." I looked at the stairs. I didn't know how careful Yummy was about such things. "I haven't seen them so I assume they're still there, hopefully piled on the bed, not on the closet floor."

Occam didn't volunteer what he might think about Yummy's willingness to fold linens, for which I was grateful. He might know an awful lot.

"Come and get it," I said to Mud.

My sister sat at the table, mumbled grace over the meal, ate while hiding yawns, and then dragged herself up the stairs as if exhausted. Monday was a school day, if the weather allowed it. For Occam and me, the night was still young and we had PsyLED Unit Eighteen reports to read, bread to bake, and maybe a midnight snack of jam, warm bread, and Sister Erasmus' wine.

At four a.m. my cell dinged. I heard Occam's ding from upstairs. Middle-of-the-night texts to both of us meant HQ and problems. I rolled over and picked up my cell.

The text said: *LaFleur, Rettell, and FireWind are en route to a new body found at a site. There's significant blood spatter, and the locals seem to think it should be our case. Are you available to respond?*

I tossed off the quilts, shoved my sock-covered feet into slippers, and pulled on a robe, making my way through the chilly house and out onto the front porch. The world was black and icy, the road down impassable. Strange pearly lightning still flickered here and there in the clouds. The only way down would be if the road melted by midday, which was usual in passing winter storms.

I considered the knowledge that I could bring heat from belowground and melt the ice. That would require a true emergency because that risked pulling the magma I had once accidentally disturbed closer to the surface. I really didn't want to be responsible for a volcano in Knoxville when it wasn't life-or-death.

Occam opened the door and stepped out behind me. He was fully clothed, wearing his coat, a gobag in one hand. When he saw the landscape, he said, "Huh."

I called Tandy on speaker and said, "Ingram and Occam here. The road down is impassable."

Occam said, "I could shift and meet transport at the bottom

of the hill. If there's a marked city or county unit nearby, they could provide transport." He looked up at the sky and added, "Dawn would be here before I could reach the address on your text."

"Stand by."

"Stand by" could mean for seconds or hours, so we went back inside and closed out the cold. Cherry padded silently down the stairs, the cats trailing slowly behind her, Jezzie braving the handrail in the unlit house. Occam's cat eyes could see better in the dark than I could, and he shucked his coat and began the process of reviving the stove's fire, moving as silently as the cats, to keep Mud from waking. The house batteries were fully charged, but if the power went out we would need them for computers, cells, heat, and hot water, so I lit a lantern and carried it with me to dress.

When I went back to the kitchen, Occam had started coffee and water for tea and had a cast-iron skillet heating on the stovetop. According to the church that was women's work, and I figured that no matter how long I lived with the man, his willingness to do things around the house would be a surprise. He had no idea how I reacted when I caught him doing something in or around the house. Or maybe he did. Cat nose and all that. A man doing housework was pure-T-sexy.

"I put another quilt over Mud and pulled her door shut so we could work." Humor in his voice, he added, "The cats are on the porch using the litter box, but Cherry might need a little encouragement."

The puppy had never seen ice, but she couldn't hold her bladder much longer. While Occam started bacon and scrambled eggs in the fry pan, I pulled on my work jacket, shoved my feet into my boots, and leashed her. "Come on, girl. Life is full of unpleasant sensory experiences, and this won't be the worst."

Cherry was not happy, but eventually assumed the position under the eave of the house and did her business. Breakfast was on the table when we got back, and Occam had put fresh water and food out for the critters.

I didn't pray for help very much, if ever, but I did thank God every day for my cat-man.

Over the course of the next hour, Tandy kept us informed as PsyLED maneuvered through the treacherous streets and arrived at the address where the DB had been reported. Then he sent their comms and their vest cam activity to Occam's computer, where we watched the unit's shuddering movements and heard their voices as they approached a residential ranch house in a middle-class part of town.

Moments later we saw the body from three different angles as they discovered it. It was female, wrapped in blankets, and, if the blood spatter was any indication, she had been stabbed to death. Blood was everywhere. It painted the walls around her and soaked into the linens she was wrapped in. She was emaciated, pale white.

The team—dressed out in sky blue booties, just in case this was a paranormal case—took pictures and gathered trace evidence, including a knife that FireWind found on the floor. Half an hour later, Rettell carefully unwrapped the body, exposing the short silk-and-lace nightgown the body wore. And her legs and arms.

"No Boot impressions," I said over the connection to HQ. "No signs of torture."

Over the connection we heard Rettell say, "Left wrist cut. Blood spatter indicates this is self-inflicted. Recommend this case be returned to local PD and we go home."

"Recommendation accepted," FireWind said over the mics. "And I believe that the on-duty OIC will hear a few words from me about trying to dump this case on PsyLED."

The on-duty OIC was the highest-ranking officer in charge. The locals had called in PsyLED without doing due diligence. I'd hate to be that officer.

Occam said, "We're off, then." He ended the connection with HQ and looked at me.

Before he had a chance to say anything my cell rang. It was a number that I had earmarked for Ming of Glass. I showed Occam the cell and said, "Uhhh."

Occam called HQ right back, told JoJo what was happening, and said, "Okay, Ingram. Answer the number associated with Ming of Glass."

I answered and said, "Special Agent Ingram of PsyLED Unit Eighteen."

"Cai," Ming's voice moaned. "My Cai is missing. They took him. Who will bring him back to me?"

"When did Cai go missing?" I asked.

"The fiiire," she said, drawing the two words out like a dirge. "The fire. The fires of hell and of my enemies." She continued in the same vein and, while I hated to be rude to the MOC, I said good-bye and ended the conversation.

"Tracking Cai's cell phone," Tandy said from HQ.

"Dyson. How did you get access to his cell phone?" FireWind asked, his tone sharp.

"You really want to know, boss?" Tandy asked.

A sigh came over the connection. "No, Dyson. I don't," FireWind said.

"His cell is on, and I'm inside it. He's . . . He's screaming."

"Are you okay, Dyson?" Rick asked. Tandy's empathic sensitivity made him acutely responsive to the pain and fear of others, even over the phone.

"Negative on that," he said, his breath coming too fast. "Worse, Soul is there. I hear her. And she's in human form. I know because she's screaming too."

"Can you patch it through?"

Audio came over Occam's laptop speakers. A man and a woman. Soul was screaming. How bad did torture have to be to make an arcenciel scream?

Still sounding breathless, terrified, Tandy said, "The weather is wreaking havoc everywhere, but I have a general location of the cell's signal. It'll take time to narrow it down, but we already know it's miles away from the location of the current active team, in weather that would strand Santa."

LaFleur said, "HQ. Did the footage from the security system at Ming's before and during the fire tell us anything about Cai?"

"Nothing we didn't know or guess. Figures dressed in black swarmed the place, armed with swords and guns. Ming's people fought back. At least one Molotov cocktail was thrown, and it was enough to activate the sprinkler system. Then it appears some type of curse was launched that shut down the sprinklers, and the place burned to the ground. More or less. If Cai was taken during the attack, we have no footage showing it."

FireWind said, "Give us what you have on Cai's signal location."

"In the general vicinity of the cell tower near Marble City."

FireWind nearly growled, "Which side of the river?"

"I can't tell yet," Tandy said.

There were lot of rivers and reservoirs in Knoxville, all of which had been dammed up to make lakes and create hydro-electric power. Getting from one side to the other of any of the rivers and lakes meant rerouting delays if you didn't plan way ahead. Which we couldn't. With ice on the roads, driving would be treacherous.

"Occam. Ingram," FireWind said. "That appears to be nearer you. It will take us forever to get to Soul."

"We can try to make it down the hill in Joh—in my truck," I said. "It has winter tires on it already. If we make it down the mountain, the rest should be manageable." I walked out on the front porch and yelled for Yummy. When the ice-covered vampire appeared in front of me with a pop, it scared the P-turkey outta me.

"*Dagnabbit*, Yummy." I ignored her laughter and said, "Occam and I jist got a case. Can you watch Mud and Soulwood until dawn? You can sleep in the guest room closet if needed."

"Sure. But I'm a little wet." She stepped in the door behind me and started dripping as the ice coating her hair and outer clothes immediately started melting. She slung a bag around and said, "I have dry clothes. A hot shower would be nice."

"Help yourself. Don't scare my sister."

"You spoil all my fun."

I raced upstairs to wake Mud. She was old enough to be at home alone—or with a trusted vampire—but I had to tell her what was happening. From the information we had so far, Occam and I would be heading into midtown. If we were on the wrong side of the river—

"Find which side of the lake Cai's signal originates," FireWind ordered.

I stopped my mad dash, listening.

"We've got ice-damaged cell towers," Tandy said. "Best suggestion, Occam and Ingram head down Sixty-two, South Illinois Avenue, and cross Melton Hill Lake. I should have more by the time you cross the water."

I dove into Mud's room and woke my sister, saying, "Work emergency. No school today due to ice. Yummy'll be in the closet, sleeping, after dawn. Sleep in, and then if you want, head to Esther's. Don't fall."

Don't fall. Advice I'd give to an adult, not my little sister.

Mud murmured in the affirmative and pulled a pillow over her head.

I raced back down the stairs, shoved into winter garb, thrust my feet into my boots, slung my vest over a shoulder, grabbed the new potted tree and my gear bag off the desk. I raced into the frigid cold, stopped to lock the door, and raced down the stairs. Halfway down, my feet went out from under me.

Occam caught my arm and held on, his were-strength halting my feetfirst plunge.

"That woulda hurt somethin' awful," I said.

"I gotcha, Nell, sugar. Always."

I knew my cat-man meant far more than saving me from a plunge down the stairs.

More slowly, we both moved out onto the ice. Minuscule sleet drops were still falling, sounding like salt hitting, sharp and shushing. The air seemed to be growing colder instead of warmer, and I feared the storm wasn't going to move away as quickly as the weather service had promised.

When we reached the truck, I saw that the bed was full of sleet that covered something mounded. "Occam? What's that?"

He slung a second, very heavy gobag from his shoulder; it clunked into the truck bed. It sounded like lots of metal. "Firewood to add weight to give the tires more traction. Chains for the tires in the canvas bag. I figured a survivalist like John Ingram would have them. Looked for some in your back storage and found them. No time to put them on the truck, but the winter tires should make a difference."

I started toward the driver's side but stopped. "You got werereflexes and this is not likely to be an easy trip. You drive?"

Without comment, he opened the passenger door for me and walked to the driver's side. That started a small bit of hades, as we slipped and slid out of the driveway and started down the mountain. I held on for dear life and knew I should have bought new winter tires for the truck. As some in the unit might say, *My bad.*

TWELVE

The weather had gotten much worse at a lower elevation, wetter, mushier, a heavy, sloppy, peppering part-sleet, part-freezing rain, part-melting-ice amalgam of *yuck*. The sound of precipitation alone made it hard to hear anything at our racing speed of less than twenty miles per hour. Visibility was poor and the streetlights were out here and there from ice building up on localized electric lines. Abandoned, ice-covered cars were all over the pike, some in small piles following accidents. The four-lane road was nothing but two slick lanes, each with two ruts, ruts that were being covered by the falling slush mired with sand and brine. Flames flickered here and there where electric lines sparked. Fire trucks traveled through the weather, firefighters putting out fires. Utility trucks and winter-clad workers repaired lines.

Tandy tried to contact us as we crawled down the main streets and, because the cell signal was so scratchy, I ended the call and pulled the comms headsets out of our gobags. I activated both and helped Occam into his before putting on my new set. Law enforcement comms were likely to be much more stable than cell phone signals now that we were in town.

Setting the mini-mics to the general channel—which would include all the people who had been at Ming's, as well as HQ—I said, "Ingram and Occam are across the lake on Pellissippi Parkway."

No one replied.

"Tan—Dyson," I amended, "Ingram here. Please acknowledge?"

He didn't.

I said, "Ingram here. Can anyone receive?"

No one responded.

"That's not the best news," Occam said grimly. "We don't know where we're going and it's nearly dawn, such as it will be, with unidentified assailants torturing Soul and Cai."

That meant we were cut off from the world, getting ready to face unknown numbers of unknown paranormals. In a winter storm. When my earth energies would be less powerful than in the summer.

We were still miles from Marble City when Tandy's voice cracked over the earbuds. "Ingram and Occam. Can you respond? Acknowledge."

"Ingram here," I said.

"What is your twenty?"

"I'm not sure what mile marker, but we just passed the exit to Tennessee College of Applied Technology," I said.

"I have a location," Tandy said, "one of five houses off Southerland Avenue." He gave us five likely addresses. "Trying to narrow it down. Get off Forty at the next exit and make your way to Southerland Avenue."

I mentally translated that and had a vague idea of where we were headed.

"It'll be one of five homes near the intersection of Southerland and Victory Street Northwest."

"We've seen what they drive," I said. "We can look for the vans."

"Backup?" Occam asked, even more grimly.

"Negative. A van with a mother and five kids skidded into a salt truck, and FireWind and LaFleur are at the scene. It's my understanding tha—" The connection abruptly ended.

The icy city passed us by, homeless people trudging with their soaked belongings through the cold, heads down against the sleet, trying to stay warm with movement. Most were headed toward the shelters.

Occam carefully corrected for a slide and managed to avoid hitting an abandoned car. Moving at speeds that approached a walk, he passed a run-down trailer park and made the turn onto Victory, cutting the truck's headlights.

The neighborhood was dark, no power, but the ice was white enough to reflect back what little light there was, and I could see. "There," I said, pointing at a house with two vans in the front yard. "White vans." I strained to see in the uncertain light. "They have a layer of ice and snow. They've been there awhile."

Occam motored on past and pulled to the side of the road.

The headsets crackled again and Tandy's voice came through with broken syllables that meant nothing.

Occam turned off the car. We both studied the house. Occam said, "I know you got this, Nell, sugar. But I'd say this to any non-were-creature except a vamp. I'd like you to stay back while I reconnoiter."

"Okay."

Occam's face was a study in stunned perplexity. I burst out laughing. "I'd be way more likely to fall on my backside than you." I patted the potted tree. "I got me some Soulwood soil, so I'll sit on the ground in this miserable icy precipitation and see what I can read underground from here. Might be something. Might be nothing."

Occam nodded and strapped on a waist and hip harness with a fourteen-inch blade. The blade had a strip of real silver along the blunt side. He checked his weapon, making sure the magazine had a silver strip down the side, marking it as loaded with silver-lead rounds. He slapped it home and pulled back on the slide. It was ready to fire when he slid it into the holster. Any vampire Occam shot or cut would be poisoned by silver.

He turned his head to me, his eyes already glowing with his werecat. "I love you to the full moon and back, Nell, sugar."

"I love you to the deeps of the roots and the heights of the limbs that cradle that full moon, cat-man."

He didn't kiss me. He simply opened the door and slid out, into the sleet, shutting me inside with the remaining warmth.

There was always survival gear in John's old truck. In a feat of calisthenics, I found a dirty blanket behind the seat, an old tarp under the seat, a trowel, a coil of rope, duct tape, and some tools, including two screwdrivers and a hammer, and his old coat where I'd stuffed it earlier. I was glad I had never cleaned out the truck. John's old stuff was mighty handy.

Taking what I wanted, I opened my own door and slid out, pulling the dirty rubber floor mat with me, along with the gear I needed. As I closed the door, darkness descended on the night. I sat on the mat with my back against the truck's warm front side panel, and where I could see the house, the potted plant between my knees. Pulling the tarp over my head and shoulders, I stabbed the ice with the trowel until I could see the ground. It wasn't frozen at this elevation, though that was changing fast as the temperature continued to drop and the freezing rain turned to pure sleet again.

Occam was already out of sight. I glared at the twig of a tree. "Play nice," I ordered it.

Scraping two handfuls of soil from the pot, I dumped them into the ice-coated depressions and sat with the pot against my thigh. I put my bare hands over the piles of Soulwood dirt and let my consciousness flow through my land and into the soil beneath.

Even had it been midsummer, there would have been little life in the ground. It hadn't been fertilized in years, it hadn't been watered through many dry summers, and when weeds did manage to take root, they had been mowed too short, chopped off right at the root. I felt sorry for the few surviving shrubs next to the house.

Even deeper, it was slow going, reading through the earth. Slow and miserable. I managed to travel through the soil about two hundred feet, and beneath the foundation. I reached the surface, inside the cement-block foundation, searching for wood on the ground that might make it easy to reach the wood that constructed the walls, but the ground beneath the house was wrapped in plastic. Protective plastic was a solid layer from outer wall to outer wall. There was no way in for me.

My comms crackled, Occam's voice so soft I could barely hear it. "Ingram. I'm going furry. I still hear screaming, and my nose tells me there's blood, but something feels off. Maintain your twenty until you hear from me."

"I can't get anything from the land," I said, pulling back through the earth. "I'm'a sit in the car and get warm. Don't freeze when you . . . you know."

Knowing I meant when he got naked to shift into his cat, Occam laughed, his voice already a scratchy growl. And then he was gone.

I climbed into the truck and turned it on. The heater blasted out warmth, and I held my hands to the vents. I was shivering, and wished I had thought to bring some thermoses of tea and coffee and something to eat. Occam would be hungry after shifting. Not like FireWind after a shift, but normal hungry. I kept protein snacks in my official car, but I had nothing in the truck.

On a good day, it would take Occam around half an hour to forty-five minutes to shift, scout around, and shift back. During the shifting time he would be totally vulnerable, yet he hadn't come back to shift near me where I could watch over him. I hoped that meant he'd found a really safe spot, but I figured what it really meant was that he didn't want to draw any attention to the truck and was protecting me. *Stupid cat.*

Overhead, a blast of pearly lightning flickered. Using my cell, I looked at the weather station for explanations of the lightning. My cell showed zero bars.

I frowned at the cell phone. Snow lightning was rare, but I'd seen cloud-to-cloud lightning several times now. Odd lightning. Pearly and prismy. I studied the sky again, but the lightning had disappeared.

Dawn had brightened the skies to dull gray when Occam loped back to the truck, human shaped, dressed, though his coat hung open and his boots weren't tied. He slid in and shut the door, his face pale in the dim light. He looked mighty hungry, but he didn't mention that. "Pretty sure the screams I heard are either mic'ed in or are a recording, being played over speakers, probably a battery-powered system.

"My nose and ears tell me no one alive or undead is in that house, but there's a lot of blood. My nose is less acute than a dog's, but the vehicles smell empty. I think it's a trap, though I don't get the musty scent of C-4 and other plastic malleable explosives, or the fruity scent of TATP." TATP was a cheap, illegal explosive used by terrorists. "No scent of nitrocellulose or accelerants or even fertilizer. But it could be something nonexplosive, like gas or a biologic." He shivered once, shaking hard all over, even in the hot air blowing through the heater. "Dang, it's cold, 'specially for a jungle cat." He put the truck in drive. "We'll go back to where we last had a signal, report in, and request backup."

I narrowed my eyes at him. "If I wasn't with you, would you jist go on in anyway?"

"No, Nell, sugar." He gave the truck a tiny hit of gas and, slipping and sliding, pulled into the street. "No," he repeated. "Once I fell in love with you, I realized that I'm not actually ten feet tall and bulletproof. And if I want to be with you for a long time, I can't rush in where fools and younger men might."

"Humph."

He grinned at the note of doubt in my tone and changed the subject, saying, "When we get to a signal, I'll put the chains on the tires, the back ones at least, so we can be safer."

I nodded and grabbed the security handle as we slid sideways onto I-40.

The sleet turned to snow and the city never opened up for the day. Electric trucks were moving from one localized outage to another, repairing power lines; city crews removed fallen trees and hauled away wrecked cars blocking roads. The weather front, which was supposed to have been transitory, had expanded to cover the eastern half of Tennessee and parts of six other states. The bad roads meant that it took time to get the people we needed on-site to check out the house and the vans, and we had to wait.

Not far off I-40, we spotted a dim light in the heavy snowfall. It was a tiny Vietnamese coffee shop that still had power and had opened despite the weather. We were able to reach HQ and report in, and were told by Tandy to stay put. That seemed like an excellent idea to me.

The shop served no tea, but I didn't care. Their coffee was made and served in a different way from any I had ever tasted, and they offered the most amazing pastries. Occam ate too much, after shifting in the cold. We had a box of coffee and all the remaining pastries boxed up to go for the entry crews when they were finally assembled. Leaving me sipping coffee and writing up our report from the target house, Occam went out and started the process of laying out the chains to get them on the tires. Men's work, according to the church, and suited to the strength of a cat-man, but it made me feel jist a mite ashamed to stay in the warmth. We waited.

* * *

At ten a.m. we were back at the house, standing in the yard, stomping our feet to restore circulation, and breathing clouds in the whiteout of falling snow. SWAT, with its tech toys and robots, had cleared the exterior, the doors and windows, and the crawl space beneath the house of possible explosive charges. T. Laine had cleared it of both mundane and potential energy triggers that would set off magical attacks.

The screaming from inside had stopped.

Because the neighborhood still had no power, we deduced that the battery on the speakers had finally failed. That was a blessing.

Snow was falling, sometimes in a heavy veil, other times mixed with sleet. The temperature had dropped. It was daylight. It was also dark and dreary and so cold my fingers were frozen inside my pockets. I had raced out of the house without proper winter gear; one set was still in the house and the backup clothes were in a gear bag in the car. Had we been able to take my car, I would have been fine. Instead my gloves and hat and extra wool socks were back at Soulwood. I'd make a point to put a backup bag in John's old truck.

In the miserable weather, Unit Eighteen was standing with the SWAT team, discussing who should lead the forced entry. Gonzales, the leader of SWAT and T. Laine's boyfriend, was giving a tutorial on barricades to FireWind, who seemed faintly amused. T. Laine stood in the background, frustrated because the interdepartmental wrangling and males in show-off mode were holding things up.

Rettell had shown up too, in a government car, but she hadn't joined us. She was sitting in the warmth, her car's heater going, watching. I figured that since she was military, she had tech to listen in on everything we said while staying warm and dry.

FireWind interrupted Gonzales, turned to T. Laine, and said, "Kent. Is there a working to blow down a door, and can you employ it?"

My head swiveled back to the group.

"Yes," she said shortly.

"Employ it."

"Yes, sir." Without looking at her SWAT boyfriend, she

turned to the door, reached inside her shirt, and pulled out her amulet necklace. A moment later she tossed something at the door and said a word too softly to catch.

The door tore off its hinges and rammed inside, crashing into something.

There was no explosion, no sound of a battering ram. Just a metallic-and-wood wrenching sound and then the door was gone.

From inside, nothing exploded. No magic happened. No one shot at us.

I bit my cheek to keep from reacting to the expression on Gonzales' face.

As speedily as the slick surface allowed, FireWind and La-Fleur raced to the door and inside, the new layer of snow giving traction we hadn't had earlier. "The rest of you keep SWAT out," Aya said softly into comms, on the dedicated channel.

T. Laine laughed. It contained a note of "they can try to get in." Occam and she moved to the door to provide backup as FireWind and LaFleur cleared the ranch house room by room, their voices live over comms.

When I could do so without laughing, I raised my head and met Gonzales' eyes. He looked a little mad and a lot stunned. This time I let my chuckle free and said, "The faster you figure out that Lainie has better defenses than you do, the better for your relationship. You'da made big bonus points to remember that today and to include her powers in your little seminar. May I speak frankly?"

Gonzales frowned at me. "Any way to stop you?" he demanded.

"No. So. Frankly speaking? You are acting dumb and stupid. And T. Laine is way too smart and self-sufficient to put up with you for long. You want her, you best be mending your ways and start using your brain. Assuming you got one."

Into my earbud, FireWind said, "Location is clear. Call for coroner. PsyLED, move in."

Calling for the coroner meant there was a dead human inside. T. Laine and Occam entered. I walked from the SWAT team to the small house and inside, through the splintered remains of the back entrance, my breath making clouds inside as well.

The back door was in pieces against the far wall, resting on top of a cheap dinette set. The house had been empty for a long time, mold on the kitchen walls, the furniture filthy, signs of rodent and raccoon scat everywhere. No human had lived here in years, not even the evidence of crack addicts I expected, or signs of squatters looking for a warm place to sleep.

I followed the voices to the front of the house.

The furniture in the living room had been shoved against two walls, and the floor in the center had been swept clean. Then splattered in blood.

In a twisted tangle of limbs and a pool of blood lay a body, male, nude, covered with wounds that were consistent with the PMs on the five homeless males. Tortured. The blood all around had frozen into scarlet crystals, flakes, and smears. It hadn't had time to dry and turn brown, but had frozen moments after it fell. He was face down, and somehow that made it easier to study the body.

I'd been raised on a farm. I was used to seeing animals slaughtered and dressed for the cooking pot, for smoking or salting, or for being made into winter jerky. Despite the death of the animals, it had always been quick and humane. This was not. This slaughter, this draining of the man's blood, had been slow and methodical and then swift and brutal. Not only inhumane but inhuman.

I walked around the body until I could see his face, swiveled hard to the right. Electric shivers shot through me. I knew him.

Cai. Ming's Cai.

FireWind tapped his mic for a private channel and said into his comms, "Jones. Cold one. Single name, Cai, human primo to Ming of Glass, Master of the City of Knoxville. Request coroner's ETA." He studied the scene as he listened. "Copy that; fifteen minutes."

Occam was kneeling on a clean corner of the floor. He angled his head to the room and tapped his nose to indicate he was telling by scent as well as by the frozen scarlet color. "Ain't often I wish I had a dog's nose, but best as I can tell, this is Soul's blood over here. Her human blood, not her arcenciel blood."

T. Laine braced against the far doorway and scrutinized the scene. She reached up to her throat and once again touched the moonstone necklace she wore beneath her shirt. A few seconds later she said into her mic, "Kent here. *Seeing* working reveals this is not a witch circle. No signs of dark magic or the torture being a sacrifice. But over there I sense magic." She pointed to a corner and walked over. She squatted and said, "Clothes. Hair. Stuff for CSI. Up close, it isn't witch magic or were-magic. Maybe some charms were kept here. No sacrifice. But . . ." T. Laine tilted her head this way and that. She touched a strand of hair on the floor. "But it does feel familiar. Like what happens when a vampire shares blood with someone. That opening, sharing, and binding. I'm guessing they drank here. But . . ." She stood and backed away. "I don't know. Something feels different."

FireWind called our contact at the headquarters of the Dark Queen and managed to get through. He described the blood at Soul's and the blood we had found here. He went to FaceTime and showed Alex the scene. Sharing a crime scene with an outside source was one of FireWind's big taboos, but I kept my mouth shut and so did the others. He returned to a simple call, the cell held to his ear as he walked into the kitchen and listened.

When he ended the call, FireWind reentered the living room and said, "Confirmed information. If an arcenciel is taken in light dragon form, they can be captured in a crystal. The person who holds the crystal can then step back through time and alter the past, sometimes only in small jumps, sometimes in larger passages of time. If an arcenciel is captured in human form, they have to be forced to shift shape into a dragon to be forced into the crystal.

"Eli Younger, of the Dark Queen's security, speculated two things. One, that they smelled the Blood Tarot on Cai and that's why they took him from Ming's when they burned the clan home. Two, that Soul was in her arcenciel form when vampires entered her apartment. They tried to capture her in a crystal but she was able to shift to human before they abducted her. That's why the two forms of her blood were in her apartment. He also speculates that they forced her to watch Cai being tortured in the hope that she would change form."

"Is there any indication that Soul and Cai knew one another?" Kent asked.

"Nothing concrete. The assistant director of PsyLED is in danger. That speculation has been agreed with by those up-line from me. It is believed that Tomás wants her to shift forms so he can ride her into the past. Reasons unknown."

"What does he *guess* Torquemada would want to change in the past?" T. Laine asked.

"Eli hinted that he and his brother have material and intelligence from a researcher and information broker named Reach, who used to rival . . ." FireWind gave one of his rare smiles, this one wry and amused at once. "Certain other hackers in the business." His expression said he was referring to JoJo. "Their information came from him. Eli agrees that Torquemada has, or once had, a captive arcenciel, based on the photographs of the old paintings acquired by Ingram and now in your electronic files.

"So far as Eli knows, there are no witches among Torquemada's group, and certainly no females of any species, so he doesn't think Cai's death was a blood-magic sacrifice. It was a message to Soul to shift forms so he could capture her. It might also have been a message to Ming to turn over the Blood Tarot."

"Then why burn down Ming's clan home?" I asked. "Torquemada had to know she kept the deck of cards there."

"Could be that Cai told them it was missing and they think Soul removed it," T. Laine said, her tone considering. "Or we removed it. If so, it may have a *tracker* working on it." She tapped her comms and said, "Jo. Put the deck in the null room until I get back. Affirmative." She tapped out and said, "She and Tandy are alone at HQ and Torquemada and his people would know we're here."

"The building and electronics are thoroughly battened down," FireWind said. "Even if he sends his humans there he can't get in."

"That's what we thought last time," T. Laine said grimly. "That's what we thought about Soul's apartment."

His face tense, FireWind tapped his comms. "Jones. Keep a tight watch on all exterior cams. I'm sending a request for two marked units to park in view of the building until we get back."

"Confirm two marked units," Jo said. "Appreciate that."

I asked, "Could the Blood Tarot, with its magical signature, combined with the vampires getting back their souls, have affected their cognition? We took the Blood Tarot, and then Ming looked more like herself at the fire."

FireWind turned his yellow eyes to me in surprise. "You are suggesting that perhaps the presence of the Blood Tarot at the clan home caused them to be especially or more harmfully affected by the return of their souls. That might explain why Lincoln Shaddock seemed like himself when fighting off the attack in Asheville."

"And Lincoln has a family now," Occam said. "Constancy and love can make a big difference to mental stability."

T. Laine said, "That makes sense. I'll do some more testing on the cards when we get back to HQ."

FireWind tapped his mic and said, "Affirmative. Send them in." To us he said, "SWAT has relinquished the site to us. Knoxville Crime Scene is on-site. PsyCSI is on the way to liaise with them here. Let's take this back to HQ."

The debrief was completed.

I was finally warm, sitting in the conference room at HQ. I had a belly full of pizza FireWind had picked up on the way here. He had also brought in five paper bags of groceries in case we got stranded. He was turning into a decent boss.

And because Mud was with family, I wasn't worried about her safety and security as much as I might have been.

All the people who were supposed to be off shift were ready to try and make it home to sleep, or else had decided to bunk down in HQ, which had a small room in back where cots could be erected for just such an emergency.

Margot lived close and was packing her gear to head out, and Aya should have been doing the same, but he seemed to be in no hurry.

I ended a call to Mud. My fearless and intrepid sister had prepped and secured the house and pipes for freezing weather and, during a break in the snow, she had trekked through the drifts to Esther's. She and the puppy were safe and I didn't have to worry about the house pipes freezing. Only that Torquemada might find a way there through the storm and try to harm them.

I stuck my fingers into the pot of Soulwood soil holding the twig of vampire tree. Silently I sent a message to my land to protect the Tulip Tree House. All I felt in return was something like a cat rolling over in sleep and flexing its claws. I had to believe that was enough. I flicked my fingers free of the dirt.

T. Laine was wearing sweats and reading reports, and was steadfastly not returning Gonzales' repeated calls.

JoJo was stretched out in her desk chair next to Tandy with her feet propped up. She was dressed in warm velour sweats and she had a blanket beside her.

Tandy was wearing fuzzy rainbow-striped socks and gray sweats.

I had changed, wearing two pairs of wool socks and adding two underlayers of T-shirts.

FireWind was wearing black jeans and a black dress shirt with boots. And a black vest that hung open in front. I had never seen him wear it and wanted to get a good look, but that seemed kinda nosy.

The werecats all wore the same clothes they had at the house where we had discovered Cai. Werecats had a higher than human body temperature and rewarmed fast. Unless they had to get naked in a sleet storm, cold didn't bother them much.

Even with Knoxville Utility Board's massive and redundant power grid, there were still outages from tree fall and ice buildup; we were prepared for loss of power. If it went out, we had a backup generator and fuel to run essential systems for a few hours. If the power wasn't restored by then, comms had battery backup power. The building was on the KUB's list of most important power needs, just below hospitals, city law enforcement, and a few of Oak Ridge's more secret research projects.

But I'd rather have been on Soulwood, with nothing but firewood to warm me. There I had water, a windmill to pump it (unless its workings froze), my stove, a year's worth of stored food, and all the amenities. If we did happen to lose power here, HQ would quickly become stinky, messy, and miserable.

"We have company," JoJo said.

I looked at the screen displaying the camera view of the front entrance. Walking through the snow, wearing jeans and a tailored coat, was Lieutenant Colonel Rettell.

Rick appeared in the hallway looking edgy, almost vibrating with awareness. Occam sat up in his chair, watching down the hallway. Aya appeared in his office door, watching.

Margot walked past Rick. "I'll let her in the outer door," she said stiffly. The werecat walked down the stairs and let the visitor in. The outer door shut behind Rettell, leaving them together in the stairwell. Margot leaned in and sniffed. Rettell stiffened like she'd been jabbed with a hot poker.

Margot said, "Well. That explains it." And led the way up.

I looked at Occam, who was watching them on-screen. The last time Rettell had shown up, Rick had acted strangely, wearing a besotted and hungry expression on his face. And then Occam had escorted me out of the building.

Rettell walked up the stairs behind Margot, sniffing the air. When she reached the top, she walked up to Rick and dropped her bags. She made fists of both hands and belted him in the gut with a hard right. Faster than I could think, she took him down with an uppercut. Rick fell flat.

THIRTEEN

Rick managed a breath, but it sounded painful. I took a step back, confused. Occam snorted and had to turn away to hide laughter. Aya's brows twitched in surprise. Rettell shook out her hands, looked FireWind over, and said, "That was werecat business, not law enforcement business."

She locked gazes with Occam down the hallway. "You best teach him some werecat manners. I'll not have my mate acting like a kit." She bent, lifted her bags by the straps, and traipsed down the hallway toward us. "You have far better mating manners," she said to Occam.

"Thank you," he said, forcing his expression to smooth. "I'm a lot older than LaFleur."

"Margot," she said. "They were together?"

"For a while," Occam said, the humor gone. "Didn't work out."

Rettell placed her bags on the big table. "Hmmm. I know a guy. I'll send an invitation and do an introduction. If they get along, I could make a transfer to a local office happen."

FireWind was standing in the open doorway. *"Mate?"*

She looked him over again and turned her back on him. FireWind's mouth fell open just a bit. The boss-boss was more than a foot taller than the petite woman, but she was unimpressed with his mass, gorgeous looks, law enforcement status, and . . . most everything.

FireWind wasn't used to being snubbed. We knew parts of his history. In his long life he had been spat upon because of the color of his skin, hated, desired, hunted, and, in recent years, honored. Being disregarded clearly wasn't something he expected or had familiarity with.

Rick stumbled to the side of his boss, one hand rubbing his

jaw, the other to his gut, his glistening white hair disheveled, strands hanging over his face. He leaned against the doorjamb as if it was the only thing holding him up, but his eyes looked clear and less haunted after the violence, and the tension running through him was gone.

"You," Rettell said, pointing at Rick. "You arranged for the werelion cubs to be turned over to responsible werecat fosters. You won four wives in Africa, in one of the black wereleopard clans there, in a battle of dominance."

My body went tight. Occam placed a hand gently on my arm, his touch soothing. *Rick won four wives? In* Africa*?*

Rettell continued. "It's said you offered them several options, one of which was to remain under your protection, so they couldn't be taken by another mate. But then you set them free to live like they wanted. They're living like queens, and the males in the area are allowed in only to mate and are then kicked out. You turned the werecat world on its head."

"And that's why you hit me?"

"No. I hit you to take you out of mating cycle, which clearly you never experienced before, even when you went home to meet your wives. And I'll hit you again if necessary. We don't have time right now for yowling at the moon and cat foolishness. When this is over, we'll talk and decide how we're going to manage this."

"She's wired," JoJo said casually. "It went active right after she hit LaFleur."

FireWind didn't shift position. His eyes simply landed on Rettell. Slowly, a smile spread across his face, as if she was a particularly interesting tidbit he might dismember for supper. "Wired?" he asked softly. The tables of power in the room had just done a one-eighty.

Rettell gave a sigh that was a tad too theatrical for the circumstances. She turned up her shirt collar and spoke into it. "I told you it wasn't going to work. Permission to go dark. Thank you, sir."

She unbuttoned her coat and tossed it over the nearest chair. Under it she was wearing a tailored dress shirt with a thin tee beneath. She peeled a tiny mic off her collar and unhooked its narrow cord from her waist. With two fingers she freed a thin black object, about the size of a lipstick tube, from her back pocket. She pushed a spot on it and handed it to JoJo. "You really are as good as they say."

JoJo accepted the device and inspected it. "Nice." A wicked smile curved her full lips. "Is this mine?"

"No."

Jo handed it back to Rettell and checked her screens again. "Nothing else live, but that's not saying she's clean. She probably has others she can turn on at will."

Rettell didn't respond to that and turned her attention back to FireWind. She said, "We need to talk about the arcenciels. Plural."

I was sipping tea from a warm cup, trying to follow the information and its importance. I had taken a seat where I could watch Tandy, our empath, who was relaxed, leaning back in his chair, elbows on the chair arms, his hands clasped in front of his lower face. Listening. He touched his nose for truth, lifted a pinkie finger when she lied, and twitched his thumb for a signal meaning: "Something isn't right, but it isn't a lie."

Rettell had taken a chair with her back to the door, which was odd for military or law enforcement, and kept looking out the heavily smoked windows to the weather. It had stopped snowing for the moment. Over her head, above the windows, were the comms screens. Using a laser pointer to highlight a still shot of the New Orleans skyline, she clicked through to a single pic of a nighttime city sky with two rainbow dragons and two blurred human forms in the air.

"The glistening bluish arcenciel is called Opal," she said. "The one that looks like liquid nacre is Pearl. We understand they attacked the Dark Queen personally, as well as one of the vampires, called Koun"—she put the red laser on each human form as she spoke—"in the street, in the days leading up to the coronation of the vampire emperor of Europe, Edmund the First. But we have no video."

"Above the street," JoJo said, her tone amused, "not in the street. *We* have video."

Rettell lasered her eyes to Jo. "When can I see it?"

"Never. Unless you finish telling us what you want," FireWind said. "And maybe not then."

"Interdepartmental proto—" she started.

"Is bullshit," FireWind said placidly, "when you wear a mic into our offices."

Rettell's eyes narrowed and her spine went even straighter.

Now that no one was being hit, I began to wish I had popcorn. I held my teacup close to my lips, sipping off and on. The bosses were doing what they called *pushing buttons*, trying to get a rise out of one another. It was a lot like what happened when a second or third wife came into a household and positions of power were sought and staked out.

So far, Rettell hadn't lied, and though she wasn't happy about everything she was saying, she was good at skirting the truth. Tandy was intrigued at their wordplay and his thumb twitched often when the military woman spoke, suggesting a lack of full disclosure.

"At another time," she said, "despite nearly killing the Dark Queen, the two arcenciels appeared at an event at the Dark Queen's headquarters in human form. We have photos if you are interested in a trade."

"We have photos," Jo murmured. "LaFleur was an invited guest."

"Of course he was." Rettell blew out a breath that sounded real this time, and not practiced or planned. "The leader of the arcenciels is Soul, Assistant Director of PsyLED, also known as She Who Guards the Rift. That rift is rumored to be on land recently purchased by the Dark Queen. Some say the rift leads into another dimension, one through which other paranormal creatures have come and gone in the last week or more. The military has decided this rift needs to be under our protection. And if possible, it needs to be closed. Permanently."

FireWind shrugged, but I could see a faint tightness around his eyes. It looked like unease. The big boss was usually better at hiding his emotions, so I had to wonder if he was deliberately letting emotions show that may not have been fully true. Like Rettell, he was good at avoiding the full truth.

"The military's hopes and dreams have nothing to do with PsyLED," he said.

"It has everything to do with you, personally. You're Jane Yellowrock's brother." She swiveled to me. "And it has to do with you, Nell Ingram." She stabbed out with a finger. "You have some sort of power over the land. We want you to find the rift for the U.S. government."

I burst out laughing. It was so unexpected I choked on the tea, tipped the cup, spilled it across the table, and started coughing as I laughed. It was a bad bout and I bent over to force the tea back out of my bronchial tubes. Occam patted my back. Others raced to get paper towels to clean up my mess. When I caught my breath, I said, "Your'un information is vastly overblown and outrageous in the extreme." *I might help some trees grow,* I thought. Between coughs I said, "The ability to recognize interdimensional physics is out of my league."

"Ingram is an earth sprite, as best we can determine. She helps things grow," FireWind said mildly.

"We have reports that she grew an entire forest using demon power."

The table went quiet. Rettell knew a lot. And she was sneaky. Usually I liked that in a woman, but maybe not when it was pointed at me. "Not my demon," I said through my coughing. "Its power had to go somewhere. It was either let the witches shoot it up into the atmosphere, where it might spin back and land on a city full of humans, or work with the witches and send it into the land. I managed to help them direct it into the land. And I nearly died. I'm not trying something like I think you're saying I should."

"Maybe your sister will. We can always take her."

Leaves rustled in my hairline, sprouting at the threat. Occam put his hand on my arm. I concentrated on calming my breathing. FireWind finally decided to take over the meeting.

"Our people will provide whatever *law enforcement* assistance you may need. You will not be taking our people off and away. You will not be abducting anyone in this county or state."

"Abduction is a strong word. There are a few useful clauses in constitutional law relating to national defense that suggest we can . . . secure a citizen's cooperation."

FireWind swiveled in his fancy desk chair, back and forth. "Has the United States government decided how to treat vampires? Or those sworn to the Dark Queen? Or the Dark Queen herself? How about the were-creatures, like you? Or beings such as I? Are we human? Are we citizens? Will the United States government *secure our cooperation*? Perhaps in a fenced-in compound on a desert military base?"

Rettell frowned.

"If not, then I postulate a lengthy and vicious legal battle would follow should the U.S. government, any of its various departments, or any branch of the military try to abscond with any nonhuman in any city where I—or my sister, the Dark Queen—might hear of such. Nell has sworn an oath to PsyLED. She works for us. She is not a *thing* to be bartered or traded. Her sister is a citizen in this county."

I couldn't leave the area of Soulwood for long periods of time. Soulwood owned me as much as I owned it. I'd sicken and die if I was gone too long. It was why I carried a pot of the vampire tree in Soulwood soil with me most everywhere I went. I figured both of my sisters were equally tied to the land.

"Hmmm," Rettell said, watching me. She turned to the screens along the wall over the windows and moved the laser pointer through a series of still shots. "Here we have a poor-quality video of a woman we believe to be Soul turning into a Bengal tiger, and another when she shifts into a light dragon, and then into a human. Her species does not conform to the laws of conservation of mass and energy, hence our scientists are of the considered opinion that she is from another dimension. Along with this thing."

On-screen was a brilliantly colored bird standing next to a tall woman. Jane Yellowrock was somewhere around six feet in height, which made the bird about five feet tall. It had iridescent feathers in blues, reds, and a brilliant fuchsia, as if an indigo bunting and several species of hummingbirds crashed into one another, leaving only the fanciest plumage, but on a Big Bird scale. "It's called an Anzu and it's a shape-changer of some sort. Our people have theorized it too came through a rift."

"Why are you telling us this?" FireWind said. "The military is notoriously close-lipped about what they want."

"We think Torquemada wants the arcenciels, maybe an Anzu, and a deck of cards called the Blood Tarot. Which is why he took Soul."

She didn't mention devil dogs or the church bloodlines. I had wondered what the Welsh *gwyllgi* had to do with Torquemada.

What if they were simply a side job, like something they came upon that was interesting but was unrelated to the other things the vampires wanted? Or maybe their blood was stronger than a regular human's? I didn't know. Not yet.

FireWind said, "I reported personally to DHS and DOD that Soul was missing, supposedly taken by Tomás de Torquemada's people. We have our best people on it, but as far as we know, when Soul wants to disappear, she simply can't be found. And we have no way to contact the arceciels you're talking about. For that you should approach the Dark Queen. I believe she's taken up residence in her winter court in Asheville, or will shortly." He didn't mention her honeymoon.

"Will you provide an introduction for me to her court?"

"No," FireWind said. "And if I did, my sister would as likely shoot me as listen to me."

"Things still tense between you?"

"What do you want?" FireWind said, spacing the words out carefully.

"We want the Blood Tarot. We want to know if it survived the fire at Ming of Glass' clan home. Knoxville CSI says they didn't find it at the crime scene where you found Cai, Ming's primo."

"We didn't find it in either place either."

No. I confiscated it. And it is in lockup about twenty feet from where we all are sitting. I didn't say that. What I blurted was, "Factions." I stopped. "Sorry."

"No, Ingram," FireWind said, now openly amused. "You have excellent observational skills. Pray continue."

I frowned at his old-fashioned use of *pray continue*. It was a lot like church-speak. "Okay. You two want the same thing, except she also wants Rick, and Rick's no good to us until she gets him alone for this mating thing and does what my sister's school friends call the 'big nasty.'"

Rettell's head went back at my term.

FireWind blinked and a surprised expression flitted across his face. He wasn't used to hearing me talk about sex.

Sex was a frank subject matter among women in the church. People had to be candid when multiple wives shared the same husband, and though I had been gone from the church for most of my life, I remembered enough. I could talk about sex without getting embarrassed if I brought it up. Not so much if my boss-boss did.

I shrugged at him and went on. "She has excellent control over her mating instincts, but it isn't likely the military sent her knowing she and Rick would go into heat."

Rettell's mouth thinned.

"Sorry about the plain talk," I said to her, lying. Returning my gaze to my boss-boss, I went on. "We have more tech and experience with paranormals than she does, except weres. She's a were-creature, and even in heat, she's got more control than most, because no grindylow has appeared, even though there are humans present."

Rettell frowned at my conclusion, her eyes penetrating. "Why do you think I have more control?"

"Because you smell like heat. That's what Occam said."

Rettell went red-faced, her frown deepening. She shifted in her seat and glanced away from me to the windows and back.

The military officer / doctor was waiting on something outside the windows. I glanced at FireWind and his eyes had followed hers, so he knew it too.

I glanced at Tandy. "She's speaking the truth, but only parts of the truth, and part of the truth she's speaking she doesn't like much, including the part about taking my sister. I think with the bug turned off, and Clementine offline for debugging . . ." I let the words trail off, pausing.

Rettell's eyes tightened.

"I think she deliberately turned on the mic while standing in a place where Jones would 'discover' it and turn it off in case this subject came up. Your'un bosses don't know you'uns in heat, do they."

Rettell didn't reply, but she didn't have to. She was red as a beet.

I picked up where I'd left off. "Based on all a that, it's reasonable to infer that she feels she should just come clean and tell you what she really wants, but her bosses told her not to. Which means if she does talk, then so should you, boss. Off the record."

Rettell flicked her eyes to the windows and back to me, watching me the way a cat does a mouse.

I knew what the look meant—she was hoping to intimidate

me, but it was too late for that. I'd been hunted by churchmen. Killed a few who needed killing.

This woman had threatened my family.

The tiniest hint of a killing smile flowed into my eyes as I pulled on Soulwood. My hands warmed. Leaves rustled in my hairline. And I let 'em.

She was surprised at my lack of being browbeaten, at what she saw in my eyes, but she pushed on. "Finding and acquiring the rift is a matter of national security," she said, her eyes locked on mine. "We need it in our possession. In return for Nell's help locating it, we are prepared to provide all the military's assistance to locate and retrieve Soul."

"You scratch my back," the boss-boss said, "is not a game PsyLED is prepared to play with the military."

"If it *is* an interdimensional rift, you can't move it," I said. "The Dark Queen's winter court is in the mountains in the middle of nowhere. I reckon you can confiscate the land, *if* you can find the rift, but so far you haven't. And if you did find it, if you build a building around it, disturbing the soil might damage the rift."

"How would *you* know that?" There might have been an implication in her words that I was an uneducated hillbilly and therefore should keep my mouth shut among my betters. Or maybe I was projecting, as T. Laine sometimes said. I glanced at FireWind and got an approving nod, so I let my thoughts and words flow, dropping deeper into church-speak. I leaned forward in my chair.

"Knoxville is a hotbed for R and D into anything paranormal, nuclear, physics, psysitope related, and magical. You ain't got diddly-squat because you're here, talking to me, an uneducated hillbilly, about interdimensional rifts.

"You'un got a way to measure multidimensions in the field? Far as I know, it has to be measured in one a them fancy labs in Oak Ridge, up the pike a ways. So no. You ain't got one."

I rested my elbows on the table, my hands one atop the other directly in front of me. My tone turned just a tad accusing. "You'un don't know how far underground the rift extends, or how far out to the sides. So you want to force me to read the land, find the rift for you, *and* tell you what it's doing."

Rettell's eyes flicked to the windows.

My own followed hers. "Ohhh. The lightning. The strange cloud-to-cloud, pearly lightning. There's arcenciels in the clouds. You military types done set a trap for this Pearl and Opal you'un been talking about. Way you been looking out the windows? I'm figgerin' you'un expect them to show up here, and real soon. And you want, but do not need, the Blood Tarot, because you jist needed an excuse to be here when your trap is sprung."

Rettell looked appalled. LaFleur and FireWind followed my eyes to the sky beyond the windows. FireWind said, "I've noticed the strange lightning."

I turned my attention back to the military doctor. "You ain't as good at hiding your intentions as you think. I been reading sneaky people since I was a toddler. It's a woman's survival skill in the church."

And we had Tandy, who was clearly more powerful than she knew. Right now, Tandy was grinning at me like a wild man, enjoying me being . . . whatever I was being. I thought about Mama taking over the women's council at church. Maybe I should go by one night and watch her in action.

FireWind said to Occam, "Search her bags for crystals that might be used to capture an arcenciel. Jones, all security cams and exterior security devices on high alert."

Occam walked to Rettell and gathered her bags, bringing them to our side of the table.

Rettell relaxed and her face softened. There was a sense of relief in her expression.

"She didn't *want* to capture arcenciels, but she has orders?" I posited.

The military doctor stared out the windows.

"Or she's a really good actor and what she's really been doing is stalling for time," I added.

Occam pulled out a velvet bag tied with a silky thread. Inside was a handful of natural quartz crystals. He fanned them out. There were no empty places inside, like Torquemada's crystals. I wondered if she knew what his looked like. Occam placed the quartz in T. Laine's hand. The witch carried them to the null room, where they couldn't be used.

FireWind said, "We have the Blood Tarot in our possession."

"Interesting," she said. "Where?"

"In a safe place," FireWind said.

Rettell gave him a tight smile.

Outside the windows, a rainbow of light blasted from the clouds. Dazzling dragons made of prisms of light dove toward the earth, swooped around the building twice, and landed on the roof. The roof cam showed blinding light, and then two human-looking beings, female, were standing on the rooftop, staring at my bed of Soulwood soil.

Rettell shoved back from the table.

FireWind moved fast and was suddenly standing in the doorway, blocking us all in. Especially Rettell. Her expression was flat and uncompromising. Her body went loose, balanced, her stance ready for combat. FireWind laughed at her, which ticked her off. The woman had a job to do, and though she might not be happy at being ordered to do all of it, she was determined to follow at least some orders.

Everyone started checking weapons, but I figured there was no good reason to. You can't shoot light. *Light* . . . "I'm bettin' that beings made of light can come through the computer wiring if they want to," I said.

Jo's eyes went wide as she ran them over her hardware.

"Alex Younger knew Soul was missing," I said. "Did he tell the arcenciels that she was taken from her home here? The Dark Queen has people who know people." The result seemed to snap into place in my brain. "The military was banking on the possibility that the arcenciels would show up here to rescue their version of a leader."

"Without the crystals, you can't control them," Rettell said. "And the only thing that hurts them is cold iron."

Both women on the roof bent from the waist and placed their hands on the soil. The rooty place in my middle twisted. I grabbed my belly and stood up from the table and asked, "Tandy, are they afraid?"

"Yes," he said, his eyes closing as he concentrated. "Very. And confused. And angry." He tilted his head, his brows drawing down. "Their emotions are not like humans'. They feel spiny, volatile, the way a cactus made of spider fangs might. I'm getting the impression of . . . insecurity? Uncertainty?" He opened his eyes. "Soul's emotions never feel this way. I'm wondering if they're young. Teenagers?"

"FireWind, they seem to like my land," I said. "May I suggest I go up there alone?"

"Proceed with caution, Ingram."

"They are *dangerous*. I have cold iron." Rettell pulled an iron blade from her duffel, which was still open on the table.

In a move faster than I could follow, Rick ripped it from her hand and stepped back. Seemed as if the wereleopard had regained his sensibilities. His black eyes were calm, if strongly focused on Rettell. "No," he said. "You will not enslave anyone."

I thought about the wives he had given freedom to. Yeah. I liked that about LaFleur.

"Ingram," FireWind said. "Go. Take comms. Be careful."

Leaving my weapon behind on the table, I stopped by my office cubby and pulled on my coat, hat, gloves, and comms set. I touched the mic on and said, "Jones, Ingram here. Acknowledge."

"You are loud and clear, Ingram," Jo said.

I picked up my potted tree and went to meet creatures who were possibly from an interdimensional universe. And teenagers. I thought of Mud and her unpredictability and belligerence. *God help me.*

I knocked on the door and pushed through. Stepped slowly onto the roof-porch. Let the door close behind me, locking me out. The snow had stopped, but the cold stole my breath, which came out like a cloud and caused my coughing fit to kick in again. "Sorry," I said, coughing, trying to catch my breath.

The two women rose from my patch of soil and faced me as I coughed. They were woefully underdressed for the weather, though neither seemed to notice the chill. Both wore filmy, fluttery gowns in colors that matched their names and also the colors of their dragon shapes, the fabric moving in the slight breeze, their shoulders exposed. The flesh of the one called Pearl had a nacre-like sheen and her gown was a pale pinkish shade. Opal was dressed in a similar gown but of every shade of blue from nearly white to a hint of black, with a flash of pink in the folds.

When I stopped coughing, I said, "I'm Special Agent Ingram with the Psychometric Law Enforcement Division of Homeland Security, Unit Eighteen." I stopped. I had almost said *What can I do for you?* But that offer might be taken literally. Paranormal beings didn't view English the way humans did. "You are welcome here, on this roof."

"You are a Keeper of the Trees," Opal said. "We have heard of your kind from times past, though we are too young to have met one such as you. May I touch the tree you carry?"

"It may bite," I said calmly. "I don't know what your blood in its bark might do to you. Or to it. But I won't forbid you to touch it."

The two leaned to each other, their heads touching.

"We will not touch at this time," Opal said, both of them standing straight. "We are young, but we have been deemed capable of learning, and therefore worthy to participate in human events and activities."

"I see." I didn't, but I was listening.

"We have come to help locate and to rescue She Who Guards the Rift. We are trying the negotiation of words."

Pearl said, "My sister is currently better at the negotiation than am I. I will kill you if need be."

"I appreciate the . . . advance notice," I said.

"We have tracked the trail of She Who Guards the Rift," Opal said. "We saw many humans at the location where her trail ended. We no longer sense her, but she is not dead. She has not passed through the rift. Therefore we think she is in human form, not trapped in crystal, and is in danger."

Pearl said, "In the matter of the negotiation of words. We will continue to search the air and the water of the rivers and the lakes to find her. If we are successful, we will contact you. If you are successful first, you will contact us." She removed a bracelet cuff from her arm and extended it to me. "Wear this."

The bracelet looked as if it had been formed in one piece from a huge pearl oyster. It glimmered in the dim light and I had a feeling that if T. Laine were here, she would see strong and amazing energies in a witch *seeing* working. "Ummm," I said.

There were lots of stories about people being captured by jewelry. I was not going to accept the bracelet if I could get out of it. "In the negotiation of words," I said, choosing my own carefully, "it's important for you to know that I'm not human. I hope you won't take offense, but it's worrying to me to put your . . . powerful communication device upon my arm. It might interfere with my own energies."

The two women frowned, identical expressions, and leaned to each other again, touching heads at their temples. Pearl then bowed down to the enclosed bed of Soulwood soil and touched it. When she stood upright, she said, "We do not know how the energies of Special Agent Ingram, with Unit Eighteen of the Psychometric Law Enforcement Division of the Security of the Homeland, might conflict with ours. You have bested us in the negotiation of words."

Before I could assure them that hadn't happened, Opal said, "The woman who practices magic and is called *witch* would be most suitable. Bring her to us."

Less than five seconds later—too quickly for T. Laine to have run up the stairs, which meant the unit was just inside the door, ready to be backup—the door opened and T. Laine stepped onto the rooftop. The door behind her didn't close completely, which reminded me I should have left it open too, and hadn't.

T. Laine gave a formal nod. "I am Special Agent Kent with the Psychometric Law Enforcement Division of Homeland Security, Unit Eighteen. I am a moon witch. May I observe the energies of the bracelet to ascertain they will not conflict with my own?"

"Once it touches you, it will be too late to withdraw," Opal said. "Observe the device as I hold it."

T. Laine said, "My thanks." She studied the bracelet in the hand of the arcenciel. I had a feeling she was studying the arcenciels too. "The energies are strong, but my own seem to be compatible. Do you wish to place the cuff on my arm, or shall I?"

"We will place it. Should we find She Who Guards the Rift first, it will vibrate and a picture of the place where she is held will appear on the surface. At that time, you will be able to hear our voices as we speak, and we will be able to hear yours. Should you find her first, you will tap here." She indicated an indention on the cuff. "You will then be able to speak to us and to call us to you. The cuff will be our guide. There will be no invasion of the privacy of listening until the vibration. We have learned that some things among humans are not for us to learn, such as the honeymoon and the mating."

My eyebrows went up.

T. Laine held out her arm and Pearl slipped the bracelet around her wrist. It shrank as if it was alive and snuggled into place.

Instantly the two women dove off the side of the building. An explosion of light came from below and trailed down the street, so bright the forms of the dragons were lost in the glare. And they were gone.

The door opened again and FireWind said, "Ingram. Kent. Report."

"I'm fine," I said.

"I feel a little weird," T. Laine said.

FireWind lunged for her.

Lainie collapsed in his arms.

FOURTEEN

T. Laine regained consciousness on the utilitarian sofa in the break room. "Water?" she croaked.

With an arm behind her shoulders, FireWind lifted her to a sitting position and held a bottle of water to her lips.

"Tell me what's happening," JoJo demanded into my comms set. She was still in the conference room, overseeing security.

"She's awake and thirsty," I said.

"What day is it?" FireWind asked Lainie while she drank.

She wrapped her hand around his, drained the bottle, and said, "It's a freaking damn Monday in the middle of a freaking damn snowstorm and I feel like I got hit by a freaking damn truck." She pushed the bottle and FireWind away to sit upright on her own. Grabbing the bracelet with her other hand, she tried to pull it off. It didn't budge. "This sucks."

"Is it affecting your magic?" FireWind asked.

"I don't know yet. Give me a bit. I need to run some tests here and in the null room." She swung her legs off the sofa and held her head in her hands as if still woozy. "One good thing, we'll know if being in a null room affects arcenciel magic."

A storm warning screen was up on the overhead system. The precipitation had stopped, the temperature hovering near thirty-three. All the snow on the ground was melting slowly into the ice below, which would only make things messier when the temps refroze at nightfall. The roads were a briny half-frozen mess. Trees were down everywhere. Ice had coated electric lines and brought them down. Even KUB's and Oak Ridge's triple backup power grid, with the arm of the Tennessee Valley Authority to back them up, were no match for localized downed power lines.

Headquarters electricity had held on, and we had Internet and comms. So far.

My brother and two half brothers, Amos and Rufus, had checked on Esther, the twins, and Mud, making sure they had firewood, lantern oil, and formula and that her pipes were okay. Sam had then made it up the hill to my house, started up my tractor, and attached the blade. Like the country boys they were, the three had scraped and snowplowed the slush off the driveways and the road, then disturbed the gravel to give tires enough traction to traverse the hill. When that was done, they checked my pipes and serviced my windmill. There were a lot of reasons to hate growing up in the church, but the attention and skill sets of family were good things.

Then to make sure "the womenfolk" were safe, Rufus was now curled up with a good book on Esther's sofa, his shotgun beside him. He was letting my sisters feed him and serve him coffee while he "guarded the house." Neither of them told him they were far better equipped to keep the house and grounds safe than him, but I was grateful he was there. My half brother with Esther and Mud, and Yummy patrolling the grounds, would provide adequate safety for my sisters. And if a small sad thought reminded me that no one had protected me when I was a young widow, the thought was small enough to push away.

I hadn't decided to stay the night at HQ, but I was leaning that way. Even with the road to my house cleared, it might take me two hours to get home. Meanwhile we were all searching for Soul and Torquemada. But the thing about being a vampire was you didn't need lights, heat, water, or power, and you could stay in a closet in an abandoned building forever and simply hunt humans in a city that was shut down. It would take authorities ages to find the drained bodies, if they ever did.

With that in mind, I checked to see the outcome of law enforcement intervention of the man who had tried to get onto my land, and of the others FireWind had taken in. All had lawyered up and had been released by the prosecutor without charges. They had vanished, of course.

Jo was teaching me how to do a deep dive on all the Spanish names Yummy had given us. I was learning how to search for the history of people on the Internet and the dark web, and it was scary how much there was out there. Some information was totally incorrect, looking as if it had been prepared with a pay-check in mind, but other things I discovered hit the nail on the head. The skill was in finding the same information in different places and not word for word, then piecing a story or a history together with names and dates and a timeline.

Background on Torquemada's people was scant except for the four high-level assistants who had guarded him before he became a vampire. I did discover that two of the original four had entered the States before Jane Yellowrock became queen, searching for the Tarot and for Soul. The two were here when vampires got back their souls. Here, alone, without Torque-mada, their maker, who would have given the vampires stability they otherwise lacked.

One was Inigo.

At some point in the last week or so, the vampires had dis-covered the devil dogs and begun to hurt them. Kill them. I needed to visit the church grounds again. I had questions to ask about the genetic lines of the people buried in church history: plant-people and devil dogs. I stood and walked to the window. The weather was horrible, but the drive to the church was easier than the drive up the hill to Soulwood.

Prepared to be shot down, I took the long hallway to the of-fice where LaFleur and FireWind worked on computers and chatted on the phone.

Occam had driven us to the Nicholson home and was sitting on the small front stoop with my father and my older brothers, watching the children play in the snow. Even the church called off school when there was enough snow to play in. At this eleva-tion and on this side of the hills, it was just cold enough to not have melted at all, the temps at just under freezing, and there were various snow forts, snowmen, and snowball fights taking place across the church grounds to keep the most active Nichol-sons occupied.

The younger children who didn't want to play in the cold were upstairs with the older girls, doing schoolwork and chores, the door to the stairs firmly shut.

The mamas, Mawmaw Maude, and I were alone in the big kitchen, me standing on the table as they took measurements and pinned bridal gown fabric. It was not the way I had planned this interview to go. They were sipping tea and coffee as was their own particular taste, mugs nearby as they worked. They were worried. My call to them had made certain they would be. But they worked well when worried, pins in their mouths, scissors and tape measures on the table.

"Was the church always polygamous?" I asked.

The four women looked at each other, communicating the way only women who had raised a passel of children together could. Mama Grace shrugged and stabbed a pin into a fold of silky fabric. My mama nodded, but she looked down too, her face set in uncertain lines as she draped a longer piece that would become the removable train.

Mawmaw said, "If she was in the church, she would know by now. If she left the church after she knew, she would have taken that knowledge with her."

They were talking about me, around me, in front of me, while sticking pins into me.

"This is church business," Mama Carmel said, her tone stern. "But I agree." She looked up at me and said, "Church business, not police business. You understand?"

"I understand," I said. Didn't mean I'd keep it secret.

"The answer to your question is," Mama Carmel said, "we always was polygamous. We'ns used to have written records back to some place near what coulda been the Mediterranean, back in Babylon times, but places changed names time and time again. Lotsa unknowns in there, we know. The records was copied over and over for a couple hundred years, but no one could read 'em, lines pointing here and there and no way to understand. The recordkeepers figgered they was fulla mistakes after the umpteenth copy, just tracing pointy lines that meant nothing like words. So at some point, they jist wrote down what they knew from the oral tradition.

"But you'un need to know that everything back before the 1300s is jist chatter. It mighta been made up. It mighta been created outta whole cloth to give import where there was none, and we'uns have come to that understanding with acceptance."

"Yes, ma'am," I said. "I understand."

"Starts out, we wasn't even Christians or a church. We was a tribe a heathens." Mama Carmel settled into a storytelling mode, her voice soft, with a telltale rhythm that suggested she had told it before. "Some a our men were particularly good warriors. After a war when only a handful survived, and they beat back the enemy to the last man, they brought back women prisoners, and men prisoners who couldn't procreate, under the care of a man who they called a chief eunuch. They brought home gold and slaves and concubines who looked different from our people, them new folk bein' pale a face with light eyes. The few remaining fighting men took in their own tribal women who had lost husbands, making them wives, and new concubines from the prisoners."

"Forced," I said.

"Is there any other way?" Mama asked.

I scowled at my mug on the table at my feet and wished for a sip of tea.

"There was no other way, not back then," Mama said sternly, "and we'uns don't blame the women, not then and not now. We'uns know that it wasn't any better within the church, not until recently, but the church is changing. Me being appointed a women's elder is changing a lotta things. Now you'un be quiet and listen to Mama Carmel. This is important."

"Yes, ma'am," I said, forcing my face into neutral and my hands to my sides as the mamas stuck pins perilously close to my flesh.

"They integrated households," Mama Carmel continued, "with a hierarchy of wives who wielded control over the concubines. But them concubines was smart and had skills the wives didn't. They taught the wives how to improve their farming and the chief eunuch taught the tribespeople how to write that pointy language. But they was different in other ways too, though the warriors and the tribe we come from didn't know it. Bringing the captured people in, that was what made us what we are today.

"From the chief eunuch, they also learned how to castrate their weak human offspring, so they could control breeding, the way we do sheep and goats and cattle. And some a them concubines had more than jist a gift for farming. They made things grow. They were bred and their daughters became wives. And sometimes even first wives, over the first tribal women, a'cause their offspring was different.

"The original tribal women bred warriors, and the concubines bred farming women. Two lines of people, distinct, and yet merged."

Mama Grace took over. "They stayed put for a few decades and taught the arts of war to the strong sons and castrated the weaker sons, making the less vicious men into farmers, tradespeople, artists. And they inbred too much. Two, three generations later, a new war started and the fighters signed on with the side they thought had the best chance of winning, and became a mercenary army. On the battlefield, they became terrifying fighters." Mama Grace's voice dropped low, as if to share a secret. "Stories called them the Dogs of War. Said that in fighting, they changed shape and became ravening beasts."

All the mamas were looking down, not one meeting my eyes.

The door opened, letting in a blast of cold. Sam stood framed in the doorway, lean and lanky. "Okay to come in? It's getting colder."

"No," Mawmaw said, her voice low and hard enough to turn him to stone. "You tell Micaiah this is the women's story. Y'all go to the church or to your house."

"The women's story?"

Mawmaw stood and whacked the table with her cane. The sound echoed in the empty main rooms. Sam flinched. The look she gave my elder brother should have broken his bones. "Git."

My brother got. While she was up, Mawmaw brought more tea and coffee to us all. Mama Grace added wood to the cookstoves. The two other mamas stuck more pins in me. I was probably shedding a little blood here and there, but not enough to stain the dress.

When they all settled back to the table, I asked, "This shifting. Did it also take place on the full moon?"

"No," my mama said. "Only in battle. We think the *gwyllgi* came from all that breeding too close, creating men for warriors and women for farmers."

Mama Carmel said, "Long before the clans traveled to settle here, in America, that tribe of carefully bred people went west, to the islands, which we think were the British islands, and they intermarried with even more different people there. Very different people. On the islands, in the farthest west-lands they could go."

Mawmaw took over the story, her townie accent clear and crisp. "The people they found in the west-lands were heathens who lived in the earth and in the trees and danced naked beneath the moon. They had been there for thousands of years, from back when there was ice over all the Earth and civilization was a single worldwide seafaring folk, one language, the language of the angels, and there was magic. The remnants of our group bred with the new tribe and again we became one."

"And then, we'uns became Christian," Mama Carmel said, "but our practice of Christianity was different from the Romans, and different from the Christians who came after. And they feared our warrior sons as abominations and our daughters as witchery."

"We'uns heard about the Welsh man," Mama Grace said. "Prince Madog ab Owain Gwynedd. He sailed west and found land. You'uns can look it up on your Google machine."

"Hold still. Not now," Mama said. "You done got stuck."

I was bleeding, but I held still.

"Secretly," Mama Carmel said, "we built or bought boats and went west, to this country. And here we'uns stayed. When the settlers came, they found us. They called our people the white Indians because we had blonds in our tribe and wove our own cloth. Later, when they forgot we'uns was already here, we faked the papers saying we come from Europe. The genes, the genes of the warrior people, the genes of the farmers, and the genes of Welsh and Irish people, they all are still there. Inside us."

Mama Grace said, "Turn a quarter turn." She pushed with a hand and I moved before she took over the women's story. "Some family lines got the farmer genes, and they birth two-thirds females and one-third males from their lines, like the Nicholsons and the Vaughns. Other clans went the other way, and produce to this day a lot of males. Like the Jackson clan. And they all mostly go into the military or the police. But no one became a Welsh *gwyllgi* over here, or a plant-person, until the last generation or so."

"The Vaughns," Mama said, "my family, were farmers and Mawmaw married into them, bringing fresh blood, or so it was thought."

"Unfortunately, the Hamiltons were originally church stock,"

Mawmaw said, "from a Lost Boy who found his way, made good, and became a proper townie, a rich and fancy townie, and he denied he had once been a part of the church. And since his name was stricken from official records, it was hard to find out who he had been or where he had come from. So when I married into the Vaughn clan, I brought back some of those genes. And when one of my daughters married into the Nicholson family line"—she sat back in her chair, looked at Mama, and blew out a breath—"we got what we got."

"Plant-people," I said.

"Plant-people," she agreed.

"The genetics have been followed for how long?" I asked.

"We'uns have records for four hundred years," Mama said. "The two groups have always been careful how often we'uns married into our own and the other lines. And careful to bring in diverse genetic lines when possible."

"Like townie girls who fell in love with the charm of a churchman," Mawmaw said placidly.

"Until Colonel Jackson began to demand girls from both sides of the lines without keeping track of who came from which family lines," I said. Carefully, I added, "And his clans began to punish more diligently from the farmer side." I was talking about Mama, who had been taken to the punishment house and had been impregnated with my half brother Zebulun.

Zeb was from mixed genetic lines, through Brother Ephraim, the Colonel's toady. Ephraim was a man whose body Soulwood had eaten, but whose soul had been trapped and wreaked havoc on me and the land and on the vampire tree until I figured out how to destroy his soul . . .

Was Zeb in danger of becoming *gwyllgi* if he got into a fight? He was younger than I was, not yet seventeen, but sometimes a danger is born, not made.

"I have to make a call," I said, starting to step down.

"You'un will not move, young lady," Mama demanded sharply. "Gracie, secure that sleeve. I have this'un."

A good two minutes later, draped in two heavy afghans to keep my dress from being seen by any wandering eyes, I stepped down from the table and moved gingerly toward a semblance of privacy, managing to not stab myself too much. I peeked out the front door, saw no men, and stepped onto the porch. It was deserted, but my red truck was running in the parking area, Occam sitting in the driver's seat. He looked up at me and I raised a single finger to tell him I needed another minute. Or several.

I dialed Sam. When my true brother answered, I said softly, "I need to talk to Zeb."

"Zeb's gone. Been gone for a couple weeks. Took off with the Lost Boys, when his best friend was taken into town. Causing mischief, most likely."

My heart dropped deep inside me. "No one reported him?"

"Ain't the church way to report a missing boy, Nellie. You know that."

"Sam, I need a list of the last two, no, make it three, groups of Lost Boys, with pictures if you can make it happen. Off the record. I also want something with Zeb's scent on it. Dirty socks. Underwear. Anything that the mamas might have overlooked since he left. And a description of the clothes he was wearing when he disappeared."

"Why? You putting tracker dogs on him?"

"It's possible that Zebulun has the potential to become a devil dog if he gets in a fight." I didn't want my brother to start thinking too much so I plunged on. "I'll get people in town to start looking for him and them. We'll capture Zeb if we can." I remembered the hair—found on the bodies. "And you should know. It's possible the Lost Boys were already taken by some bad vampires. So yes, brother mine. I need a scent item."

My brother took in a slow whistling breath. "Zeb spent the night here after he had a fight with Daddy. I don't think Sara has washed the sheets on that bed. I'll check and bring them to your truck right away. And, Nellie? I can't imagine killing my half brother. But we'll be watching. If one of them things comes to the church land, it won't make it off."

"Any of the young men sent out of the compound might be in danger of changing."

"So we could have a pack of 'em attacking here?"

Or on my land. "Don't start a panic. This ain't contagious. Just let the menfolk know and to be aware. And get that scent item to Occam."

"On the way with it now."

Back inside, I said, "I thank family. I'm honored to have

been trusted with the women's stories. I need to get back to work."

My cell started to ping as Sam sent pictures and descriptions of Zebulun and the latest batch of Lost Boys. As I stood, helpless and full of pins, the mamas took final measurements and began to unpin me enough to get out of the gorgeous dress.

Occam's cell was propped on a cell phone holder so he could use both hands to drive. Even with chains on the tires we were sliding on the ice. The streets should have been deserted, but they weren't. Restaurants were doing a booming business, gas stations were well lit, beer sales were high, and takeaway food trucks were open; the city, which should have been shut down, was partying—which meant the streets were full of yahoos doing ice donuts, tailgating-style beer parties had been set up in parking lots, and bonfires were blazing in backyards.

I had just gotten off the phone with FireWind, LaFleur, and Kent, letting them know that my underage half brother, who had been friends with Arial, was missing and now might be a prisoner of Torquemada's band of blood-servants. Sam had sent me names and photographs, and I had forwarded them to HQ comms.

I asked JoJo the one question that had been burning in my heart. "Will you check the testing and see if there were devil dog hairs on the clothes found at the house where Cai died?"

There was a click and the ambient noise changed. Jo had taken me off the official line. "I don't have to check, Country Hick Chick. There were. You okay?"

The cold shaft of fear I had felt with the mamas solidified. "No. Not really. Okay. Thanks."

I disconnected and made a call to Brother Thaddeus Rankin of Rankin Replacements and Repairs, and his son, Deus. The two had kept my house in good shape and repair when I was a widder-woman, and they also belonged to a church that helped the homeless, including, as needed, any church boys dropped off in the night. They hadn't seen any church boys lately, which was unusual, but they promised to keep an ear to the ground and put out some feelers.

I also studied the description of the clothes Zebulun had

been wearing when he disappeared, wondering if they matched any found at the abandoned house where Cai was found.

While I talked with HQ, Occam had been waiting on a return call from the Montana Bighorn pack's leader.

As we skidded toward HQ, Occam's call was returned. He pulled the cell from the holder, pressed it against his ear, and said, "Thank you for taking my call, sir. Yes, sir. Yes, sir. I know, sir. Yes, sir." Followed by a short silence. I glared at Occam because he could have put the leader on speaker, but I had a feeling that he had things to hear that he didn't want me to know. "How are they integrating, sir?"

He shot me the side-eye and pulled off the road into the parking lot of an empty storefront, a lot that had no tailgate party, and idled the engine. "That's . . . unfortunate, sir. Were the two permanently incapacitated?"

I turned in my seat, pulling a knee up and tucking a foot under the other leg. And glared at my cat-man.

"Yes, sir. I understand, sir. There is a concern that we have more in Knoxville on the loose. Yes, sir. That makes sense. I'll run the ideas by Regional Director FireWind and let you know what he says about sending one of the portable null rooms to you on the next military flight out. Yes, sir. Regardless of whether we ask you to take more of the *gwyllgi*. My pleasure, sir. Yes, sir. And to yours."

The call ended. He looked at me, shrugged with one shoulder at what he saw on my face. "Let me tell this to FireWind so I don't have to say it twice."

I nodded. How did Occam even have the contact number of the alpha of the Montana pack? I knew that Soul had helped save Occam when he was first released from the silver cage the traveling carnival had kept him in for two decades. Had Soul taken him to the Montana pack? I had never asked him about his past, knowing that some things were too painful to be poked and prodded, and had to be offered. So far, his offerings had been only the highlights of his salvation, not the full truth, just like I never talked to him much about John and what happened in my life with him. Details were often painful and unnecessary at first. And sometimes forever.

"FireWind," Occam said when the boss answered. We were on speaker this time. "Occam reporting. I just got off the phone with the leader of the Montana Bighorn pack. They've had an incident with several of the juvenile *gwyllgi* we sent. They were found this morning partially drained of blood, in a bunkhouse used as a holding pen for *gwyllgi* who can't control their shifting and are unable to remain in human form. It's a safe house of sorts, but to protect others from the dogs rather than the other way around, and before you ask, yes, it sounds like a prison, though a nice one, with wide-screen TVs, video games, human food, teachers, and counselors.

"The teenagers were drained by a vampire who disabled the guards and got inside. This morning, the pack tracked her and killed her, but she may not be alone.

"Two of the juveniles have received transfusions and no one sustained lasting damage, but the pack wants a portable null room. I know the Nashville coven had one ready for Kent to take to the Arizona PsyLED office, but I think consideration should be made to the Montana Bighorn pack, especially if we end up needing to send them more devil dog kids."

"I think that's wise," FireWind said. "I'll see how fast I can get a portable null room there, and how fast Kent can be ready to go. However, with the weather, flights will be undependable at best."

"Also, sir, he offered two werewolves to track the vampires here."

There was silence over the phone and Occam looked at me again, his mismatched eyebrows raised. "Call him back," FireWind said after a moment. "Tell him we're dealing with logistics and shipping but will get him a null room posthaste. Thank him for his offer of a tracker, but . . ." He stopped. And he laughed shortly and said, "Remind him that FireWind can shift into a very large wolf and track. And we have Occam, who has a very good nose as well. Next time you make a call to the leader of another paranormal group or species, no matter your personal relationship with them, discuss it with me. *First*." The call ended.

"Oops," I said.

"Not oops. I deliberately went over his head, and he knows it, because I was the most likely to get through. But he has to lodge a formal protest for form's sake."

"I don't understand."

"FireWind and the pack have a difficult history. They have little interest in talking with him, even decades later. And where the pack is concerned, my personal connection will always come before FireWind's order."

He turned in his seat, mirroring my position, but he clasped his hands around his knee, not reaching to me. That body language said something about his state of mind, and so I gave him the space I thought he needed.

"Just like you talking to Mud or Esther," he said, "would come before a discussion with FireWind. Family first."

"The Montana pack is your family?" I asked carefully.

"Soul took me to them when I was set free. I stayed with them for months. They helped me recover. Taught me to shift to human, and to control my shifting. How to hunt. Gave me family, as much as a feral wildcat can have in a wolf pack."

His lopsided grin was charming and I curled my fingers tight to keep from stroking his jaw in a gesture for cat comfort. Instead I nodded, accepting what he was telling me. "Okay. Did you arrange for the *gwyllgi* to go to the Montana pack in the first place?"

"Soul and I did."

"Thank you. Despite what they might become, I want everyone who was hurt by the church's history to get help, and to have an opportunity to become better people."

"Mmmm." Occam gave a single twitching nod, though his eyes were glowing with his cat, and with nothing human. And "Mmmm" was not exactly agreement. He returned to the onerous job of driving through freezing streets.

The pikes had been re-scraped and heavily brined, along with most of the major city streets, and there were piles of dirty snow everywhere. The schools would be open tomorrow, and I needed to get home before dark so Mud could have her school night with me. But I had another call to make too, one I had been avoiding because I didn't want to talk to Gomez at UTMC. But since I was chicken, as we drew near HQ, I called PsyCSI and spoke to the harried-sounding person who answered, "PsyLED CSI, Pinchot."

FIFTEEN

"This is Special Agent Ingram with PsyLED Unit Eighteen."

"What can I do for you, Ingram?"

"Can you give me an update on the forensic postmortem of the human found at the abandoned house this morning, as well as the evidence collected?" I gave the case number, and added, "Specifically, what can you tell me about the tufts of hair you and Knoxville CS took into evidence there?"

"UTMC will be doing the post in the morning. You're welcome to observe. We're still processing trace evidence. What do you want to know about the hair?"

"Everything that wasn't human based."

"Sure, sure," she said, in what sounded like a verbal tic. "I'm not a hair specialist, but sure," Pinchot said, and launched into lecture mode. I had discovered that techs in general—unless grumpy and sleep deprived—were talkative and liked to share their information and knowledge base. "Okay. The nonhuman hair found at today's crime scene. First, though, to know why I'm saying this: human hairs, unless artificially dyed, are generally consistent in color and pigmentation through the length of the hair shaft. Animal hairs may exhibit radical pigment color changes in distribution and density in a short length. We call these changes banding, and in animal hairs, banding can often be used as identifiable features as to species. Morphologically and microscopically, the nonhuman hair samples were similar to cases a while back. Hang on. I have to pull up the case files for the species name."

"No need." I spelled out *gwyllgi*, and said, "It's pronounced gwee-shee."

"Yeah. That's it, thanks. Now I won't have to look that up for my report."

I heard typing as Pinchot entered the information into a computer.

"The hairs from today match the banding of the known *gwyllgi* samples. They also match as to the combination of longer guard hair on top and a shorter fleece hair used by some species as thermal protection, *gwyllgi* included. *Gwyllgi* guard hair can be varicolored, but the tip is always black. The fleece hair is also universally a buff color near the skin and black at the tips. Total match with today's sample."

"Thank you. May I send you a photo of what a missing teenager was wearing? For you to compare with the clothing found at the crime scene?"

"Sure, sure. Send me anything you got."

"Okay. Pic on the way to this number. Can I hold while you compare?"

"Sure, sure. Hang on." Horrible music came over the speaker.

Minutes seemed to drag by as the hideous music played on a loop that surely had been designed to make listeners hang up. That was likely a good psychology to help overworked techs and clinicians.

The music ended and Pinchot said, "We have a match."

My heart fell to my knees at her words.

"Do you have a name?" the tech asked.

"Affirmative." I cleared my throat. "Missing teenager. The clothing belongs to Zebulun Nicholson. I'll make sure the family is notified of the possibility of his . . . being in imminent danger, and PsyLED will also issue a BOLO." A BOLO was a law enforcement term for "Be on the lookout for."

"Is he young enough for an Amber Alert?" she asked.

I went blank on Zeb's exact age. "I'll check. Probably."

"Go for it. I'll make a note that PsyLED Eighteen is handling notifications."

"And, if necessary, may we bring in a tracking animal to sniff the clothing to help us track the kid? Would you allow a sniff test?"

"In the lab? I think it would be fascinating. I'll run it by my boss. Give me a number and I'll get back to you."

I gave my number, ended the call, and slanted a look at Occam. "Family before work," I said. "The clothing matched what Zebulun was wearing when he took off."

"There's no proof that fangheads have your half brother. If he was with a group of homeless boys, they may have scattered."

"Yes. But I know what law enforcement thinks about coincidences. The vampires may have stumbled on the devil dogs when hunting for blood donors. They may have stumbled on plant-people when Ming sent them our way, chasing the Blood Tarot. But however they found us, they surely know my kin are different, just by the taste of the blood. And if Zeb was being tortured, he could have sent them our way, all on his own. You know, 'Stop hurting me and I'll tell you about my half sisters.'"

Occam pulled into the parking lot of HQ and idled the truck. "Your family kept records, even during the Inquisition. We should be wondering if some or all of them fell into the hands of Torquemada back then. Maybe following the case with Jackson and the church and the FBI, someone went looking at Vatican records."

"I've heard different stories about the family and religious persecution. And the Inquisition was here in this hemisphere as well as in Europe. But Mama says my ancestors were mostly in the mountains here by the time Torquemada showed up. I'll tell you later. Right now, I need to read my land deeply, to see if I can find any traces of the souls of the priests. There was one time the land couldn't digest a soul without a lot of help from me. I have to wonder if it's having trouble now."

Occam held out his hand and I took it. His fingers were warm, werecat-warm, and wrapped around mine. My woody nails were hidden in the shadows, which was good.

"We'll report in, finish up written reports," he said, turning off the truck. Occam leaned over and plucked two leaves from my hairline. I accepted them and tucked them into a pocket. "Then we can call your family, have them issue the necessary alerts, and go pick up Mud. I'll fix supper while you read the land."

Occam elected to lope from Esther's to the house, start a fire in the Stanley stove firebox, and get things started for the evening meal, leaving the truck for Mud and me to pile her stuff in later and crawl up the hill at ice-speeds. I also figured he planned to run on alone to avoid my prickly sister. I couldn't say I blamed him.

As the truck cooled, Mud opened Esther's door, letting out Cherry, and I watched her run up to Occam and gambol around. Satisfied the puppy was going for a run with my cat-man, I entered the madhouse that was Esther's home.

My half brother left the house as I entered and nodded at me before he got in his beat-up truck to drive away. His expression said he wouldn't be back anytime soon if he could help it.

Inside, I put on tea. I took over changing a very stinky baby, burping Noah, rechanging his newly wet diaper, and putting him down for a sleep. After pretreating the diapers in the toilet, I put a load of cloth diapers in the washer to soak with Clorox and homemade laundry soap. Mopped up a spill in the kitchen. Changed another very dirty diaper from Ruth and went through the process again, this time agitating the diapers a bit before letting them soak longer. I removed dry clothes from the dryer, dumped them on the kitchen table, removed the dirty sheets from all the beds, put them in an empty laundry basket for the next wash, folded the clean clothes, and put them away before putting fresh sheets on the beds.

My sisters worked around me in the too-small space, chatting about the weather, asking about how the townies were doing, talking about the "wonder chicken" that was still laying two eggs a day, even during the shorter days and the colder weather, and the black snake Mud had carried from the henhouse to a hole in a tree. She had also carried some chicken straw to keep him alive. Black snakes ate poisonous snakes and rats and were mighty handy to have on any farm of any size, but not when they got into a coop. Snakes in a coop got lazy and fat eating eggs.

I listened and felt the cares of the day fall from my shoulders. Even my worry about Zeb eased in the warmth and familiarity of chores and true sisters and babies.

"Tea's ready," Esther said, taking down mugs from a tall shelf. Mud got out honey. I sat with them, unfolded clothes in my lap. As one, we all blew out a hard breath and grinned. "Thank you," Esther said.

"My complete pleasure." I sipped and nodded at the taste. It was an herbal, with rose hips and dried apples and chamomile. "Mud, is this yours?" I asked.

"Yup. I'm'a call it Baby's Finally Asleep tea when I sell it to the townie women. I'm'a whisper to them it's even better with a shot a wine in it."

I spluttered into the tea.

"Not enough to hurt a nursing baby," Mud said, indignant. "Jist a tablespoon."

"Don't laugh," Esther said. "She's right. Ohhh, my feet hurt."

Some people said even a trickle of alcohol could hurt a nursing baby, but the two were spouting church wisdom. "Mmmm," I said, changing the subject. "I noticed when I drove up you're a little low on firewood. I'll remind Sam to split more tomorrow and pick up some chicken feed. You need anything else from the feed and seed store?"

I took down a list and texted it to Sam. Then, as casually as I could, I asked, "Anything new or different about the land or the trees?"

Esther's face went from quietly happy to suspicious in a heartbeat. "Why you'un askin'?"

I laughed and held up my hands as if to ward off a blow. "Nothing, nothing, nothing. I promise. It's just the first snow since you moved here and, since the trees of your house are alive, I just wondered what you could tell about the land through the wood floor."

"Oh. I ain't tried that. Can you do that? Read the land through the floors a your'un house?"

"Yes. And I wondered if it might be even easier since your walls and floors are still alive."

"Well," Esther said, looking around the small living room. I figured she would refuse to do anything related to her being part plant, but she surprised me when she slipped off her shoes and socks. "Let's see."

I know shock showed on my face. Esther was willing to read the land with no prodding? The weather outside might be proof that hades had frozen over.

Mud kicked off her shoes too, so I unlaced my work boots and toed them off. We sat around the table, bare feet on the wood floors, hands spread flat on the table. "Now what?" Esther asked.

"Just think about the trees and the land and how it makes you feel."

"Safe and protected," Esther said instantly.

"Usually happy and loved," Mud said. "But I can't get past the floors."

I took Esther's hand and Mud's and said, "Mud, let's try now."

Together, we pushed through the unfamiliar wood—I felt Esther's presence and Mud's through our feet and our joined hands—and into the earth beneath her house. The mental virtual landscape below us opened, widened, deepened, earth that was dark and sleepy and warm. "Ohhh. Yes," Mud said. She sighed long and soft, as if relaxing in a warm bath.

We all went silent, sharing breath, until Esther said, "We got us some thriving chestnuts. I'm thinking about encouraging a grove. You'uns okay with a grove of chestnut?"

We all murmured agreement.

"That green man is still here," Esther said. "He seems a mite upset."

"Esther, use sign language to tell the Green Knight we want to visit with him," Mud said.

"I don't know how to sign no language, but I done gave him a fierce look and he backed away, like a man should when a woman's mad."

I smothered my laugh.

Wood, living and breathing, was everywhere, strong and resilient, elastic and bending to the air, resistant to, and yet responsive to, snow and ice, full of sap running high and life running deep into the earth. Life and trees, shrubs, vines, fungi, molds, all showing minuscule mutations and health and strength. So much strength. Esther's acre had spread into my own as if joining forces and, like my own, had crossed the drive onto the Vaughns' land and crossed beneath the main road into the empty land there. Her power had claimed a good five acres altogether, and her life force—and the life forces of the twins—had made the land healthy and fecund and bountiful. It was wondrous.

Mud whispered, "I want me some land. I . . . *want*. I want this, what you have and what Esther has."

Quietly, I said, "I been planning to deed you a few acres. You'll have to tend it like Esther's."

"I don't tend nothing," Esther said. "It just is."

"Oh, you tend it," I said. "You tend it by loving your babies and by protecting your babies. The land knows what you feel and what you do. So it helps to protect you and the babies."

"I hear screaming," Mud said.

Leaving Esther on the surface to bask among the trees, I followed Mud's lead, dropping below the tangle of trees and roots, plummeting deeper, deeper into the land beneath. I was familiar with the land all around Oliver Springs, the broken ledges and crumbling scree, even deep into the dark weight and heaviness of the tectonic plates, and deeper yet, to where the spirits of the deep stirred from time to time.

What's that? Mud thought at me. I rose to her and saw the small magma pool I had allowed to rise.

A mistake, I thought back. *Don't tell the land you're cold. It might send warmth.*

Mud laughed and then thought, *I still hear screaming.*

That was bad. *Where?*

Right here. Beneath Esther's yard.

I rose higher, following my sister's mental voice, back up through massive rocks and broken boulders, through water tables, limestone, loam, and deposits of pure clay. To a place in the earth that was filled with energy, energies trapped beneath a shelf of granite a hundred feet or more below the house.

They were red and electric blue, thorny and sharp, a burning green the color of olives. All the energies were indeed screaming. I knew what they were. I had seen trapped souls before, and I knew the land couldn't quite digest them, and the afterlife they should have entered couldn't quite accept them, not in this form, for whatever reason.

I thought at Mud, *The energies are the souls of the vampires that died here a couple nights past. They're still present in the earth and are fighting being absorbed into the next life.*

Hell? They're trying to avoid hell?

Wouldn't you? If that's where they're going? And would heaven be any better for souls like theirs? We have to help them to cross over.

Why? Mud asked.

Because when energies are trapped, they cause problems. Ancient lore tells us that when the deepest spirits of the life of

*the Earth are roused we get earthquakes, tsunamis, shifting of
the poles, even the shifting of the Earth on its axis. But I'm not
sure how to make the souls go on. It's different every time.*

I was trying to figure out how to exorcise the spirits, when a
ball of energy dropped into the unbalanced, erratic, screaming
souls. The ball was composed of burning energies brighter than
my own, brighter than Mud's, brighter than all the vampires
taken together, like a ball of lightning, plasma and power, but
with intent. The sureness of the energy ball, the pureness of its
light, should have meant safety, but it didn't. Something about
the fierceness of it meant fear and pain.

I pulled Mud and myself away, darting behind a shelf of
granite, to watch. The ball cracked open, into a clawed hand.
Lightning ripped from the fingertips in jagged lines and slashed
across the screaming souls. The lightning clawed into the damaged life forces. Shredded them to strips and fragments. And
fed them to the earth.

They were bad, Esther said. *They wanted my babies. Can't
nobody evil be near my babies. Not now. Not never.*

They didn't have time to make peace with the afterlife, I
thought.

Don't matter for the willfully evil. The lightning in the
clawed electric hand sizzled again. *Not on my land.* The last
four words thundered into the earth.

Yes, I thought. But didn't let her hear the question on its
heels. The uncertainty, doubt, and maybe the fear of what my
sister was becoming.

We all three eased out of the land. We were still sitting at the
table, holding hands. Mud's hands were cold and shivering, her
eyes wide and fearful.

Esther released us and got up to check on the babies. "Holy
Moses," Esther cursed. "My babies got leaves."

Mud and I looked at each other and nodded. We had leaves too,
but we could groom ourselves later. We walked into the twins'
room and found them lying in their bassinets, sound asleep. From
their bald scalps grew tiny forests of scarlet maple leaves.

With little pinching motions, Esther nipped off each leaf.
Silent. Her face tight with anger and worry. The babies slept
through the shearing, and when she was done, my sister gath-

ered up every leaf and carried them to the kitchen, where she tossed them into the woodstove.

Esther had leaves too, but I didn't say that. I couldn't think of what to say that wouldn't make things worse and Esther had always hated platitudes. "Get your'un shoes on. It's time for bed." She shooed her hands at both of us, her eyes not meeting ours.

Esther had just sliced and destroyed the souls of vampire priests, with a power stronger than any I had ever seen.

I had one other thing to tell Esther before I left. "Zeb ran away. An invading group of vampires got him. We don't know if he's alive or dead. An Amber Alert went out on him."

Esther stilled. "I like Zeb. Hope they find him."

"Me too," I said softly.

The truck made it up the road, and Mud, silent and troubled, went inside, carrying her things. I put my gear on the third step with a clomp and dropped heavily onto the second one, which had been shoveled and swept clean while we were busy at Esther's. Occam was a treasure.

The wood step was frozen and chilled my backside through my clothing. I was tired and frightened and breathed deeply, seeking the calm of Soulwood, waiting on the visitor I had felt when I pulled my own spirit from the land after reading Esther's and watching her kill.

Yummy, who had been patrolling, walked up across the hill from the south, across the three acres I kept clear of trees, her strides strong and steady, crunching through the snow and ice. She settled beside me with that vampire grace I sometimes envied. My breath made clouds in the darkness. Yummy didn't breathe.

"Nice night," she said after a time.

When she spoke, her words still made no clouds of vapor. She had been outside on my land long enough for her body to acclimate to the ambient temperature. Which meant she was likely below freezing to the touch. Did vampire bodies freeze in the cold? Did they have some mechanism that kept them from freezing? *Antifreeze?* How rude would it be to ask?

Frantic nervous laughter tried to rise through me, but I shoved it down.

"It's cold," I said.

"It is."

Behind us, the Christmas tree lights came on, casting pale reds and blues and greens over the snow. I could hear Occam and Mud talking, their words blurred by the walls. Vampires could hear better than humans, but I didn't ask what they were talking about. I pulled my knees up and eased my coat down over them, wrapping my arms around them to conserve body heat, and waited.

"I have houseguests," Yummy said eventually. "Ming showed up on my doorstep at dawn, Ming and six others."

"That sounds"—*horrible*—"crowded."

"It was. Ming isn't used to being an unwanted guest in someone else's lair. She lacks—let's call it social graces. I found them a place to live. They're moving into the new place tomorrow night. It's a rental unit and will not be up to their standards, but it was the best I could do on short notice, until they can get the clan home and the barns rebuilt."

"Cai is dead," I said.

I felt the jolt rush through her. "How? When?"

"Last night, we think. Torquemada and/or his men tortured him, bleeding and reading, and killed him. I was going to call Ming tonight and tell her."

"My job. I'll do it." After a time she said, much more softly, "It'll destroy her."

"I'm sorry."

"Me too. Cai was a bastard and a pain in the butt, but he was loyal. And he loved Ming with all his heart. My kind don't get true love often in this undeath." The tone beneath the words was angry, not sad, and I wondered if she was thinking about Inigo or the vampire who made her and then abandoned her. "When can we have his body?"

"Tomorrow sometime. I gave your number to the forensic coroner's people to contact. I'm sorry," I said again.

"Me too. I'll head home to tell her, if you're okay with that."

"I'm okay. Don't get your throat torn out or your head ripped off."

"Not on my list of ways to die."

"You have a list of ways to die?" I asked, surprised.

"You don't?" she asked, sounding equally surprised. And then she was gone with a little pop of sound.

"No," I said to the night sky, which was black and sparkling with stars. I closed my eyes and breathed, feeling the tension ease away with each exhale.

The door behind and above me opened. Cherry raced outside and leaped off the porch, landing in deep snow. She bounded up and landed again.

"Goofball," Occam said from the doorway.

"Yeah." I stood and walked up the steps to Occam, and inside. I was pretty sure I was shaking like a leaf—which was actually pretty funny since I had quivering leaves in my hairline and eyebrows and at my fingertips. I went straight to the refrigerator and poured myself a double serving of Sister Erasmus' wine and chugged it down. Then I pinched off my leaves, tossed them and the others I had collected in a pocket during the day into the firebox, and started putting dishes on the table.

After a hearty meal of cheese toast made with day-old bread and leftover soup, Occam said, "We ain't seen a grindy in a week or more." He took a bite of the greasy goodness of bread and cheese, chewed, swallowed, and lounged in the old turned spindle-back chair. The wood creaked.

"Okay. I know that," I said. "Even though Rick nearly changed into his cat, totally out of control, and we have Rettell in town and all that . . . were stuff going on?"

Occam nodded. "Even though. The Dark Queen supposedly helped free an angel from a partial binding and also banished a demon. That might have been the same night that the vampires got back their souls. From what Alex Younger said, the angel's last words to her were that the curses—and we don't know which curses—are either gone or changed. That might have been around the last time I saw a grindylow."

"But we don't know exactly what kind of change, if any," I said.

"The Dark Queen's put out the word, requesting blood and saliva samples donated from every were-creature she can get to agree. She owns a privately run laboratory in Texas that will analyze the samples to see if the were-taint is gone."

"She thinks you'un all might not be contagious anymore?" I asked. I wasn't sure why that sent a shiver of fear through me. It would be a good thing, right? If Occam couldn't infect anyone? And then I understood my spurt of fear. If he couldn't infect someone else, he didn't need me. Were-creatures couldn't infect plant-people. We were acceptable mates to were-creatures. Now . . . Now Occam could have anyone.

Does he still want me? "You think your curse is gone?" I asked. "Do you feel any different?"

Mud looked back and forth between us as she nibbled on her cheese toast. Church children grow up in a psychologically charged environment where they learn early on to be aware of all the emotional currents flowing through an extended family.

"Can't say the last full moon was any different," Occam said, "but I've been hurt. I need my moon shifts more than most." He shrugged. "Maybe just the werewolves were changed, and the change has to do with the insanity of all their females. But FireWind wants all of us to be tested. He's making it an organization-wide mandate. I just wanted you to know." He shrugged again. "I don't care one way or another, but Margot would be thrilled. Her options for finding a mate are pretty limited in Knoxville."

Casually, I said, "Your options of finding a mate just got a lot bigger."

"Done got my mate, Nell, sugar," he said in his Texan accent. "If you're thinking about backing out, you can stop right now. You can't get rid of me, and I ain't going no place."

My heart heated instantly. I was both relieved to my bones and also a little ashamed that I'd doubted him.

Mud sighed. "True love is so amazing."

Occam chuckled, the sound part purr. "It shore 'nuff is, Muddy girl."

A knock sounded on the door. Occam started to stand, but I said, "It's Yummy. Please let me get that."

He glanced at the clock on the old desk and nodded. "We're expecting a wolf shortly. Not a wild wolf. A FireWind wolf."

I stopped halfway to the door. "What's that?" I asked, confused.

"FireWind is a skinwalker and he has some wolf teeth for genetic material as a pattern. He's going to shift into a wolf and sniff your missing brother's pillowcase."

While he was talking, I slipped off my house slipper and put a bare foot on the floor. Through it, I felt the alien presence of a creature on my land. Not big-cat. Not fox or coyote. Bigger. Rangier. Trotting across the ice. Wolf. Aya. A huge *wolf*.

I was used to big-cats. All the were-creatures in Unit Eighteen were cats. I had seen the boss-boss in jaguar form, and to me he was a jaguar, same as werecats. But he wasn't. FireWind could be any shape or form as long as the mass-to-mass stayed within the genetic-code-acceptable range. Aya was . . . other. And now a wolf.

"I gotta see this," Mud said, darting forward.

"This is work," Occam said, catching her shoulder. "You can watch through the windows, but stay inside. We don't need to confuse his scent with ours. And your scent and Nellie's scent will have some family overlay with Zeb's through your mother."

Mud settled narrowed eyes on Occam. "You know about Mama? About Brother Ephraim punishing her?"

"I know. I'm sorry your mama had to go through that."

Mud nodded. "I'll stay inside."

"Me too," I said, privately relieved that I wouldn't have to confront my boss-boss when he was a big bad wolf. I opened the door and welcomed Yummy with church hospitality, and stepped aside.

"He's nearly here," I said to Occam.

"Who's nearly here?" Yummy asked.

Occam looked at my bare foot resting on the floor and a corner of his mouth twitched. "Nell, sugar, you got the best security system on the planet."

Occam maneuvered past Yummy and out the door, stepping into the cold.

"Nell?" Yummy asked.

"Aya FireWind is gonna come here as a *wolf*," Mud said. She raced around cutting off lights so we could see him, but the wolf must have been at an angle just below the porch. We unabashedly crowded around the front windows. I cracked one so we could hear.

"Evenin', FireWind," Occam said. "'Preciate you coming.

Ingram and her sister are inside to keep from contaminating the scent pattern. You ready for the scent item? It's in the truck." There followed a silence and then Occam said, "Hang on." He glanced at me in the window, before trotting down the steps into the icy white blanket.

Moments later, a massive black wolf stepped up the stairs to the porch, his eyes yellow and glowing. They settled on Mud and me in the window. FireWind gathered himself and leaped the few feet to the window, landed, and rose up on his hind feet, resting his paws on the window ledge. Mud squeaked and flinched. I crossed my arms and glared at him. FireWind chuffed, white clouds coating the window and blowing into the air. Mud made another high-pitched sound and the wolf's tongue dangled out the side of his mouth, comically.

"I reckon you do have a sense of humor," I said, "or you do when you're a wolf. Don't worry, Mud. He won't hurt us. He's just jerking on his chain, like a junkyard dog."

FireWind could hear us. His yellow eyes narrowed and he growled. I had no idea what to compare that sound to, but it wasn't at all like Cherry's mock growls.

Yummy growled back. The hair on the back of my neck stood at attention.

Mud crossed her arms, adopting my stance. She said, "That's a dog threat he's making right there."

Yummy leaned to the glass and said, "Don't threaten me, *dog*. I'd be more likely to kill you first."

"Us'un too," Mud said, her face fearsome as a hurricane.

Well. *I'm sure my boss-boss won't be happy with me now.* But I was very happy with my fighting sister. Churchwomen don't fight. Mud was no longer a churchwoman.

Occam walked silently up the stairs to our boss and I was pretty sure my cat-man was figuring where to shoot him to do the most damage. FireWind dropped his front paws to the porch, head down, blowing clouds of mist, and stared at Occam, shoulders raised, ears flat, his yellow skinwalker eyes glowing.

The pillowcase Sam had sealed in a plastic zip bag—the pillowcase Zebulun had slept on his last night on church land—was in Occam's hand.

Moving slowly to keep from riling the wolf-shaped and wolf-acting FireWind, Occam opened the baggie. FireWind stuck his head inside and sniffed. And leaped backward across the porch as if he'd been hit with a cattle prod. He shook his head, his ears rotating all over the place. He sneezed mightly. And then four more times. He did the yoga down-dog position and rubbed his nose with his front paws. And he sneezed, repeatedly.

"Gwyllgi?" Occam asked, his words laconic. "Devil dog?"

Our boss-boss nodded his head up and down and then sneezed three more times, his ruff standing straight up. Mud laughed. FireWind shook his head as if shaking off a punch, then pushed off with all four feet, clearing the railing and the eight feet or so to the ground in a single leap.

Occam resealed the baggie and came inside, a cat-sly smile on his face. He shut out the cold and said, "Boss-boss clearly never smelled a *gwyllgi* while in canine form. The scent is strong enough to choke a goat even in cat form." He tossed the baggie to the desk and laughed when the house cats scattered off the tree at the residual scent.

Mud and I went to the kitchen and put on tea and coffee. Mud had taken my fresh bread to Esther's. I had started a new batch rising and checked to see if the loaves were ready for the oven yet. Not quite. I ladled up a bowl of soup for the boss-boss and scrambled six eggs. He'd be far more hungry than when a were-creature shifted. Weres used the rotational and gravitational force and energies of the moon to shift shapes. FireWind used calories. He'd be starving. I dug out three of my protein bars, made with tuna, canned salmon, and mushy oat groats. They tasted terrible, but the protein made the taste bearable, according to the werecats.

"Mind if I stay around and watch the rest of the show, before I start patrolling?" Yummy asked.

I looked her over, decided she had been well fed at her lair before driving back over, and nodded. "Don't encourage my sister. I need this job."

Just as I dished the odd meal up, FireWind entered the house. He wasn't wearing a coat, just black jeans, black cloth shoes, and a black dress shirt. His black hair was flowing and loose, down to his hips. His eyes were glowing yellow in that skin-walker way.

Mud softly mouthed, "Wow," but didn't say it aloud.

Ignoring us all, he lifted a leg over a chairback, settled into its seat, and raised the bowl of hot soup with his hands. He drank from the bowl, emptying the food without chewing the veggies, noodles, and meat I had quickly chopped in. With a grunt that might have been the word "Thanks," he scraped the eggs into his mouth with the spoon, six eggs, six bites. He didn't chew them either. But he did sigh with the last swallow and said, "Nell, that was delicious. Thank you." Before he tore into the three protein bars.

There was little chewing with the bars either so I placed three glasses of water at his elbow and poured him a cup of hot coffee. He downed a glass after each bar. When he was done, he took the warm cup in his hands and breathed the coffee-scented steam.

"The coffee might be strong enough to get the stink out of my nose. I can detect canine scent in cat form. In wolf form it packed a punch, musky, filthy, strong," Aya said.

Mud, who was holding the baggie, leaned toward Occam, fists balled at her sides, her short hair falling forward. "That's not a *filthy thing.* That's my *family*," she said, her voice soft as falling ice and twice as cold, her body suddenly trembling with fury. "My *half brother.* And his friends. And they had no choice in what they were born, and nobody never taught them how to control what they was or how to be better. So you'un take that back."

When FireWind didn't respond except to raise his eyebrows, she leaned in until her nose nearly touched his where he sat at the table. Leaves sprouted across her hairline and in her eyebrows, and her head looked like an entire forest of mighty trees. "Fine. You wasn't brought up right, to apologize. I get that. But you watch your mouth, *dog.*"

FireWind's face went fully human in shock.

I burst out laughing. "Be nice, Mud," I said through my laughter.

"No. He thinks he's better than other paranormal people. He looks down on plant-people and werecats and probably even Jane Yellowrock even though he's her brother. He's stuck-up and mean just like the bullies at school. And if he don't apologize, he'll wish he had. If not, every patch of ground he touches for the rest of his life will sprout thorns and try to trip him and tie him up."

I was pretty sure none of us could make that happen, but I understood a good threat when I heard it. And I too had caught the insult in his words.

"You have my deepest apologies for speaking out of turn and without forethought." FireWind took the baggie from her hand. "I'll find your devil dog half brother. I'll bring him back to you alive and well if I can. My word on it."

Mud backed away from him and looked at me. "I do not like bullies."

FireWind turned to me and said, "You do know your sister is terrifying, don't you?"

"Aren't we all?" I asked.

SIXTEEN

The dream was sharper than memory, the trees lifting their roots from the earth, but not to race across the landscape like in some fantasy movie. Rather, to shake out the rocks and ancient bones that were tangled there. Disgorging the bones of the plant-people who had been buried beneath the trees. Jumbles of bones fell free: old fragile bones of the aged, strong bones with full sets of human teeth and the weapons of warriors, and the young, delicate bones of children who never made it to adulthood. So many bones. The skeletons assembled themselves and stood, staring at me out of eyeless sockets. Generations of bones. Four were holding their heads under their arms, a brick still wedged in their jaws.

The Green Knight rode up to the standing bones, a banner on a tall stick secured behind his thigh, a mace across his spine. A sword was sheathed at one hip. He carried his lance and a shield. With no guidance I could see, his warhorse turned to face me. Snorted. Blowing green smoke.

Impaled on the lance was the body of a black wolf. Dead.

I sat straight up in bed. Awake. Bones gone. Trying to catch a breath. Gasping. Heart pounding as if I had sprinted a mile at a dead all-out run.

Torquil made an unhappy sound and shook herself. I was alone except for the one cat, the other two upstairs with Occam. Cherry was with Mud.

Torquil crawled onto my lap, only her white body and legs discernible in the dark, her black head invisible, like a headless cat. The house was cold and so were my feet. I scratched Torquil, and then pushed her from me, into the warm spot my body left behind as I slid from the bed and into my slippers. The main room was warmer, the fan returning the warmer air in the rafters down the walls.

Quietly, I added a log to the coals in the firebox. Checked the bread on the hob. The loaves were perfect. With one bare foot, I searched the land. Yummy patrolled. So did FireWind in his more usual jaguar form.

Taking one of the frying pans I kept on the cooktop in the winter, I wrapped it in an old towel, carried it back to bed with me, and slid it where my feet went. I picked up the once-feral cat and put her on my chest so her purrs could soothe me. But I didn't sleep.

We stopped at the bottom of the hill, sliding for a few feet before the brakes caught. We were in my car, not the truck, because the main roads would be completely clear of ice in an hour or two, and the truck's chains would just slow me down then.

School was on a two-hour delay, but even with the postponed opening, it was too slippery for Mud to walk to the bus stop at the bottom and cross the street to the other side, to the edge of land that was now growing a forest of vampire trees, maples and chestnuts. Oddly, not a single car slowed down to gawk at the new trees, probably concentrating on the icy roads and their own concerns. Everything seemed normal, except that Tuesday felt like Monday, and the roads were slick with black ice and the populace seemed to have forgotten their winter driving skills.

"So not fair," Mud grumbled. "I could still be in bed." She was yawning, bored, sleepy eyed, and fell back to sleep in the backseat as I drove. She didn't even bother to wave before she joined the line of wilted-looking kids at the school entrance, dropped off by family for early arrival, probably for the same reasons I dropped Mud off.

At HQ, Occam's fancy car was parked, no dents, no signs he'd run into a tree or a snowbound car. I checked in, admiring the bank-vault-style doors that now protected us, and planned to spend the day following up on every missing person report and any reports of a small pack of large feral dogs.

Close to ten, FireWind stopped in the opening of my cubicle, his fingers on the low walls to his sides like supports. When I looked up, a question in my eyes, I caught his gaze tracking the abundance of growth in the window. He had kindly given me a cubby with a south-facing window and, on the ledge, I was growing three lettuces, two spinach plants, basil, a small rosemary, two kinds of thyme, two mints, and, in its own pot, the new vampire tree sprout.

"It looks like a forest in here."

"It looks like a farm in here," I corrected. Inside something twinged, and the woody roots in my middle and along the bones in my hands quivered, as if in pain. Surprised at my body's reaction, and not willing to let the boss-boss see that, I asked, "Can I help you?"

"You are a strange and difficult woman," he said. "And I fear your sister will be worse."

I frowned. "You turn into any animal you want. Rick and Margot and Rettell and Occam turn into werecats. Soul turns into a dragon made of pure energy or a Bengal tiger. I grow leaves. Honest to God, boss-boss," I swore, "why are plant-people any weirder?"

A smile ghosted across his face and was gone. FireWind said, "I am sorry I upset your sister with thoughtless remarks about your brother's scent."

"Half brother," I murmured, squinting down at my keyboard. "Zebulun."

"I visited Soul's apartment last night before I went home," FireWind said.

He hadn't asked a question or given me important information, so I waited.

"Zebulun's scent was in Soul's apartment."

My mouth opened to reply, but all the potential words stopped. Possibilities flashed through me. "He musta disappeared 'bout the same time Soul did." My face squashed up in thought. "How'd Zebulun's scent get to Soul's? How did he even know about Soul?"

"I was hoping you might tell me."

If Zeb had been working with the bad guys, he mighta been

with them when Soul was kidnapped. If Zeb had been kidnapped *with* Soul, then he mighta been there as a prod for Soul to cooperate. If Zeb had been following the bad guys, then he mighta entered Soul's place after they took her. Or . . . if he knew of Soul through my family, then he mighta been there on his own, looking for help. He mighta followed her scent to her apartment. FireWind had to know all those possibilities.

When I said nothing, and didn't look up from my fingers on the keyboard, FireWind walked away, his strides silent on the flooring. Opal and Pearl were searching for Soul. Rettell had been looking for the two arcenciels in the area. So were Torquemada and his heinous band of men. And they were drinking from devil dogs. And looking for the Blood Tarot.

Good Lord a Mercy. Arcenciels were made of light. I remembered wondering aloud if creatures made of light could travel through fiber-optic cables in their pure energy form and get into information systems.

I saved my work and walked to the conference room, where Tandy was manning comms. "Tandy."

He looked up from his keyboards, his odd reddish pupils widening as he focused on me.

"If a being of light wanted to, could they crawl through the fiber-optic cables, override all the firewalls and encryption, and get information?"

He blinked, his eyes turning away. Blinked again. "JoJo and I have been researching that, Nell. We can't rule it out. But if it is possible, and if an arcenciel is in the hands of an enemy, they might be forced to try. There are a lot of unknowns about your question."

"If it's a possibility, then no security systems set up by the government, any government anywhere, any private company anywhere, are safe. I can't see how any system *can* be safe from light."

Tandy met my eyes again, his bright with delight. "Your brain works in such strange ways."

"Trauma victim." I pointed at my chest. "We always think in terms of saving ourselves from attack. And also, well, I was thinking about attacks by a light being who worked for the government. I remember hearing a while back that Soul can break her way out of a crystal if she's captured. Is it true?"

"We've heard similar things from the Everhart witches in Asheville, the same witches related to Lincoln Shaddock. We've also heard that from the Dark Queen's people. Soul hasn't verified it."

"If she was being forced to help the enemy, even in human form, Soul might be leaving traces for someone to find. And if we locate her, and she's close to a fiber-optic cable, maybe you could set up an escape route for her. A way for Soul to get away from a captor if they forced her into her rainbow dragon form. It might mean having a big crystal here at HQ that she could get into, and that she could then break."

A smile spread across his face, brightening the Lichtenberg lines there. His eyes went off into the distance, unfocused, problem solving. "Beautiful," he said.

I wasn't sure why *beautiful*, but he was seeing things I couldn't, so I shrugged and nodded all at once.

"JoJo and I have been working on several different ways to locate her and to get her free if we find her, each based on any particular current form—human, tiger, dragon, probably others we don't know about. We'll have to have several methods available to rescue her. Yes," he said, "I'll add fiber-optic cables to the list. And when Jo wakes, in"—he checked the corner of a screen—"two hours and twelve minutes, we'll work on it together."

"I want to look through the locked closet where we keep the arcane weapons," I said. "Maybe something will come to me to help us get her back."

"I'll buzz you in. Sign in and out."

"Will do." At the closet, I swiped my ID and opened the door when the green light appeared over the doorsill. Inside were items we had collected at various magical scenes, and items we had from PsyLED central and the military's R&D department. There were null sticks. Weaponized amulets for T. Laine's sole use. An emergency box of sky blue antimagic unis. There was a large crystal—one without an arcenciel-shaped space inside—on the top shelf, and I texted Tandy to remind him we had one.

At the bottom of the closet, sitting on the floor, were three empty containment vessels. Containment vessels were used to capture and hold any demon, uneasy spirit, noncorporeal magical being, or whatever we might find harming humans, provided we could get the magical thing inside. We'd had them since the demon situation, when local witches had had to . . . help me with a demon. It had been difficult, and would have been immeasurably easier had we had the vessels back then.

Rumor had it that PsyLED HQ in Langley had a whole null room, in a level five secured space, built from reinforced concrete, that was full of the vessels, imprisoning everything from djinn to fae. Rumor was often based on fact. I wondered what I could capture underground, like evil souls who refused to pass on. I wondered if an arcenciel could be caught in one. And what Soul would think of that question.

I signed out one of the vessels, locked the closet, and went to my car, where I secured it in the backseat. Each containment vessel cost enough to buy a mansion. I hoped I didn't have a wreck and total the car and harm the vessel. I tossed my army blanket over the vessel to disguise it from opportunistic passersby, and locked my doors with the fob.

Back inside Unit Eighteen's HQ, I wandered to my cubby. As I walked, still trying to make sense of Zeb at Soul's apartment, I had a second bit of blinding brilliance—though I was the only person who would ever notice that brilliance—that I should track every overnight report of annoying *howling* dogs.

Minutes later, I hit pay dirt. There were four reports of howling dogs. I raced to tell the bosses. LaFleur assigned Occam and me to check them out.

A bit after lunch, my cat-man and I drove toward the first howling dog location. It was near the Egwani Farms Golf Course, where we slogged through the rough—that's what golfers called the brush and unmown grass around a hole—to discover a litter of puppies and an abandoned mother dog in distress trying to deliver a pup that was simply too large for her small body. Fortunately there was a veterinary office a few blocks off the golf course and it only cost us a small fortune to have the bitch seen to, the puppy birthed, and a week's boarding paid for until the vet could try to foster the small family.

The second howling call wasn't much better. It was a small dog that had been attacked by predators and eaten. The tracks didn't resemble devil dogs', more like a small family of foxes', so we didn't spend much time at that one.

The third howling call had come from behind the Kroger in

Seymour, on the far side of the river. The body in the snow had once been human. He appeared, from the lack of blood, to have been dead and frozen before he was eaten, and he hadn't been tortured, which gave me some comfort but didn't help him at all. We took pictures of the body, which was lying face down, with a naked back and arms exposed.

As Occam followed animal tracks into the surrounding area, I called in the death and studied the animal tracks around the body. I was guessing that a hungry pack had feasted here, and compared them to pictures of devil dog tracks from back when I was a probie.

They were not the same.

Occam trotted to me, his body long and rangy, his hair hanging into his face. He opened the door and levered himself into the driver's seat, turned the car on, and cranked the heaters up to high. As we waited for the local police, wildlife, and crime scene people to arrive, Occam stared ahead at the body, silent. I could practically feel his turmoil, but I gave him space. I grew up in a church where women who pestered a man oftentimes had a black eye at the next worship or devotional. I knew the signs for when to not ask questions, and after a few long minutes, when the seats got warm and the air heated, he finally asked the questions I knew he had been avoiding.

"Nell, sugar? You think this man was one a your Lost Boys? And you think *gwyllgi* . . . ate him?"

"No, cat-man," I said gently. "His hands are too old, his body too stringy. This was a homeless man, maybe a vet, which breaks my heart. He had military tattoos on his upper arms, and scars that mighta come from service injuries."

Occam blew out a breath and said, "I'm right glad to hear that. And also not glad."

"Lookee here." I turned so he could see my footprint research. "Coyote tracks have this little bump in the . . . I guess you call it the palm, of each front foot, and the toes all point directly forward. The coyote back feet are different and have a much smaller palm, with usually only two toenails showing. But here." I handed him my cell. "These are pics of *gwyllgi* tracks. Note the palm on the back foot is larger than the coyotes', and the outer toes point more out to the sides, like regular dogs. But unlike regular dogs, they have longer claws that often curl down and lift the toes just a bit. We don't have any *gwyllgi* tracks here."

"Okay. So a homeless man, already dead, was eaten by local coyotes." He looked into the rearview. "Local LEOs are here. Let's turn this over to them and check out the last scene."

On the fourth site of howling dogs, we got lucky.

Occam called it in to HQ, asking for marked cars to seal off the area.

I called it in directly to FireWind, saying, "Aya. I think we found *gwyllgi* tracks in the snow. The devil dogs appear to be being tracked by humans. Or maybe vampires. And the track line is melting. If you want in on this, in wolf form for tracking, you need to get here fast."

FireWind was typing, the clackity keys not stopping as I spoke. They went silent and he said, "Address?"

I gave him the address in Kingston, near an assisted living facility.

"Is there a place I can shift?" As in, get naked and change forms in private.

"We can make something work," I said.

After hanging up, I stared at the crime scene.

The site was bloody, the kid's body torn apart. But not by dogs or wolves. By vampires. The skin had been scalded off his lower legs. Then he had been drank down, unhealed fang wounds torn through at the throat, groin, and shoulders. It wasn't a feeding. It was an attack.

The boy's arms and lower jaw had shifted form, into a reddish black devil dog. It looked as if he'd died in midshift.

There were devil dog tracks all around, most overlapping the human shoe prints. I had a bad feeling the young man had been tortured to death as a way to force him into *gwyllgi* form. And maybe as a way to call more of his kind to the scene.

I knew him. Gad Purdy. He had been one of Zeb's best friends, along with Uriah, from the Lambert clan, which made him my cousin to one degree or another. Zeb had played with Gad, Uriah, Harmon Stubbins, and two boys from Colonel Jackson's faction growing up, and though the friendships had been tested when social services had raided the compound and taken

the womenfolk away from the Jackson alliance, Zeb's friendship with Uriah and Gad had survived.

The Tennessee Department of Children's Services and the
Department of Human Services had been after the church for
human trafficking and child endangerment, and everyone knew
I had played a part in the government agencies descending on
the church. I figured everyone still living on the compound had
strong feelings about me and the role I played in the raids and
the continuing legal oversight.

But Gad . . . He and Zeb had been close. I opened my tablet
and looked at the names on the list of Lost Boys that Sam had
sent, knowing what I'd see there. Uriah, Gad, and Harmon were
among the most recent group of Lost Boys sent to live away
from the church.

Uriah was the reason Zeb had run away, to be with his best
friends.

How many of the church boys—young men—were devil
dogs, created to be shape-shifting warriors, bred to fight and to
kill? And what had Torquemada known or discovered about
them? Had he discovered something in the Coda?

Overhead, in patches of blue sky, prisms of light danced and
flickered. Arcenciels flying over the city. Even as I had the
thought, an arcenciel darted down and hovered above the body,
wings flapping, gusting a downdraft. Pearl. She hissed at me,
somersaulted, flipped her tail, and disappeared.

FireWind appeared around the corner in human shape, dressed in
jeans, his white dress shirt, and a PsyLED navy jacket, a comms
system on his head, the mic at his mouth, a gobag on one shoulder.
Comms were crackling in my earbuds with FireWind ordering up
PsyCSI and connecting with Kingston PD and the state lab.

He walked straight to Occam and said, "Secure location to
shift?"

Occam walked around the corner and up to a small notch in
the warehouse wall that I hadn't noticed. He turned his back to
the notch, FireWind slipped into it, and Occam kept a lookout,
glancing at me once to make sure I was okay. My cat-man,
keeping watch over me. It wasn't necessary, but I was learning
to find his protectiveness kinda sweet.

Minutes passed. In the distance, police unit sirens wailed as local cops sped to the scene, running lights and sirens. I got out of my car, adjusted my jacket so my weapon, badge, and name tag could be seen.

A marked city unit pulled up and slid to a stop on the icy slush. I walked carefully across the melting ice as the skinwalker black wolf slid out of the notch, the gobag the man had carried, now around his neck, twined with his comms system. FireWind approached the body, walking into the breeze, sniffing.

I held up my ID for the officer. I pointed at the wolf and said, "He's with us. Tracker dog."

"Ain't got no vest or leash," the officer said.

"Don't need one," I said back.

The cop made a huffing sound of disbelief. Occam joined us, so I fell back. I heard him begin a soft-voiced conversation and I joined FireWind, watching as the boss-boss began a sniff-search.

The black wolf stopped on a patch of ice-free parking lot and studied the body. Sniffed high in the air and then dropped his nose and began to make large circles. Nose to the ground, he went off into a patch of trees, returned, went off a hundred feet or so toward the road. Came back.

Other law enforcement units arrived and took charge of sealing off the crime scene.

FireWind trotted to me, which I didn't expect. I'd have expected him to go to Occam. The black wolf sat at my feet and looked up—not that far, as he was a huge wolf—into my face. He tapped the ground with a paw four times.

I asked, "Four priests?"

He shook his head no, which looked so funny I had to force a laugh down. And then I figured out what he was saying. My heart sank.

"Four Lost Boys."

He nodded, waiting.

This was going to be a game of Q&A. I wished Unit Eighteen had bought the button thingy, where a dog could press a button and get a word spoken aloud. We hadn't planned to use the boss-boss as a working dog. Hindsight and all that.

"Was one my brother? Half brother?"

He nodded once, his glowing yellow eyes on me.

"Was it vampires that killed Gad Purdy?"

He nodded. Tapped the ground five times. Five vampire priests. He had their scent.

"Can you track them all?"

FireWind nodded and shook his head. I took that for a maybe and figured it depended on a lot of factors. He grabbed the mic of his comms in his teeth and pulled on it just as Occam reached us.

Occam dropped low, onto one foot and the other toe, looking from the comms to the wolf. "You want a comms set with a GPS on it? So we can follow you on a tracking app?"

FireWind nodded.

"Okay. I'll stick a GPS device on it."

FireWind nodded. His tongue lolled.

Occam carried FireWind's rolled handful of clothing and shoes to our vehicle and rummaged in his largest gear bag. A minute later he returned to the boss-boss wolf and threaded a GPS device onto the gobag near the comms system around FireWind's neck.

"Do us a favor," Occam said. "Stick close to roads as much as possible. Assuming they didn't have a vehicle close by and disappeared in that, Jones and Dyson should be able to follow you as you track them. If you get close, make a sound so we'll know to find you on foot."

FireWind made a chuffing-woofing sound.

I tapped my mic. "JoJo? You got that sound? You ready to track?"

"Affirmative. FireWind, can you hear me?"

FireWind made a different sound. Kinda like a low-pitch, basso whistle.

"You can call in your team and we'll take them down," Occam said. "We'll stay close. If you run into trouble, you make a third sound. We'll come weapons drawn."

FireWind growled, low enough to make my chest vibrate.

"Copy that," Occam said.

Jo said, "It's got a range of one square mile, boss. If we lose you, you may not know it, so I'll check in every three minutes. If three minutes go by and I don't check in, backtrack until you hear me."

FireWind made the basso whistle of affirmation and trotted

into the woods. Behind us, two different CSI teams pulled up and parked. Occam said, "I'll stay and work the scene. You follow FireWind.

"Jo?" he said. "If they get more than five miles away, inform me and I'll stop here and follow."

"Copy that, Occam," she said.

"Jo?" I said. "Now that we know these are church boys—men, I guess—and all but one are eighteen, there's no way to create a missing person report, is there?"

"Their families can."

I blew out a sad, tired breath. "The church doesn't care about Lost Boys."

For a former churchwoman, tech could be trying. Nothing about tech was intuitive. By the time I figured out Jo's map and tracking screen on my tablet, FireWind was three-quarters of a mile away and I had to hustle to keep him in range. I took side streets that wove in and out of neighborhoods and across major thoroughfares, and still I lost him twice. Both times I extrapolated based on his general direction, asked Jo for advice once, and managed to cross his path again. However, he was headed exactly nowhere in an awkward direction in terms of streets. Until he approached a bridge.

I realized FireWind was tracking Zebulun heading home.

I tapped my mic and asked, "FireWind. Are the boys still together?"

He made the yes sound.

"Are . . . Are they in human form?"

He made the growl-negative sound.

"They're in devil dog form, ain't they?"

He answered yes.

"Are they still being followed by a bunch of vampires?"

He made the affirmative sound again.

"FireWind, I have a feeling they were heading to the church. Being chased by crazy vampires. In the middle of the night."

He made the low growling sound. I had no idea what it meant in this case, except something bad. I sighed into my mic. "Yeah. I agree."

Zebulun had gone cross-country toward the church. In devil

dog form. Vampires were fast. When they ran, they popped air out of the way. How had Zeb stayed ahead of them? Zigging and zagging. Never stopping. He and the other three boys were killing themselves trying to get away.

As I drove, now able to get slightly ahead of FireWind, who was following by scent, I punched a button on my steering wheel and told the system to call Sam.

"Nellie," Sam said, his voice sounding distant. "Hang on, let me wipe off my hands. I'm greased up to my elbows working on the old horse-drawn plow, replacing the connection rods."

I heard water running and splashing, and his voice continued in the distance. "We have horses, and we have old equipment that costs less to keep working as long as we can rig parts, and with supply line problems and the cost of fuel, it's getting cheaper to use the old stuff for a while. Mama Carmel says we'uns ain't no Mennonites, but I say we *are* farmers so we got to find a way to make a living." His voice came clear again. "What's up, sister mine."

"Zebulun has been confirmed as a devil dog. He shifted last night when one of the Lost Boys was taken and killed by vampires at some point in the night. Zeb was heading toward the church. Four-footed. If he hung on until dawn, if the vampires didn't catch him, he's likely either still trying to get there, or is on the church grounds, hiding."

"Nell—"

"He can't help what he is, Samuel Nicholson," I said sternly. "Not any more than I can help what I am or Mud or Esther or the twins. And what he is ain't contagious so there ain't no reason to shoot to kill. You'uns get your kids to safety and set a trap. And capture him and any of the others who show up in dog form. *Alive*. You hear me?"

"Nell—"

I hung up on my brother and gunned the motor in an ice-free patch of road. I spoke into the comms system. "FireWind. Did you hear that? I'm heading to the church."

I heard a chuffing sound as I took the next left. I told FireWind which roads I'd be using to take me to the church. "I'll need you to tell me where—or if—they crossed over onto the church grounds."

He chuffed again, and suddenly he was just in front of me.

All two-hundred-plus pounds of black wolf standing in the middle of the street.

I slammed on the brakes and skidded on a patch of ice before the tires caught. I opened my door and yelled, "You stupid dog. I coulda hit you'uns!"

FireWind's head lifted as if he smelled something stinky, his eyes holding me down.

"Ummm. Okay, sorry, boss-boss. You scared the heck outta me." When he didn't move, sitting in front of my car as if blocking it, I asked, "You wantin' a ride? I'm in a hurry. Best make it snappy."

FireWind's eyes went squinty, staring me down. He trotted very slowly into the scrub at the side of the road and I pulled over, still breathing too fast in reaction.

I heard a click and LaFleur said over a private channel, "Ingram." I realized he—and everyone else at HQ and in the field—had been listening in on everything I said.

"Ummm. Sorry, boss. I didn't mean to be . . . whatever that was . . . to the boss-boss."

There was a hint of laughter in his words when he said, "We'll meet at the entrance of the compound."

"It's as good a place as any to start hunting, but Zeb was never stupid. If he's heading home, he'll go in through a back way. Like through my land. So I'm heading home and will start searching at the boundary."

"I see. One of us should go to the compound's entrance. I'll send T. Laine there. She may have some amulet that will let her find magical tracks. I've never asked that particular question. Where else should we start searching?"

"If all of the remaining kids are in dog form, and if they all managed to evade the vampires and cross the river safely, then either of the properties to the sides of my land are likely entrances. So go up my road, past Esther's, then hike in on the left for the Stubbins property, which is where the kid named Harmon Stubbins is most likely to seek sanctuary, or drive past my house and park on the right where the deer stand used to be. The one all a y'all destroyed when you was keeping the churchmen from spying on me. If you're four-legged, I suggest you track right, into the Vaughns' property, around the house out of sight, and back toward the church."

Rick said, "I'll send a cat to the Vaughn boundary where the church land meets yours, and two others will take the Stubbins side. I'll meet T. Laine Kent at the front gate."

He went silent, and I stared at the scrub on the side of the road, glad it was clumped and piled with ice. Otherwise I was sure I'd be staring at my naked boss-boss.

"Are you and FireWind all right working together?"

It would be hard going, steep uphill on icy footing, to the top of my land, where the new cell tower perched. Then a cliff drop down to the church land. I was about to say we'd take forever, but FireWind, in his gobag clothes, walked out of the scrub, wearing light sneakers, and slid into the passenger seat. His black hair was loose and flowing, not braided, and he looked warm despite the lack of layers. Just the jeans, white shirt, and sneakers.

"We'll be just fine. Ingram out." I turned off my comms as my boss-boss opened the door and slid smoothly into the passenger seat. The door closed softly.

I swiveled in my seat and said, "Something you ought to hear, FireWind."

"Other than your apology for your tone?"

"I apologize for my tone. I'd have felt a lot worse and my tone woulda been a lot meaner if I'd hit you with my car."

FireWind inclined his head as if he understood I had been angry for almost hitting him. He pulled his hair around and began to braid it.

I reached into the console, found a rubber band, and placed it within easy reach. "There might be a lonely woman or two in the church compound who will offer you something. Food, drink, wine, rest, a bathroom break, cookies, bread, steak, and their own bodies. To accept *anything* from anyone, other than my family, implies a distinct and unmitigable interest. You will be considered interested in the possibility of marriage if you accept anything up to sex, and married by the church if you sleep with anyone."

FireWind's black eyebrows climbed toward his hairline. "Thank you for the warning, Ingram. If I am in human form, I'll make certain to decline with the *proper gentility*."

As opposed to my fussy tone. Gotcha. I didn't say that part. I pulled into the traffic and headed home on the ice-patchy roads. Overhead, sunlight broke through, and everything every-where glistened. It was so bright I stuck my hand into the console again and found a pair of sunglasses by feel and slid them onto my face. I also reached behind the seat and grabbed my gobag, the one with the food bars in it, and placed it on the console near the elastic. He'd be hungry.

FireWind finished braiding his hair and tied off the end, opened and devoured three protein bars, and drank a large bottle of water. When he had wolfed it down, a thought that made me smile, he took over comms and told the entire team what he'd discovered as he tracked the kids.

My hands clenched on the steering wheel when he described the scene where one of the injured devil dogs had fallen behind. The vampires had captured him. There was no indication if he was still alive. It wasn't Zeb. But that didn't make it okay. Three kids still on the run. Last night. Alone.

Expecting FireWind to shift back to wolf, I parked my vehicle in front of my house and ran around to the back at the shed-porch. The door stuck from all the wet weather, and I had to put some muscle into a hard yank to get it open. The door rammed back, into me, and dislodged the rusted iron horseshoe that had been hanging over the door since I moved in with John and Leah. It nearly hit me on the head and I caught it in midair, surprised but rather proud that I had seen and caught it. I set it by the low step and searched for a machete, a rope, a carabiner, and my leather yard-work gloves.

Cherry went nuts and raced into the enclosed space, accepted some pats, and went back inside. The cats peeked out the back window, decided I wasn't interesting, and vanished.

Instead of shifting, FireWind followed me and when I came back out said, "I need a weapon."

I handed him the machete.

"I need a *gun*," he said. He held up the machete. "Not a *knife*."

"Wrong. That's for you to cut yourself free if the tree objects to you being on the land. And a gun won't help you fight the tree."

"Ingram. What—" He stopped. "You think the tree will object to my presence?"

"It knows you as a cat." I shrugged and led him back to the car. Together, we drove as far up the hill as possible, to a spot where the snow was still solid and pristine except for animal tracks. I parked, got out, and dropped the car's floor mat to the ground, sat on it, and put both hands flat on the ground.

"Ingram." His voice was hard and commanding. I opened my eyes and focused on him. "Attempt to *not* get buried in roots this time."

I gave him my happiest grin, watched his face react, and shoved myself into the earth, through the snow, and found the roots to the vampire tree. I closed my eyes and it reached for me, showing me the close-up face of the Green Knight, no visor but looking mad. To FireWind I said, "Give the land a drop of your blood, right here in front of me."

"No. I do not share my—"

The earth erupted around FireWind's feet and before he could move, roots and vines had climbed to his knees, over and beneath his jeans. He didn't twitch except to say, very softly and very . . . politely, "Ingram?"

"You left the machete in the car, didn't you?" I asked.

"Mmm-hmm."

"Don't fight it. The more you fight it, the worse it gets. And it will take your blood if you don't give it." I let a faint smile cross my face. "It grows thorns four inches long."

I heard a folding knife open and felt the drops of blood hit the snow-covered earth. They splattered into the Green Knight's hand and trickled over his gauntlet. To the Green Knight, I thought, *This is my superior, a skinwalker. He has hunted on my land in cat shape. You know him. He means me no danger. He's welcome on my land. Have others of my family, in the form of devil dogs, crossed my land?*

I saw a vision of dogs racing past. One vampire followed. The thought came, *Not yours.*

I jerked at the words. The knight didn't talk to me.

The vision changed and I saw vines and roots and thorns trap and pull the vampire beneath the ground. *Not yours,* he repeated.

He meant *Not Yummy.* He showed me an image of a vampire, male, naked, pierced by thorns all over, trapping him with a long thorn through his belly like a stake. Inigo was asleep, buried in the land not far from me. Sam and my half brothers would be very unhappy that two dogs and a vampire had gotten so close to the church in the night.

How had a vampire gotten so far up my road?

The Green Knight showed me the vampire getting out of a car on the Vaughn property and walking-popping after the devil dogs. He had been moving so fast that the vines hadn't been able to trap him until he stopped.

Between my knees, the earth moved. I opened my eyes to see all the gold that had been on Inigo's person. Six rings and two solid gold chains with crosses on them had erupted out of the ground. There was also a terminated quartz crystal on a gold chain. At this rate I'd be rich. I closed my eyes.

Where did the dogs go? I thought at the knight.

Here.

I saw a vision of the Nicholson house. Under the foundation, curled up next to the entrance to the root cellar, were two dogs. They were shivering and afraid. The way a tree feels when fire, or a farmer, is near.

How did they get through your branches? I thought at him.

I saw an image of dogs growing hands. Bleeding on the tree. Offering a sacrifice. With the hands they went high, into the limbs. The vampire had been less . . . wise.

Okay. Yes. They are mine, as is the skinwalker.

He thought at me, something that might have been *Mate?*

No! A . . . political alliance. Does the skinwalker in human form have safety to cross the land?

He nodded once.

The vines and roots withdrew from FireWind and the boss-boss got back in the car really fast. I said, "The tree accepted your sacrifice and it won't eat you now."

To the tree, I thought, *I have given the shape-shifter in human form a sharp instrument to carve a way through to the land where you were . . .* I searched for the right word and there wasn't one. *Where you were born. After we are there and safe, I will ask you to please seal the breach behind us. Will you do this small request?*

He nodded.

I almost said thank you, but stopped in time. To some para-normal creatures of myth and legend, the phrase *thank you* meant a gift given and a gift owed. I didn't want to owe the tree anything.

You are gracious. I opened my eyes and was pleased to see a single root pull away from each hand. Nothing had penetrated my flesh. I made fists. The roots under my skin were again more prominent, contracting and relaxing with the motion of tendons and muscles before they settled deeper into my flesh. Dang tree had—what?—put a communication device into me?

At the thought, the vines in my flesh and the rooty place in my belly quivered as if an ax had struck home. *Holy moly.*

However. This was something I would have to deal with, emotionally at least, another time. I wasn't sure I could deal with it on a power-struggle level ever.

I opened my eyes and tapped my mic. "FireWind and I have acquired the trail of two *gwyllgi* and one vampire at the hard north boundary of my land, where it meets the church boundary. I recommend all the big-cats shift form and head to the church as humans, in your cars. The tree feels—" I stopped. Hungry? Territorial? Possessive? I settled on: "Difficult."

I stood up, grabbed the pad I'd been sitting on, and crunched across the snow, back to the car. I noted Aya had gotten in the driver's seat, not the passenger seat. I had the fob, so if he'd intended to take the car and leave me, he couldn't.

"This time when you leave the car, bring the machete," I said. "You'll be hacking a way through, and sniffing out where they entered the land. I want to know how they and the vampire trailing them got through to the church compound."

"Certainly. I accept my new job description." There was a hint of amusement and sarcasm in the tone.

I chuckled. I'd heard Daddy use the same tone when his wives ganged up on him.

SEVENTEEN

It was easier going than I had expected. FireWind narrated the blood trace as he hacked and sniffed with his human nose, asking questions, which I didn't answer, and saying things, which I didn't reply to, and ending up in a running monologue that included things like: "How did the dogs get up the tree? When the vampire jumped up there too, he left behind a blood trail." Hack, hack, sniff, sniff. "A great deal of blood here. All vampire." My underdressed boss-boss pressed a hand to a tree, and his eyes followed the blood up, into the branches. "He climbed the tree, following the dogs, but either he was injured by a fall or the tree hurt him. Did the tree put out vines with thorns?"

I didn't reply. FireWind, who was not usually so talky-talk, kept talking, hacking a path through the trees for us, and sniffing.

"Here's a hole where the vampire landed. More blood trace. But why does it smell like more blood is underground?" He knelt at the depression on the ground, a place where snow and mud and leaves and broken branches were all mixed together. He looked up at me, a frown firmly back in place.

"You are growing leaves in your hair, Ingram."

I made a soft sound, trying to figure out how I was going to get my half brother and his last remaining friend somewhere safe.

Still kneeling, FireWind went back to examining the site and expounding on his discoveries. "Dogs dropped from the tree and landed at the spring just there, drank water, rested a bit. Ah. This explains how they climbed the trees. They have both handprints and back paw prints. They're both dog and human, like the hybrid forms my sister can make. They climbed back up there, on that tree. The vampire stopped here." He indicated the depressed area where the ground had been disturbed. "I think he had a machete too. Look at this cut on this young tree."

It was bleeding red sap. I said, "The fence is just ahead. The church installed one at the top of the hill, after the last group of people just dropped straight down. That means climbing."

"Or." He looked up at the sky through the bare branches. "We can go over like your brother did." He pointed up, into the limbs of a vampire tree, where bloody thorns suggested how the boys had gotten over, though not how they had managed the cliff on the other side of the fence. Vampires could handle the fall. Boys not so much, not even in *gwyllgi* form.

I pulled the rope out of my pack, released it, and slipped the carabiner through the loop at the end, ready to tie it to the tree. I said, "Boost me up. I'll go over first and you follow."

Without response, the boss-boss boosted me up so I was sitting astride a wide limb with no snow or ice but signs of blood on some thorn tips that fell off as I watched. I secured the biner to the rope and tied a loop in the other end for my foot. I patted the tree. "Thanks for the way over. You can close up the way through now."

To FireWind I said, "Come on up." The boss stepped back, took a flying leap, and swung up into the tree like a kid on monkey bars, to land straddling the limb behind me. It looked a lot like the Wild West way of mounting a horse, and from the softness on his face I figured he thought about that too.

"We can do this one of two ways," I said, facing forward so I could tie two loops in the rope—one at the bottom, one about five and a half feet above, give or take. Girls in the church weren't taught rope tying except for gardening knots, but I had been a farmer with John. I knew my knots. "You think you can let me down with my foot in the loop? Without letting me fall or bang against the cliff wall too much?"

"I'll let you down," he said, "and then shift to wolf and get down my way."

"You'll be real hungry. Try not to eat too many people."

The boss-boss snorted.

A shape-shifting creature on church land. Three of them, counting the boys under the Nicholson house. Lordy mercy. I just nodded, pulled on my gloves, grabbed the upper loop with one hand, and put my left booted foot in the loop at the bottom.

FireWind eased me off and down, and the cliff went by at a steady rate as he lowered me hand over hand. Skinwalker strength.

When I was on the ground, he dropped the rope and I coiled it around one shoulder. Checked my weapon. Wished I had a tranquilizer gun. I didn't want to kill a devil dog. Not even one who had been the result of Mama being punished. My half brother had never done a single thing wrong in his whole life. He deserved a chance to live. If he could control himself and not eat people. I thought about his human-shaped hands. That had to be a hard form to achieve, so maybe the boys had learned some control the hard way—by running from enemies who wanted them dead.

Noises came from the cliff wall, and I stepped away to avoid being hit by rocks, boulders, or dead tree limbs that FireWind might knock loose. Shortly, my boss scrambled down the cliff, leaping from one tiny outcropping to another, and landed in wolf form near me, black against the snow that was still on the ground here.

I dug three protein bars from my bag, opened them, and tossed them to FireWind, one at a time. Doglike, he snapped them from the air, fangs flashing. I gave him some water from a bottle, which was messy, but he grunted what might have been thanks. No longer starving, he nosed the ground and began a systematic sniff-search for where the boys had likely landed.

I followed him as he found and trailed the devil dog scent. The fleeing boys had kept to the back of the houses, and under oversized greenery, leaving few tracks, and since we took the same route, no one noticed the humongous wolf and me. Yet.

On the heels of that thought, I saw Balthazar Jenkins and two other men walking away from the general direction of the Nicholson house. I grabbed a handful of FireWind's ruff and he stopped, looked up at me, and then followed my eyes. Jenkins was part of the Jackson clan and he had never been fond of me. He was among the faction that had wanted me dead when I was twelve. They moved out of sight.

When we got to the root cellar entrance at the Nicholson house, FireWind sat and stared at the entrance to the root cellar and then at the wood door that led to the underside of the house's foundation. With his right front paw he tapped the ground.

"Two boys?" I asked.

He nodded.

"In dog form?"

He nodded.

"No vampire under there, sleeping away the day in undead form?"

He shook his head no.

"Do me a favor and stick close by me so you don't get shot."

FireWind showed me his teeth, but more like a "they can try" expression than a Big Bad Wolf eating Red Riding Hood–type snarl.

Before I faced my family, I reported in to HQ. Rick had shifted to human shape and was waiting at the front gate with T. Laine. I ended my report with the words, "FireWind in wolf form and I are going to talk to Daddy about sanctuary for the Lost Boys under the house. You want in on this family gathering?"

"Wolf form? Is he in danger from your family?" T. Laine asked.

I laughed and said, "I have no idea. I guess it depends on how cute he can look and how well he wags his tail."

This time I got FireWind's full fangy snarl, but I just laughed more. For some reason, the huge wolf and the man wearing the form no longer scared me. For a former churchwoman this was more than satisfying. It was something to celebrate.

With the wolf at my side, I walked around the house to the Nicholsons' front door. There was something almost symbolic about walking in armed, wearing a badge, a paranormal creature at my side. I was a churchwoman no more.

I knocked. FireWind sat beside me, his head reaching my midchest.

The little'un who answered the door squealed and threw herself at the wolf, screaming, "DoggieDoggieDoggie!" She latched onto FireWind's neck and squeezed. My boss froze, his yellow glowing eyes wide as a human's. He seemed to forget to breathe. His amber eyes met mine in horror.

I grinned, wondering where I got the mean streak, patted his head, and said, "Nice doggie."

Mama Grace was suddenly standing in the doorway, her eyes as wide as FireWind's.

"Morning, Mama Grace," I said. "I assume the toddler with

her face buried in fur is one of the grands? This is FireWind, a wolf, but very playful, and very safe for the young'uns."

Mama Grace was holding her chest as if her heart was about to pound out of it. She said, "Dear Lord Almighty. My gran'baby, Annah. Nell. Get her away from the wolf. Please."

Not letting anyone but the wolf see my amusement, I peeled the little girl away from FireWind's neck, lifted her by both arms, and placed her in her gramma's arms, finally seeing her face. She was ecstatic at the big-dog hug. "She's grown a foot for sure," I said. "May we come in?"

"Both of you?" Mama Grace squeaked, her grip so tight on Annah the little girl cried out.

From deeper in the house, I heard Daddy's limping footsteps and the faint thump of his cane.

Mama Grace was rattled, so I slid into church-speak again to provide comfort. "I promise the wolf won't hurt no one. Did Sam tell you'un about the . . . the boys? FireWind's helping me track 'em and we'uns need to talk to Daddy. Then y'all might want to call in the leaders of the Nicholson faction."

"And him?" Her eyes traced quickly from the wolf to something behind him.

I glanced back and then to Daddy over Mama Grace's shoulder. "That's my other boss, Rick LaFleur. Yes. Him too."

Daddy took Mama Grace's shoulder and pulled gently, guiding her back into the house and toward the kitchen. He took her place in the doorway, blocking it, standing taller than I'd seen him stand in quite a while, back straight, no weight on the cane, and looked his guests over, evaluating. "Welcome to my home," he said. "Hospitality and safety while you're here. Guests are safe in my home so long as they don't bite no one." He stared at the wolf, clearly recognizing the wolf wasn't a normal wolf. "If they bite, then they get shot. With silver."

In the background we all heard multiple shotguns being readied for firing. Three young men appeared next to Daddy, my half brothers Zeke, Harry, and Rudolph, each prepared to protect the home. With silver, which would probably kill FireWind. And kill a devil dog, come to think of it. And it was my fault they were loaded with silver. I had told them to be on watch.

"Family council," I said. "Impending crisis. Adults only. Kids upstairs, not outside to play."

All sorts of emotions crossed Daddy's face. In one I caught a hint of blame, directed at me, for bringing trouble to his door.

My heart went cold. New leaves sprouted in my hairline, rustling. FireWind turned his head and sniffed my side. He looked at Daddy, sniffed, and a low rumble started. I thought it was an earthquake, but it was the wolf. Growling. Protective.

I put my hand back on his head and said softly, so only Daddy and the three boys could hear me, "I am not responsible for the actions of generations of evil men who forced women to be their sex slaves, nor for evil men who ousted their sons, throwing them into the cold to live or die, when they reached their majority. *I* am not responsible for the twisted and twined bloodlines that produced plant-people or devil dogs. *The church is.* So if you want to blame someone or shoot someone for the mess you find yourselves in, you blame the church's way of life for however many hundreds or thousands of years they lived this way, and bred with other species of paranormals and created what we are today. You blame *them.* You shoot *them.* Not me, not my friend who is trying to help, no matter what he looks like."

Daddy opened his mouth to speak, but I wasn't done.

"I've been hounded and threatened and manhandled and shot at all my life with little to no help or protection from *family.*" I leaned in, my eyes locked to my father's. "I'm here to help. But it will be the last time I'll help if you cast blame my way. Mote, see spar," I said, reminding him of a Bible verse.

Daddy blinked, his blue eyes unexpectedly growing wet. "I'm sorry, Nellie. It's always easier to blame others than to take responsibility. Welcome into your'n home, and your guests with you'un."

He turned and thumped back to his favorite rocker. He sat and said, "Family council. Beccah, take the young ones upstairs. Everyone sixteen or over stays, boys *and* girls. We got trouble. And we'll face it together, as we always do."

Zeke murmured, "Throw them into the cold?"

Harry joked like the teenager he was, "That's cold, man."

Rudolph whispered to me, "You'un're talking about the Lost Boys, ain't you'un? No one will tell us about them. And Zeb done took off looking for 'em."

"Yes, Rudi, I am talking about the Lost Boys and the devil

dogs. And the plant-people like me." I plucked off a leaf from my head and held it out for them to see before I stuck it in my leaf pocket. "Put them rifles on safety and back where they go. You'uns ain't shootin' nobody today."

A silent human-shaped wereleopard and a Cherokee skin-walker at my back, I walked into my childhood home.

After the necessary introductions were made, coffee was poured, and pound cake had been offered and politely refused, Rick said gently, "Thank you for agreeing to speak with us. Some of the Lost Boys were captured by vampires for food."

All the mamas and most of the kids gasped softly.

I spotted my brother in the background. Sam wore a hard expression on his face, as if he already halfway knew what was about to be discussed. When he saw me looking at him, he nodded once.

LaFleur didn't wait for questions but plowed on. "Somehow they got away, and the vampires pursued them. We think Gad Purdy was captured and killed by vampires last night, though full identification is still pending. His death forced the others in the group to shift shape into *gwyllgi* and run. Two of those are under your house."

"Two devil dogs . . . are under *our house*?" Daddy repeated.

"Yes. They stink of shame and confusion," Rick said. "They are afraid of what they have become and what is happening to them. They are seeking shelter. And hospitality. They are not inherently evil. They simply *are*."

Daddy accepted a cup from my half sister Sabtah, then sipped his coffee and rocked for a while, the runners not quite smooth on the old floors, thumping softly. The mamas and the elder boys and girls watched him, their eyes drifting often to my leafy hairline and odd woody fingernails, to the black wolf now lying at my feet, and to the beautiful, white-haired, Louisiana-born, Frenchy-looking man sitting in the chair at my side. "And who are these shape-shifters beneath my family home?" Daddy asked.

Sam turned his blue eyes to me, his gaze affirming that he already knew who we were talking about. His lips thinned into a hard line.

"Zebulun Nicholson, for certain, and a boy we think might be Uriah Lambert are under your house. They are, we think, in dog form."

FireWind chuffed agreement.

LaFleur said, "Special Agent Occam has sent word that Harmon Stubbins came through the Stubbins property and may be hiding in one of the outbuildings there. All the boys we have identified except your son, Zebulun, were among the last group of Lost Boys ostracized by the church."

I moved in my seat to catch Daddy's attention. "Zebulun is only half Nicholson, through Mama, so really half Vaughn. His other half is through Brother Ephraim," I said gently, "from the Jackson side. Had he been your'un, he mighta been a plant-person. Or not. Or he mighta never changed at all, because maybe he'da stayed here safe, and not been forced to fight for his life on the streets. Fighting for one's life seems to force the change on us, plant-people and devil dogs both."

All the mamas looked down at their laps. Their hands were tightly clasped, the stress showing in their faces.

"You said they had to fight. Them dogs we let you'uns send to the werewolves for training?" Daddy questioned, his eyes on FireWind and then traveling up to Rick. "Some were real young. The Colonel's faction let them be attacked? Made them fight until they shifted into abomi—" He stopped. "Until they shifted into devil dogs?"

"Yes," LaFleur said. His pure white hair caught the light like a halo, his black eyes sparkled, and his prematurely lined face caught the shadows and the light. I watched a few of my half sisters eye him as potential husband material. Rick ignored the interested looks from girls young enough to be his daughters, maybe, and continued. "Or subjected them to biting and other . . . exceptional means . . . to force the change." He meant torture, like the Boot, but he didn't say it. "Except for the very few who were born in dog form, even the very young children had been traumatized to force the shift."

Daddy shook his head, the motion weary and despondent. "I made a decision and a promise to Carmel when we first married that we'd never let our own go to the Lost Boys without our help. We'uns put away money jist like we done for the girls as dowry, so I could find a place for them in town, get them jobs, help them join the military, or help them go to trade school if the church forced them out. We figured when the next batch came up to be transported away, some of our'uns would be forced to make a decision what they wanted to do with their lives." Daddy looked at his sons, love in his eyes. "Sam was a keeper. Amos and Rufus too. But that was my three, all I could keep as my own. Zeb, Zeke, Harry, Rudolph, Rethel, and Narvin woulda been among the ones to be judged and removed come spring."

My half brothers exchanged startled looks, and Rethel and Narvin looked to be getting mad.

Sam stared at the floor, his jaw working as if he silently chewed words he wanted desperately to say aloud. He had already known his younger half brothers would be sent away. From the tension in his shoulders, I could see he had fought against it and lost.

"It might yet kill me," Daddy said, his voice breaking, his eyes welling and going red, as if the tears burned like acid. "Kill me to let my boys go. But I won't be able to fight the ruling of the other church elders." He pulled his handkerchief and blew his nose, wiped his face, and rocked again, the runners thumping, thumping on the wood floorboards in the silent house. He watched the five of the six sons he had named, as they took in their likely fates. Didn't any of them look very happy about being thrown out. "You'uns'll have a start. Best as I can do. But I never thought about one of mine being a devil dog."

"But Zebulun isn't yours, sir." Rick turned his attention to Mama. "What do you want us to do with your son, Mrs. Nicholson?"

Mama flinched just the tiniest bit and focused on FireWind. "Mr. Wolf Man. Nellie trusts you'un. Can you'un take him?"

FireWind shook his head no, the motion odd on his wolf body.

"FireWind is not always a wolf, Mama. He has no pack."

Rick LaFleur said, "Your boy will need a pack."

To the gorgeous white-haired man sitting beside me, Mama said, "Can you'un capture him and send him to the werewolf pack, where the others went?"

"We can. It's expensive for the pack to feed and clothe and educate the boys. The church has been making payments for the ones there now, but it isn't enough."

"How much more does the church need to pay?" Daddy asked.

LaFleur named a figure that made me want to cry and made Daddy wince. "And if you send them more boys," my boss added, "that will increase the cost of board and school."

"We'll find a way," Daddy said. "I'll talk to the elders."

"*We'll* talk to the elders," Sam said. "All our faction. Amos, Rufus. You too."

The elder brothers nodded. Sam wasn't the eldest Nicholson son, but he had always led the way.

LaFleur's cell made a faint sound and he looked at the face. "Occam and Rettell have the boy located at the Stubbins farm," he said.

"Can you'uns get the boys to safety?" Mama asked. "They get caught here, they'll get kilt. Burned at the stake at the very least, by the factions that hate anything not fully human."

Knowing I was speaking cruel words, I said, "It's easy to hate something not fully human, while denying you, yourselves, ourselves, are not fully human, and probably never have been."

Mama closed her eyes and bowed her head so low I could see only her bunned-up hair.

LeFleur said, "I've tracked canines before. I had the presence of mind to bring a large cage. It's out front of your home in the pickup truck. PsyLED can take them in and arrange transport." He looked at his cell phone again and then at FireWind. "Kent is on premises. She has a *sleepy time* working readied. Once she casts it, would you be willing to pull them out from under the house? Then we can go to the Stubbins farm and get that one."

"A vampire's buried on my land," I said, "asleep with thorns in his belly, underground."

"Will he be safe there until dark?" Rick asked.

I shrugged and answered truthfully, "I don't know."

"We can try to backtrack from the crime scene"—Rick meant where the Purdy boy was killed—"to the rest of the vampires and hopefully stake them and arrest them while they're asleep. We have the Dark Queen's permission to take them. And save Soul and free any other prisoners."

FireWind chuffed agreement and stood. He trotted to the door.

LaFleur said, "Thank you for the hospitality and the coffee. Ingram, we'll see you at the Stubbins farm."

"He ain't eaten," I said, indicating our boss-boss. "He needs meat."

"I'll take care of that," Rick said. He and FireWind walked through the door and out into the warming day.

Which left me alone with my family.

"It's time to tell the young'uns the women's stories," I said. "The men and boys too. They have a right to know who they are and where they come from. And what they and their offspring might become."

"What do you mean, what we might become?" Harry asked.

Sam's face looked like stone. "And our children?" Sam asked. It seemed he hadn't heard the women's stories either. I wondered if SaraBell, his wife, had known. He looked at his father. "Daddy? You'un said we got no problems. You'un and the mamas keeping secrets?"

The resultant anger of the Nicholson parents was not pleasant. But it did afford me the chance to get out before Mama turned her ire on me for letting the secret cat out of the invisible bag.

I got to the rear of the house just as FireWind backed out, pulling the second *gwyllgi* by the scruff of the neck. My half brother's eyes were closed to red slits from the spell T. Laine had cast, but most of his face and his hands were still human. He was scrawny, his black coat ragged and bloody where the fight and the thorns had torn it.

Both boys were loaded into a large cage, with water and dog food in bowls and several fluffy blankets placed at the back for when they woke up afraid and trapped.

Sabtah ran out of the house, carrying two bags. "Change a clothes for both," she said. "And Zeb's things. I . . . Tell him I love him."

"I will," I said softly. "I'll see if I can get a mailing address so you can write letters."

"Don't bother. Daddy won't let me write." With those terse words, she turned and ran back inside.

The members of Unit Eighteen got into the two vehicles they had driven to church land. The rest of the team was waiting for us at the Stubbins farm. FireWind, still a wolf, rode with Rick in a pickup truck with the *gwyllgi* cage in back. I rode with T. Laine, her car leading our short caravan to the abandoned farm of a former church member clan. She didn't need directions. We had covered a nasty crime scene there once already. We didn't talk; I wasn't in the mood and T. Laine seemed to understand that.

When we arrived at the Stubbins place, on the shadowed side of a steep hill, the property was still iced over and slick. Lainie's tires were unable to get traction up the drive, so we parked and walked the slippery hill, stamping down with each step to break the ice until we reached the side of the abandoned house where Occam and Margot, in big-cat form, had trapped the devil dog. Rettell had shifted to human and was dressed in a pair of sweats and thin sneakers. She was holding a weapon in a two-hand grip, her aim centered on the dog, in the corner of the low wall in front of the house.

T. Laine tossed an amulet at the dog. The dog stumbled and went down, asleep in a heap. Lainie turned and touched Rettell's shoulder, murmured something to her, and pressed down on the military service weapon. Rettell removed the round in the chamber and holstered the gun. "The military wants the dogs," Rettell said.

T. Laine said something else.

"You think I don't know that? So when the dog got away, into the snow, and LaFleur sent his people to chase, I was ordered back to HQ. That's my story. That's what needs to be in your reports."

The military woman went to the pickup truck and climbed into the passenger seat, her back to us.

Rick raised his brows. FireWind chuffed, a clear interrogative.

T. Laine said, "JoJo found her orders. Tandy confronted her about them last night and she didn't even bother to lie or deny. Rettell came for the arcenciels, but her orders were amended when the devil dogs appeared on scene. She didn't know they were *young*. And now the military knows about the Montana Bighorn pack having some. The pack needs to beef up their security."

FireWind growled, the sound vibrating.

T. Laine looked surprised. "You already knew," she stated.

"FireWind spoke with the pack leader last night," Rick said. "He's aware there's danger. He updated his defenses, moved his people, and is prepared to take in more *gwyllgi*. The dogs are fierce and strong, and most have integrated well with pack life." His face went hard as if reliving something bloody and terrible. "Today's military has never fought a fully trained and equipped shape-shifter pack. If they show up there, FireWind says they're in for a surprise."

Today's military . . . But perhaps a military in the past had fought a pack of shape-shifters? Maybe with FireWind part of the fighting?

"Is the Montana pack a safe place for the boys?" T. Laine asked.

"You got a better idea?" Occam asked. He had shifted and trotted around a building in human form, wearing lightweight clothes. "They stay here, they stay doped up and in cages. We don't have the skills, the personnel, or the facilities to keep humans safe from them, and them safe from humans. They'll be safer there than here."

FireWind showed his fangs in what might have been amusement. Or a threat. It was hard to tell. But it looked as if we were colluding to keep the military from knowing about and confiscating our *gwyllgi*.

Aya jumped over a low gate half-buried in drifts, as if the ground wasn't slick, and gently picked up the reddish black dog in his jaws like a grown wolf might lift a puppy, his fangs not piercing flesh. He carried the boy to the back of the truck, where Rick took him in his arms. His black jacket and shirt were immediately smeared in blood and mud and covered with black dog hair. Moving gracefully, his hands and motions gentle, he loaded the dog into the cage with his friends and piled the blankets closer.

FireWind leaped into the bed of the truck and lay down next to the cage, his jaw on his front paws, his eyes on the boys. I had expected none of the kindness they showed the church boys. Many of the churchmen would have killed their own *gwyllgi* outright. But these men, who knew nothing about them, were being kind. It made me ashamed of my own family.

Rick locked the cage, pulled a tarp over it to keep out the worst of the wind. "Margot. Shift, and you and Occam go pick up lunch for us all. I'll drop Rettell off at HQ with Jones and Dyson and see that the boys are put on a plane to Montana immediately."

"How are you going to get a flight out today?" I asked.

Grimly, Rick said, "The Dark Queen has a small jet. I plan to beg for her help." He looked at the truck. "With the military involved, I have a feeling she will agree, and might even foot the bill."

Without waiting for us to respond, Rick got in the truck next to the big-cat he was in heat with, and drove off in the direction of HQ.

Margot trotted off behind a wall to shift. T. Laine, Occam, and I stood in the cold, waiting.

"Rick didn't want to call Jane Yellowrock," I said.

"No. Pretty sure he didn't want to contact her on her honeymoon," Occam said, "but this is a personal request. Not a PsyLED request. The DQ is responsible for things vampires do, and vampires killed a human kid and forced others into *gwyllgi* form and then chased them until they were . . ." He stopped when T. Laine looked away. Softer, he continued. "This falls under her responsibility as queen. She'll help. And if she shows an interest, and claims the devil dogs, the military is likely to back off. Word is, Yellowrock is trying to form an alliance with all the vamps, all the packs, and independent paranormal creatures to force the U.S. government to recognize them as citizens or set them up permanently as independent nations, under the same part of the Constitution that governs the tribal Native Americans. She even approached the covens."

I glanced at Lainie, who was staring across the small abandoned farm, her eyes unfocused. "How did that go over?" I asked her.

"The council of covens said no thanks." Her voice was unyielding, defensive.

I let the tone and the information settle inside me. Occam had said the queen was trying to set up *independent* paranormal creatures. T. Laine was one of very few covenless witches. I wanted to butt in and ask more questions, but her lips turned under as if holding in her thoughts, as if every choice came with problems attached.

"Pizza," I said.

"I could eat pizza," T. Laine said, accepting the change in subject with relief. "*You* need to talk?"

"No. Except to say that my family is both horrible and wonderful. I kind of . . . hate them while I love them. You know?"

"Yeah. Family is always a mess. So are covens, especially when the one you were born into lets you down. Then you have chosen family and . . ." She stopped, her face screwing up.

Margot was stepping gingerly across the ice in human form, dressed in sweats that hung on her.

Suddenly Lainie laughed. "Chosen family. That's us. Unit Eighteen. Even with asshole FireWind in charge."

I gave a small snort. "Yeah. A witch, a bunch of were-creatures, a skinwalker, a guy who reads emotions, a human hacker."

"And a plant-woman. She plays a very important part for the rest of us. She and her land are the soul of us."

EIGHTEEN

The day had warmed. Lunch was very, very late, and tasted even better because of the stress and the hunger: more take-out pizza with a salad from my window box garden, a silent meal while we all typed up our after-action reports. I had already switched my chair for another and so the seat didn't feel maggoty.

FireWind, still in wolf form, ate his own take-out food, an entire rib section—the part of a steer that provided the rib eye roast, rolled rib roast, and standing rib roast—on the floor of the break room, the raw meat on a newspaper to absorb the blood. He finished it fast and went to shift into human, padding down the hallway to the locker room.

There were a lot of things going on politically in the world, things I kept abreast of through online newspapers and media sources, because that was one church teaching I agreed with: know your historical politics, current politics, and legal rights; know what is at stake in every election and with every law passed or vetoed—or you lose your rights and history repeats itself.

But the politics of the microcosm were harder to keep up with: the politics in law enforcement, the petty disagreements between agencies, the changes in financing and diversion of tax-payer money, the change in leadership in different organizations, who had been caught with their hand in the cookie jar or the honeypot and who hadn't, who was on the way up and who was on the way down, who was a dangerous hothead and who was cool under fire.

FireWind had been in law enforcement in one capacity or another, under one name or another, for a hundred years. The addition of a queen over the vampires and the total reorganization of the European and North American vampire political power structure wasn't something I understood at all. But it was clear that Aya was torn between the protocols and demands of PsyLED, the military, mundane law enforcement, the dithering of Congress about the status of paranormal creatures like us, and the power offered by his sister, the queen. That kind of internal struggle about external political struggles was affected by history, love, family, and the demands of honor. All that pulled at him.

Or at least that was how I read his silence and the emotions that flitted across his usually stoic face as he returned and ate ten pounds of deli beef in one sitting. FireWind finished his second lunch and reached for a piece of pizza. It disappeared in two bites. He went into the break room and returned, his eyes settling on Occam. "Thank you for cleaning up the bones."

"Thank Margot," Occam said, not looking up from his computer.

"Not a problem," Margot said, not waiting for the thanks, her fingers flying over her keyboard.

Aya returned to his chair and wiped his hands fastidiously before saying, "The vampires have Soul. They may have more devil dogs held captive, possibly being tortured. Their lair will not be where we expect it to be. It may be much more heavily fortified than we expect, or we may find the trail simply disappears. I will have the best nose and the best defenses if we are attacked, so if we find them, I will shift back to wolf form. We have three hours until sunset. I want everyone in human form except me."

Rick frowned, but no one argued. It had been phrased as an order, and when FireWind used that tone, he expected to be obeyed.

"Rettell. Have you informed your chain of command that PsyLED headquarters in Richmond has placed restraints on your removing any paranormal creatures? And that if you attempt to do so, you will be disarmed and placed in a cell?"

"I didn't phrase it quite so blatantly," the woman said with a twisted smile, eyebrows high, "but they are aware that the Dark Queen is *personally* involved, *while on her honeymoon*, and that she is most unhappy at having to 'deal with politics during this joyous and private occasion.' That's a direct quote from a certain three-star general who had plans for *gwyllgi*. Jane Yellowrock's personal interest has changed things." Her brows arched up higher. "Must be nice to have family in high places," she said, in what sounded like a direct challenge to FireWind.

"I didn't make the call," FireWind said calmly, "though I would have had Rick not taken it upon himself to speak to an honorable and kind woman who has the power to help others instead of use them."

Rettell glared, knowing the barb was aimed at her personally as much as at her bosses. "I have free rein at this time and permission to act as I see fit. Within reason."

FireWind asked, "'As you see fit'? If we find a more dangerous situation than expected, can you offer resources?"

"Yes," she said, "but that horny wereleopard sitting across from me and I need some time off soon, because me beating him up won't work much longer."

"I'll authorize forty-eight hours' PTO for him once the vampires are contained or true-dead."

"Good enough." The lieutenant colonel didn't seem very happy about getting Rick alone. She didn't seem very happy about much of anything right now. Mostly wry, irritated, and maybe a little bit tired of the politics of being a female werecat in a male-human-run world.

It was late afternoon when we returned to the site of Gad Purdy's death. The city's and PsyLED's crime techs had been over it extensively, and the body had been removed to PsyLED's headquarters in Richmond for a more thorough necropsy than UTMC could do. Not an autopsy, done on a human. But a necropsy, done on an animal. Gad had died horribly, and still mostly in devil dog shape. There was little we could learn at the scene itself. The snow was gone, the blood washed away, leaving the site clean-ish, but even with the cleanup, FireWind's nose was on high alert. He was tired and scrawny, having shifted several times in twenty-four hours, but he'd eaten a huge raw turkey and another twenty-pound roast after he shifted back to wolf, so he wasn't looking too terribly starved.

Before he shifted, he had told us he planned to start at the center of the previously bloody site and work out in a spiral, tapping the pavement every time he found a scent marker that was vamp or *gwyllgi*. In a system worked out by LaFleur and Rettell, FireWind used his right front paw for vamp and his left front paw for one of the boys, and he ignored the scents left by techs, cops, and others, such as our small group.

The wolf started in the center of the kill scene, and with the first sniff, his hair stood on end and he began to growl, that low, ominous vibration I had felt at the Nicholson clan home. He put his nose down and sniffed, his nostrils quivering, his entire body tense and taut, his tail down in a rigid position. Moving outward, the black wolf began to walk in a growing spiral.

The rest of us worked the outer perimeter, finding tracks in the melting snow. But there was little to say how all the primaries during the crime had arrived at the location or left it. Even the vampire tracks appeared in the woods at the edge of the parking lot and then seemed to disappear into nowhere. And with the snow melting, I feared that scents and prints would trickle away faster than we could keep up.

But FireWind was smart. After he had been over the entire site and trotted into the woods, all around the parking lot, and all around every building near us, he trotted up to me. Irritated, he bopped me on the hip, shook his head at me, showed me his teeth, and made noises that sounded as if he had stomach cramps. "If you need to poo, go poo in the woods," I said.

He chuffed at me in a sound that was full of irritation, and loped to LaFleur.

The wolf repeated the irritated sound and jogged back to the area of the kill scene, then raced and leaped into an open dumpster. He didn't stay inside long enough to sniff it out. He just leaped back out of the dumpster, landed, and bounced up and down on his front paws.

"Soundboard?" Rick asked.

Aya chuffed his *yes*.

Rick said to the rest of us, "Leann and I ordered a soundboard off an online store. PsyLED refused to budget for it, so we used personal funds. We recorded words and alphabet for it last night."

We . . . So many uses of *we*. And *Leann*, not Rettell. I turned my head to hide my smile.

Rick and Rettell got a soundboard out of her government car's trunk and unrolled it on the cracked pavement.

The uniformed woman said, "It's a one-of-a-kind button and word soundboard, created for intelligent creatures—were-creatures—to talk to the human-shaped." Across the top were three rows of the alphabet in QWERTY formation for words that had to be spelled out. Across the bottom were buttons for complete words, punctuation, and emotional context.

FireWind familiarized himself with the soundboard and tapped out, "Vampires up. Landed here." The recorded words were vaguely Rick-like, but metallic too, as if there had been some kind of filter on it.

FireWind walked to the dumpster and tapped it with a paw, then looked up at the building beside us, to which I had paid no attention. It was an empty but well-kept warehouse.

FireWind returned and tapped, "In."

"They were inside the warehouse?" I asked.

FireWind tapped, "Yes."

"Are they there now?" Occam asked, glancing at me, probably all worried that I might be in danger. He was smart enough not to say so.

FireWind tapped, "No."

"They had a vehicle?" LaFleur asked.

"Yes," the board's pseudohuman voice said.

"Okay. Let's get a warrant and go inside to see what might be still there," Rick said.

We got a warrant fast. The snow had kept crime down and the judge was available to issue it almost instantly. As there was no owner around to complain, and the paper warrant was on the way via marked unit running lights and sirens, FireWind had T. Laine break the chain, and the door swung wide. The building had electricity, lights on in the entry.

After telling us he would sniff out the place first, we were prepared when the black wolf went in, sniffing for weapons, blood, hostages, vampires, explosives, magic, and rodents. That last one he hadn't actually sounded out on the keyboard, and was just me thinking. I didn't speak the word aloud, but I wore a grin when I entered the building, weapon drawn, heading right, in front of Occam, where we cleared offices with no furniture, no electronics, in a building that had minimal heat and less insulation in the metal walls.

Once the smaller rooms and functional bathrooms were cleared, we joined the others in the large area to the rear. There was nothing in the great open space but mattresses on the floor, and cages.

Eight cages. All were empty. Most had bowls on the floor and blankets in the back, larger than but similar to the cage PsyLED had procured for the *gwyllgi*, who were on their way to Montana. Four of the cages had blood on the bars and mesh sides; urine and feces were puddled on the floors.

Two cages were encircled by quartz crystals, tied onto the heavy-duty wire with string, like bizarre Christmas decorations. One cage had broken crystals, the other had fully intact crystals. All the cages were large enough for humans to stand up inside, and when he saw them, LaFleur said a word that might have been a curse. Or a prayer. "Scion cages," he said. "Was Soul kept in one?" he asked FireWind.

The boss-boss sniffed around both cages with crystals and pawed the one with the broken crystals.

I stared at the cage with its dangling broken crystals, jagged edges sharp as scalpels. Each of the quartz crystals had a space inside for an arcenciel. I could almost *see* Soul breaking crystals meant to imprison her.

From a corner, FireWind yipped, tearing my attention away. The wolf was staring at a ladder that went up into the metal roof supports. At the top was a small door, cracked open to the cold daylight outside. He yipped again as Occam reached him.

"Is this how the boys got away? Up the ladder and out the small door there?"

FireWind gave Occam a look suggesting that was obvious.

Occam holstered his weapon and swung up the ladder, climbing fast. "Dried blood on the rungs," he said, "and dried clear stuff, like Soul's blood in arcenciel form."

Rick and his . . . girlfriend. I couldn't make myself think *mate*, as in something forced on humans. They were still at the cages, kneeling or crab-walking in front of them. "Boys in these cages." She pointed, sniffing each cage. "One of them human, without devil dog genetics."

FireWind was beside her and nodded agreement, his snout wrinkled at a stench even I could smell.

Rettell lifted the broken lock on the cage with the shattered crystals. "Soul got free, so did the other prisoners, and it looks as if it all happened at one time. There had been eight captives. And Soul didn't come to HQ. So we have to presume she was recaptured, in her arcenciel form, and for whatever reason is unable to break the crystal she's in. If they know how to ride the dragons of light, we may be in serious trouble. And Soul certainly is."

Coming through the cracks around the high trapdoor, shades of blue light swept inside, playing across the near wall and metal roof like light reflecting off water. Occam reached up a hand and flicked the door. It swung wide and an arcenciel stuck her head—her massive, horned, fanged, glowing head—inside the too-small door. When she spoke, she sang, her words like a bird. "I am Cerulean." The high tones echoed off the metal all around. "She Who Guards the Rift has been taken. She is fighting being ridden to our destruction. Come, come, come. We have not much time! Follow. Follow!"

She ducked her head back out.

FireWind galloped across the floor for the outer door we had left open.

The others of the unit followed him.

Occam slid down the ladder, his hands and the insoles of his boots on the outer rails. Together we took up the rear, and I dove into his fancy car as we fishtailed out of the parking lot, chasing the coruscating rainbow in the sky. I had driven to the crime scene with Occam, and I steadied our gear and my potted tree with my feet on the floorboards.

"You think it could be a trap?" I asked.

"Sure it could, Nell, sugar. That's why we'll let the wolf go in first." He grinned like a maniac as he took a turn too fast, gunning his fancy car. "Cats always let the stupid dogs lead. In our case, the early bird might get eaten and the watching cat then gets the bigger prey. Like turducken but with werecreatures."

"*Cats,*" I muttered. "Just please don't bring home a vampire head and leave it in my boot."

My cat-man seemed to find that statement entirely too funny.

* * *

Our small line of vehicles followed the arcenciel across the sky, spreading out onto side streets as her altitude increased, making it appear that her direction was less certain, as we once again approached the river, heading for the hills to the east. We passed out of Knoxville and into the Great Smoky Mountains National Park, onto roads better suited to my car or John's old truck, roads that headed directly uphill and quickly became rutted, washed out, unused, and uncared for.

Finally Occam pulled over, and we grabbed gear and locked the car before climbing into the two cars behind us. I ended up with Lainie, and Occam in the car driven by the lieutenant colonel. Rick was driving the car ahead, with Aya, and now totally out of sight. As my door closed, Lainie asked me, "You think he'll get a more useful car now?"

"No. Never," I said, as she punched the gas to catch up. I wasn't sure how I knew, but I did know he'd never trade it for a more reasonable vehicle. That fancy car was Occam's baby. "But he might start driving John's old truck to work and leave it at the house when we get—" I stopped.

"Married. It's okay to say it."

The back of her car fishtailed over black ice as she took a turn onto a dirt road too fast.

"Married," I said, then changed the subject. "We got less than an hour before the sun sets and the vampires are fully awake. And we got no vampires to fight them with."

"No. But you do have a witch. And they don't have a witch. Advantage to us."

"They got *gwyllgi* they could send to attack us."

"*Sleepy time* workings will knock them out. Already tested and proved. Go ahead. Hit me with another worry."

I laughed. "I'm glad you're with us, Lainie. We need you." When she didn't reply, I added, "That was appreciation for my friend, who will be honored as my friend no matter what she does, where she lives, or even if she marries a SWAT guy."

"Don't make me get all misty-eyed while I'm driving," she said, shooting a grin my way before returning to the road.

I said softly, "I just need you to know that PsyLED has been a huge step into a real life for me, and you have been a big part of that. A big part of me accepting what I am." Fighting tears, I looked away, out the window at my side. "I love you, witchy woman."

"I love you too, plant-woman."

She slung the car in a sharp turn and braked hard. "Stupid wolf!" she yelled. "Sorry. Stupid wolf, *sir*," she yelled again as we rocked in our seats. But she didn't sound sorry. T. Laine had barely missed hitting FireWind, who was standing in the middle of the narrow not-really-a-road. He stood with his back to us, his black fur making him a silhouette among the shadows, almost invisible. He was staring at the sky.

"Think he's going to howl?" T. Laine asked.

I laughed softly, watching the boss-boss. I followed FireWind's gaze. Overhead, three arcenciels danced against the sun, brilliant against the last of the snow front's clouds. I pointed into the sky. "They've been in Knoxville awhile," I said. "First time I saw them, I thought it was lightning. Like a snow thunderstorm, but I never heard the thunder."

An arenciel who looked like liquid pearls flashed through the clearing and away. Lainie's bracelet glowed once.

"Okay. I'd say we're here, then," Lainie said. She cut off the engine and began to gear up. I simply sat and studied the setting.

We were on the crest of a cleared hill, the snow nearly melted even at this higher altitude.

To the left was an early 1900s farmhouse, a square one-story with a wraparound porch, a pyramid roofline, gabled windows on each side, bedrooms beneath the eaves. A bathroom had been added onto the back porch at some point, an antique tub visible through a rotted exterior wall. The house had been abandoned for decades, the roof caved in here and there, with evidence of water damage, rot, and termites. The windows had been broken out and the wraparound porch was rotted through. The open roof system meant sunlight entered every day; there was no way that vampires laired here.

On the near side of the house, there were two doors in the foundation, the small shape and location suggestive of a coal chute and bin, but there was no sign of a root cellar, which was odd in a house this old unless it was located beside the coal chute, with access from inside the house.

The arcenciels were flitting through the sky, diving toward FireWind and away.

I turned my attention to the overgrown yard. There were no saplings, which indicated that someone had mowed the yard in the last year or two. Through the tall, winter-brown weeds, there were trails, made by animals, humans, and/or vampires. No cars in the area, but the dirt road had tire tracks everywhere, so it was used by someone, even if it was just locals out with ATVs.

I checked the sky again and grabbed my gear.

Sunset was minutes away. Dusk would follow shortly after, the time when vampires rose to face the night. Just to be on the safe side, I texted Yummy where we were, sending her the GPS pin. I didn't ask permission. If my vampire friend wanted to come, she could.

Standing by T. Laine's vehicle, I geared up: vest, stakes, null sticks—one in my front pocket, one in my back pocket—and all the goodies FireWind might suggest. I added a rechargeable tactical flashlight from my gear bag, one that had been advertised as having three hundred thousand lumens. I liked hefty flashlights and had several, the better to bonk bad guys on the head after they were blinded by the light.

I also borrowed a floor mat from T. Laine's vehicle. I held it up in the air, asking for permission with the gesture.

"Help yourself," she said.

I stepped into the weeds, some of which were as tall as me. Occam walked through the tall grasses to me and stood close as I dropped the rubber floor mat and spread my army blanket on top of it, crushing the weeds down to leave a puffy-looking mound that crunched when I sat. The ground here was drained well and the soil under my blanket wasn't muddy. I put the new, small vampire tree sprig between my knees on the blanket, gave it a fierce glare, and touched one finger to the ground.

Nothing grabbed me. No roots, no weeds, no vines, no thorns. The soil under me was thin, a scant layer of dirt and vegetable matter, as if it hung on to the broken rock of the mountain beneath with desperate claws. I placed more fingertips on the ground and let my consciousness trail around, finding an area that had once been a vegetable garden; an old, covered well lined with rocks and long dried out; a chicken coop, fallen into

a heap. A burn pit was off the far side of the property, filled with
rusted, scorched cans, jars, household goods, paint cans, plas-
tics. There were also spots where petroleum products had been
dumped and burned and had poisoned the ground.

I found the foundations of the house and the coal bin, heavy
with a layer of coal dust, along with the remains of an old coal-
fired heating system and a rusted water heater. I delved deeper
around the house itself, back and forth, scouring a narrow trail,
and so far there was no root cellar.

Delving deeper, I dropped into the stone heart of the mountain, the rock so close beneath me. The stone was broken,
slanted, a mixture of jagged granite, quartz, and feldspar miner-
als, with smaller pieces and dirt in layers above and beneath the
broken granite.

I followed the largest table, a straight, almost smooth slab
with shattered edges. At the upper edge, I fell through into air
and yanked myself back underground. About twenty-five feet
down, a narrow cave opened up under the house. There was a
spring in it, water halfway up the stone walls, flowing away
from the house and into the hillside in small openings. A small,
weak ley line was knotted above the springhead, below the
waterline, and it tied off far away to the ley line along the Tennessee River. More stone canted up to one side and then the
rock heart of the hill fell away to the valley below.

The ley line was interesting, but other than that, there was no
magic in this land, nothing unexpected, no blood or graves. But
I did spot what I thought might be the root cellar near a boulder
about thirty feet from the house.

As I pulled back close to the surface, something gently
touched me, pressing. Air. A second front was moving in, dry
cold air stirring, chasing the wetter winter storm away.

The wind had changed direction as warm areas lost trapped
heat and cold air moved back in. It would quickly refreeze
patches of half-melted snow. The earth breathed. The grasses
rustled. Trees to the sides clacked branches.

I opened my eyes. Occam was kneeling in front of me, staring at my hands. His cat wasn't close to the surface, not gleam-
ing through his human eyes, and he seemed pleased.

I lifted my hands. My fingers were a tad knobby and rooty,
and I had grown leaves on my fingertips, but I hadn't been in-

vaded by local plants, and the potted vampire tree looked just like it had before I started my read. Pulling the leaves off my fingernails, I tucked them into my pocket before I let Occam haul me to my feet. I put the tree and the blanket back in T. Laine's car and nodded to FireWind. "This place seems fine. Mostly a lot of rock and one small, water-filled cave with a springhead and tiny ley line. T. Laine will want to make note of that, I'm sure. No other signs of magic."

"No root cellar for a vampire lair?" he asked.

I gestured to the house. "Coal bin at the house. That's all. Root cellar might be that way, away from the house—which is kinda strange—" I gestured. "Under a slanted rock."

Occam frowned. "There were root cellars in Texas, always close to the house." He lifted his head to the arcenciels still in the sky and wandered toward the edge of the hill. He was holding a psy-meter 2.0 and extended the wand to the crest of the hill I could see beyond the house. As he measured for the four different kinds of paranormal psysitopes, I put away the floor mat and rechecked my gear, waiting with the others for the psy-meter to read if there were energies for paranormal creatures: were-creatures, vampires, Welsh *gwyllgi*, or even witches.

Rettell moved around the side of the old farmhouse. Rick's eyes searched the area until he spotted her. The tension between them had altered in the last two days. Now instead of the crazies, it had strong elements of sexual and emotional attraction. There was no way they had found time to consummate their relationship unless they'd jumped into a closet at HQ, but they looked ready to do so at the earliest opportunity.

The black wolf suddenly appeared, standing near the house.

Ignoring Rick, Rettell looked at the sky, hunting for the winter moon. It wasn't visible, still below the horizon, so the power of the moon wasn't active on were-creatures yet. But it would be, and soon.

Occam handed the psy-meter off to Rick and knelt. The wolf loped up to them. Rick said softly, "Do you need the soundboard?"

FireWind shook his head no.

"Do you intend to sniff around and tell us how many humans and vamps have been on-site?"

FireWind nodded yes and trotted off, nose down.

Rick said, "The rest of you, pair up and gear up. Vests, wood stakes, null stakes, silver and traditional rounds, one member of each team with silver, the other with traditional. Stay paired. Everyone human shaped. Do not become separated. Comms on."

FireWind circled, circled, until he came to a hard stop on the drive and turned at a sharp angle. He trotted about twenty feet in the opposite direction of the house to a hillock with a rounded, oval-shaped boulder sticking from one side, not far from where I thought the water-filled cave was located. Occam and I followed, the occasional patch of snow crunching beneath our feet, tall grasses swishing. I could see the edge of the hill. It fell off, a long way down. On the other side was the sky, bright clouds, and the setting sun. The cleared hill offered a view down on Knoxville's lights and the Tennessee River Valley floodplain. As a housing site it was amazing, and I was stunned that a developer hadn't snapped it up for high-end town houses with a view.

FireWind climbed to the top of the hillock and made a chuffing sound. We all moved through the winter dry weeds to the hillock and I spotted two wooden doors set flush, butting up to the boulder. Root cellar doors. Good, well-made, strong root cellar doors. New ones, unlike the wood of the rotting house.

Studying the entrance, I walked around the low hillock. "It's a really odd place for a root cellar unless it's also a natural cave that abuts a rock shelf I found. I guess the shelf could be tied into this boulder." I hadn't looked far enough this way when I was reading the land.

The unit converged on the doors. The hasp of the lock was broken, but the two doors were closed tightly, almost as if wedged together.

Overhead, jarring against the pinkening sky, muted rainbows flashed in blues and purples and hints of shell. A pearlescent sheen touched the underbelly of the low clouds. Three arcenciels were dancing in the sky: Cerulean, Pearl, and Opal were not enough to attract attention when in the city and competing with city lights, but here in the hills where darkness reigned, there was no doubt what they were. Rainbow dragons. Angry rainbow dragons.

Cerulean slammed to the ground in front of FireWind. To his credit, Aya didn't flinch.

I did, though. It was like a bolt of bright blue lightning hitting the earth. The power shot through my shoes and into my bones like a lightning strike.

When my eyes cleared from the glare, I saw a female-ish form, standing in front of the boss-boss. She was tall, improbably lean, brilliant blue, and totally naked. She carried two rows of breasts as if she fed a litter at a time, and had what looked like horns at her spine, shoulders, hips, and groin. A crest rose along the center of her head and down her spine and it moved as she breathed, opening like a frill with each breath.

The arcenciel spread her hand in front of FireWind's snout. Her fingers were webbed, with three fingers and a thumb that might correlate with the design of a hand, but with several more spiny finger bones that pointed out to the side and others to the back along her arms to her elbows. They looked like spines on fish fins.

"Mermaid form," Occam said in my ear, "siren. Interesting."

"He who walks in the skin of predators," she said, her tones dulcet and breathy, like a quartet of wood flutes, like a song, a melody meant for the heavens and not the Earth.

LaFleur stepped up, his white hair caught in the evening wind blowing up the hill, swirling. It picked up the blue lights of the arcenciel. "He who walks in the skin of predators cannot speak the speech of humans while in this form. I will speak for him, the words of his will and intent."

"I accept your words," Cerulean said.

LaFleur said, "We attend your words."

"There are two caves. One has a water source that empties from the hill, three of my dragon lengths below the crest. It trickles to the valley. The water cave contains energies that repel my kind. The other cave I have entered and have observed. It is long and winding, with openings to the air in three places." Cerulean pointed. "There are this many drinkers of blood within." She held up four fingers of one hand and two on the other for a total of six. "And this many humans." She flashed her open hands at him four times.

I had no idea if that meant thirty-two or four times the spines too. Rick didn't ask, and Cerulean continued.

"Three of the humans are also young shape-shifters of the canine family and they are injured. She Who Guards the Rift is there. She is captured in a crystal. It is a small crystal. I have been locked in a crystal and ridden by blood drinkers. One like this one"—she pointed at FireWind—"but female, set me free. You will go inside and you will set She Who Guards the Rift free or your people will die at my hand."

Opal hit the earth beside Cerulean, and even before the pale blue and pink lights dimmed, she said, "This is not the words of the negotiation, sister."

Cerulean's voice altered into the notes of ill-tuned wind chimes. "I do not *negotiate* with lesser beings. They will obey as in the olden times or I will destroy them."

T. Laine said, "Will you be able to kill all of us before one of us kills you with cold iron?"

Rick pulled a small blade from a sheath at his side.

Cerulean stepped back quickly and hissed at him. Her teeth were like shark's teeth and there appeared to be several rows of them. She turned to Opal and said, "You will use the words of the negotiation with the lesser beings." In another blast of light, Cerulean changed shape and flipped into the air in a spiral. From above us she said, "I will go back into the air cave through the opening down the hill. I will be ready to fight when you enter and will eat them from behind."

Pearl landed beside Opal. Both looked more like human women than Cerulean and were again clothed in filmy, silky gauze that waved in the swirling wind. Pearl handed LaFleur a paper rolled like a scroll. In tones like bells and harp strings, she said, "This is the shape of the cave for beings who cannot fly and who must walk upon the earth."

Rick unrolled the paper and T. Laine moved to stand beside him. The rest of us stayed well back. Rick knelt so that FireWind could see the scroll.

I didn't have cold iron on my person. I used that for cooking and keeping the fires burning. Maybe I needed to get one of the churchmen farriers to hammer out an iron blade for me.

"Here," Opal said, pointing to the map, "are the human prisoners." She moved her hand. "Here, we will emerge. There will be three of us. We will try to save the humans and the dog shifters here; however, the energies in the water cave will impede our power and ability to . . . forward fly. Soul is here." She pointed. "You must find Soul and release her and incapacitate the blood drinkers so that we may eat them."

"Tell him the truth of the witch working, sister," Pearl said.

Opal leaned in slightly and her voice lowered, more like wind in a large reed flute than wind chimes. "Soul should *not* have been able to be captured and contained in a crystal. She alone has a witch working that keeps her free. Therefore, she is there by her will and her choice, for many reasons, only some of which we may know, and some of which we may not."

"Would the speaker of the negotiation tell us those reasons," Rick asked, talking as strangely as the dragons.

The dragons leaned into each other, silent, Opal gesturing with one hand.

Pearl leaned back and said, "We think she was taken in human form, and could not shift to escape without being caught in the crystal. She was captured with a Dog of War. For reasons we do not understand, she later shifted shape and was captured in a crystal. She has a working to escape from her crystal and yet has not escaped. Perhaps she allowed herself to be taken as a lure, so that you will follow and find and save her and the dogs. Or perhaps her witch working is no longer effective."

Opal added, "Soul is She Who Guards the Rift and also Keeper of the Rift, as well as many other titles of honor. She said that vampires and humans have a powerful item that the vampires want and so does she. She has been searching for another rift, and it is believed that the item might guide her to one. We think . . ." She stopped and looked at her sisters. There was more silent communication. ESP.

There was a time when I didn't believe in ESP, until the land and the Green Knight started talking to me in my brain.

Pearl picked back up. "Soul has been searching for a magical item she calls the cursed deck. There is a small possibility that it is in the cave system, hidden. Perhaps this was the only way that the Keeper of the Rift could get the drinkers of blood to bring her to their lair."

"Yes," Rick said, sounding as if he understood and agreed with their words. "Sunset is approaching. Are you able to follow time as humans do?" he asked. "Hours and minutes?"

"We understand your limited concept of time. It is sixteen of your minutes until sunset. At dusk, the vampires young enough to still be asleep will awaken. It would be best if they were staked by then."

Aya smiled, showing wolf teeth, and made a low-key growl of agreement.

"Yes, it would," Rick said. "We will enter through the door here in three minutes."

"We three will enter from the back of the air cave. Beware the small star."

In a blink, they were gone.

"Small star?" T. Laine asked.

Rick unrolled the scroll again and placed it on the ground at FireWind's paws. He pointed to a tiny star on the paper. "I don't know what it means, but once we're in, and the vampires have been immobilized, check it for abnormal energies."

"Underground, it felt like a ley line," I said. "I figured T.—Kent would look into it after."

"Nice," she said, and her face, which was usually pugnacious, was lit with anticipation.

"For now," Rick said, "check the doors for energy traps."

T. Laine tossed a small amulet at the doors, opening a *seeing* working. We could all see what she saw, which was wood and old nails, but nothing magical. She bent over the doors, running her hands over each board and each crack, touching, feeling for dangers no one else could spot. "This side of the door is okay. Can't tell you what's on the other side, like maybe a fishing line attached to a handle on that side, with a bomb on the other end, or a shotgun, or any number of things. We know people are on the other side. If I blow the doors off like I did at the abandoned house in town, I could hurt someone inside."

"And there was a small cave filled with water there, where the star is, the ley line they said was bad." I pointed to the map. "If we disturb the ground here, it's possible we might create an opening and flood the cave where the hostages are." I shrugged. "Or not."

"Everyone to the sides," LaFleur said. "I'll use a crowbar from the top."

We repositioned as the senior special agent in charge of Tennessee and seven other states, as well as Unit Eighteen, walked through the reedy weeds with a faint whisper of sound, moving gracefully, like the cat he had become, his white hair catching the tints of sunset. He was dressed in black jeans, a black shirt, and a tac vest with weapons enough to fight off a horde of mythological beings. Orcs or something.

Rick climbed the small hill and lay on his stomach, with his upper body draped down, near the top of the doors. T. Laine followed him and lay down beside him. She opened a *protection* working that we could all see in the glow of the *seeing* amulet that was still on the ground. "It won't be total protection, because the crowbar will make a constant break in the ward, but it will be better than nothing."

"I'll only lose my hands, not my head?" Rick said, his tone darkly amused.

"Pretty much," she said.

Rettell growled.

"Best I can do, cat-woman," Lainie said.

Rettell stepped to the left of the door, ducking behind the edge of the hill, weapon in hand. She was dressed like Rick, black clothing and tactical gear.

FireWind took position to the doors' right, hunched low, ruff bristled high, shoulders tight, to leap into any fray. Occam and I got low to the ground, covered our ears, and opened our mouths to deal with possible concussive results.

Rick raised his crowbar back and high over his head. With a grunt, he brought it down, ramming it into the crack between the doors. The blow hit true with a shattering, splintering crash. A fracture opened in the narrow space between the doors. He reared back and brought the crowbar down again. The wood snapped and broke. Multiple fissures ruptured through the wood. Only blackness was visible beyond. The third blow created a crevice big enough for a dog to wriggle through.

FireWind gathered himself to leap through. Stopped. Backed away two steps.

From inside the doors, a weak moan rose.

Soft weeping.

The words, "Nonononononon."

I knew those sounds. They were the sounds of children in terror.

Church children. Zeb. My brother.

ɲINETEEN

FireWind tapped his front paw four times and whuffed-growled.

I said, "I count four voices. Two are little children. Toddlers. No church children that age are missing. There's something . . . I don't know. Wrong. Not real? Aya?"

He tilted his head one way and then another, his ears moving all around, catching the sounds from the tunnel. Occam, at my side, leaned forward, his shoulders high, catlike, and the other werecats followed suit.

Occam asked, "Is it a recording? Like in the house where we found the body?"

I shook my head. "I don't know. But it feels wrong," I said, this time not making it a question. "Maybe something faking being children to pull us in."

"Null sticks," Rick ordered. "One in your off hand."

My off hand held the flashlight, but I could make do. I tucked the metal stick into my jacket sleeve and rolled the cuff to hold the stick in place. From the cave came increasing screams of pain and terror, but . . . I had heard real pain and terror. This was off.

"No gasping," I said, figuring out what was missing. "The breath is all wrong."

"Ingram," LaFleur said. "Shine your light in. Kent. Throw in an *illumination* working amulet as soon as you can see how far back the light goes."

Lainie blew out an exasperated breath and dug into a small gobag at her waist. "I don't know why you always expect me to have every kind of working amulet on me. Sir."

"Because you are exceptional at your job, Lainie," he said with a faint smile, "if a bit snarky."

FireWind, who liked more formal communications and no chitchat on an op, snapped at the air.

While they talked, I eased to the broken doors and shined the beam of the flash all around. It had once been a small room with cement-block walls and floor, and metal ceiling, all overlaid with planking and attached wood shelving. There had been jars and tins and bottles and cans on the shelves, and those on the side walls were still there. The back wall, however, had been constructed as a false wall, a hidden door, and someone had broken through into darkness on the other side.

T. Laine said, "Ready." She tossed the amulet into the dark, past the broken shelving and jars.

On the other side of the broken shelving was a cave, one I had missed in my read of the earth. The right wall was the ledge of stone I had read under the earth, but I hadn't bothered to read around the ledge's sides. It canted up at an angle on the other side of the root cellar, becoming the roof, making the cave a triangle, and the left wall was a different-color rock, gray with shiny stuff in it, like mica. The floor was smooth granite. In its center was a dried pool of blood.

"We'll lose access to comms," Rick said. "Stay in visual contact."

A boy screamed in fear. Real fear. It shivered the air.

FireWind dove through the doors, breaking them with his massive body. Dashed in. Shoved me to the side.

I tilted. Falling.

Occam caught my arm. Righted me. Took my flashlight.

Rick grabbed the top framing of the door. Somersaulted down. Drew his weapon. Stepped inside to the left.

Rettell followed, stepping to the right. The two of them provided cover and cleared the first part of the cave space.

Occam glanced at me. Accepted a handful of wood disks from T. Laine. Leaped into the dark, and raced in front of them, disappearing.

"Kent and Ingram at our six," LaFleur said. "Check out the star on the map. If it's clear, follow. If you reach a fork, stay put. We can smell our way out. You can't." He disappeared into the dark after the wolf, my cat-man, Rettell on his six.

"That is so not fair," T. Laine said. From her expression I had a feeling she was calculating a working to follow scent. Or maybe she already had one. Together we stepped inside and walked gingerly through the broken glass, seeing ancient tomatoes, peppers, what might have once been green beans, all brushed to the sides of the small room with piles of dried beans and mice droppings everywhere.

The frugal part of me ached for the lost foodstuffs, but the law officer in me proceeded into the cave. It was much larger than it had appeared from the view of the doorway, leading off along the hill and around a bend. The star had to be to the side of the root cellar's intact left wall. We turned to face the false wall. It was wood set into the solid stone of the small cave.

"The ley line is probably there." I pointed at and through the rock. "In the same place as the star on the map."

T. Laine activated another *illumination* amulet and moved to the left. She cast the *seeing* working—it was more complex than usual. I could see what she saw, tangled twisted energies of a ley line.

I touched the wall and pulled my hand back. "That cave is much bigger than I realized and it's filled with water, just inches away on the other side of this wall. If we do anything wrong, the pressure of the water might break through into here."

"How much water?"

"A lot." I thought back to the read of the land. The old, dried-out well had once sunk into the water-filled cave. The water table had dropped over the years, and the well was dry, but the water just below the well was still there. "A human can be pulled under by a two-foot-high wall of water if it's flowing fast and hard enough. A pressure change at the star energies might knock down the whole wall."

"And we'd drown," T. Laine said. "In a few feet of water. The cave slopes down. The rest of the unit would be trapped and drown too," she added. "Gotcha. Let's go."

"Walk slowly," I said, "and I can keep in touch with the land as we move."

"Copy that."

I let my thoughts drop, connecting through my boots and into the cave floor beneath me. The contact was precarious at first because I had to lift each foot with each step, losing contact. I swiveled in place, facing the rest of the cave where Unit

Eighteen and Rettell had gone. A wave of vertigo washed through me. I reached up to touch the slanted wall that formed the ceiling, and found both my balance and a third contact point with the land. I reached out with my plant-woman senses and traced the contours of the cave. It moved deeper into the hill, some parts steep, some with broken roof rock blocking passages.

From the blackness of the cave, a scream rose, an ululation of agony. It was the scream of a vampire at true-death. I secured my flash and drew my weapon, triple-checked that the magazine was loaded with silver-lead composite rounds. To my side T. Laine touched her necklace, the moonstones hidden beneath her shirt. A tint of energy blossomed.

"*Protection* working," she informed me. "Not worth much against *gwyllgi* or vampires, but it might slow them down. A little. Maybe."

"I love your confidence," I murmured.

T. Laine made a snorting sound. "Country Hick Chick, you're picking up some city snark."

"Townie snark." I probed the stone beneath my boots and fingertips, sweeping my mind into the darkness, seeking the sound of the vampire dying, and my friends. "Unit Eighteen are all alive and uninjured. No one is bleeding," I said. "They have staked some vampires, all in a pile, too close together to read the number. Devil dogs are there too. Some unmoving but full of fear. Can you feel the moon rise even underground?" I asked the moon witch.

"Always. The moon pulls on the Earth, on its seas, on the crust of the planet where we live. As soon as it's above the horizon, my personal power to draw from the reflected sunlight and from the direct attraction between Earth and moon will increase, but my access to the power of the tidal forces is uniform." She seemed to connect my question to the information I had just provided. "Now tell me why you ask?"

"Two vampires and at least one devil dog are still free. And awake. And moving our way. I have a feeling we'll need all our power."

"You're just full of good news. And I hate caves, by the way. And not being connected to comms."

"Let's go, but slow. I need to maintain a connection between my body and the cave." With careful slow steps, I continued, one foot or hand always on the stone. I got used to reaching ahead with each step, and pushed my boundaries, but that meant staying focused. I holstered my weapon. "Can I try something?"

"Nothing kinky," T. Laine muttered. "I don't swing to plants."

I blew out a silent laugh. "Can I put a hand on your shoulder and see if I can find the earth through your magic?"

T. Laine stopped dead. "That's a circle. Sharing power." Her voice went strident and penetrating, echoing through the cave. "That's a freaking damned *circle*."

I met her eyes, which were wide in the darkness. "Oh. I didn't know. My sisters and I can meld and share each other's power."

"You can share raw power? Without drawing a circle?"

"Ummm. Maybe? On Soulwood land." We hadn't tried it anywhere else. And I remembered Tandy talking about energy and power and how all energy and matter was the same thing. Could we use Soulwood power, plant-woman power, *yinehi* magics, away from the land, as a team? "Try?" I asked.

"Hell yeah, we'll try it, but not here, in this place, where we could be attacked while our attention is elsewhere."

"Oh."

T. Laine and I had stopped, so I closed my eyes, seeking ahead. "The cave moves around the crest of the hill and down to a second water table, where a stream exits the mountain and falls to the valley. There's a dead body ahead to the right. And . . . something vile." I dropped my voice. "Blood. Welsh *gwyllgi*. Alive. And it isn't a kid. It's . . . It takes up a lot of space. It's huge."

"So we have two vamps and probably an adult devil dog between us and the unit, and we're between them and the door."

"Ahead. If the vampires attack, get me some blood. Even if it's just a drop." I felt the shock run through Lainie. She forgot my gifts could drain vampires. "I don't know about devil dogs," I said. "I don't know if I can use their blood down here or not. It could be too similar to my own."

"Where are the arcenciels?" she asked.

I probed deeper. "Two levels below. They're . . . I don't know. They're all in one place."

"Can you feel Soul?"

"No. She must still be in crystal."

"Or dead or never here."

"Or that," I acknowledged.

"In which case the arcenciels set us up."

There was nothing to say to that. We continued deeper into the cave. The floor descended, the angles changing. We moved around broken boulders where a cave-in had brought down part of the ceiling.

The cave turned more to the right, winding into the mountain. Stalactites and stalagmites began to appear, mere bumps on the floor and ceiling. A tributary cave opened to our right.

"Wait." I stopped and closed my eyes.

We were moving around the hill and down. The cave that branched off to the right canted down hard and fast. A pit. There was water at the bottom. Not a lot of water, but an underground stream running across the pit's floor, before disappearing again into a crack of the rock wall.

"This way." I led us into the wider tunnel.

The slab of rock above us angled away and the roof was growing higher. Echoes resounded, indistinct voices.

A low vibration seemed to move through the walls but wasn't sound, not exactly. More a microvibration. A microtremor. Air moved through the cave system, the earth breathing.

We turned sharply and found the way ahead partially blocked by a cave-in. The largest boulder was bigger than my car. Even the smaller ones would crush a human flat.

A faint drumming began, the sound almost a counterpoint to the vibration.

"Vampires moving fast, right toward us," I said.

T. Laine grabbed my jacket and dragged me to the side, not touching my skin.

The floor shifted angles. Rocks moved beneath my feet. I gagged as my perspective changed.

Lainie shoved me to the cave floor.

I caught myself on stone. My knuckles scraped, abraded. My blood brushed the stone. My gift reached for the land, reached for Soulwood. Reached for power.

I fellfellfell through, into the deeps. Into the earth. Layers upon layers of stone and rock and gravel and water tables. Sand, clay, sources of magic there and there and there, magic all around and beneath me. I clutched at the stone, nails scrabbling. My hands pulsed as the roots inside of me sprouted leaves and tiny vines, pressing against the stone, searching for a place to take root and grow. *No. No.* I pulled back on the energies. *Not here. No sun. No life.*

I pulled my mind and energies back, fighting to control the roots moving inside me. My hands aching, my belly hard and gnarled like the roots of a tree. But they stopped moving, stopped *wanting*. When I had them under my control, I turned my attention up, to the surface. Roots, so many roots. The sensation of life all above me, of magic all around me. Witch magic. I pulled my attention in, close to where I sat. Close to where Lainie stood.

"Shhh," T. Laine whispered.

I explored the energies she had opened over us. I had been around her long enough to recognize an *obfuscation* working over us, to keep us from being noticed. It was a foot from my hands. Closer to our skin, a shield called a *hedge of thorns* working, and a *seeing* working, all at once. If any of the three beings coming our way saw us through the *obfuscation*, they would get hurt trying to get to us. But eventually something would get through. The feel of undeath pounded closer. Two vampires raced past in little pops of sound.

They were escaping. Neither was bleeding. My magic was useless to drain them without blood. And then they were gone, out, into the dark of night.

The *thing*, the stench of wrongness, the adult *gwyllgi* I had detected earlier, was standing six feet away. It was sniffing the air. Without opening my eyes, I saw the shape of it, half-human-shaped, half-dog-shaped, and the magic of it, foul and bloody and without pity. Dog of War. Dog of Darkness. Ancient Welsh terror unleashed upon the Earth. When I opened my eyes, he had a human face with a dog nose. I knew him. Balthazar Jenkins, cousin to Boaz Jenkins, one of the men who had actively tried to bring the churchmen to devil dog shape.

Balthazar stepped toward us. Closer. Pushed his nose near, sniffling, snuffling. Moving only my eyes, I looked around.

We were in a small crevice of rock between the rock wall and the car-sized boulder from the cave-in.

The devil dog was hunched over us, less than eighteen inches from my face, a huge, skeletally thin creature, its hairless belly concave, as if it had been starved. The rest of it was covered with shaggy black hair. It had abnormally segmented fingers and toes that ended in elongated, razor-sharp claws. But it was Balthazar's eyes that drew me. They glowed red in the darkness.

He snuffled closer. Blew out rancid breath, the stench like rotted meat. He made a slack fist with his left hand and pointed his index finger. Like a child who didn't know what to expect, the finger slowly pointed toward the *hedge of thorns* as if to tap on the cave wall. I felt its energies, a ball of poison on the earth, a thing that was not supposed to be, bred with purpose. Bred to kill.

The vibration in the earth changed pitch. And I knew, in an instant, just before the *gwyllgi*'s talon touched the *hedge of thorns*, that the vibration I could feel in my bones was the bedrock of the earth, a spirit of the hills, the sleeping, quiescent life force of an ancient granite sentience deep in the earth. It felt . . . restless. *Hungry.*

Small things came together in my mind, as the *gwyllgi*'s talon slowly approached the *hedge*, our only protection. Things I had seen and felt and even partially put together. Things that were part of my secret hidden soul, my innermost profound power.

The earth's innate, overwhelming, terrible capacity for life and for destruction fed on the blood of sacrifice, fed on battle-fields. Life ate the dead.

Like Soulwood.

Soulwood, who was a young spirit of the deep, a new creative entity with purpose and power. And I was its Keeper. Through Soulwood, I could wake all the spirits of the deep. I could feed them, feed their dreadful *hunger.*

And the Dogs of War were both the servants of the *hunger* and the *hunger*'s preferred food. The earth breathed. The earth vibrated.

The claw inched closer.

I had first encountered a Sleeper deep under the earth at the *gwyllgi* house of Roxy Benton, the man whose family had left the church, and who had helped Colonel Jackson breed the Dogs of War into existence again—the Welsh *gwyllgi*, feared shape-shifters in battle—by drinking the blood of vampires. The Sleeper beneath Benton's house of horrors had been restless, ready to wake, wanting blood, stirring, stirring in uneasy sleep, creating tremors, microearthquakes. Like now.

The *gwyllgi* touched the *hedge*. Tapped on it. It sounded as if he was tapping on rock.

He snuffled.

We don't smell like rock. We smell like meat.

I closed my eyes and put my bloody knuckles against the stone. I shoved myself into the deeps. Pressure built around me. Heat and cold, water and clay, rock and magma. I searched for the local ley line, not the one in the water cave but the one beneath Knoxville, that ran more or less along the Tennessee River Valley. The largest Sleeper beneath Knoxville was covered with a thin membrane created from the energy of that ley line. That membrane reached up into my hills. From here, Soulwood glowed softly in somnolent silence. Knowing where I was in relation to my land, I traced the ley line from Knoxville and found where a thin line branched off, twisted into knots, and touched the Sleeper of this hill, as well as the Sleepers of the nearby hills.

The sentient, self-aware life force of the earth.

If the Sleeper awoke, we'd have an earthquake. People would die. The magma chamber I had inadvertently created might rise. More people would die. On the surface, I reminded my body to breathe. And I sent a sensation of peace into the Sleeper.

The *gwyllgi* tapped again. He breathed in deeply. Snarled. His lips pulled back, revealing fangs that had no correlation in the dog or wolf world. The growl trembled into my chest before fading away.

I forced panic down. I breathed. I pulsed peace into the land.

On my third breath, third pulse, the Sleeper quieted. The vibration from it eased.

Magic cascaded over my skin. Lainie cursed, not caring that she spoke aloud. I could smell her sweat. Hear the strain in her voice.

I opened my eyes again and saw the dog's face right in front of me, its eyes on mine. The *obfuscation* working had either failed or Lainie had dropped it to concentrate on the shield. The devil dog could see us, smell us.

A growl from the adult *gwyllgi* grew. Louder, more . . . *hungry*, to rend and tear meat. Much like the *hunger* of the land to destroy and drink down life. I knew *hunger*. The land knew *hunger*. It had been starved. Balthazar *hungered*.

The dog's fingers and claws were touching the *hedge of thorns*, had pressed into the energies of the working. His snarl went wider, the rumble of his growl deeper.

A drop of saliva drooled from his mouth and hit the floor of the cave. *There*. It wasn't blood, but it would do.

I looked at my hands. Roots had grown from them into tiny cracks in the rock floor and into the pile of boulders. I was trapped. But my trap was also a weapon. I closed my eyes again and felt through the rock, through those small cracks, slipping under the *hedge of thorns*. And up, to the energies of the devil dog. I drew on the saliva, using it to sprout through the rock and up, around the ankles of the dog. Lightly, barely touching. Curling up his legs. Silent as the grave.

When I reached his knees, I let the vines grow thorns. Taking my power into my hands, I yanked back on the roots. Tightening. Knotting. Sending the thorns into his flesh. And I drank him down. And down. Letting the earth here feed.

I didn't let the land take his life, not completely, just enough to drop him where he stood.

He fell. Whimpering.

"Son of a witch," T. Laine cursed, in the way of the witchy women. "Son of a witch on a switch. You did it."

Through the tunnel, light billowed. All the shades of topaz and pearl and the prism of quartz. All the shades of the rainbow, of sunlight, of shadow, and moonbeams, a nacre-lit brilliance of light and energy. A serpent face with curved, spiraled, spiked horns and bone white teeth and fangs blasted around the cave bend. *Soul*. Someone had freed her.

Or she had freed herself at last.

She stopped. Swiveled her head to the dog, her eyes the colors of moonlight on ice clouds, the tints of moonbows, focused. She noted he breathed, his blood pumped. He was still alive. Her massive maw opened. She scooped the dog up. Chomped through his legs, leaving his dog ankles and paws shackled with my vines.

She stared at me as she swallowed, her frills rippling. Her body undulated. She moved on, passing us. Over twenty feet long with massive back legs and claws like scythes, her entire body was covered in glistening scales and horns and spines. A blazing dragon of light and energy, of movement and intensity.

I fell over, into the dark. My last thought, before blackness could take me, was that if I had known Soul was coming, I'd have waited. I'd not have grown into the earth again. I wondered if I was a tree. And if the vampire who had tortured the Lost Boys into becoming Dogs of War had gotten away.

I woke on the surface, wrapped in a blanket, sitting in Lainie's car in the dark, the engine running, the heater on, the seat temp turned up high. My body ached. My bones ached, a deep-down spirit ache. I was shivering, but not teeth-clacking cold as I often got when working with the land. I had experienced worse. My hands were bandaged again. I twisted in the seat, trying to find a comfortable position, moving the blanket so I could see some skin. My fingertips were leafless. Not rooty. They looked like human skin.

Occam spoke from behind me, and I jumped. "No visible damage," he said, his words pointed, his voice a cat-scratchy purr-growl.

I turned in my seat to see behind. He was stretched out on the backseat, his legs at an angle that looked human uncomfortable but cat relaxed. However, his eyes were glowing the gold of his cat, the way they got when he was fighting a shape-shift. His scratchy voice told me he wasn't okay. I decided his cat might interpret me meeting his gaze as a challenge, so I turned back around.

"You had to cut me free again," I stated.

"I did. It was different this time."

"Different how?"

"I thought you were going to bleed to death when I cut the roots next to your hands. The roots had grown from your flesh, through the ground, into the severed feet of the *gwyllgi*. The roots were draining the feet of the dog. Feeding on the flesh. Rooting into the flesh because there was no soil to root in."

I adjusted the blanket to make a tent over a heating vent at my feet, trapping the warm air, giving myself time to think about that. "I bet T. Laine thought that was . . . freaky," I said, using a term she might choose.

"She started mumbling about the nature of magic and power and energy and mentioned the words *quantum mechanics*."

"She's been talking to Tandy, I assume." When Occam didn't reply, I went on with an explanation. "The vampire tree is slowly merging with Soulwood like some kind of symbiotic life-form, inside me *and* growing on the land. It works with Soulwood's energies, with my energies. You know it eats meat to survive. I know that. I ain't never hid it. Are you upset because I'm a cannibal?"

"No. Human meat is foul, but it will stave off starvation. I'm upset because when I cut you free, the roots in the dog died. And when they died, they . . . They spoke."

I went very still. The vampire tree in the virtual reality we could share had finally started speaking. I thought a kind of hallucination, a onetime thing. Or, if I was honest with myself, I had hoped that was the case. Seems I had been wrong. There was no sound in the car except the whisper of the heated air and the quiet engine. Softly, I said, "What did they say?"

"They said, 'No.'"

"Oh . . . That's . . ." I stopped. That was *terrifying*.

"Without a larynx," he said. "Without lungs. Rubbing themselves across the rock to make a sound. They said, 'No.'"

Just a sound. Just a vibration on stone that Occam interpreted as a word.

But I knew it was more than that.

"I carried you out of the cave," he continued. "When we got back to the car, the potted tree had grown so large it took up the entire backseat. I had to cut it out in pieces."

I didn't want to ask, but I had to. "Did it talk too?"

"Not right away." He went silent for a while, the car a comforting drone, the heated air trapped beneath the blanket, warming me. He spoke again, his voice deeper, more catlike. "I carried the pieces and the pot to an old burn pit behind the house and lit it all on fire. It screamed, Nell. It screamed, 'No,' over and over. We all heard it."

"The tree is sentient. It wants to reproduce. It wants to claim land and territory. It mutates every time it comes into contact with the blood of plant-people. It may mutate when it comes in contact with devil dog blood too, since that's also church-bred blood. I don't know. But burning anything is smart, the way I burn my leaves."

"We need to destroy that be-damned tree."

"How?" I asked. "The churchmen and I tried burning, herbicides, cutting, and, I think, explosives. It just comes up somewhere else and finds a spot to thrive. And it thinks. Not like a person, but it seeks survival and reproduction and mutation. I honestly don't know if there *is* any way to destroy it."

Occam said nothing.

"The vampires?" I asked.

"Two got away. The others are in custody and will be taken to HQ's null room in silver cuffs. The Dark Queen's security team have arranged to pick them up. They'll bleed and read them and put them in her jail if they're guilty of hurting and killing the Lost Boys, which they are."

The Dark Queen. The person who put my life on a new track, into law enforcement, into the world outside the church. I looked out the windows. "The moon is up. Do you need to shift?"

"Yes. The cats have left already to go back to Soulwood. They will shift and run and hunt and study your tree. I'll shift and join them as soon as we arrive."

"You're upset."

His breath was a rasp of anger. "I'm going to lose you, Nell. You're going to go too deep, too long, into the land, into that *damned* tree, and you won't come back." The words sounded as if they had been wrenched from him. "And I can't bear it. *I can't.*"

Tears gathered in my eyes.

Occam sucked in another breath. "But I have you today," he said, "and today is all I'm promised. We'll go to your land. You will be inside your house and safe with your sister. You and Mud will be safe," he insisted. "FireWind and T. Laine will stay here and make sure the devil dog children and young men are taken to the Montana pack."

"Zebulun?"

"Landed in Montana. Your parents signed the papers to send him. Your daddy talked to the pack leader, which was no small honor for him. Money for Zeb's upkeep was wired over, like sending him to camp for the year. He's safe." Occam paused and I could hear him breathing. "Your father spoke to Zeb. He's settling in well."

He stopped talking, but I could tell he wasn't finished. "Zeb confirmed that Tomás is possessed with a demon. The demon talks to people. It revealed itself to the boys."

"That can't be any kind of good."

"No. The pack alpha says he's getting a medicine man or woman to come read the boys and make sure there's no demon taint in them. If there is, they'll handle it."

I sighed softly. My half brother was a Dog of War, a teenager, and might be possessed. How could a kid grow up healthy with all that? "Okay."

The words sounded as if they ached to speak. "I love you, Nell, sugar, to the full moon and back."

"I love you, cat-man, to the heights of the branches and the depths of the roots."

TWENTY

T. Laine drove Occam and me down to his fancy car and she returned to the top of the hill to help FireWind—who was back in human form, exhausted and too lean, too skinny, and with only a handful of protein bars to eat—deal with the caged devil dogs. Occam and I were silent as he drove to Soulwood, picked up Mud from Esther's, and parked near the others' cars. My car was in the yard, having been brought home by someone at some point.

Rick and Rettell were already roaming, making a mating ruckus that I hoped wouldn't keep the neighbors on nearby farms up all night. The cries and screams carried, echoing everywhere.

The land told me that Margot was trotting into the dark, alone. I didn't want to think about that too much.

Occam made sure that Mud, Cherry, and I were safely inside and slipped back out to strip and shift. Full moon wasn't far away. There was an old were-creature saying: "The urge to shift and to hunt waxes strong three days out, abides the three days of, and wanes three days after. Nine nights of pleasure and nine days of hell." Occam needed the release after the cave and the situation there.

There were a lot of things I needed to do, like read the after-action reports by the others to learn what had happened down in the cave, and find out where Soul was and where the other arcenciels were, and what Lainie might be doing about the ley line in the springhead cave. But none of that mattered. I was too tired. I kicked off my boots, turned on the Christmas tree lights, and plopped onto the sofa. Mud fed the critters and started banging around in the kitchen, full of teenaged energy and irritation and maybe some angst.

"I'll fix dinner in a bit. Don't you have homework?" I asked.

"This was the last day before winter break. No homework for weeks!"

She threw a fist into the air, a gesture no church girl would ever make. It brought tears to my eyes, which I quickly hid.

"You want mac and cheese and tuna salad?" she asked. "I'm fixing supper tonight."

I almost said "That sounds awful" but changed it to "I'll eat anything you want to fix."

"Mac and cheese and cat food it is."

I chuckled. Minutes later, I fell asleep.

I knew it was a dream, but it was also a form of reality. Quantum mechanics and all that stuff . . .

The Green Knight sat on his stallion, on the crest of a low hill, overlooking a battlefield in a narrow valley. His body was full of arrows, the shafts sticking out here and there. He bled from numerous sword cuts.

His beautiful horse was bleeding, standing on three legs. The stallion had been hamstrung, blood pouring down the injured back leg. He was out of the game.

Not a game.

A war.

A war between life and undeath.

In the valley below the knight lay felled trees bleeding from stumps, branches intertwined on the ground. Vampire trees. All dead. Destroyed.

At the feet of the horse, Mud, Esther, the twins, and I lay in a tangled bloody heap.

"Nnnnn. Nnnnn," I tried to shout, tried to deny what I saw. But I was frozen. I was dead. I was too late to save my sisters.

"It's a dream. Wake up!" a voice demanded.

Dream. A dream, yes. Not real. Not yet. I fought to wake. Fought to move. The dream held me in place.

A hand gripped my shoulder. Shook my body. My left leg fell off the sofa and my bare foot hit the wood floor. "Wake up, Nellie. Wake up!" Mud's voice was panicked. "There's vampires at the house. I can see them in the moonlight."

I woke. Hard. Clearheaded. "I'm awake."

I sat up, on the sofa and yet still in the land. In my vision

Mud was with me. We were alone on the hill in front of the house. The forest all around was upright, deep in winter sleep, standing, uninjured. But the trees knew, Soulwood knew, that danger walked the land. The battle hadn't happened yet. Not yet. But the enemy was here.

"Vampires," Mud whispered, warning.

"Yes." I remembered what T. Laine had said about circles of power, and that the way my sisters and I merged our visions was similar to a witch circle. I unwrapped my bandages, pulled off my socks, placed my bare feet on the boards, and held out my hands. "I'm in the land. Try to see what I see."

"Yes. Okay." Mud kicked off her shoes, sat on the floor in front of me, and looked at my hands. They were weird and rooty, but Mud grasped them as if they were normal. The vision of the forest and the valley came clear, but it wasn't the vision of my dream. *Thank God. Not the vision of my dream.*

We were on the hill, the house behind us. The trees were standing and alive. The Green Knight was armed and healthy. The dream hadn't been a current reality but a possibility, because the warhorse wasn't maimed and the knight was unbloodied.

Just as in the first time when I guided Mud and Esther to meet the tree, the horse now wore Mud's mark, a bloodred handprint on his face. The knight stood beside his warhorse, his standard a war pike, the handle buried in the ground, a pale green war banner flying, as if claiming the hill.

The green cloth banner displayed a different crest: a tree in full leaf, similar to the tree of life, but with roots reaching deep, and blood falling from the green-leafed branches. The cloth billowed in an unseen, unfelt wind.

The knight was in full armor, his shield on his left arm, his sword in his right hand. On his back and at his sides were strapped a mace, a hand ax with a steel knob and a spike opposite the blade, and a flail, its three smaller spiked balls secured with a leather strap. Various blades were on his belt at his waist and hips.

Mud and I were barefoot. Each of us wore a dress with long hair bunned up. Churchwomen clothing. In the vision, I changed us fast, one blink to the next, both of us with shotguns, wearing jeans and sturdy boots, flannel shirts, short hair to our shoulders. I had my sidearm, still loaded with silver-lead rounds. In the vision, leaves grew from our hairlines, trailing down our backs, and from our fingertips. In the vision, I sent vines snaking down our arms and legs, across our hands, not binding us, not touching the ground, not part of the vampire tree. Part of us. Plant-women. Instead of vampire tree vines, they were *our* vines, encasing us in flexible, movable, portable armor. *Our* armor. Our defenses. The defenses of the land.

"Not skin," Mud murmured. "Woody, pliable, bendable vines at joints and for movement. But here and here and here"—she pointed at arms, legs, thighs, chest, belly, back—"ironwood. Harder. Stronger."

I followed her instruction.

"Fanghead teeth will snare at joints," I said, "and break on the ironwood if they try to bite us. If they shoot us, the rounds won't penetrate ironwood."

The wood of the vines hardened and twisted.

"And weapons of thorns," I added.

They grew beneath the vines, ready to react, ready to punch out and kill. On the hill that fell away to the curving road, Mud and I stood, facing the wood line, staring over the place I had buried my dogs after the churchmen killed them.

As if the thought of dead dogs had brought her to us, Cherry burrowed between us, onto Mud's legs, whining. "It's okay, girl," Mud said. "It's okay." The dog was panting in fear. But we weren't afraid. We were plant-women.

The Green Knight was to our left.

Here, in this reality beneath the land, two vampires walked from the Vaughn farm, across the road, across the graves of the dogs, and separated. They didn't look like vampires did in real life. They looked like an empty outline representation with fangs, like something a child might draw. The Green Knight's vision of them was bare and sparse, based on the vampire blood he had tasted when the land ate the ones at Esther's house, and also when he buried Inigo. But one of the vampire figures was smoky dark. The stick figure was coated with demon smut. Tomás de Torquemada.

The stick figures moved to either side of the hillock where the Green Knight stood guard with us. The small hill where my house stood.

Behind them trailed two adult devil dogs, these much more realistic. The land had probably known the genetics of devil dogs much longer. Generations of churchmen had been buried in the ground, long before I was born.

The vampires and the dogs spread out, making harder targets.

Beneath the vision, the Sleepers were settled, silent, unmoving.

In the vision, there was no wind. There was no sound. Yet vampire feet vibrated on the earth, no matter how vampire-stealthy they moved. The land knew they were *here*, whether they moved fast or slow. The land knew. The Green Knight knew. Mud and I knew. They were *here*.

From the side, from the Vaughns' land, a black blur appeared, a wolf, running. A blacker shadow-cat raced at his side. Behind them, another cat sped. FireWind, Rick, Rettell.

The vampire without the demon smut drew a gun. He fired four shots, two and two. FireWind fell. The earth thumped beneath my feet as he fell, tumbled, and lay still.

Rettell fell.

Rick went still as death for an electric heartbeat.

He screamed. Cat scream into the night.

His mate had fallen. He stood over her body, protecting her. Quivering with the need to attack, the need to protect. His cat undecided what to do.

But the intruders were not moving. The Green Knight lifted a hand and the ground sprouted vines. Long and sinuous. They curled up the legs of the vampires and the devil dogs. Just long enough that they stood still. The tree had them.

Buying us time.

I *knew* the breath and blood of the injured through the trees. They weren't dead, but they were full of silver. The skinwalker wolf and the Asiatic cheetah would die if I didn't do something.

"Nell?" Mud murmured aloud, her voice panicked.

Don't take the weres or the wolf, I said to the knight. Then, aloud, I added so my sister could hear, "Not Rick. Not Aya, or Leann. Tell the tree not to take them."

In my mind I heard Mud talking to the knight.

To my side, I felt Occam. He had squeezed in through the cat door and climbed onto the sofa, sniffing me all over. He licked my jaw, turned, and raced back outside.

The demon in Torquemada recognized the life in the tree. And attacked. Death spread out from where his flesh touched the tree, the demon seeking entrance to the tree, to the sentience there. The knight leaped to the back of his horse and drew his sword.

Rick screamed out a challenge.

I reached out to him through the earth. *Be still. We're here.* I didn't know if he heard, but he went silent, standing over his mate.

"Not dead," I said aloud to Mud. "Use your life. Feel their hearts beat. Feel the pain in their bodies. First thing we do is heal them." I sent pulses of healing into Rettell, the most seriously wounded of the two. "We're going to do surgery. You've seen animals butchered. Seen the vet work on animals in the barn. You know anatomy. Feel the holes in her chest." I sent a thin shoot of vine into the hole of the first round. Moving deep, moving fast. The blood was black as tar, tainted, the way paranormal blood got when silver was involved. There was silver in her chest. Silver was poisonous. Silver kept were-creatures from shifting, from healing. She was a young were. She'd be dead fast.

"The rounds are silver-lead," I said to Mud, "solid, not frangible. Watch." I sent small vine shoots to knot around each of the broken arteries and veins, closing them off. With the main part of the vine, I traced the path of the first round until I found it. I wrapped the poison with wood, sealing it away from blood and tissue. Pulsed life into the torn flesh. Began to pull the round out.

"I can start on FireWind," Mud said.

I felt her move away. FireWind was wheezing. I didn't know what silver did to his kind, but if he couldn't shift, he'd die, no matter what.

"Look in his lungs," I said.

On the land, the vampires and devil dogs fought the vines and the thorns.

Only feet away from them, the cheetah whimpered. Dying. I pulsed in more life and decided quicker was better. I yanked the vine-tangled round out of Leann's chest. She didn't react. That was bad. I shoved a fresh vine into the other hole and found the round more quickly. It had done less damage, and I got it out fast.

I drew on the life of the land and sent the healing of Soulwood into her, making her mine, making her the land's, but there was no help for that.

In the real world, Occam leaped from the dark, snapped at the wrist holding the gun, and bit down. Bone crunched. The gun fell, Occam nipped it up and sped away. In an instant he was back, weaving back and forth between all the trapped beings, biting each, leaping past, swiping with claws. Buying us time. Vines grew up around Leann's cheetah body. Made a cage around her, thorns pointing outward. Protecting her. "Shift when you can," I whispered aloud, hoping she could hear me, figuring I had spoken to the military woman in the yard and also in my house.

Rick seemed to hear. He leaped away as the thorns made a protective cage around her. Occam nudged him with his nose, as if saying she was okay.

I transferred my attention to FireWind.

In the house, Mud's hands in mine were icy. She was panting in time with the black wolf. The wolf on the grass out front and also in the earth.

Still tied to the sleeping strength of the earth, I sent calm to Mud, healing into the wolf, following her vine into the skinwalker's lung. Right lung. Lots of blood. I found the round in it. Circled it, wrapped it with a vine. And then I said, "Okay. Mud. We'un's gonna have a mess of a time getting it, 'cause it went clean through the lung, broke a rib, hit his shoulder blade, and bounced back in. So we're gonna have to stop some bleeding first. You'un tie off the bleeders on the entrance while I tie off the bleeders on the ricochet entrance and start figgering which way to pull the round out."

"If'n you'un push it back through the body, here and yon, it'll do more damage. Push to the shoulder blade," she suggested. "Once we'uns get it beside the shoulder blade, we can stabilize it there."

"He'll have to have surgery to get the round out, but I reckon that'll do."

"We'uns talking all churchy."

"Mmmm. We are, ain't we? Get to work."

In my mind, Mud said, *I'm working. It's a lot harder than butcherin' a hog.*

I'm not a damned hog. FireWind. Sensing us in his body.

You'uns say cussing things like that and I'm'a leave the silver in and let you die, Mud said. *Shut up or die.*

I was so proud of my baby sister I'd have hugged her if I hadn't been trying to save the wolf.

Stiffly, his mental voice frosty formal, FireWind said, *Forgive me. This is . . . interesting. And extremely painful. May I suggest you move quickly? I believe I'm dying.*

Did I say shut up or die? Mud asked. *Hush.*

I pulled the poisonous round in under FireWind's shoulder blade and fortunately it had hit the lower part of the scapula and stopped. It could likely be felt from the outside, and it would take a doctor only a minute to excise it.

The other round had passed through his upper leg, a clean shot. From deep in the earth I sent healing into the silvered wound and watched the blackened blood and flesh turn back to wolf-red.

When we were done, Mud and I pumped FireWind full of life and pulled back to the surface.

I was exhausted. I just wanted to rest, to sleep a bit, like the Sleepers, maybe. Just curl up and let everything go. Eyes closed, I took a breath. I smelled smoke. In the vision, I opened my eyes.

Smoke filled the three acres of lawn and my dormant garden. The trees near the street were on fire. The vampire tree. Not cut down, but burning, dying, like the knight had warned.

Occam was in the house again, on the kitchen floor, shifting into human.

I dove back into the earth and found the knight's vines twisted tighter to the vampires. They were still trapped, the knight in a battle royale with the demon in Torquemada. I didn't sense the poison of accelerants on them, in the air, or on the ground. So where had the fire come from? I sent my awareness up the vines, up the unknown vampire's legs and torso. There was no indication of matches or even a lighter, and the trees and the ground were still all wet from the snow and ice, so there was no way the fire started without an accelerant. I stuck the vampire full of thorns all over. Aimed for the place in his belly where he could be paralyzed by wood. Missed.

I pulled away from the first vampire and inspected Tomás. He too carried nothing to start a fire. And vampires were highly flammable, so why would they start a fire while trapped on the burning land in the first place? It didn't make sense. I studied the vampires carefully.

At the edges of my mind, I sensed a third vampire, mostly forgotten in the hurry of the last day. Inigo was still trapped beneath the land, thorns in his body, but the stake dislodged. He was screaming in pain, but had no way to start a fire. I staked him again and withdrew, back to the vampires trapped by the tree, close to the house.

I saw-felt-discovered an anomaly.

Tomás de Torquemada wore a broken crystal on a chain around his neck. In his pockets were gold coins, and several gold crosses wrapped in lead bags to keep him from burning at the touch of the holy icons. Beneath his clothes were wounds. Massive wounds, half-healed. There were four wounds altogether, round, except for one area on each that was serrated. Two wounds were on his left chest in front, two on his left back.

I checked the other vampire, the unknown. He too had been wounded, and the wounds were lined up just like on Tomás, four, front and back.

They were bites. The vampires had been bitten by something bigger than even the wolf. Bigger than an adult Dog of War.

"Oh," I said aloud in the cold house. "Oh dear."

Things that hadn't made sense, made sense now.

Soul had been a prisoner of the vamps, caught in human form, and yet she had emerged from the cave in dragon form. She ate a devil dog on the way out. She left some *gwyllgi* in the cave alive. Why?

Chasing the vampire who got away?

The bites?

Arcenciel bites? Arcenciel bites made the bitten crazy. Crazier. Tomás de Torquemada was possessed by a demon. He had worn a crystal on his chest in the old paintings, a crystal trapping an arcenciel. Now he wore a broken crystal on his chest. So . . . his crystal had been broken at some point recently, freeing the arcenciel he had worn trapped for centuries.

It bit him and bit the other vampire with him? Or Soul did? And no one ate the vampires as Soul had eaten the adult devil dog.

Soul had been caught—allowed herself to be abducted, but not to save the devil dogs. One of the other arcenciels had said Soul knew how to get out of a crystal, she had a working of some kind that she hadn't shared. So maybe she allowed herself to be ensnared because she was tracking a trapped arcenciel. One worn by Tomás de Torquemada. That made sense.

The trapped dragon had not been among the three we knew

of, Pearl, Opal, and Cerulean. The dragon in Tomás' crystal had been there for centuries and recently gotten free. A dragon had recently—very recently—bitten Tomás. The same dragon? Had it happened in the cave when the others of Unit Eighteen had gone on before me? Before that? Had she escaped before we had ever reached the cave on the hillock? That made sense. No way to prove it.

I wondered what had happened down there, why Tomás had run off like his pants were on fire. Or why Soul had followed. But I was guessing she had been on the trail of the fourth, unknown arcenciel, who was now . . . breathing fire onto my land, trying to kill vampires.

Did dragons really shoot fire? They were made out of energy. So I'd guess they had that ability. Just like with healing the wolf and the werecat, first things first.

Dragon fire.

I was suddenly standing on the hill, Mud beside me, her hand in mine. I said to the Green Knight, *Send moisture up the roots and branches and put out the fire.* I looked out over the field of battle. *What happened to the* gwyllgi?

Mud thought, *A blast of light went from there to there, and the devil dogs were gone. Chomp chomp.*

To the Green Knight, I asked, *Did a dragon eat them?*

The knight bent his head down and back up. A nod. So maybe Soul was here. Or maybe only an angry arcenciel, a stranger. Maybe devil dogs were just tasty treats to arcenciels. Either way, the dead dogs weren't my biggest concern. My concern was what happened to the dragons. How many were here, which ones were here? And did they all know we were friends?

I felt a vampire race across my land. Yummy. The Green Knight knew her. She was envisioned as part of the landscape fully fleshed. Swords in each hand. With slinging motions, she cut the wolf and the cheetah free of the thorny cages, sheathed the shortsword.

I had forgotten about the wolf and werecheetah. The fire was raging closer.

One-handed, Yummy picked up Leann by her front paws and slung her to relative safety. The werecat flew through the air and landed and bounced at my feet. As if the massive wolf weighed no more, Yummy repeated the process with FireWind, though he flew considerably less far. Rick raced to his mate and lay down next to her, licking her head with his tongue.

"Gross," Mud said.

Near Yummy, fire spread and crackled. If a wind popped up, this would spread. And Yummy was terribly flammable.

She raced to Tomás, swung her longsword back.

Yummy, I said.

She shouldn't have been able to hear me through the land. But she stopped at the highest point of her backswing. "Nell?" She did a fast pirouette. "Where are you?"

You came through the trees. I smell your blood. So I might be inside you. Anyway, be careful about cutting them free. I think they were both bitten by an arcenciel. And Tomás is demon possessed. If you kill him, the demon may take you.

"Fuck. Bites make our kind crazy. And now we have an arcenciel-bitten, demon-possessed vampire."

Yummy resheathed her longsword and pulled stakes from her waistband. Faster than I could follow, she staked both vamps in the belly. They slumped in the vine cages and into the thorns that had pierced their flesh. Yummy proceeded to cut them free.

The vampires were mine. If I wanted them. I drained a little undeath from them, and the Green Knight slapped his hands together hard enough for me to stop.

I turned to him and looked up, way up, at him on the huge horse. *What?*

He touched his mouth and shook his head no.

They— I thought about it a second as the fire blazed closer. *They taste bad?*

He nodded. Had they tried to heal themselves from arcenciel poisoning by drinking from a *gwyllgi*? Was that why Tomás had been chasing devil dogs? I sent my sister a sense of comfort, but all I felt in return was a blazing hot anger.

To the tree and the earth, I said aloud, "More water in the trees. Hurry."

Yummy had cut both vampires free. She carried them by their sword belts, stepping over the wolf, and dropped them near Rick and Rettell. In the vision, she dropped them right at Mud's and my feet. I knew Yummy couldn't see me in the visionscape, but somehow she knew where I was, even if only instinctively.

In real life, my cell phone rang. I released one of Mud's limp, icy hands and opened my eyes in my house. I glanced at my cell, saw Esther's name, decided it could wait a few rings.

Mud was deeply under the land, eyes closed, leaning against the couch at my feet. Cherry was curled at her side and thumped her tail when she saw me moving. The puppy whined, a high-pitched sound of fear.

I soothed her as best I could and said, "It's okay, girl. Good girl. Stay."

I rearranged Mud, laying her flat and putting her head on a sofa pillow. She murmured something when I covered her and her puppy with a crocheted afghan. I made it to my feet like an old woman with arthritic knees, and went to the kitchen for water.

I answered my cell and put it on speaker, but my mouth was too dry for *hello*. I managed to say, "Yeah?"

"Your'un woods is on fire, sister mine."

"I see that. You okay?"

"I got me a woman, a crazy fanghead, sitting in my front room. You'un tell me. She tried to stick her fangs in me, so I stabbed her."

In the background I heard Ming of Glass laugh. The tone had a ring to it that sent faint chills across my flesh. Vampires could mesmerize. They could make humans afraid. Make them fall in love, make them do and be all sorts of things. This laugh sounded nothing like that.

Thoughts flashed through my mind. Ming had never been totally sane. The vampires here had been bitten by arcenciels. We had never figured out if Ming had been bitten too at some time. Was that the real reason why Ming was crazier than other vamps who had gotten back their souls?

Without a pause, sounding as calm as I could, I asked, "Are the babies okay?"

"They's got vine cages all around their bassinet with foot-long thorns pointing up. *You'un tell me*. This house is like a fairy tale and a insane asylum all mixed up together."

I chuckled. Now would *not* be a good time to tell my sister that she was unconsciously directing the fairy-tale insane asylum protections.

"I'll call back," I said. "I'll send one of the werecats to stay with you and to keep Ming in her place. Keep the knife out and handy."

"I ain't stupid, sister mine. But I am growin' leaves and vines outta my fingers, and thorns in weird places."

"Good. Use all that as weapons. If the vampire has any sense at all, she knows you can use the thorns. Stake her in the belly with them if you get the chance." Vampires also had preternaturally good hearing, so Ming could hear my part of this conversation.

Esther thought about that for a moment and said, "Humph." The call ended.

I finished the water, poured another glass, and walked barefoot onto the front porch, leaving Cherry and Mud and the cats inside. Bare soles on the wood, I reached through the land and made sure the were-creatures on Soulwood were okay. Or at least not dead.

They were all moving and no longer in cages. So they seemed fine. Sorta.

Rick and Rettell had taken off together and were otherwise engaged on the far side of the property. I quickly withdrew with a soft "Sorry," though it was unlikely they heard me, what with their caterwauling.

I searched for Occam and discovered him in the backyard. He'd been scouting. From the land, I knew he had been all over the front area, sniffing the bodies; he'd gone onto the porch, where he had no thumbs to get inside, and raced back down, all around the house and garden and grounds. In and out through the cat door in the back. Not panicked but not a happy cat.

I reached out to him and thought, *Can you hear me, cat-man?*

I can hear you, Nell, sugar. Surprise filled his emotional tone, but no doubt, no questions.

Ming's at Esther's. Tried to bite her. Can you go help? I'm good here. Yummy is here and I'm'a put her to work too. If Yummy hadn't been bitten.

Why is Tomás here and why fire? Occam thought at me.

Tomás is probably still after the Blood Tarot and the only place he can think to find it is here. And with Ming at Esther's, he probably thinks we're all in one place at one time. As to fire, I think an arcenciel that had been trapped in Tomás de Torquemada's crystal got free. I think she set the fires trying to burn

Tomás. The vampires out front have been bitten by the dragons. I need to know if Ming has been bitten. And though you ain't asked, I think the devil dogs was dinner to angry arcenciels.

That's what I'm smelling on Tomás and this other fanghead, he thought at me. *Arcenciel venom.*

Yup. Stake Ming. Check for wounds. Be safe, cat-man.

Heading to Esther's. Be safe, Nell, sugar.

I walked to the front windows, water in one hand. No weapons out. "Yummy," I said aloud, reaching out through the land to her, reaching through the blood the land had tasted. Yummy had vampire hearing and she could hear me from inside. "Come here, please."

There was a pop of sound and Yummy appeared on the porch. She was fully vamped out, with thin fangs and huge black pupils in red sclera. She was wearing some kind of vampire armor, and carried a lot of weapons, both blades and handguns. She stood two inches away from the window glass, her swords out to the sides, a look of fury on her face. If she had been warm-blooded, and had needed to breathe, she'd have fogged the glass.

I wasn't afraid of her. I wasn't afraid of much of anything right now, but I probably should be. "Who's the other vampire? The one with Tomás?"

"I don't believe you've had the pleasure of meeting Bishop Don Alonso Suarez de Fuentelsaz," she said aloud to me. "Or you can call him Don Psycho, either works for me. What do you want, plant-woman?"

"I want to talk, and not outside in the cold. If you wish to be welcome in my house, which includes this porch, you'll put away your weapons." Watching her, I drank down the second glass of water.

Yummy snarled and sheathed the blades.

I reached out to her and into her blood. I couldn't pulse life, because she was undead, but I could pulse calm, clearheaded thinking. I opened the door and stepped back as she entered, looking less angry and battle-riled. I said, "Tomás and Alonso Don Psycho were bitten by an arcenciel. We've been thinking for a while that Ming may have been bitten too. I'll know in a minute or so. Has an arcenciel bitten you?"

The look of fury dropped slowly from Yummy's face. Her

eyes bled back to human even more slowly, but fast enough for me to know she wasn't a current danger I'd have to kill. Relief washed through me like an icy stream and I breathed through a tightness in my chest I hadn't recognized.

"Bitten . . . ? No. But Inigo came to my lair before I woke last night. Before dusk, stinking of sunscreen. I haven't seen him since. I think he's true-dead or would have called me."

Before I could tell her Inigo was still undead, buried in thorns at the boundary of my property, she went on.

"I have no idea how he got into my house, but Ming was there too, so . . . she might have let him in?" Yummy's eyes flashed to me once before she realized the door was still open and took the knob in one hand. "He tried to kill me."

Cold air flowed in through the open door.

Yummy stared out at the dark. She twisted her head back at me, moving like a lizard, which made my skin crawl. Her face was set in hard lines of sadness, a brokenness that I recognized, brokenness from betrayal—betrayal by her maker, betrayal by her lover. Even Occam had walked away from her.

I wondered how many others she had lost over the years of her life. *Unlucky in love,* I thought. In church-speak it was a curse for a woman.

Her voice toneless, Yummy asked, "Bitten where?"

"Chest."

Faster than my eyes could follow, she leaped across the porch and to the ground. Yummy pushed aside Alonso's tunic and ripped open his shirt, exposing the bite marks. She hissed in a breath she didn't need. "I hope it hurts like the fires of hell, you filthy pig."

The wounds looked half-healed, punctures that had become infected under the skin, and were now infecting the entire torso. The center of each fang mark was full of pus. Streaks of red, green, and a sickly yellow ran outward from each toothmark in a gruesome pattern, like a dying star. Alonso was dying.

TWENTY-ONE

Yummy walked to Tomás and ripped his clothes open. She sighed out the unneeded breath. The grand inquisitor was even more infected. His entire chest was swollen and puffy, a multi-colored mass of infection. There was a gold chain around his neck and attached to the chain were two parts of a long quartz crystal, broken in half. She ripped them off his neck and wrapped the chain around her hand.

I walked out onto the porch in bare feet, and closed the door behind me.

Walking back to Alonso, Yummy sat beside him. She placed her hand on his chest and closed her eyes as if reading his body. "They were bitten days ago," Yummy said, "and the dragon injected venom. A lot of venom. They don't always do that, but she did this time. Venom, just a single hit, makes my kind mentally unstable. A full injection? Like this? I don't know. Maybe kill? Maybe take them over and control them?"

"How do you know all this about dragon bites?"

"When we were together, Inigo told me the church never destroyed the secret things of other religions, other societies. The church kept the stolen books, the tablets, the scrolls, the crystals, the devices. 'The church *knows* things.' That's what he said. 'They know how the world will end. They know when.'

"And when they ran their own names, as many priests have done, through the encoded words hidden within the Hebrew text in the Torah's Coda, Tomás discovered how he would die the second time. The ancient texts suggested that he'd be redeemed, that he'd then be killed by a dragon, and that he'd be buried." She stood, leaving the horrible wounds visible in the night, her eyes on his face. "Inigo discovered he would be killed on a tree after he was redeemed. I didn't put redemption together with the

idea of getting back souls, but I guess if you're a priest, you have
to have a soul in order to get it redeemed."

Inigo's death hadn't said anything about a dragon. Only Tomás'
death prophecy had. *Interesting.* "Is there an antivenin?"

"For dragon bites? No. They live or die." She shrugged.

I let that thought roam around in my head a bit, and then
snorted like one of the mamas, a little contemptuous. I closed
my eyes and sent my thoughts into the land beneath my frozen
bare feet and considered. It would take time to visit with the
land and inspect the ground and think things through. But the
tree lived *in* the land. He . . . it—whatever it was—knew things
already.

I asked the Green Knight, both aloud and in my thoughts,
"The vampires who were eaten by the land at Esther's. Did they
have blood that was contaminated, like these guys? But maybe
not so bad yet?"

"Dayum, girl. You're getting spooky on me."

I ignored her.

The knight nodded, that single slow nod, the green glint of
his eyes barely visible through the helmet's protective ocular
slits.

"So the land has tasted dragon through its venom?"

He tilted his head to the side, which wasn't an answer. With
one finger he pointed at the vampires, crumpled on Soulwood.
The land had tasted enough to give them a full shape and form
now, recognizable as who they were. Finger extended, he waited.

"Don't kill them. Don't eat them."

The finger remained pointed at them. He had spoken to me
before, but it had to be difficult.

I thought about what he might be asking. This time I sent just
my thoughts, because Yummy didn't need to hear this question.
*Wood can incapacitate vampires. Maybe enough roots and
vines would eventually kill them, which is not what I'm planning. Is it possible to heal them from the venom? Is that what
you're asking me if I want you to do?*

In what might be best described as an overlay, resting on top
of the image of Soulwood, the knight sent me a vision of vines
coming out of the ground and piercing the wounds of the vampires. I saw the bodies pulled underground, the turf and soil
turned as if plowed under. Beneath the ground, the roots and

vines coiled against the bodies, the life of the land cleaned out the evil, the poison, depositing the venom and the infection far underground. Breaking it down, cleansing it, leaving the vampires underground but not, maybe not, true-dead. Inigo had told Yummy he'd "be buried." He hadn't actually said *true-dead*.

Is that what is happening to the vampire you first buried? Near the church land and the long cliff?

He nodded, too slowly for me to be fully certain.

The vampire with the . . . with the dark spirit energies inside. What will happen if you heal him? Will the demon get free?

The knight nodded. More certain, and though his expression didn't change, I got the feeling of worry, concern, and that sensation of trees dying. I remembered Brother Ephraim. His filthy soul had been trapped in the land. It had taken a lot for me to destroy his devil dog evil. I wasn't certain I could kill a demon.

"Let me think about that," I said aloud. I eased out of the ground to see Yummy, sitting beside Alonso, watching me. "What?" I asked her.

"You talk to things I can't see. Beings I can't see. And when you do, you— Okay, don't take this the wrong way. But when you talk to the nothings, you sort of glow."

"I what?"

"I'm not sure if any creature but Mithrans and *maybe* witches in a *seeing* working can see it, but you glow."

Dang it, I cursed silently. Did I only glow when I was talking to the Green Knight or also when I communed with the land? If I was gonna start glowing all the time . . . *Dang it!*

"Do you still love Inigo?" I asked.

Yummy laughed. "I don't think I ever loved him, but the attraction is still there."

"Well, he ain't true-dead yet. He's buried underground with thorns inside him while the tree and the land heal him of a dragon bite. You're about to see what happened to—"

The frozen ground around the two vampires erupted with thorned vines, whipping in the air. Yummy jumped just a bit, in surprise.

The vines wrapped around the men, every limb, joint, finger, coiling all around their torsos and heads. Beneath them the ground quivered, shook, rattled.

The bodies were pulled beneath the surface.

"Like that."

"Dayum. Dayum dayum dayum."

In her shock, her accent had sounded a little like Rick La-Fleur's. I didn't let my amusement show but it was a near thing.

I had put my cell phone in my back pocket. I pulled it and called headquarters. JoJo answered. I said, "Just listen. I'm'a make this fast. I got three vampires staked and full of dragon venom. The land is—" I thought about listening ears. "*I'm* trying to heal them of the poison.

"Inigo was buried last night. Tomás and the vampire named Alonso attacked my property with two adult devil dogs tonight. Dogs were eaten by an arenciel, I think, and then that arenciel set my woods on fire. Fire's out now, but it was a mess."

"Nell? Where's FireWind? Rick and the others? No one is answering their comms or cells."

"Oh. They's all critter shaped, getting healed too. It'll be in my report. Now hush and listen.

"The vampires are underground in my front lawn, but not true-dead, but are infected at the bite sites. Yummy says the arenciels can inject enough venom to hurt, or a full load that will kill vampires."

Cautiously, Jo asked, "Can you keep them underground until a time of FireWind's choosing?"

"Yes. But why?"

"If they survive, we'll need blood donors at hand when they rise or they might drink down you, your kid sister, and all your chickens, but that's something we can deal with later."

Yummy made a face at the thought of drinking chicken blood.

"Okay. Right," I said. "I'd hate to heal them only to have to kill them again. Yes. I can do that."

"Then I say do it. Is that all?"

"No. Ming is at my sister's, and is acting crazy too, so maybe she was bitten when her place was torched. Or maybe long before that. How'd I know? The twins are okay for now, but Esther might kill Ming. Occam's on his way there to check her out and assist in staking her. Permission to detain Ming, check for wounds, and bury her too if she's bitten?"

"That . . ." JoJo Jones stopped. "Ummm. That's above my pay grade."

"Can Yummy decide?"

"Better than me," Jo said. "The political implications of detaining the Master of the City to heal her, versus letting your sister and fiancé kill her, seem obvious to me, but maybe not to vampires."

All vampire-formal, Yummy said, "I give permission. I now know what arenciel venom smells like. My former mistress has smelled like the venom of arenciels for decades."

"That's . . . interesting? When did she get bitten . . . Never mind. Okay, Jones. Ingram out." I ended the call and closed my eyes. Instantly I met the eyes of the Green Knight. He had taken off his helmet. His beard was green and braided, and his hair pulled back in a queue. But his eyes were greener than I had ever seen them, and intense. I spoke aloud. "Take extra care of healing the vampires if you can," I said. "And the vampire I'll put out for you at my sister's. That's four in total."

He gave that regal nod.

"But the one with dark energies, I want to see if we can work together to . . . to . . . expel the energies from the vampire and help catch the energies."

The knight lifted his hand. It no longer wore a gauntlet. In fact, all his armor was gone, leaving him wearing a really long shirt and leggings of some sort. His warhorse was behind him, chomping grass, ears twitching.

In our vision, I was dressed in the plant armor. Should be itchy, but it wasn't.

The knight pointed down. The ground rippled and shifted and a vampire's body erupted from the earth. Tomás de Torquemada.

"Okay." In my imaginings, we were standing at my car. In the back was the gear I had packed in preparation for stopping some big bad ugly evil thing. I pointed at the containment vessel. I wanted to capture the demon in a containment vessel.

He showed me Yummy, who was talking to FireWind. FireWind in human form. The boss-boss reached out to grab my arm, as if to shake me.

"Stop that. She wasn't talking to you," Yummy said. "She was talking to the land or to something in the land."

"How do you know that?" the boss-boss asked.

"You're not shaking her," Yummy said, sounding stubborn. Protecting me.

I opened my eyes. I wasn't sure when I had gotten here, but I was standing beside lumps of earth and vines that buried two vampires. I said, "Jo. I'm going to Esther's to bury Ming. Then I'm going to try and lure a demon into a containment vessel and trap it. Occam is at Esther's. I have Yummy, an anemic FireWind with a silver round in his shoulder, and an even more anemic Rettell with silver-poisoned blood, but who is also in heat and mating with Rick on-site. No one is going to be much help."

"I'll be a great deal of help if you feed me first," FireWind said.

There was a click on my cell and I switched calls to T. Laine. She said, "I'm driving lights and sirens your way, ETA fifteen, Country Hick Chick. Where's LaFleur and Rettell?"

"Busy. Do not ask. See you in fifteen, if I live that long." I ended the call and looked over to where Tomás and Alonso had once lain. Neither one was visible, but the land where they had fallen was humped up and suspiciously grave shaped. I shook my head.

To Yummy I said, "I like the armor. You up for us figuring out a way to get Ming into the yard and letting the land take her down?"

Yummy laughed. "I can get her outside. Watch and learn, *Country Hick Chick.*" With that, Yummy strode into the dark, looking a lot more like a warrior than I ever would. And I'd never hear the end of that newest nickname.

"You're'un gonna need all this," Mud said from behind me. "Shoes, jacket, weapon harness, and car fob is in the pocket."

I had felt Mud wake and walk across the porch, down the steps, and across the raised bed, jump off the low wall, and join me on the grass. Every step. When I married Occam, I needed to be very careful where my cat-man and I got physical, because it was possible that Mud would one day be as aware as I was.

I swiveled around to my not-so-little sister, who was bundled up against the cold and laden with my gear and boots. I accepted the socks she held out. I dropped to my backside and pulled them on over my frozen feet, yanked on my boots, and laced them. I slid into the shoulder harness, checked the weapon to make sure it was loaded with silver-lead rounds, and grabbed the jacket, which was warm from the house. It felt like heaven on my cold body.

As I dressed she said to FireWind, "It's commercial. Fastest protein I can think of." She was holding out a jar of peanut butter and a spoon, which he took.

"Thank you."

"You understand you have to stay up here, safe, right?" I asked both of them. FireWind nodded and said, "Mmm-hmm," his mouth full of sticky peanut butter. I glanced at Mud. "With the boss-boss and whatever werecats show up . . . after?"

"Gross. Yes. I get it. But I'll be with you in the land." She sat on the ground and placed her hands flat on the earth. "Better hurry. Yummy's already there."

"She would be," I grouched. "Be safe, sister mine." I beeped my car to start and took off for Esther's, hoping I wasn't already too late.

I pulled up, my headlights illuminating the house. Esther's Tulip Tree House had gone into full protective mode, and had grown thorns like spikes, the size of Yummy's smallsword.

Yummy herself stood at the edge of the yard, near the closest vampire sapling, her eyes on the weird house. She shook her head slowly. I had a feeling she was remembering the time tree vines had suddenly gotten protective and attacked her.

Occam, in human form, and wearing only a light shirt, pants, and thin cloth sneakers, came around the back of the house and up to my car. I cut off the engine and Occam opened the door, sliding into the passenger seat. He sat tall, watching Yummy, and he didn't look cold at all, when my feet were still aching from contact with the ground.

Without looking at me, clearly knowing what I was thinking, he said, "I'm good, Nell, sugar. What's Yummy getting ready to do?"

"Get Ming out of Esther's house. Yummy confirmed Ming was bitten by an arcenciel a long time ago. She might have been bitten again." I shrugged slightly. "I have her permission to pull her under and try to heal her."

"Looks like I'm behind on the latest," he drawled.

"I'll catch you up when I can." I handed him a stake. "Your job is to stake Ming."

"Sounds easy enough."

My breathy laughter whispered through the car. "That's the spirit. Sure. Very easy. I'll be unhappy if you miss our wedding, so don't get your head torn off."

"Not planning on it, Nell, sugar."

Yummy stepped into my car's headlights, which I had left on. She shouted, "Ming of Glass! Attend me!"

The door flew open. Ming stood on my sister's porch, thorns growing up toward her feet. She was dressed in fighting leathers like Yummy's, but scarlet. She was wearing swords and knives. And she looked really, *really* mad.

"You dare to demand of me?" Ming said. "I am the Master of this City. You are the blood clan leader of a few weak Mithrans."

As Ming spoke, Yummy sniffed, scenting the air. She glanced back at the car and nodded once, officially confirming what she had said: Ming had been bitten, and bitten again recently.

Ming sneered. "You are nothing."

"Noooothing?" Yummy said slowly, separating the syllables in a way that somehow implied derision, shrugging slightly, deliberately provocative. Holding Ming's total attention and giving Occam and me time to get out and onto the ground, which we did, sliding out of the car, pushing the doors almost closed. Occam crawled around the car, stealthy as a hunting cat, and knelt beside me at the front wheel.

The words slithering like snakes, Yummy hissed, "Ming of Glasssss. My lair still stands, and my primo wasn't taken from me and . . . murdered. Unavenged."

Ming froze, unmoving as a block of ice.

"Oops," Occam whispered.

Yummy had just questioned Ming's right to be the master of a city and of a blood clan. Using Cai.

Ming threw back her head and screamed. I clapped my hands over my ears. The ululation was similar to the sound vampires made when they were dying, but lower pitched, a basso roll of vibrations that made my head ache.

Yummy screamed in response, "You are not worthy to rule! *¡Prepárese para la muerte!*"

"Well, hell," Occam said. "I'm pretty sure that was Spanish for 'Prepare for death.' I probably," he added, his words overly slow and Texan and with a lot of cat *rrrowl* in them, "should have staked the Master of the City before the swordplay started."

"Best-laid plans of mice and cat-men," I murmured.

Ming leaped off the porch, drawing swords. Yummy already had hers held high and low. Ming was still in the air when the swords clashed.

Steel glinted in the headlights. They slashed, lunged, cut, blocked, swords clanging and ringing.

I closed my eyes. Plunged into the deeps. I woke the land.

The Green Knight and I were standing on our battlefield, he in armor, astride his warhorse. In the center of the battleground two warriors engaged in battle. Steel and flesh. Hot emotions. Cold bodies.

Mud joined us in the vision beneath the ground, her body warm and steady against my cold one. Both of us in our plant armor, and oddly, both of us armed with swords and shotguns. I figured Mud had brought those. We watched the land's vision of the fight: Two bipedal undead, steel clashing. Occam, crouched to the side. Then first blood was drawn. Cold blood.

The earth knew Yummy's blood. Familiar. *Belonging.*

Ming's blood followed. A single drop from the thinnest slice. But it was enough. Her blood was different. Tainted. The tree separated and identified the abnormalities in her blood. Arcenciel venom.

Watching, sensing, I shaped my mental sword into a fist of thorns. Mud, following my lead, shaped hers into a trap-like thing, with snapping jaws and teeth. But the vampires moved too fast for us to differentiate the feet we needed to trap, popping back and forth across the lawn.

As if we were inside each other's minds, my true sister and I followed the battle. Together, we sent roots tunneling through dirt and pressing aside rocks, growing, surrounding the fighters, beneath them, ready to spring.

More of Yummy's blood flew, a thick cold spray. She was losing.

Beneath the surface of the land, Esther strode to us and stood, a churchwoman with a meat cleaver in one hand and a whiplike vine covered with thorns in the other. "Holy Moses,"

she whispered, as she watched the fight. The power of the land
rose up in her, filled her.

"Now." Occam rose and stepped toward the fight. He appeared on the battle scene, part of the conflict. He was half
human, half cat. Claws like rakes.

Belonging.

Yummy fell.

Occam-cat leaped. High in the air above the battle. Off the
earth.

Ming raised her sword high. A backstroke meant to decapi-
tate him.

Together Mud and I *reached* through the sacred ground,
sending life. Vines sprang up, thorned traps. Esther's vine
whipped out. Snapping.

Occam flew through the air, spinning, tucking. Beneath
Ming's death stroke.

Vines erupted, thousands of shoots making a steel thorn
glove and a barbed thorn trap. Together, my sisters and I snared
Ming's feet. Caught her arms. Twined around her body, piercing
her with living wood stakes.

Still in the air, Occam-cat hammered his stake into Ming's
body. Through her armor. Into the undead flesh of her belly. She
faltered. The downstroke of her sword shifted as Occam tumbled to the side, his trajectory altered.

Ming's stroke tracked him, heading toward Occam, somer-
saulting in the air.

The Green Knight was suddenly behind Ming. Just *there*.

He grasped the sword handle. Stopped its fall.

Occam slid by the sharp edge.

Mud and I yanked. Down and down. Pulling Ming through
the ground. And beneath it.

The roots and thorns beneath the ground were wood. Wood
could make a vampire true-dead. I had to hope the vampire tree
would keep her alive. Though I admitted to myself that if Ming
died, I wouldn't grieve much. Under the ground, we shoved the
stake in more securely. Deeper.

"Holy Moses," Esther said again, cussing in church-speak.
"That there blood-sucker is gonna die."

I opened my eyes.

Esther was looking at Yummy. The vampire's body was limp, stretched upon the land, her blood scarlet on the green. Ming's final strike had sliced deeply. Her neck was half-severed. Gouts of blood had emptied onto the earth, feeding the land. Now it trickled. Her flesh was pale as paper, white and bloodless.

"Sister mine," Mud said. She took my hand. We closed our eyes.

Mud and I were armored, standing in front of Yummy, hands clasped. I felt another hand take my free one. Esther, joining us, a churchwoman fierce and free to act as she needed. I was so proud.

Power slammed through us.

"Sisters mine," Esther said.

"Sisters mine," I said.

"Sisters mine," Mud repeated.

Behind me, I heard the words, "Rule of Three."

Together we three slid into the body of the one who *belonged* to Soulwood. Mud's vines seized the sliced jugular, guiding Esther's uncertain hand. I worked on the carotid. With tiny scarlet roots, fine as silk thread, I began to stitch the large artery back together. I had never studied how to make surgical stitches, but I knew how to finish a seam in a dress so it looked pretty, would never ravel, and was extra strong.

The scarlet root of the vampire tree, of the Green Knight, grew thin and thinner in my hand, but with a firm and pointed tip. With the threadlike root, I pierced the narrow-walled vein and guided it over, under, through the root's circle, creating a loop, pulling the delicate elastic blood vessel together. Next stitch went on the other side, overlapping, then higher, lower, inside and out. Clean and neat, just like the samplers I had embroidered as a child. This was much better work than I had done on the were-creatures. I wished I had thought about fancy sewing stitches instead of knotting off.

Inside of Yummy, her heart beat once.

She was still alive. Or as alive as an undead could be. But she had wood inside her, and wood was dangerous to vampires. She would need blood, and a lot of it, if she woke. While I hated to stake a friend, pulling her underground to finish healing might be smart. I turned and found Esther's roots, paler than mine, the

lovely delicate pink of the walls of her home. I knotted my
thread and broke it. With the tip, I patted Esther's thread. *I need
to secure her so she can't hurt us if she wakes,* I thought at her.

As if from far away, I heard Esther say, "I can take over for
you." She shaped her root and thrust through the artery wall
next to my knot. Her stitches were much more tiny and precise
than mine.

I checked in on Mud and then let my thin rootling travel
through Yummy's body, along her blood vessels, to her belly, to
the spot where vamps could be impaled with a wood stake,
which would make them fall to the ground essentially lifeless.
Lifeless-er? Undead-er?

The small area in her flesh, about a four-inch square, was at
and below the navel. At that centerline point, a stake would pierce
the descending artery that fed the lower body. For reasons never
determined, that particular strike would immediately disable a
vamp like a potent tranquilizer. Wood was ineffective as a para-
lyzing agent anywhere else except the heart, and a heart strike
could be deadly to a young vampire like Yummy. I intended to
create a stake and stake Yummy's belly from inside.

When I reached the spot, just below her navel, I widened my
focus. I spotted a loose tangle of nearly microscopic . . . things.
It was something I had never seen before.

Of course, I had only recently seen a vampire body from the
inside. I tightened my mental focus on the twisted things and
frowned. It was a slack knot of nerves and neurons, looking
vaguely like a pile of yarn half-unraveled from a sweater or
shawl, slightly kinked and spiraled with long arms like starfish.
Like what I thought brain matter might look like under a microscope.

This supple mesh of nerves was not something I had been
told about at Spook School, and had not seen in the postmortems of vampires I had watched there, though working from the
outside, the relaxed snarl wouldn't have been noticeable. The
only way to see it was if this particular slice of tissue had been
viewed through a microscope. It also was not something humans had, or any animal I had seen butchered for meat. This . . .
this was something new to me. This thin layer of neurons might
be why vamps dropped deader when staked. I wondered if even
they knew about it.

I followed the nerves from the snarl and they traveled to Yummy's stomach, then to her heart. There, two long odd-looking nerves branched off and followed her carotids up to her brain. How strange.

I pulled back and considered what to do about Yummy potentially waking up hungry and draining some human to death. Since I had no idea what damage I might do to her while I worked from the inside, I encouraged a root to grow from the ground, outside Yummy's body. I forced life into the root to sharpen one end, to thicken the stake, harden it off, and then I shoved it through Yummy's belly, through the bunched nerves and into the big artery. I broke off the part outside, leaving the wood inside her.

Moving back up Yummy's body, I checked in on my sisters. The carotid and the flesh of Yummy's neck had been stitched together. All she had to do now was drink blood and heal.

Of course, if I was wrong about wood only doing major damage in the belly and heart, I had just killed my vampire friend, using wood to sew her together. If there had been another vampire or six around, I'd have made sure Yummy was healed in the Mithran way, but that hadn't been an option and I hadn't known if Yummy would survive until help could come. So I took a chance. I offered up a prayer for my friend and pulled out of Yummy, trailed by my sisters.

I opened my eyes. At Esther's porch, Margot was curled against the foundation, human shaped, naked, and steaming in the cold. Panting with pain. Gripping an old iron ax-head. The ax-head the land had spewed up only days past.

The field of battle at the Tulip Tree House had a lot more people than when I started work on Yummy.

T. Laine was bent over Rick, who was lying between two vehicles on the road, shifting shape into human. I gave him a boost of energy to speed the process because he was breathing hard, and seemed to need help.

A few feet away Rettell rolled to her feet, human, naked, armed with a weapon, ready to fight.

Occam, in his cat form, was fighting a human, the two of them dancing as vines tried to trip only the human. Occam bit down, his fangs savaging the man's leg. The stranger's blood splattered onto the ground.

Hunger . . .

The man pulled a gun. He fired. Straight down.

Occam fell.

My heart crumpled. I tried to rise, but my legs were asleep. I fell over.

The ground erupted and snarled around the shooter. Pulled him down. Mud grunted, working with Soulwood's power. "Son of a bitch," my baby sister muttered. "Got you."

"I got your'un man," Esther called from the porch, her bare feet on the cold wood. "He won't die. I promise. But there's more humans on the land, still. You'un stop 'em."

I had to trust her. I had to. I closed my eyes, searching Soulwood. I found three more humans, armed. The land and I wrapped them in thorn baskets, piercing their flesh, the land tasting, neither of us caring if the invaders suffered. Their blood tasted of vampires. Blood-servants of Torquemada and his fangy goons.

Do not eat them, I instructed the Green Knight and Soulwood. *They are mine.*

I pulled back to Occam and dove into him, seeing the fine and perfect stitches my contrary sister had placed in the flesh of the man I loved more than my own life. His heartbeat was fluttery and weak, his breathing too fast.

I pushed life and healing and power into him. *You'un die and I'm'a kill you deader, cat-man,* I thought to him.

Ain't my plan, Nell, sugar. Dying ain't my plan.

TWENTY-TWO

Asperity in her mental tone, Esther said, *So that's how you'un do it. I got him.*

My sister, who had feared magic for as long as she had lived, shoved healing into Occam. The ground beneath him erupted into blooms and leaves.

He began to shift.

I nearly sobbed with relief. It would take him longer than usual to shift into his spotted leopard. He was injured. But he was going to make it.

Naked as a jaybird, Margot prowled around the house, keeping Esther and the twins safe. Protecting Occam while he shifted and healed. Rettell was dressed now in thin pants and a sweatshirt, but barefoot, walking the perimeter. Rick was human, fighting to breathe. Through the land, I said to him, *You got sexing on the brain so much, you ain't got nothing left?*

Rick waved the finger of one hand at me, telling me to go away.

"Stupid man," I said aloud.

Lucky man, he whispered through the land. *Luckiest man on earth.*

I shook my head at him and found my sister. In reality Esther was sitting on the porch, guarding the twins. Spiritually, she was beneath the earth, helping Occam.

I opened my eyes and tried to stand. Didn't make it upright by myself.

T. Laine caught me on my shoulder and shoved me back down, steadying me. "At least you're still alive," she said. "But you better pull out of the earth real fast, plant-woman, or you may not come back."

"Why?" I managed.

"You're going all tree on us again. And while I have some arborist training, it isn't enough to bring you back to flesh."

I looked down at myself. My fingers were sticklike and my hands were woody. I was having trouble breathing deeply, as if my lungs weren't working right. Mud was holding my hand, and hers was completely human looking. I held up her hand. "How?" I asked.

"I just told my brain to not let my body change. We been learning about matter and energy and vibrations in school, and how's they all the same thing. You know. In science class."

"Told. Your brain," I gasped, breathing too shallowly.

"It's our brains is what's letting us see in all these places, sister mine. It's our brains interpreting energy and affecting matter. Or we'uns crazy as a bunch a drunk raccoons. One or t'other."

It was very much like what Tandy had said. I'd think about it all later. I closed my eyes and looked at the Green Knight. I thought at him, *You ready to put Operation Contain a Demon into practice?*

He gave me that regal nod.

Okay. When I get there, bring Tomás to the surface.

To . . . más?

The Green Knight was talking to me. In English. *Holy Moses.* I thought at him . . . it, saying, *The vampire with the dark energy.*

The Green Knight nodded again, all elegant and stately. I needed to learn how to do that.

Mud was in the house, though not without argument, guarding Cherry, the cats, and the house itself. With her were Esther and the twins, the babies squalling at the top of their lungs, even though they had been fed and burped and changed and sung to.

Occam, still extraordinarily weak, lay in cat form near my knees, his breathing almost fast enough to be called a pant, though he would have argued the canine comparison.

T. Laine sat on the steps to the house, magical and mundane weapons scattered to either side in a pattern she could find easily in the dark. She had cast a *seeing* working over the property.

We didn't know how long it would last, but for now we could all see magic like witches did.

Leann Rettell, Margot Racer, and Rick LaFleur were fully clothed and sitting in a car, weapons ready.

FireWind was again in black wolf form and had devoured a side of smoked bacon delivered by my brother Sam. He sat on the porch, ears perked, alert, golden eyes shining, ready to help T. Laine or me. Not that he could actually help us.

The captured humans had been released from their thorned cages, handcuffed, and carted to the city lockup for trespassing and weapons charges. That was the best and worst we could do to them.

It was well after midnight and I was so tired I wanted to cry. But we had one more job to do. One more thing to accomplish before we could turn the vampires—who were guilty of torturing and killing humans, and currently captured in the land—over to the emissaries of the Dark Queen's court.

Jane Yellowrock had people on the way over from Asheville, led by a vampire called Koun. They were flying in via helicopter to beat the dawn, so we had to hurry. Hurry to free and then capture a demon, and turn over the vampires to the Dark Queen. And manage not to release the demon and get one of us possessed.

I placed my ratty pink blanket on the ground in front of the lumps of dirt that covered Torquemada and his friend. Don something, that started with an *A*. Whatever it was. I half fell to the blanket and crossed my knees, which snapped and popped like green sticks breaking. I put my hands on the ground and dropped into the bliss of Soulwood. There was no need of a potted tree to bring me close to the knight and to the earth of Soulwood. I was here. They were here. We were here.

Rule of Three?

Lainie's voice had mentioned that during the fight at Esther's house. Sooo, the three of us were stronger together?

The containment vessel I put beside me, tilting it so I could remove the lid without fumbling. The Blood Tarot was propped against the vessel, having been brought from HQ by a very confused county deputy running lights and sirens.

Bait. The deck was bait. In case that was what the demon

wanted, and maybe had been using Torquemada to acquire. It was an educated guess put forth by Tandy, who, along with JoJo, was manning comms at HQ and liaising with county officials. Just in case some unseen and unplanned-for scenario happened and we needed human backup.

Keeping in mind Mud's words about how not to go rooty and turn into a tree, I instructed myself to become and stay human shaped. Nothing happened: the stiffness in my knees didn't improve, my hips didn't stop aching, and my fingers didn't look less bumpy and knotty. Ah well. I stroked Occam once along his cat body. I had all that I needed, right here, beside me. Hands to the winter dry grass, I scratched my woody nails into the ground and slid into the earth.

Breathing out, relaxing, I let Soulwood gather me up and hold me. I shared with my land all that I was, and all that I hoped, all that I loved, all that I wanted. It wasn't prayer. It was hope.

I closed my eyes and slid my thoughts down. And down. Bypassing the vampires lumped in the ground near me, I moved out, beyond the borders of the land marked on the deed, to edges of the land Soulwood claimed. And even farther, to the land the vampire tree was claiming. I located each animal, few out this late, most sleeping in dens or nests or in small herds or clutches. I caressed each non-vampire-tree, each interconnected thing that was simply and solely the life of Soulwood. Beneath me, the land sighed and slept and suffused me with something that might have been love, though it was a love as unlike human love as the day was from the night. It was *other*. Ancient. Beyond my understanding. The *Earth*.

The darkness here, in Soulwood, beneath the trees and the ground, seemed to have texture, as if I could brush my fingers across the lack of light and feel it prickle on my skin, light like bioluminescence. Sleeping in winter. Not aching with *hunger*. The land had fed well and its *hunger* was satiated. For now.

On the surface, my body sighed. I reminded myself I didn't need to become a tree.

I stepped into the visual pasture created by the Green Knight.

To him I saluted, lifting a weapon that looked like a spear made of living wood, with blossoms at the base of the sharp point and vines trailing from the end. I was armored in wood and, in the vision, was growing leaves and thorns and a few small scarlet flowers here and there. I looked like a walking bower. Or maybe like the knight's vision of Soulwood.

I thought, *When I open the vessel, you best be gone or it might take you in too. And maybe watch out for that demon who tried to take your power. All this stuff we're getting ready to do is dangerous.*

His horse's hooves became restive beneath him, dancing in place.

The containment vessel was an equal opportunity energy vacuum, sucking in anything noncorporeal. I figured the demon could only hurt the tree if the demon could visualize Soulwood the way we did, and also understand that the tree was self-aware and sentient. A tree in the real world would not appear to be a likely host for a demon. I hoped it was still confused about the powers in my land.

Overhead in the green sky, a few stars shone through leafy branches. As we walked, the bracken around us seemed to grow taller, the stones sharper and glowing with phosphorescent moss, lighting our way.

Together we approached the mounds of buried undead. Here, deep in the life of Soulwood, in the vision of the Green Knight's place within the land, the two vampires lay in the fetal position, unrotting flesh pierced by thorns with wooden stakes in their bellies. In the vision, maggots writhed within the bodies' wounds. But within each vampire there were sparks glowing, things that danced or writhed and twisted.

I stopped, in the vision standing directly in front of them, and studied the bodies and the sparks. In each body, there were sparks of life and power. The one with two sparks was Alonso. One spark was as green as the sky above, as green as the knight himself. The other spark was red. In the other body there was a third thing, one I had no name for, this one not just a speck of darkness but a blackness so deep it seemed to be an entity all its own. Torquemada's undeath, his tattered soul, and his demon.

I looked at the knight. *Any suggestions on how I get the demon out?*

He turned his head left, then right once.

I figured.

T. Laine had told me what to do. "Get in close, aim the vessel at the body, then open the lid and yank out the stake at the exact same moment. And hope for the best."

Bring that body to the surface, please. I indicated the one with two sparks and a darkness. *Remove the thorns when it's on the surface, but leave the stake in place. And then get out of the way.*

The knight gave a scant nod. I opened my eyes.

On the surface, only a foot from my knees, the dirt began to quiver and shake. The ground rolled aside in miniature landslides, and the body began to appear. Wrapped with pliable roots. Skin pale as moonlight. Drained of what blood he once carried. Dirty and smeared with his own blood. Pierced with thorns. Hundreds of thorns, all over him, the viny roots wrapped tight around every limb, every digit. The land and the knight had drank down his blood, sharing the sustenance.

Tomás' clothes were ragged. His hair was gnarled and matted with soil, blood, and thorns. His fangs were fully out, three inches long. His beard was thin and pointed. On his chest was an old scar, a cross-shaped wound, like a healed burn. Silver-branded vampire flesh. Had he been branded by placing a silver cross on his chest? His dark eyes were open but sightless, vamped out, blacker than the night sky. Dirt coated the surface of the eyeballs.

In my mind I heard Mud murmur, *Gross.*

I wanted to laugh, but it wasn't funny. Not at all.

As I watched, the thorns all slowly withdrew. They made soft sounds of suction as they left the flesh, faint *squicks.* The roots rolled to the side and coiled upon the ground. The tips quivered slightly. The knight wasn't pulling them beneath the earth.

The stake was still in place. I'd have to reach over his naked leg to grip it and there wasn't a lot of the stake protruding from the belly. I'd have to shove my hand against his cold undead flesh to grip it. Mud had been right. *Gross.*

I repositioned the vessel between my knees, setting the Blood Tarot on the body, beside the stake. I reached to Tomás and pressed my fingers against his undead, blood-smeared flesh. His body was cold as the grave.

Something halfway between horror and hysteria burbled in

the back of my throat for a moment before I squelched it. The breath I took shuddered. I shoved at the cold flesh, trying to push it away from the stake, but the stake moved with it. I shoved harder, as if trying to compress his belly to his spine. The stake went too, back and forth with the surface of Tomás' belly.

I was going to need tools. Like John's pliers in the covered back porch. I started to speak when T. Laine knelt on the far side of me. She was holding a pair of fifteen-inch-long straight-nose locking pliers.

"Not my first unstaking," she said. She opened the locked pliers nose a little wider than the end of the stake. Gently, she shoved the jaws down along the stake and inside the flesh. She locked them tight on either side of the stake. "I'll unstake. Do me a favor. Don't drop the vessel."

"I promise." I blew out a breath and stretched my shoulders.

"On three," she said, "like, one, two, three, and then open the vessel."

I gave a jerky nod.

"One. Two," she said, establishing rhythm. "Three."

Everything happened at once, overlapping, overlaying, like Aya shuffling the tarot deck.

She yanked the stake.

I twisted the lid.

Tomás de Torquemada leaped to his feet.

A millisecond later, the vessel's top fell open.

T. Laine dropped back.

Tomás de Torquemada fell upon her.

The vessel roared with a silence so intense it stole every sound from the world.

His fangs buried in Lainie's throat.

The roots attacked.

Beneath the earth, the Green Knight charged forward. His warhorse thundered. I raised my spear.

From the dark, Yummy screamed a wordless challenge. Hurtled to us.

The Blood Tarot rattled in its box.

T. Laine fell back.

Tomás fell with her.

Yummy popped to my side. She raised her sword and brought it down.

Tomás ripped his fangs up.

Blood flew. Massive gouts.

Yummy severed the spine of Tomás de Torquemada.

A mist rose from somewhere and vanished into the vessel.

Two sparks flew toward the opening, one red, one blacker than night. The red of undeath. The utter absence of light of the demon.

Yummy's sword stopped a hair's breadth from cutting through and slicing into T. Laine.

Lainie's blood pumped. Pumped. Everywhere.

Yummy dropped the longsword and from somewhere a shortsword appeared in her hand. She slid it between the vampire and the witch. Cut upward, toward herself. Severing Tomás' blood vessels.

A second spray shot out. Doused T. Laine's face. Mixing with her blood. Healing vampire blood.

I tried to set the lid back in place.

Silence. Intense silence. Like nothing ever imagined.

Yummy batted Tomás' head away.

T. Laine's blood pumped.

Yummy cut her own arm.

I had seen only two sparks. The demon and the undeath. Not the green of Tomás' soul.

The collection vessel roared. I quaked trying to get the lid aligned with the vessel's open mouth. It clunked into place and I shoved it down. As I did, two green sparks flew into the vessel.

Two.

Tomás was dead. T. Laine . . . ?

Yummy dropped to her knees. Her blood flowed over Lainie's throat.

T. Laine lay still.

I shoved the vessel away and leaned over her. She had no throat to check for a pulse. Just gouged meat.

Tomás had killed my friend. And her soul was contained in a vessel with his soul and with a demon.

Yummy cut another place on her arm, deeply. She bled more onto Lainie. Reached with her free arm and took my nerveless hands. She placed one on Lainie's chest and the other onto the dirt. "Fix this."

She hadn't seen. Hadn't seen Lainie's soul sucked into the vessel.

I reached into the land. Reached into the life of Soulwood.

Reached for Mud and Esther.

Yummy cut herself again. Sharing her healing blood all over Lainie's wounds. The vampire's bleeding stopped. Her skin started to regrow.

"Mercy, Jesus," Esther prayed as she fell to my side. Next to T. Laine.

"That ain't good," Mud said, kneeling on my other side and placing her hand on top of mine.

I reached deep, deep, deeper and found a Sleeper of the earth, silent, full of life. With one finger, I brushed the thin lining of the Sleeper. Gently, I slid just a hair of its life away. Mixed it with the life of Soulwood, pulled yet more from the vampire tree. I wrapped them together, twisting, pulling, as if making thread from three different kinds of wool. Tight. Strong. Twirling the life forces into one.

Help me, I thought at my sisters. We shoved the odd fusion of energies into T. Laine.

Nothing happened.

I reached for the knight. *I need life for her. Energy. Electricity. To restart her heart.* Once I got her heart started I could figure out what to do about her soul.

I have no fire, the knight thought. *Fire is evil.*

Kneeling on Lainie's other side, Rick began chest compressions.

Yummy clicked her fangs open and pricked T. Laine, licking the healing flesh.

Time passed. Probably only seconds, but it felt like forever.

Aya stepped into my field of vision, saying, "I've called EMS." He had clearly shifted too many times recently. He looked gaunt. He'd traded flesh for the power to shift shape. He elbowed his way in next to Rick and switched off for compressions, his fists laced and arms straight, his body rocking, pumping on T. Laine's chest, hard and fast.

With her own fangs Yummy ripped her inner wrist and held it to T. Laine's mouth. "Stupid witch." To us she snarled, "What are you waiting for? Do your magic."

I said aloud, "She died at the same time as Torquemada. Her soul was sucked into the containment jar. If we can get her heart started, we can open the containment jar and let it free . . ."

"Nell. You will not," FireWind said, his breathing loud as he compressed her chest.

I didn't reply. He had a small point. I had no idea how to get just one soul out, or how to keep a demon in. A demon might come out, leave Lainie's soul behind, and take her body.

"They use a defibrillator in school," Mud said. "They showed us how to use it."

"We don't have one." I took her hand. "There *has* to be something *we* can do."

Together we dove back into the land. In the visions of the land, T. Laine's body looked like a carcass. Mud, Esther, and I shoved life into Lainie. Mud and I sent *ourselves* into her, and . . . nothing. Not a spark of life.

Nothing.

Nothing.

I started to open the vessel.

"Nell. Do not," FireWind said.

I hesitated.

FireWind sounded winded when he said what I had been thinking. "We have no idea what might happen if we open it again. The demon would surely get out and possess one of us. No idea if Lainie can get back out and into her body if we *do* open it."

I looked to the side and something glinted on Tomás' bloody chest. A silver cross. The same one that had burned into his chest? The brand . . . He wore it all the time? I ripped it from him and said, "Let's see what happens."

Before anyone could stop me, I opened the containment vessel. Instantly I rested the silver cross across its wide mouth. Silence descended on the clearing. The demon's lightless evil roiled against the silver and whipped away, back inside. "Come on," I whispered. "Lainie. Come on."

Nothing happened.

Margot, who had avoided me since our private conversation about her belonging with the unit, landed near Mud and squeezed in. Her cell phone was on speaker. "Yes. I know I'm not a witch, Aunt Sheshema, and I know the *wyrd* isn't a witch working. But I have to try. Her soul is trapped in a containment vessel of some sort. Give me the *wyrd. Give me the* wyrd*!*" she demanded when her aunt didn't reply. "Or I'll tell Uncle Jeremy about you smoking again."

"You a bad child. You mama be ashamed if she knew you threatening me."

"Don't make me tell her about the—"

"You'll need something of power for an exchange," Sheshema said.

Mud grabbed a vine on the ground and said, "Give me some roots, you damned tree." She twisted it around her hand. The root broke off in her fist.

"We have a thing of power," Margot said, taking the root Mud held out. It coiled slowly in her hand like a snake dancing. "And we have this." She lifted the Blood Tarot in its box.

"Hold the items of power over the vessel containing the woman's soul," Sheshema ordered.

Margot held the root and the cursed deck above the silver. "Done."

"*Njoo. Ishi.*" The syllables rang in the clearing, fighting back the unnatural silence. "Say it with me. Every being of power in the place. Say it. *Njoo. Ishi.*"

We all joined in. Even Mud, Esther, and me, knowing we were saying witch words of power, words we would be burned at the stake for if some of the churchmen knew of it.

"*Njoo. Ishi. Njoo. Ishi. Njoo. Ishi,*" we chanted.

Sparks appeared at the mouth of the vessel.

Margot held the vine over the vessel and I moved the silver.

The vine was yanked into the containment vessel. Instantly the Blood Tarot followed, bending, folding shape as if space itself altered, allowing the tin box to fit into the vessel's mouth.

Green, green sparks appeared. Bloomed into glowing white mists, two tiny clouds with no shape, no form. In the darkness of the yard, the shimmering mists erupted from the mouth of the vessel. I slammed the silver cross back. Trapping, I hoped, the demon.

But the mists didn't look for their bodies.

"They's out and free," Esther said, "but they ain't going into the body."

"You can see them?" Margot asked.

"'Course I can see 'em. I'm a plant-woman," Esther sniped. *Which one is Lainie?*

Sheshema and Margot continued to chant. And we followed, saying, *"Ishi. Ishi. Ishi."*

Mud reached over, slapped FireWind's hands out of the way, stopping the compressions. She grabbed a soul out of the air and commanded, *"Live."* And she pressed the soul against Lainie's chest. Held the spark there.

In a wash of blackness, the silver cross and the other mist were sucked into the vessel. Gone. I slammed the lid into place and pressed it down. Tossed the vessel to FireWind.

With her other hand, Mud grabbed my wrist, and I added my power to hers and Esther's. Together we three shoved the soul she held into Lainie.

Let it be T. Laine's, I prayed. *Let it be T. Laine's.*

Lainie's body bucked.

"Ishi. Ishi. Ishi." The chant rose around us. *"Ishi. Ishi. Ishi."*

Mud looked at the sky and said, "Elohim. I ain't always been happy with you'uns. But you'uns is more powerful than all this nonsense. You'uns need to fix this." She brought her fist down hard onto T. Laine's chest.

Lainie's body bucked again. And she took a breath.

We all went silent. Watching. The breath slowly escaped her slack lips.

Seconds trickled by.

Lainie sucked in a breath. Sat upright, knocking us all away, her arms flailing.

"What is it? What's happening?" Sheshema asked. "She dead? She back?"

Lainie gasped a dozen breaths. Held her hands to her chest. Her face was contorted with agony. She bent forward, over her knees. Sucking breaths. She cursed softly, over and over.

"She's breathing," Margot said. "She's cussing."

"Her body breathing. Who's in it?" Sheshema asked, her tone challenging.

"What were we saying?" I asked as I watched T. Laine breathe, and wondered who or what was actually inside her. "Those words, *Njoo. Ishi.*"

"A *wyrd* working of sorts. A prayer, really," Margot said. "One my auntie created. She's a Christian and she only uses prayer, so her workings have never been tested. This was sort of a test run."

"A test— And?" Aya demanded.

"It's Swahili for *Come. Live.*"

"The bishop gonna skin me alive," Sheshema said.

"No, he ain't," Mud said, "'cause we finished it with a church word. We called on one a the oldest names of God."

Power. Energy. Intent. Quantum stuff. And God. I shivered with cold. Stared at my friend.

"Son of a witch," Lainie whispered, rocking back and forth.

Tears sprang out of my eyes and rained down my cheeks. *Son of a witch* was witchy cursing.

"Where's the elephant that was sitting on my chest?" she demanded.

"She's alive, Auntie," Margot said. "She's alive. You did it."

"Let me talk to the woman who finished off the working," Sheshema said. "I want to hear the final parts."

Margot said, "It's a kid who grows leaves in her hair, not a witch. Have fun." She handed Mud the cell phone and crawled up to Lainie. She sat next to her and encircled her shoulders with her arms.

Lainie laid her head on Margot's shoulder. "That was freaky. What happened?"

Almost casually, Margot said, "Your throat got torn out and you died. Your soul got sucked into the vessel with Torquemada's and a demon."

Lainie laughed and coughed. When she could breathe, she asked, "Only that? No elephant?"

"No elephant. FireWind and Rick did CPR while Yummy fed you, and everyone else sat around with their thumbs up their collective butts. Nellie captured the demon. Then we figured out your soul was missing, so Nell disobeyed FireWind and opened the vessel. She figured out how to keep the demon inside and let you out. My auntie gave us a *wyrd* prayer to pull your soul free. And Mud figured out which soul was yours and how to get it back into you. It was a community effort."

Lainie tilted her head to FireWind. "You wouldn't let me out? Fuck you. Sideways."

The boss-boss laughed, and was still laughing when he said, "Turns out I was wrong about the demon escaping and possessing one of us. My deepest apologies, Kent. I'll approve you two weeks' PTO to heal from the broken ribs I gave you keeping your body alive while the unit figured out how to save you."

Mud reappeared and handed Margot her cell. To Lainie, Mud asked, "How do you have sex sideways?"

I interrupted quickly, "No sex talk."

"Mindy," FireWind said, using my sister's given name. "How did you know which soul was Kent's?"

"I'm a plant-woman. I know things," Mud stated, her expression Nicholson-mulish.

Her defensive tone made me afraid that she had taken a wild guess. Mud was often impulsive, but she had seemed so certain this time, as if she had known, not flipped a mental coin.

I dropped my head back and stared up at the night sky. I said, "Before anyone gets comfy, we have to release the other two vampires under the earth."

"This is an order," FireWind said. "This unit has done enough tonight. We can take care of vampires tomorrow night."

"Thank you," I said. "I'm a mite tuckered."

Before I could get the words out fully, the sky overhead rippled with light, pearly, prismed, scintillating light.

Esther whispered, "Leviathan." She darted to the house and her babies.

Breathing hard between short phrases, I said, "I had hoped for a break. But the arcenciels are here. From the light show it looks like they're here in force. Three arcenciels at least. Ain't we lucky."

FireWind murmured something in another language and turned away, dialing his cell.

"They're pretty," Mud said. "They dangerous?"

"Very." I looked down at myself. I was covered in the blood of vampire and the blood of my friend. But my hands were not as rooty and knotted as before. I felt my belly. It was less woody. But I was heavily leafed out. I was a forest at my scalp and nails. I could feel them unfurling in my boots.

I needed a shower and time to wash the blood off me and out of my hair. As Mud might say, I was kinda gross. Right now I had no time for a shower or to groom my leaves.

Mud, still kneeling beside me, whispered, "After all this, are we'uns gonna get eaten?"

"I hope not. And if we do, let's plan to give them a whopping case of indigestion."

Mud giggled nervously and slid an arm around me, under my shoulders. I forced myself to my feet, my baby sister helping me stand straight. If the dragons came to kill us, there was no weapon that could harm them except cold iron. I thought fleetingly of the rusted ax-head the ground had given up at Esther's when all this started. Of the iron horseshoe that had fallen off the shed not so long ago. Of John's old woodworking tools.

Four arcenciels landed. I recognized Pearl, Opal, and Cerulean. The new one was a topaz and sapphire creature who didn't take on human form when they landed. In size, the new dragon looked more like a teenaged human, but was built like a lizard with horns, standing upright. She was smaller than the others, maybe younger.

She hissed at us.

The lizard was likely the one that had been inside Tomás de Torquemada's crystal, which had to be a horrible experience, but all I could think of was the green lizard on the old commercials and wondered if she spoke with an Australian accent. I breathed out a silent laugh, and Mud elbowed me in the side.

"Stop that," she said. "Them's guests."

"Sorry," I said. But I wasn't. I was simply too tired to be properly hospitable.

From the heavens came a greater light. A big, *big* dragon. The light was blinding, like a million rainbows shining through fog, a mist that hadn't been there a moment past. She landed, remaining in dragon form, and walked closer to the others until they were under her wing, which she kept raised like a rainbow umbrella. She wrapped her tail around them, creating a barrier between us.

FireWind stepped closer and said, "Soul. It is good to see you . . . looking well. We have been concerned."

"The business of dragons is none of yours," she said. The voice sounded like Soul, if the words had been put to music, to bells and strings and woodwinds. To a melody straight from heaven.

"The safety of our friend is our business," Aya said, his words gentle.

The dragon cocked her head. "'Friend' . . . " Her eyes were

round as plates and glowed with inner light. That light blasted out and we all turned away. When I blinked away the glare, Soul, in her human form, was holding Ayatas FireWind and Rick LaFleur in a hug. Or killing them. With my burned retinas it was hard to tell for sure.

"I forgot for a moment—for a while more than that—what it meant to be human. Forgive me. I made your jobs harder," she said, her silver hair floating on the air, her gossamer dress billowing. "I'm sorry. I stepped outside the bounds of my official duties as assistant director of PsyLED."

No one spoke into the silence, all of our faces showing the confusion we felt.

"You mean because you bit vampires?" Rick asked.

"It was the only way to save all of the prisoners they had trapped," Soul said.

"How many?" FireWind asked, stepping back first from the physical contact.

"Let me give my final report to close my case," Soul said. "Do you have a recorder?"

"Yes. You can dictate to JoJo at HQ on my cell phone," Rick said. He tapped the screen and said, "Jones. Record."

"Copy that, LaFleur. Recording."

Aya stepped back, standing on my other side from Mud. His hair was still loose and he had pulled it back out of the way in a long tail that draped over his shoulder. He was dressed in only thin street clothes and a light jacket and should have been cold, but seemed impervious to the temperature, his expression remote yet his yellow eyes intense, watching his boss.

Soul produced a torn piece of paper from the glowing veil of her gown. She handed it to Rick. "Add this number to the call, LaFleur."

Rick had a momentary reaction, barely visible in the dim light. He tapped his screen and a moment later a sleepy, grumpy man answered with, "This better be good."

Soul replied, "Mackey. This is Soul. This is my final report. It's being taken by Unit Eighteen HQ, but you said you wanted to be kept in the loop."

"Hang on," he replied. There was ambient noise and the sound of a door closing. In a much stronger voice he said, "Soul. I've been worried."

"And who is this?" Jo interrupted. "For the record."

"This is Director Mackey of PsyLED," he said.

"Thank you, sir," she said, her voice crisp and not at all awed to be on a late-night call with the boss-boss-boss-boss in DC. A man who had obviously been awakened from sleep.

Soul said, "For the rest of you who were not in this loop at all, for the last month I have been on a clandestine assignment for Director Mackey, with the express permission and cooperation of the president of the United States, and the Dark Queen."

"Soul. Before you start," the director said, "were you successful?"

"Yes, sir. I was," Soul said.

"Thank God. And are you okay?" the director asked.

"I am well, Mackey," Soul said. "Thank you. For my final report, this is Assistant Director of PsyLED Soul. Rick, will you list the others?"

LaFleur said, "Jones. FireWind, all the same special agents, and civilians, are still present except Esther, Ingram's sister. Also present on the ground are arcenciels Pearl, Opal, Cerulean, and an unknown arcenciel who has been approved by Soul."

Rick put the cell into Soul's hand and stepped back.

"A bit of backstory," she said. "My kind had been trapped in crystals for millennia. The magical, or humans strong enough and who knew the proper *wyrd* and the proper rituals, could, and did, capture us for our magic. The rare being or group of beings who captured three of us had immense power, power to ride us, using our gifts to walk into the past and change the direction of the present and the future. Some Mithrans and Naturaleza were intent upon riding us, to go back into the past. They never had one coherent purpose, which likely saved us all, each working to their own ends. We knew that some wished to destroy their own kind. Others wished to find, capture, and ride all arcenciels. Others wished different things.

"Over the years, I located and released many of my kind who had been trapped in crystals and allowed to languish. Jane Yellowrock released at least one other before she came into her full power.

"When she became the Dark Queen, there were two outliers, Tomás de Torquemada and Ming of Glass, each who had in their possession a trapped arcenciel.

"Already in my report, many years ago, prior to my taking human form and joining PsyLED, I located and released Vréfos, who had been captured in quartz crystal for two thousand years. Unfortunately, later, Ming of Glass and her sister were both bitten. Their sanity has been precarious since.

"Three months past, Ming of Glass was bitten again when she tried to abduct me. This resulted in a form of psychosis that was exacerbated by the return of her soul."

Yummy walked up, and Soul stopped. Her eyes flinty hard, Soul said, "What is *that* doing here?"

"Fighting Ming and saving your people," Yummy said. Sarcasm in the words, she added, "I await your thanks."

"There will be no thanks. Your kind are vermin." Soul turned her back on the vampire.

Yummy laughed, her tone sharp enough to cut iron. In her hand she held an ax, the ax from Esther's house. She tossed it at the feet of the arcenciel. Cold iron. Soul didn't flinch, but the other arcenciels moved further into the dark, and out of the *seeing* working. Yummy laughed again.

Ignoring the ax-head, Soul said, "We heard that Tomás de Torquemada, who had an arcenciel in crystal, had come out of hiding in the Vatican, and that he was intent upon trapping and riding more arcenciels, planning to come to this country to accomplish his ends, since this was the only rift he might get near, and hoping to trap one of us."

"What were his ends?" FireWind asked.

"He wished to bring the Inquisition to full and supreme power. To destroy every infidel in the world, and to allow what he called the only *one true church*, the Holy See, the Roman Catholic Church, to remain. He had the Coda. He knew when the world sat on a precipice. He knew what levers to use and what people to kill all through the history of the last four thousand years to bring this to pass. All he needed were arcenciels. He would have ridden back in time repeatedly. Had he found two more arcenciels, one of which was in Ming of Glass' lair, he might have destroyed all that we know.

"This possibility was determined to be not only a national security risk but a risk to the entire world. Director Mackey and I agreed that I would go undercover and stop him.

"As some of you now know, I had learned a new *wyrd*, a way

to break the crystal from the inside. Alone of my kind, if I were captured, I could break myself free. With the permission of National Director Mackey of PsyLED, the chairman of the Joint Chiefs of Staff, and the president of the United States, I made myself bait. But I did not plan on being approached by Welsh *gwyllgi* asking for help to escape Torquemada. Nor was I prepared for Torquemada's men to approach me in my apartment within minutes of his arrival. I bit my attackers, shifted to human form, and allowed myself to be captured when the boy was taken."

"Zeb?" I asked.

"Your kin. Yes," Soul said.

Shock like icicles ran down my limbs.

"I'm sorry to say, Director," Soul said, "that there was not time to apprise you of my change in plans before I was abducted by Torquemada's people. They took my cell phone," she said wryly. "I've lost track of how many days I spent in a cage in a warehouse, but once I discovered the location of the only remaining trapped arcenciel, I devised a way to get the others out. I set many of the young *gwyllgi* free, killed all of the adults I could find, and bit all the vampires in the warehouse before I allowed them to capture me in my light form. Once they took me to their cave, I escaped and brought my people to safety."

I slid my eyes to FireWind.

His mouth was turned down in a fierce scowl. "Several young devil dogs, little more than boys, were tortured in your human presence."

"I knew their names," I said.

"Nothing was more important than finding the last arcenciel," she said.

"Forgive me if I quarrel with that assessment," I said, fighting for breath, fighting to hold down my fury. *"You should be in jail."*

FireWind whipped his head to me, his yellow eyes blazing.

"I happen to agree," Soul said. "The boys deserved to be free. They were nothing but food to the vampires, young and old. I erred, put away the duty I swore to uphold, in favor of saving my own kind. Hence, all arcenciels will return to our world through the rift, and I will close the rift as we leave. Director. Please consider this my formal resignation."

"Soul," Mackey said softly.

"I cannot remain here. When I said this was my final report, I meant that in the sense of my final report forever. I still hear the screams of the tortured. I wish to—must—return home. I must heal. I am done with this place. End report."

In an instant she shifted to her light dragon form and spread her diaphanous wings. She leaped for the sky. Pearl, Opal, and Cerulean leaped after her. Only the lizard-shaped dragon remained.

"Soul wept," she said, her voice rubbery and elastic, as if her larynx was made of balloons. "No arcenciel weeps for humans. They live such a short time, a flower in a field, a mist that appears in the dawn and then vanishes away. You are nothing to ones such as we. This mission, allowing the dog-boys to die to achieve her ends, it broke her. We do not understand her foolish grief." The unknown arcenciel spread her wings and shoved off with her lizard legs, joining the last of her kind in the sky.

When they were gone, Margot lowered her camera. She had taken video of the entire conversation and of Soul's final report. She turned off her phone and walked up to me. "I apologize."

"For what?" I asked.

"For not realizing that you were just as alone for half of your life as I was."

"You'un fit in here pretty good."

"I do, don't I? We do."

I smiled and said, "Yeah. We do."

"Coffee one day next week? Girl talk?"

"I'd like that. But right now, I'm 'bout to pass on out."

TWENTY-THREE

Three days before Christmas, long after the last arcenciel had vanished from the face of the earth, and after the buried vampires had been released from the land, I was standing in the center of my house, wearing a dress so beautiful it made me want to cry. I stroked my hand across the fabric and wondered at the silky feel of it.

Mud handed me my bouquet of bare stems: maple, oak, and poplar, tied together with freshly green-leafed-out stems and fall-scarlet-leafed stems from the vampire tree. It symbolized the seasons and the life of the land. It stood for Soulwood and the Green Knight.

The vampire tree had donated its stems from the new sapling I had cut down in the front yard the day before, the sapling that came from Tomás de Torquemada dying true-dead on my lawn. There was still a lot of sawdust and wood chips from that epic event, and the tree had been cut up and dragged to dry at the edge of the property. Later it would be cut and shaped into a pretty table for the house.

The vampire tree wasn't happy about being harvested, but it was partially mollified to be part of the ceremony.

"You look amazing," Mud said. She was beaming, her dress a vibrant green we had raided from among Leah's things and that looked perfect on her. "I love you, sister mine."

"I love you too, Mud."

She opened the door and crossed the porch, walking slowly down the steps of our home, between the rows of our family and friends.

Before she reached the front of the raised beds, where Daddy stood, leaning on a cane, Occam walked to the bottom of the stairs and stopped. He was dressed in a black tux. He stood

there, his hands clasped in front of him. His head down. I had
never seen him in a tuxedo and he took my breath away. He was
almost totally healed, his dark blond hair to his shoulders, his
skin scar-free.

I walked out of our home, took two steps onto the porch. My
dress, layers and folds of blue gray silk, whispered against me.

Occam sniffed the air, scenting me, and raised his head, as
if expecting a blow. His eyes met mine. I felt the punch with
him. All that love. All that need. All that wanting. Slamming
into him. Into me.

Tears filled his eyes.

Tears filled mine.

Leaves tickled my hairline, growing into the circlet I wore
just in case that happened. We had planned this, this one private
moment before the others saw us.

Occam held out his hand. We both smiled. Love stretched
between us, a living thing, bright and warm, and so full I
thought my physical heart might break. Occam placed his other
fist against his heart as if he felt the same thing.

Mud reached the front. Daddy nodded.

We weren't in church, so a recording of the Wedding March
started. Everyone stood and turned. And saw me standing there.

Mama gasped and said, "My baby!" The mamas hugged.
Mud beamed with pride.

I wanted to run to Occam. I wanted to fling myself down the
steps toward him, into his arms. He laughed, seeing the desire in
my eyes, and I laughed with him. Totally inappropriate, both of us.

My heart in my eyes, I walked sedately down the steps. I
took his hand, cat-warm around my icy one. He tucked it into
the crook of his elbow. Together we walked down the aisle toward Daddy. Daddy, who was going to marry us. I had refused
to be given away like a piece of meat, but Daddy was an elder
of the church, he was officially a preacher, with a paper and
everything, so I had agreed he could perform the ceremony.

Occam and I passed my family on one side, and our friends
on the other. The mamas were standing together on the front
aisle. Esther and the twins sat with my true brother and sisters
and their spouses on the next aisle. Then the rest of that side was
full of the half brothers and sisters and a few real young ones,
the next generation of Nicholsons.

Occam and I reached the front of the raised beds. I handed Mud my bouquet. Everyone sat.

Daddy cleared his voice. He said, "Dearly beloved . . ." And began the formal, church-approved wedding service. But a few lines in, he changed it, and his words shook me.

"Each moment has to be lived in that moment. Because the moment after will not be the same. Each joy. Each sadness and sorrow. Each success. Each grief. Each spring of blooming and leafing"—Daddy looked at the scarlet leaves in my scarlet hair—"each summer of growth, each harvest, and each winter of sap rising and root strengthening, each season gives us something that leads to living. And each must be lived in that moment. This is a moment of joy.

"You have vows. Occam, speak your vows."

"I loved you from the first moment I saw you, Nell, sugar," my cat-man said. "I will be your help and your protector when you want one. I will never crowd you, never push you. And I will love those you love, and cherish those you cherish, until my dying day." His cat-eyes glowed. "I love you to the full moon and back. I will love you forever, until my soul is freed from this body, and will cleave to you through all eternity."

Tears trickled down my face.

"Nell, you have vows," Daddy said.

"Occam, I was afraid of you when we met, afraid of myself, afraid of love and caring and being vulnerable. You taught me how to trust again, you gave me hope and taught me joy. I love you to the deeps of the roots of the strongest trees, to the heights of the tallest branches. I will love you through the seasons, through the years, and when I die, I will die loving you with all my heart and all of who I am. Forever."

"Please exchange rings," Daddy said, his voice rough with tenderness. "Occam, repeat after me. 'I take thee, Nell, as my wife, to love and to hold and to cherish.'"

"I take thee, Nell, as my wife, to love and to hold and to cherish. Forever." Occam slid the slim gold band onto my left ring finger.

"Nell, repeat after me. 'I take thee, Occam, as my husband, to love and to hold and to cherish.'"

"I take thee, Occam, as my husband, to love and to hold and to cherish. Forever."

I slid the ring onto his finger.

"I now pronounce you married," Daddy said. "You may kiss the bride. And may you live in harmony and joy for the rest of your days."

Occam kissed me, a soft pressure of his lips on mine. The audience clapped and cheered, and my husband and I turned to face our family by blood, marriage, and choice. And to face the home that was now ours. Forever.

ACKNOWLEDGMENTS

Mud Mymudes for all things planty and doggy, and for beta reading and PR.

Beast Claws! Best street team evah!

Lucienne Diver of The Knight Agency, as always, for applying your agile and splendid mind to my writing and my career, and for being a font of wisdom.

Thanks to Katie Anderson for the glorious cover design.

As always, a huge thank-you to my longtime editor, Jessica Wade of Penguin Random House. Without you, there would be no books at all.

Read on for an excerpt of the first book
in Faith Hunter's *New York Times* bestselling
Jane Yellowrock series,

SKINWALKER

Available wherever books are sold!

I wheeled my bike down Decatur Street and eased deeper into the French Quarter, the bike's engine purring. My shotgun, a Benelli M4 Super 90, was slung over my back and loaded for vamp with hand-packed silver fléchette rounds. I carried a selection of silver crosses in my belt, hidden under my leather jacket, and stakes, secured in loops on my jeans-clad thighs. The saddlebags on my bike were filled with my meager travel belongings—clothes in one side, tools of the trade in the other. As a vamp killer for hire, I travel light.

I'd need to put the vamp-hunting tools out of sight for my interview. My hostess might be offended. Not a good thing when said hostess held my next paycheck in her hands and possessed a set of fangs of her own.

A guy, a good-looking Joe standing in a doorway, turned his head to follow my progress as I motored past. He wore leather boots, a jacket, and jeans, like me, though his dark hair was short and mine was down to my hips when not braided out of the way, tight to my head, for fighting. A Kawasaki motorbike leaned on a stand nearby. I didn't like his interest, but he didn't prick my predatory or territorial instincts.

I maneuvered the bike down St. Louis and then onto Dauphine, weaving between nervous-looking shopworkers heading home for the evening and a few early revelers out for fun. I spotted the address in the fading light. Katie's Ladies was the oldest continually operating whorehouse in the Quarter, in business since 1845, though at various locations, depending on hurricane, flood, the price of rent, and the agreeable nature of local law and its enforcement officers. I parked, set the kickstand, and unwound my long legs from the hog.

I had found two bikes in a junkyard in Charlotte, North Carolina, bodies rusted, rubber rotted. They were in bad shape. But Jacob, a semiretired Harley restoration mechanic / Zen Harley priest living along the Catawba River, took my money, fixing one up, using the other for parts, ordering what else he needed over the Net. It took six months.

During that time I'd hunted for him, keeping his wife and four kids supplied with venison, rabbit, turkey—whatever I could catch, as maimed as I was—restocked supplies from the city with my hoarded money, and rehabbed my damaged body back into shape. It was the best I could do for the months it took me to heal. Even someone with my rapid healing and variable metabolism takes a long while to totally mend from a near beheading.

Now that I was a hundred percent, I needed work. My best bet was a job killing off a rogue vampire that was terrorizing the city of New Orleans. It had taken down three tourists and left a squad of cops, drained and smiling, dead where it dropped them. Scuttlebutt said it hadn't been satisfied with just blood—it had eaten their internal organs. All that suggested the rogue was old, powerful, and deadly—a whacked-out vamp. The nutty ones were always the worst.

Just last week, Katherine "Katie" Fonteneau, the proprietress and namesake of Katie's Ladies, had emailed me. According to my Web site, I had successfully taken down an entire blood-family in the mountains near Asheville. And I had. No lies on the Web site or in the media reports, not bald-faced ones anyway. Truth is, I'd nearly died, but I'd done the job, made a rep for myself, and then taken off a few months to invest my legitimately gotten gains. Or to heal, but spin is everything. A lengthy vacation sounded better than the complete truth.

I took off my helmet and the clip that held my hair, pulling my braids out of my jacket collar and letting them fall around me, beads clicking. I palmed a few tools of the trade—one stake, ash wood and silver tipped; a tiny gun; and a cross—and tucked them into the braids, rearranging them to hang smoothly with no lumps or bulges. I also breathed deeply, seeking to relax, to assure my safety through the upcoming interview. I was nervous, and being nervous around a vamp was just plain dumb.

The sun was setting, casting a red glow on the horizon, limning the ancient buildings, shuttered windows, and wrought-iron balconies in fuchsia. It was pretty in a purely human way. I opened my senses and let my Beast taste the world. She liked the smells and wanted to prowl. *Later*, I promised her. Predators usually growl when irritated. *Soon*—she sent mental claws into my soul, kneading. It was uncomfortable, but the claw pricks kept me alert, which I'd need for the interview. I had never met a civilized vamp, certainly never done business with one. So far as I knew, vamps and skinwalkers had never met. I was about to change that. This could get interesting.

I clipped my sunglasses onto my collar, lenses hanging out. I glanced at the witchy-locks on my saddlebags and, satisfied, I walked to the narrow red door and pushed the buzzer. The bald-headed man who answered was definitely human, but big enough to be something else: professional wrestler, steroid-augmented bodybuilder, or troll. All of the above, maybe. The thought made me smile. He blocked the door, standing with arms loose and ready. "Something funny?" he asked, voice like a horse-hoof rasp on stone.

"Not really. Tell Katie that Jane Yellowrock is here." Tough always works best on first acquaintance. That my knees were knocking wasn't a consideration.

"Card?" Troll asked. A man of few words. I liked him already. My new best pal. With two gloved fingers, I unzipped my leather jacket, fished a business card from an inside pocket, and extended it to him. It read JANE YELLOWROCK, HAVE STAKES WILL TRAVEL. Vamp killing is a bloody business. I had discovered that a little humor went a long way to making it all bearable.

Troll took the card and closed the door in my face. I might have to teach my new pal a few manners. But that was nearly axiomatic for all the men of my acquaintance.

I heard a bike two blocks away. It wasn't a Harley. Maybe a Kawasaki, like the bright red crotch rocket I had seen earlier. I wasn't surprised when it came into view and it was the Joe from Decatur Street. He pulled his bike up beside mine, powered down, and sat there, eyes hidden behind sunglasses. He had a toothpick in his mouth and it twitched once as he pulled his helmet and glasses off.

The Joe was a looker. A little taller than my six feet even, he had olive skin, black hair, black brows. Black jacket and jeans.

Black boots. Bit of overkill with all the black, but he made it work, with muscular legs wrapped around the red bike.

No silver in sight. No shotgun, but a suspicious bulge beneath his right arm. Made him a leftie. Something glinted in the back of his collar. A knife hilt, secured in a spine sheath. Maybe more than one blade. There were scuffs on his boots (Western, like mine, not Harley butt-stompers) but his were Fryes and mine were ostrich-skin Luccheses. I pulled in scents, my nostrils widening. His boots smelled of horse manure, fresh. Local boy, then, or one who had been in town long enough to find a mount. I smelled horse sweat and hay, a clean blend of scents. And cigar. It was the cigar that made me like him. The taint of steel, gun oil, and silver made me fall in love. Well, sorta. My Beast thought he was kinda cute, and maybe tough enough to be worthy of us. Yet there was a faint scent on the man, hidden beneath the surface smells, that made me wary.

The silence had lasted longer than expected. Since he had been the one to pull up, I just stared, and clearly our silence bothered the Joe, but it didn't bother me. I let a half grin curl my lip. He smiled back and eased off his bike. Behind me, inside Katie's, I heard footsteps. I maneuvered so that the Joe and the doorway were both visible. No way could I do it and be unobtrusive, but I raised a shoulder to show I had no hard feelings. Just playing it smart. Even for a pretty boy.

Troll opened the door and jerked his head to the side. I took it as the invitation it was and stepped inside. "You got interesting taste in friends," Troll said, as the door closed on the Joe.

"Never met him. Where you want the weapons?" Always better to offer than to have them removed. Power plays work all kinds of ways.

Troll opened an armoire. I unbuckled the shotgun holster and set it inside, pulling silver crosses from my belt and thighs and from beneath the coat until there was a nice pile. Thirteen crosses—excessive, but they distracted people from my backup weapons. Next came the wooden stakes and silver stakes. Thirteen of each. And the silver vial of holy water. One vial. If I carried thirteen, I'd slosh.

I hung the leather jacket on the hanger in the armoire and tucked the glasses in the inside pocket with the cell phone. I closed the armoire door and assumed the position so Troll could search me. He grunted as if surprised, but pleased, and did a thorough job. To give him credit, he didn't seem to enjoy it overmuch—used only the backs of his hands, no fingers, didn't linger or stroke where he shouldn't. Breathing didn't speed up, heart rate stayed regular; things I can sense if it's quiet enough. After a thorough feel inside the tops of my boots, he said, "This way."

I followed him down a narrow hallway that made two crooked turns toward the back of the house. We walked over old Persian carpets, past oils and watercolors done by famous and not-so-famous artists. The hallway was lit with stained-glass Lalique sconces, which looked real, not like reproductions, but maybe you can fake old; I didn't know. The walls were painted a soft butter color that worked with the sconces to illuminate the paintings. Classy joint for a whorehouse. The Christian children's home schoolgirl in me was both appalled and intrigued.

When Troll paused outside the red door at the end of the hallway, I stumbled, catching my foot on a rug. He caught me with one hand and I pushed off him with little body contact. I managed to look embarrassed; he shook his head. He knocked. I braced myself and palmed the cross he had missed. And the tiny two-shot derringer. Both hidden against my skull on the crown of my head, and covered by my braids, which men never, ever searched, as opposed to my boots, which men always had to stick their fingers in. He opened the door and stood aside. I stepped in.

The room was spartan but expensive, and each piece of furniture looked Spanish. Old Spanish. Like Queen-Isabella-and-Christopher-Columbus old. The woman, wearing a teal dress and soft slippers, standing beside the desk, could have passed for twenty until you looked in her eyes. Then she might have passed for said queen's older sister. Old, old, *old* eyes. Peaceful as she stepped toward me. Until she caught my scent.

In a single instant her eyes bled red, pupils went wide and black, and her fangs snapped down. She leaped. I dodged under her jump as I pulled the cross and derringer, quickly moving to the far wall, where I held out the weapons. The cross was for the vamp, the gun for the Troll. She hissed at me, fangs fully extended. Her claws were bone white and two inches long. Troll had pulled a gun. A big gun. Men and their pissing contests.

Crap. Why couldn't they ever just let me be the only one with a gun?

"Predator," she hissed. "In my territory." Vamp anger phero-mones filled the air, bitter as wormwood.

"I'm not human," I said, my voice steady. "That's what you smell." I couldn't do anything about the tripping heart rate, which I knew would drive her further over the edge; I'm an animal. Biological factors always kick in. So much for trying not to be nervous. The cross in my hand glowed with a cold white light, and Katie, if that was her original name, tucked her head, shielding her eyes. Not attacking, which meant that she was thinking. Good.

"Katie?" Troll asked.

"I'm not human," I repeated. "I'll really hate shooting your Troll here, to bleed all over your rugs, but I will."

"Troll?" Katie asked. Her body froze with that inhuman stillness vamps possess when thinking, resting, or whatever else it is they do when they aren't hunting, eating, or killing. Her shoulders dropped and her fangs clicked back into the roof of her mouth with a sudden spurt of humor. Vampires can't laugh and go vampy at the same time. They're two distinct parts of them, one part still human, one part rabid hunter. Well, that's likely insulting, but then this was the first so-called civilized vamp I'd ever met. All the others I'd had personal contact with were sick, twisted killers. And then dead. Really dead.

Troll's eyes narrowed behind the .45 aimed my way. I figured he didn't like being compared to the bad guy in a children's fairy tale. I was better at fighting, but negotiation seemed wise. "Tell him to back off. Let me talk." I nudged it a bit. "Or I'll take you down and he'll never get a shot off." Unless he noticed that I had set the safety on his gun when I tripped. Then I'd *have* to shoot him. I wasn't betting on my .22 stopping him unless I got an eye shot. Chest hits wouldn't even slow him down. In fact they'd likely just make him mad.

When neither attacked, I said, "I'm not here to stake you. I'm Jane Yellowrock, here to interview for a job, to take out a rogue vamp that your own council declared an outlaw. But I don't smell human, so I take precautions. One cross, one stake, one two-shot derringer." The word *stake* didn't elude her. Or him. He'd missed three weapons. No Christmas bonus for Troll.

"What are you?" she asked.

"You tell me where you sleep during the day and I'll tell you what I am. Otherwise, we can agree to do business. Or I can leave."

Telling the location of a lair—where a vamp sleeps—is information for lovers, dearest friends, or family. Katie chuckled. It was one of the silky laughs that her kind can give, low and erotic, like vocal sex. My Beast purred. She liked the sound.

"Are you offering to be my toy for a while, intriguing nonhuman female?" When I didn't answer, she slid closer, despite the glowing cross, and said, "You are interesting. Tall, slender, young." She leaned in and breathed in my scent. "Or not so young. What are you?" she pressed, her voice heavy with fascination. Her eyes had gone back to their natural color, a sort of grayish hazel, but blood blush marred her cheeks so I knew she was still primed for violence. That violence being my death.

"Secretive," she murmured, her voice taking on that tone they use to enthrall, a deep vibration that seems to stroke every gland. "Enticing scent. Likely tasty. Perhaps your blood would be worth the trade. Would you come to my bed if I offered?"

"No," I said. No inflection in my voice. No interest, no revulsion, no irritation, nothing. Nothing to tick off the vamp or her servant.

"Pity. Put down the gun, Tom. Get our guest something to drink."

I didn't wait for Tommy Troll to lower his weapon; I dropped mine. Beast wasn't happy, but she understood. I was the intruder in Katie's territory. While I couldn't show submission, I could show manners. Tom lowered his gun and his attitude at the same time and holstered the weapon as he moved into the room toward a well-stocked bar.

"Tom?" I said. "Uncheck your safety." He stopped midstride. "I set it when I fell against you in the hallway."

"Couldn't happen," he said.

"I'm fast. It's why your employer invited me for a job interview."

He inspected his .45 and nodded at his boss. Why anyone would want to go around with a holstered .45 with the safety off is beyond me. It smacks of either stupidity or quiet desperation, and Katie had lived too long to be stupid. I was guessing the rogue had made her truly apprehensive. I tucked the cross inside a little lead-foil-lined pocket in the leather belt holding up my Levi's, and eased the small gun in beside it, strapping it down. There was a safety, but on such a small gun, it was easy to knock the safety off with an accidental brush of my arm.

"Is that where you hid the weapons?" Katie asked. When I just looked at her, she shrugged as if my answer were unimportant and said, "Impressive. You are impressive."

Katie was one of those dark ash blondes with long straight hair so thick it whispered when she moved, falling across the teal silk that fit her like a second skin. She stood five feet and a smidge, but height was no measure of power in her kind. She could move as fast as I could and kill in an eyeblink. She had buffed nails that were short when she wasn't in killing mode, pale skin, and she wore exotic, Egyptian-style makeup around the eyes. Black liner overlaid with some kind of glitter. Not the kind of look I'd ever had the guts to try. I'd rather face down a grizzly than try to achieve "a look."

"What'll it be, Miz Yellowrock?" Tom asked.

"Cola's fine. No diet."

He popped the top on a Coke and poured it over ice that crackled and split when the liquid hit, placed a wedge of lime on the rim, and handed it to me. His employer got a tall fluted glass of something milky that smelled sharp and alcoholic. Well, at least it wasn't blood on ice. Ick.

"Thank you for coming such a distance," Katie said, taking one of two chairs and indicating the other for me. Both chairs were situated with backs to the door, which I didn't like, but I sat as she continued. "We never made proper introductions, and the In-ter-net," she said, separating the syllables as if the term was strange, "is no substitute for formal, proper introductions. I am Katherine Fonteneau." She offered the tips of her fingers, and I took them for a moment in my own before dropping them.

"Jane Yellowrock," I said, feeling as though it was all a little redundant. She sipped; I sipped. I figured that was enough etiquette. "Do I get the job?" I asked.

Katie waved away my impertinence. "I like to know the people with whom I do business. Tell me about yourself."

Cripes. The sun was down. I needed to be tooling around town, getting the smell and the feel of the place. I had errands to run, an apartment to rent, rocks to find, meat to buy. "You've been to my Web site, no doubt read my bio. It's all there in black and white." Well, in full-color graphics, but still.

Katie's brows rose politely. "Your bio is dull and uninformative. For instance, there is no mention that you appeared out of the forest at age twelve, a feral child raised by wolves, without even the rudiments of human behavior. That you were placed in a children's home, where you spent the next six years. And that you again vanished until you reappeared two years ago and started killing my kind."

My hackles started to rise, but I forced them down. I'd been baited by a roomful of teenaged girls before I even learned to speak English. After that, nothing was too painful. I grinned and threw a leg over the chair arm. Which took Katie, of the elegant attack, aback. "I wasn't raised by wolves. At least I don't think so. I don't feel an urge to howl at the moon anyway. I have no memories of my first twelve years of life, so I can't answer you about them, but I think I'm probably Cherokee." I touched my black hair, then my face with its golden brown skin and sharp American Indian nose in explanation. "After that, I was raised in a Christian children's home in the mountains of South Carolina. I left when I was eighteen, traveled around awhile, and took up an apprenticeship with a security firm for two years. Then I hung out my shingle, and eventually drifted into the vamp-hunting business.

"What about you? You going to share all your own deep dark secrets, Katie of Katie's Ladies? Who is known to the world as Katherine Fonteneau, aka Katherine Louisa Dupre, Katherine Pearl Duplantis, and Katherine Vuillemont, among others I uncovered. Who renewed her liquor license in February; is a registered Republican; votes religiously, pardon the term; sits on the local full vampiric council; has numerous offshore accounts in various names, a half interest in two local hotels, at least three restaurants, and several bars; and has enough money to buy and sell this entire city if she wanted to."

"We have both done our research, I see."

I had a feeling Katie found me amusing. Must be hard to live a few centuries and find yourself in a modern world where everyone knows what you are and is either infatuated with you or scared silly by you. I was neither, which she liked, if the

small smile was any indication. "So. Do I have the job?" I asked
again.

Katie considered me for a moment, as if weighing my re-
sponses and attitude. "Yes," she said. "I've arranged a small
house for you, per the requirements on your In-ter-net Web
place."

My brows went up despite myself. She must have been pretty
sure she was gonna hire me, then.

"It backs up to this property." She waved vaguely at the back
of the room. "The small L-shaped garden at the side and back
is walled in brick, and I had the stones you require delivered
two days ago."

Okay. Now I was impressed. My Web site says I require close
proximity to boulders or a rock garden, and that I won't take a
job if such a place can't be found. And the woman—the vamp—
had made sure that nothing would keep me from accepting the
job. I wondered what she would have done if I'd said no.

At her glance, Tr—Tom took up the narrative. "The gardener
had a conniption, but he figured out a way to get boulders into
the garden with a crane, and then blended them into his landscaping. Grumbled about it, but it's done."

"Would you tell me why you need piles of stone?" Katie
asked.

"Meditation." When she looked blank I said, "I use stone for
meditation. It helps prepare me for a hunt." I knew she had no
idea what I was talking about. It sounded pretty lame even to
me, and I had made up the lie. I'd have to work on that one.

Katie stood and so did I, setting aside my Coke. Katie had
drained her foul-smelling libation. On her breath it smelled
vaguely like licorice. "Tom will give you the contract and a
packet of information, the compiled evidence gathered about
the rogue by the police and our own investigators. Tonight you
may rest or indulge in whatever pursuits appeal to you.

"Tomorrow, once you deliver the signed contract, you are
invited to join my girls for dinner before business commences.
They will be attending a private party, and dinner will be served
at seven of the evening. I will not be present, that they may
speak freely. Through them you may learn something of import." It was a strange way to say seven p.m., and an even
stranger request for me to interrogate her employees right off

the bat, but I didn't react. Maybe one of them knew something about the rogue. And maybe Katie knew it. "After dinner, you may initiate your inquiries.

"The council's offer of a bonus stands. An extra twenty percent if you dispatch the rogue inside of ten days, without the media taking a stronger note of *us*." The last word had an inflection that let me know the "us" wasn't Katie and me. She meant the vamps. "Human media attention has been . . . difficult. And the rogue's feeding has strained relations in the vampiric council. It is *important*," she said.

I nodded. *Sure. Whatever. I want to get paid, so I aim to please.* But I didn't say it.

Katie extended a folder to me and I tucked it under my arm. "The police photos of the crime scenes you requested. Three samples of bloodied cloth from the necks of the most recent victims, carefully wiped to gather saliva," she said.

Vamp saliva, I thought. *Full of vamp scent. Good for tracking.*

"On a card is my contact at the NOPD. She is expecting a call from you. Let Tom know if you need anything else." Katie settled cold eyes on me in obvious dismissal. She had already turned her mind to other things. Like dinner? Yep. Her cheeks had paled again and she suddenly looked drawn with hunger. Her eyes slipped to my neck. Time to leave.

Ready to find
your next great read?

Let us help.

Visit prh.com/nextread

Penguin
Random
House